ANDREA KANE

THE SILENCE THAT SPEAKS

MIRA

Recycling programs
for this product may
not exist in your area.

ISBN-13: 978-0-7783-1769-2

The Silence That Speaks

Printed in U.S.A.

To our newlyweds, Wendi and Will, whose union adds a whole new and precious dimension to our lives. Wendi, you've always been the joy in our hearts, an amazing friend, daughter and human being. And now we have Will, your wonderful husband—a fine man we're proud to call our son.

We love you both so much and wish you a lifetime of joy and the happily-ever-after you deserve.

1

Madeline Westfield never saw the car coming.

It was late at night, and chilly for the beginning of November. She'd turned up her coat collar, and was waiting to cross Park Avenue at East Eighty-Eighth Street. Lost in thought, yes, and with more than enough reason these days. She was an emotional wreck. But navigating between pedestrians, taxicabs and speeding motorists was second nature to her. She'd been a Manhattan resident for most of her life.

She'd watched for the walk sign to flash from red to green. Even then, she'd paused briefly to glance around.

The crosswalk was still.

She took her initial steps into the street.

The screech of tires was her first warning. Then came the flash of motion from her peripheral vision.

Her head snapped around, and she came to a dead stop, staring like a deer in the headlights. A black SUV was roaring in her direction. It veered sharply at her, leaving no doubt that its goal was to hit her head-on.

Self-preservation kicked in. She lunged away, hurling herself backward and crashing to the sidewalk, a pile of wet leaves doing nothing to cushion her fall.

The impact of her body slamming against the concrete rocketed through her. Her head struck the ground—hard. She cried out in pain, saw stars.

Somewhere in the dim recesses of her mind, she heard the screech of brakes and the sharp swerving of tires, and the terrifying thought occurred to her that the driver was going to try again.

"Miss, are you all right?" a gravelly male voice inquired as the man it belonged to rounded the corner.

Madeline had never felt such great relief at the sound of another human voice. She looked up to see an elderly gentleman, with a full head of white hair and a lined face, holding a leash. The Brussels griffon at the other end of the leash was eye level with her. He trotted over to take a sniff.

"No, Max!" the man said. He was staring down at Madeline, his forehead creased in concern. "Did you trip? Can you move?"

He hadn't seen what happened. He wasn't a witness.

As Madeline opened her mouth to speak, she heard the SUV's engine roar in the distance as it sped down Park Avenue.

"I…" She shifted her weight and winced. Her right side was killing her. Her head was throbbing violently. And "Max" looked like two dogs, not one. Double vision. A concussion. Not to mention some major bruises—possibly even some broken bones. As an RN, she recognized the signs.

Seeing the agony in her eyes, the man reacted.

"I'm going to call 9-1-1 and get you an ambulance." He took out his cell phone.

Madeline nodded her thanks. She tried again to move, and was rewarded with jolts of pain. She inhaled sharply, causing shooting pain in her chest. So she lay there quietly and waited.

The ambulance seemed to take forever to arrive. Maybe it was the pain talking. Or maybe it was her nerves. But she finally saw the red whirring light and heard the siren. Lenox Hill Hospital was nearby. That's where the EMTs would transport her. It wasn't the hospital she worked in, but she did know some people there.

Not that it mattered. She passed out as they arrived at the E.R.

When she came to, she was in a hospital bed with a bandaged arm, a taped midsection and an ice pack resting on her hip. Her head felt like a jackhammer was splitting it in two.

She lay there for a moment, willing her mind to work. Then she remembered what had happened and everything inside her tensed up.

It hadn't been an accident. It was attempted murder. That SUV was gunning for her. The cops wouldn't believe her story. Why would they? They hadn't believed her the first time. And that had only been a robbery. Now someone wanted her dead.

She flinched, knowing she had a concussion, a few broken ribs and a badly bruised hip. She wished she had some painkillers—anything to take away the throbbing and to knock her out. She wanted to sleep. She knew she couldn't. Not yet. Not until the doctor saw her and checked out her neurological responses.

She'd be here overnight. They'd keep her for observation. Then, if she remained stable, they'd let her go home.

A wave of panic set in, followed by utter resignation. She couldn't do this alone, not anymore. She'd put off the inevitable for as long as possible. It was time to get help—and from a specific source.

Seeking out that source was going to be even more painful than her injuries.

2

It was 8:45 a.m.

The Forensic Instincts investigative team was hard at work—but not on a case.

Instead, they were scrambling around their Tribeca brownstone, trying to get the place into some semblance of order before their next job applicant arrived.

Having just wrapped up a high-profile corporate espionage case, they'd normally be debriefing. Instead, all their notes, reports, follow-ups and computer files were in uncharacteristic disarray. The phone was ringing off the hook. Their voice mailboxes were exploding. And this was *not* the way Casey Woods intended to run her company.

She'd made her position clear several weeks ago. The minute their current case was closed, they were hiring a receptionist-slash-assistant. From a small start-up investigative firm, they'd catapulted into a highly sought-after company, thanks to the combined efforts and stellar results achieved by their brilliant team.

Until now, there'd been the six of them, each of whom was a critical and integral part of FI. Starting with Casey herself—who was the company president and behavioral expert, and who had the extensive academic credentials and professional experience to be the firm's anchor—every member of the FI team had a stand-alone résumé.

They were no longer New York's best kept secret, and their client list was growing daily. Thus, the need for someone to man the front desk and to assist the team as needed.

So far, they hadn't had much luck.

At the moment, Casey was upstairs on the fourth floor—the floor that served as her apartment during the few hours that she actually lived there—running a brush through her shoulder-length red hair and adjusting the collar on her green cowl-neck sweater. Hero, Casey's bloodhound and the team's human scent evidence dog, was already poised in the bedroom doorway, waiting expectantly for his mistress to leave her apartment and go downstairs to her *real* home: Forensic Instincts.

"I'm coming, boy," she told him, looking in the mirror and giving herself a quick once-over, before heading for their morning interview. "God knows what we have in store this time."

Ryan McKay was still downstairs in his man cave, affectionately known as his lair, which filled the entire basement level of the brownstone. It was the technology center of Forensic Instincts, complete with their servers—Lumen, Equitas and Intueri, from the Latin words for *light, justice* and *intuition.* Part data center, part electronics lab, Ryan had more high-tech equipment than a small university.

Despite its serious purpose, Ryan left enough room to maintain two areas of personal space—his free weights and fitness section, and a small competition ring for his self-built robots.

Right now, he was enjoying neither. He was printing out pages from FI's just-closed case.

While the pages were printing, he was on his iPad, reading the latest issue of *Sound on Sound* magazine. The software review of Audio Detracktor was compelling. The reviewer described how it was developed by three of genius college students—a math whiz, a computer geek and a musical prodigy. Audio Detracktor would analyze an audio file, separating the component tracks and instruments into layers. Each isolated layer could be played independently, giving the listener the ability to hear insignificant sounds in a rich recording. *Sound on Sound* had written about experimenting with Eric Clapton's "Layla," Gene Vincent's "Be-Bop-A-Lula" and Paul McCartney's "Yesterday." They were even able to isolate the sound of a flying guitar pick bouncing off the floor. Guitarists would often lose their picks in midperformance, which is why they always carried extras with them. But to actually hear the sound of a tiny plastic piece hitting the ground? Awesome.

Just as Ryan was about to swipe to the next page, his iPhone began vibrating in his pocket, reminding him of a scheduled meeting. Glancing at his calendar entry, he scowled at its purpose. Interview. Emma Stirling. Another teenybopper receptionist he had to talk to.

He understood Casey's decision to establish a more professional office environment, as well as to get some help answering the phones and doing odds and ends. But he'd lobbied strongly for a virtual assistant, aka software, installed on one of their servers. A virtual assistant was smart, predictable, *not* female and never took a coffee or bathroom break.

The perfect receptionist.

Casey and Claire had overruled him. They felt a personal touch was needed. A flesh-and-blood human being, not a machine. Marc was indifferent, although he saw the value of both. And Patrick had been married long enough to know when to avoid a losing situation.

Ryan's pocket buzzed again. Time to stop procrastinating and get this over with. Full of attitude, he marched upstairs ready to meet and nix Emma Stirling.

The rest of the team was already congregated in the second floor's main conference room, pouring coffee and settling down around the sweeping oval conference table.

Marc took a gulp of black coffee and eyed Ryan. "Nice of you to join us." A corner of his mouth lifted. "You look thrilled to be here."

Ryan scowled. "You know how I feel about this. I was about to do something useful—like order a cool state-of-the-art app while I was preparing the case wrap-up. Instead, I'm here, ready to meet another substandard candidate."

"Great attitude." Claire walked over just in time to hear Ryan's statement. "Did it ever occur to you that we might find a white elephant? There are still a few of those out there, you know."

"Is that a prediction, Clairevoyant?" He loved to get at her with that nickname he'd coined.

"No." She shot him a don't-get-me-started look. "It's an optimistic fact."

Patrick was already seated, scratching Hero's ears.

He glanced over at them. "Play nice, kids. We have a reputation for professionalism to uphold."

"Yes, we do." Casey seated herself at the head of the table. "And, like it or not, we're going to eventually have to hire someone. My standards are as high as yours, Ryan. Maybe higher. But I'm not giving up. This place is *not* going to continue as chaos central."

"I hear you." Ryan got himself some coffee and turned to peruse the group. "So should we do rock, paper, scissors to decide who's going downstairs to let this one in?"

"I can handle that electronically, Ryan." An invisible computerized voice echoed from everywhere in the room, and a wall of floor-to-ceiling video screens began to glow. A long green line formed across each panel, pulsing from left to right, bending into the contours of the voice panel.

"Good idea, Yoda," Ryan replied. "Disarm the Hirsch pad when the doorbell rings and advise our job candidate to come upstairs. That alone should scare the shit out of her."

Casey couldn't help but smile at Ryan's assessment. As for Yoda, Ryan's extraordinary artificial intelligence system, he'd become an honorary FI team member. Sometimes, it was hard to remember that he wasn't human. Then again, he'd been built by Ryan, who was *very* human. Bottom line? Ryan was a genius and Yoda was omniscient.

"Has everyone reviewed this candidate's application?" Casey asked.

"Yup." Marc was his usual straightforward self. "She sounds like a juvenile delinquent who never did hard time."

"She sounds like a kid who needs a chance," Claire

chimed in. "She was bounced from foster home to foster home and spent a lot of time on the streets."

"I have to agree," Patrick said. "I know she's got a juvie record, and that would normally turn me right off. But in this case—her parents died in a plane crash when she was eight. There were no relatives to take her in. So she spent ten years in the system. That's tough."

"And we're not exactly squeaky clean ourselves," Marc commented drily. He glanced at Patrick. "Other than you, Special Agent Lynch."

"Not so much anymore," Patrick retorted. "You've corrupted me."

The whole group chuckled.

"Yeah, we're the maverick investigators," Ryan said, coining a phrase from an article written about them. "So, if this girl has a brain, I'm willing to cut her some slack."

"Some slack?" Casey repeated, shooting Ryan a look. "I'm hoping you'll do more than that."

"I wouldn't count on it. I still think a virtual assistant would be the best choice." Ryan held up both palms to ward off oncoming arguments. "But I've accepted that I've been overruled. So let's get this show on the road."

Right on cue, the doorbell sounded.

"Applicant number twenty-seven has arrived," Yoda announced.

"Punctual." Casey glanced at her watch. "Okay, Yoda, go ahead and let her in." She interlaced her fingers on the table in front of her. "Oh, and, Yoda? Leave out the applicant number when you announce her. Just stick to her name. Applicant twenty-six nearly took off when you made that reference. Let's not scare off applicant twenty-seven. It's starting to sound like we're scraping the bottom of the barrel and each one of them is it. Either that, or we're looking for perfection and can't find it."

"That would be accurate," Yoda pointed out.

"True, but we don't want to intimidate the girl before she even gets upstairs."

"Very well, Casey. Name only."

Yoda's words were punctuated by the beeping sound of the alarm system as he disarmed it.

A loud *thunk* resounded in the FI hallway as the large steel bolt retracted, unlocking the front door.

"Please enter the building and proceed to the second floor," Yoda instructed the young woman at the door. "Make a right turn into the main conference room. Your interview will be conducted there."

"Thanks." Without so much as a flinch, Emma Stirling walked through the foyer as the door bolt reengaged behind her. She climbed up the winding staircase, and paused on the landing to run her fingers through her hair and adjust her tote bag on her shoulder. Then she entered the conference room.

She fought back a smile as she saw the all-too-familiar startled reaction from the team at large. It was the same as everyone who'd read her history. They were expecting a scraggly looking brat from the streets. Instead, they were getting the equivalent of a prep school cheerleader—all blonde, blue-eyed and composed, with a fashionable short skirt and a formfitting top.

She'd worked hard to perfect that image.

"I clean up nice," she said, putting aside the looks of surprise and assessing the challenge she was about to face.

Emma had done her homework.

The pretty, authoritative redhead at the head of the table was Casey Woods, the president of Forensic Instincts and a brilliant analyst of human behavior. On either side of her were two hot guys—one dark and brooding, the other sexy and charismatic—Marc Devereaux and Ryan McKay, respectively. Marc was Casey's right hand, a former navy SEAL and former FBI agent in the Behavioral Analysis Unit in Quantico, Virginia. Quite simply, there was nothing Marc couldn't do or couldn't make happen. Ryan was nothing short of a techno-wizard and a strategy genius.

The willowy blonde who looked like a fairy princess was Claire Hedgleigh. Emma didn't quite get what it meant, but Claire was a claircognizant and had an amazing psychic gift that took her into scary but productive places to help solve cases. The older conservative-looking guy was Patrick Lynch, a retired FBI agent with over three decades of law enforcement experience, and who grounded the team when they pushed the boundaries a little too far. Oh, yeah, and the cool bloodhound sitting up tall, ears erect, was Hero—an FBI-trained human-scent evidence dog whose olfactory sense was second to none.

Pretty thorough, Emma thought with an internal grin.

"Job candidate Emma Stirling," Yoda supplied. "Twenty-two years old. Currently unemployed and available immediately. Have a seat at the table, Ms. Stirling."

"Yes, sir," Emma replied, looking around to see where the voice was coming from. It was the same voice that had greeted her in the doorway.

She placed her tote bag in the empty chair next to Patrick, but remained standing.

With self-taught courtesy, she proceeded to walk

around the conference room table, shaking hands with each team member. First, she squatted down to stroke Hero's ears. "He's great. What's his name?" she asked.

"Hero," Patrick responded. He helped her to her feet and shook her hand. "I'm Patrick Lynch. Nice to meet you."

"Same here." She moved on to Marc and Ryan, who were sizing her up as they greeted her. She made sure to touch each man's arm with her left hand. Men appreciated that in business introductions.

As she approached Claire and Casey, she tripped and toppled forward, struggling to right herself as they caught her.

"I'm sorry," she said, her face turning bright red. "I get clumsy when I'm nervous. And I'll never get used to high heels."

"We hear you," Casey said with a chuckle. There wasn't a woman alive who didn't understand the battle between fashion and comfort.

"We certainly do," Claire echoed, intent on putting the poor girl at ease. "Men don't have to juggle looking great and professional without limping home. It's one of the hardships of being a modern woman."

"Thank you for understanding." The color was fading from Emma's cheeks as she regained some of her composure. Sheepishly, she made her way back to her seat and gratefully sank into it.

Once she was settled, Yoda continued. "Application and résumé displayed on the main screen."

As he spoke, the large middle screen lit up, and Emma's paperwork appeared, the pages arranged side by side.

"That's just the good stuff," she told them, having

glanced up at the information displayed. "I'm sure you know the rest."

"We do." Casey leaned forward and studied the young woman. "We've all read every word. The bottom line— you were a juvie. According to our research, you were guilty of a lot more than you were convicted of. You were incredibly good at getting off."

Emma startled. "What?"

"Not the reaction you were expecting?" Casey asked. "Sorry. We're nothing if not thorough. We're also not easily shocked. Or were you hoping we would be and that we'd bounce you out of here so you could feel vindicated and like you'd put one over on us?"

"I…" Emma was visibly taken aback.

"I like the wide-eyed innocent thing," Ryan commented. "You've got a great combo going there—a disarming exterior and an iron core."

"You're smart, too," Marc added. "You did research on each one of us." He read the surprised widening of her eyes that she fought to conceal. "The way you studied each of us as you walked around—which you made sure to do," he explained, answering her unspoken question. "Like you were making mental connections. That was your tell."

"Wow, you people are just like the articles say." For the first time, Emma looked impressed. "So let's say I came here to mess with your minds, and you figured me out. You also guessed I was a lot guiltier than my record shows. Then why are you interviewing me?"

"Why wouldn't we be?" Casey asked.

"You just said so yourself. I'm a criminal."

"A *former* criminal," Patrick qualified.

"And a good one," Ryan said, ignoring Patrick's

scowl. "Here at Forensic Instincts, we not only admire excellence, we demand it. Also, you've got guts. Guts are a requirement for working here."

"True," Casey said.

"Plus your background piqued our interest," Claire couldn't help but interject. She pointed at herself. "And before you size me up further, yes, I am the soft touch of the team. I felt a pang of compassion when I read your history. That's the upside. The downside is that none of my team members is as squishy as I am. So you'll have some convincing to do."

Emma acknowledged that with a nod. "I figured as much."

Casey raised her chin. "Do you want this job?"

"Yes."

"Why?"

"Because it sounds way cooler than the other jobs I was applying for."

"But you didn't think you'd get it."

"Truthfully? No."

"Honesty. Another refreshing virtue." Casey glanced around the table, making eye contact with each team member and reading their reactions.

Emma used that time to look around again, puzzled as her gaze searched the room. "I don't know where it's based, but I like your virtual intelligence system. How come you didn't make that your assistant?"

"Smart girl," Ryan muttered.

"Because Yoda is overworked," Marc answered for the group.

"Yoda?" Emma grinned. "Great name."

"*Really* smart girl," Ryan muttered again.

Only half listening to Ryan's wisecracks, Casey was

eyeing Emma as their job applicant kept asking questions. What was going on in that cunning little blond head?

The girl was sharp. She was a walking contradiction. And she had a curious mind. She had the brains and the balls to fit right in.

But was she trustworthy? Loyal? Those were key requirements in Casey's hiring practice.

Only one way to find out.

At that moment, Emma pushed back her chair and rose. "I want this job. What do I have to do to get it?"

"Prove yourself," Casey responded.

"How?"

"A probationary period. Say, three months. Minimum wage. Show me unwavering loyalty to Forensic Instincts—the company and the team. Hard work. *Good* work. No bullshit. No games. Up front all the way. Then we'll talk."

"Fair enough." Emma paused, chewing her lip. "In that case, I guess I should start out on the right foot, boss." She reached into her tote bag and groped around for a minute. "Here you go." She pulled out Patrick's wallet, Claire's bangle bracelet, Marc's switchblade, Casey's day planner and Ryan's iPhone, placing each item in front of its respective owner. "No bullshit. No games. Up front all the way."

You could have heard a pin drop as the team members each stared at their just-confiscated belongings.

"And who knows?" Emma added with an impish grin. "I might even teach you guys a thing or two."

3

Emma was still getting used to the coolness of having her own desk and swivel chair in an alcove right off the front hall of the renowned Forensic Instincts.

Maybe if she played her cards right, she'd get business cards, too.

The doorbell rang, and she snapped to attention, grabbing her new scheduling book.

"Our nine-thirty prospective client has arrived," Yoda announced. "Ms. Madeline Westfield. She's listed in your appointment book on the left page, third column."

"Yes, Yoda, I see that." Emma grimaced. "Cut me some slack. I'm trying to learn. At least give me thirty seconds before you jump in."

A brief pause. "That seems fair and acceptable. I'll program my database accordingly."

"You do that." Emma rose and walked to the door, punching in the dummy alarm code Ryan had assigned her. Only the inner circle got the real code. Not the newbies on probation.

She opened the door and automatically ran through the physical assessment she'd learned during her pickpocket days, when she'd sized up her potential marks.

Madeline Westfield was pretty in a haunting kind of way. Mid-thirties. Chestnut-brown hair, classily styled and just grazing her shoulders. Fair skin. Deep, dark eyes. Medium height. Cute figure. Casually but expensively dressed in a cashmere coat, from beneath which peeked a sweater and pants that screamed designer. A badly bruised forehead—from a bad bang, not physical abuse—and an anxious look in her eyes.

The ideal client—rich and needy.

"Good morning," Emma said brightly, extending her hand. "You must be Ms. Westfield. I'm Emma Stirling. Welcome to Forensic Instincts."

"Thank you." Madeline clasped her hand briefly. Her palm was icy. She was peering around. She was nervous. Emma wondered what that was about—the upcoming meeting or whatever had brought her here.

"The team is waiting for you right in there." Emma gestured at the cozy meeting room down the hall. "I'll take your coat. Can I get you something—coffee, tea, water?"

"Coffee would be lovely, thank you," Madeline said, shrugging out of her coat and handing it to Emma. "Just black."

"No problem. I'll show you in and then bring it to you."

Emma led the way, escorting Madeline straight to the open door. With a brief knock, she glanced at the team. "Ms. Madeline Westfield is here for her appointment." She noted the steaming pot of coffee on a trivet in the middle of the center table. "Should I pour?" she asked Casey.

"No, thank you, Emma. We've got it. Just shut the door on your way out."

"Okay. Let me know if you need me." Emma left the room, closing the door to give them their privacy and heading back to her desk—and to Yoda's tutoring.

Madeline stood just inside the meeting room, tightly clutching her handbag. She looked stiff, as if she was in pain, and there was a bad bruise on her forehead.

Casey was about to open her mouth when she caught the odd, strained expression on Madeline's face. She was staring at Marc. And Marc had a look on his face that Casey had never seen before—a look of stark, raw emotion.

"Maddy?" He rose slowly to his feet.

"Hello, Marc." She attempted a smile, but it didn't quite reach her eyes. "It occurred to me that you might not realize I was the one who was coming here today."

"No. I didn't." Marc's emotions shut down and his usual unreadable expression snapped back into place. "The appointment didn't list you as Madeline Stanton."

"Westfield is my married name."

"I see."

The silence was so awkward that even Casey was hard-pressed to break it.

But break it she did.

Coming swiftly to her feet, she stepped forward and extended her hand. "I'm Casey Woods. I see that you and Marc already know each other, so I'll introduce the rest of the team."

No questions. No observations. No belaboring the all-too-blatant reality.

Madeline's relief was visible. "I'm so happy to meet you," she said, shaking Casey's hand. Her gaze shifted to the area rug, where Hero was lying beside Casey's chair. "What a beautiful bloodhound."

"Hero is a human-scent evidence dog," Casey explained. "He's part of the Forensic Instincts team."

"Then he must be remarkable. Your company's reputation speaks for itself."

"Well, let's see what we can do for you." Casey ran through the rest of the introductions, poured Madeline a cup of coffee and gestured for her to have a seat on one of the buttery-soft caramel leather tub chairs in the room.

There were three other identical tub chairs, casually situated around the two matching leather couches. Sure, the room also had some high-tech equipment, but it wasn't center stage. There was no point in making the place look like an interrogation room. Living rooms were far more relaxing, and leant themselves to calmer clients who were open and honest about their reasons for being here.

Madeline politely accepted the cup of coffee and gingerly sat down. Casey noted that she swiveled her tub chair ever so slightly away from Marc and kept her gaze fixed on Casey.

Those weren't acts of anger. They were unconscious acts of emotional protection.

"I don't know where to start," Madeline said.

"Start wherever you're most comfortable." Casey sat back, ostensibly relaxed, but reading every tell that Madeline displayed. Ryan had run a preliminary background check on her, as he did on all their prospective clients. But nothing beat an in-person assessment. And, in this case, there was an additional—and very personal—nuance to observe.

"We'll ask questions as we need to." From Casey's

peripheral vision, she noticed that Marc had opened his portfolio and was ready to take notes. Business as usual. Marc preferred to go at it by hand, and then transfer his conclusions into the computer. It also wasn't a shock that he hadn't done more than a cursory read of Ryan's report. He liked to go into a first meeting with just the facts and a clear mind.

Evidently, that method had backfired this time.

"Do you mind if we record this conversation?" Casey asked. "It helps us refocus on any details that might become important later on."

"Not at all," Madeline replied. "Just as long as everything remains confidential."

"Absolutely." Casey nodded. "I assume you received the confidentiality agreement that I messengered to you?"

"I did. And I reviewed it with my attorney." Tentatively, Madeline leaned down, reached into her purse and extracted a folded document. "Here's the fully executed original," she said, unfolding the page and handing it to Casey. "I kept a copy for my records."

"Good. Then let's begin." Casey sipped at her coffee, then called out, "Yoda, please turn on Inspector Gadget."

Ryan grinned, proud of yet another of his accomplishments. Inspector Gadget was the iPhone hack he'd programmed into each team member's iPhone, which turned the cell phones into secret listening devices. With Yoda in control, the iPhone microphone and cameras could be activated, streaming audio and video over the best available network, for live viewing and/or recording by the team.

"Inspector Gadget activated," Yoda announced.

"Go, go, Gadget," Ryan muttered under his breath with a quiet chuckle.

Madeline was looking around, her eyes wide and puzzled.

"Yoda is our artificial intelligence system," Casey explained. "Ryan built him, so he's smart but safe."

A tentative nod. "Okay." Madeline still looked bewildered. Then again, everyone did the first time they heard Yoda.

"Go ahead and tell us your situation," Casey said.

Madeline cleared her throat. "Someone is trying to kill me," she said bluntly. "I have no witnesses and no tangible proof, so the police can't help me. Can you?"

"Who would be trying to kill you and why?" Marc spoke up for the first time, his demeanor all business.

"I have no idea." Madeline couldn't meet his eyes. "That's the problem. But my apartment was broken into a few weeks ago. Yes, items were stolen, but the way the place was trashed so violently, I don't believe that robbery was the reason for the break-in. And then three days ago…" Madeline touched the bruise on her forehead. "Someone tried to run me down when I was crossing the street. It wasn't a drunk driver. It was very deliberate and very professional. I'd just stepped into the road when the SUV came at me. I literally had to fling myself back on the sidewalk to avoid getting killed. I have broken ribs and a concussion as souvenirs."

Patrick's forehead creased in thought. "If that's the case, then whoever's behind these attacks is convinced that you not only *have* something, but that you *know* something," he said. "Otherwise, they'd just be going after your possessions, not you."

"So you believe me?" Madeline's voice was weak with relief.

"We have no reason not to," Casey replied. "You make a solid argument."

"But the police…"

"The police have to operate by a certain set of criteria that we don't have to." Casey kept it short and sweet. "So let's move on to the obvious questions. What's changed in your life recently? New relationships? New job? New routine?"

"None of the above."

"Then let's start close to home. Tell us about your husband."

"*Ex*-husband," Madeline corrected. Almost inadvertently, she darted a quick glance at Marc, then looked away. "Conrad's and my divorce was final last month. But we were separated for six months before that. It's hardly new."

"Tell us about him, anyway," Claire asked.

Madeline sighed, not a sigh of anger, but one of weariness and resignation.

"Conrad is a brilliant cardiothoracic surgeon—one of the top three in the country. He was…is…the head of the cardio unit at Manhattan Memorial Hospital. He's also a very complex man."

"How so?"

"He's bigger than life. Always striving for perfection. He not only needs to excel and to surpass others, but to surpass himself. And when all the pieces fall into place, he's unstoppable. But when they don't…" A helpless shake of her head. "He's his own worst enemy."

"Did you say he *was* or he *is* the head of the cardiothoracic surgical unit?" Casey asked, having not missed Madeline's hesitation over the past or present tense.

"Is. He's just taken a leave of absence."

Something about the way Madeline said that gave Casey pause. "When you say 'a leave of absence,' do you mean an extended vacation, or a sabbatical to go abroad and study some new aspect of his craft?"

"Neither." Madeline looked down at the floor for a moment, then met Casey's gaze. "This isn't common knowledge, but Conrad has been staying at Crest Haven Residential Treatment Center. It's a private facility in Connecticut."

"I've heard of it. It's a top-notch mental health facility."

Madeline nodded. "This has been a devastating time for Conrad. Three months ago, he lost a dear friend who he'd just operated on. He's never forgiven himself. I doubt he ever will."

"Why did he operate on a close friend?" Casey asked. "As I understand it, that's ill-advised."

"It is. But the friend was Ronald Lexington, the hospital administrator. The surgery was a delicate one, and Ron wouldn't allow anyone but Conrad to perform it."

"Wow." Ryan let out a low whistle. "Talk about pressure. That's a tough one to live with."

"It must have taken a huge toll on whatever was left of your marriage," Casey said tactfully.

"Our marriage was already over." Madeline's reply was straightforward, but she was fiddling with the pleat of her pants leg. "We'd been talking on and off for a year and a half about separation. The divorce process was already well under way when this happened. But no, our relationship wouldn't have been strong enough to hold up—not given the severity of Conrad's reaction or his resistance to share his pain with me."

"Was he sharing his pain with anyone else?" Ryan asked.

Claire winced. There was brilliant but blunt Ryan. "Anyone that you know of—like a colleague or a clergyman?" she asked, trying to soften the glaring implications of Ryan's question.

A small smile curved Madeline's lips. "I'm not offended. I doubt Conrad was having an affair. That's not where his head was. I also doubt he did much sharing with anyone—that's just not his nature. So, for the record, I doubt I'm being hunted down by a jealous lover. The gossip mill runs wild in the circles we traveled in. The fact that our marriage was ending was common knowledge. As was the fact that it was an amicable divorce. We wished each other well. We still do."

"What circles did you travel in?" Patrick asked.

"Oh, we had a real-life soap opera going on." Madeline grimaced. "An elite social crowd of high-profile doctors and their spouses. It was compounded by the fact that I work in the same hospital as Conrad. I'm an emergency room nurse. So I was in the middle of the drama both professionally and personally. It was exhausting. I'm a private person, so I'm struggling to extricate myself from it as quickly as possible. But after five years, it's not easy, despite the divorce."

That opened the door to a whole separate cluster of questions and suspects. But Casey was studying Madeline's body language. She was no longer sitting up straight and tall. She looked drawn, exhausted, pale. And every time she shifted in her seat, she flinched. The woman was clearly in a fair amount of physical pain. And the only motivator that had gotten her here today was fear.

This interview had barely gotten started. But it was about to end.

"You're a nurse," Casey said. "Why do I get the feeling you used your clout to check yourself out of the hospital sooner than the doctors would have advised?"

Another pained smile. "Probably because you're perceptive—which is one of the reasons I want to hire you. Although I am on extended leave, pending my doctor's permission to return. That, I couldn't wiggle my way out of." Her smile faded. "I'm terrified. I know someone wants me dead—and I have no idea why. Or when the next attempt on my life is going to be. I don't feel safe anywhere—not at home, not doing errands, not even at the hospital. Please. I need your help."

Casey glanced around the room, reading her team's expressions. Their usual procedure was to meet privately and make a group decision as to whether or not to take on a case. But Casey was reluctant to make Madeline wait when she was clearly in pain.

Plus, Casey knew her team. She knew what their reactions would be.

Except for Marc. This time, he was a huge question mark. So she saved him for last.

First, Patrick. He gave her an indiscernible nod. Ditto for Ryan. Claire's lips mouthed the word *yes*.

Everyone accounted for. Casey angled her head in Marc's direction. He was still writing—although Casey suspected that was more to keep himself occupied than it was to jot down notes about what was being said. Marc had a steel-trap mind, plus Yoda was taping the interview.

Well aware that Casey was looking at him, he raised his head and met her gaze. With an expression that was totally nondescript, he blinked his assent.

That settled that.

"If money is the issue, just name your fee," Madeline interrupted the silence to offer. "Conrad gave me a generous settlement. I'm sure we can come to terms."

"I'm sure we can." Casey rose, extended her hand. "Consider yourself our client. We still have a lot to go over with you, but not today. You need to be in bed, recuperating. How did you get here this morning?"

"I took a cab. I live on the Upper East Side."

"I'll drive you home," Patrick said at once. "I'd like to check out your apartment."

Once again, Madeline reached into her purse. "I have a copy of the police report, if that helps. It lists the items that were stolen."

"Great." Patrick took the sheet of paper she unfolded. "That eliminates our having to contact the precinct. But actually, I'm more interested in seeing what specific areas of the apartment were ransacked. It might give me a clue as to what the intruders were looking for."

"I hadn't thought of that."

"Also, while we're driving, I'll contact my security team and arrange to have a guard assigned to you immediately." Over the years, Patrick had compiled a number of retired FBI agents and police officers to make up his expert security team. "That way, you'll be safe and you'll have peace of mind."

"Thank you." Slowly, Madeline stood up. "I truly appreciate it."

"We'll be in touch tomorrow," Casey said. "If you're up to it, maybe I can stop by your apartment and talk to you there. I'm sure you'll be more comfortable in your own home."

A nod. "I'm sure I would. I'll wait for your call, then." She paused, for the first time turning to look directly at Marc. "It was good to see you again, Marc," she said softly, gripping her purse as if for moral support.

Marc met her gaze. "Good to see you, too."

Patrick escorted Madeline from the room.

The rest of the team chatted briefly, and then disbanded, already divvying up assignments.

"Marc." Casey stopped him before he could leave the room. "I need your input for a minute. Could you hang around?"

"Sure." He stopped in his tracks, not looking the least bit surprised by Casey's request. He knew her. And he knew what she wanted.

He remained silent, waiting for her to initiate the conversation.

Casey crossed over and shut the door, turning around to face him. She folded her arms across her chest. "Want to tell me what that was all about?"

"Not really."

"Fair enough. I'll ask only what I need to. You answer only what you want to."

"Shoot."

"What was the nature of your relationship with Madeline, and based on that, do you need to bow out of this one?"

Marc shoved his hands in his pockets. "Madeline and I met when I was a SEAL, stationed in Norfolk, Virginia. She was a nurse at Bethesda Naval Hospital. I went for a checkup. She was on duty. We hit it off. We got involved in a personal relationship. It ended. And no, I'm not bow-ing out. She and I haven't seen each other in years. Plus, you know me. Nothing prevents me from doing my job."

"Yes, I do know you. And I've never seen you react to another living soul the way you just did to Madeline Westfield. You were in love with her. That's obvious. It's also quite a departure from the Marc I'm used to. So you can understand my concern."

"I understand it. I'm assuaging it. It's not a problem. Am I excused now?"

Casey studied him for a long moment. Then she nodded, stepping aside. "Yes, Marc, you're excused. I won't bring this up again unless it becomes necessary."

"It won't." He was already heading out.

Casey stared after him as the door shut in his wake. "If you say so," she murmured.

4

By the time Madeline unlocked the door and let herself and Patrick into her East Eighty-Second Street apartment, she was weaving on her feet.

Patrick scanned the place. It was damned impressive—modern furnishings, all chrome and leather, lots of windows, gleaming parquet floors, serious artwork on the walls. This postdivorce apartment must have cost Madeline a pretty penny.

Then again, she'd been married to a renowned cardiothoracic surgeon. He had to be rolling in money. From the preliminary information Ryan had provided them, Madeline's original home—the one she'd shared with Conrad on East Seventy-Second and York—was a multimillion-dollar duplex, so this apartment was small potatoes in comparison.

Still, compared to Patrick's modest home in Hoboken, New Jersey, this was a showplace.

Having assessed the foyer, the dining room and the sunken living room, Patrick's gaze settled on the cocoa-brown leather sofa near the wall of panoramic windows. "Go lie down," he instructed Madeline, pointing. "I can look around myself. I'll fire questions as I need to."

"Thank you," Madeline said, making her way gingerly across the hall.

Watching her slow, unsteady progress, Patrick changed his mind and opted to take her arm and assist her down the two steps to the living room, leading her over to the couch. He stood there until she'd settled herself on the cushions and covered herself with a multi-colored afghan.

"Can I get you something?" he asked. "Coffee? Soup?"

Madeline smiled. "You're an excellent host, especially since *I'm* the one who should be asking *you* those questions."

A return smile. "I'm not the one with the concussion and broken ribs. Plus, I'm not bad in the kitchen. My wife is the cooking wizard, but I can certainly heat up a can of soup."

"I have no doubt. But honestly, I'm fine." Madeline graciously declined his offer. "Thank you, though. It's nice to know there are still some gentlemen out there. Your wife is a lucky woman."

Patrick chuckled. "There are times when she would challenge you on that." As he spoke, he surveyed the room, focusing on specific areas of interest.

Madeline followed the line of his scrutiny. "You're eager to get started. Go ahead."

Nodding, Patrick noted that the apartment appeared to be pretty tidy, despite the gaping spaces where electronic equipment had once stood. "Clearly you did a thorough cleaning and rearranging since the break-in. I need to know not only what was taken, but where most of the ransacking took place. Once I get a handle on that, I'll get started looking for what the intruder wanted."

"Okay." Madeline nodded, her arm sweeping the room. "As you can see from the hollow spaces, all our... *my*," she corrected herself, "electronic equipment was taken—a fifty-inch flat-screen TV, audio components, DVD player—you name it. The DVDs on the shelves had collapsed all over the floor, thanks to the fact that the intruders stole the statues that were holding them in place. The same applied to the matching statues and DVDs in the master bedroom. The kitchen drawers were emptied onto the floor. The credenza and the vitrine in the dining room were rifled."

"Did they take the silverware in the kitchen? Or any china or collectibles that were in the dining room?"

"Neither. A few of the costlier sculptures from the dining room were gone, but all the paintings throughout the apartment were left on the walls."

"Some of those paintings are valuable," Patrick noted, scanning the walls again. "Which is another indication that robbery wasn't the real motive here. Keep talking. What other rooms were disturbed?"

"The second bedroom was a disaster."

Patrick's brows rose. "And that room is for...?"

"I use it as a den. I have a futon, bookshelves filled with books, a small desk and some computer equipment. I also have a wall safe in there. I opened that right after the burglary. Obviously whoever broke in couldn't figure out the combination because the safe was locked, and when I checked, none of my jewelry, personal papers or cash was taken. Oh, I also have some old file cabinets in the room. The intruder went through those, too."

"How do you know? Were the contents dumped? The files sticking out?"

Madeline shook her head. "Everything looked perfectly in place—not a sheet of paper to be found. But I double-checked, anyway, just in case. I know my filing system, right down to my old recipes. Sure enough, the files were all out of order, as were the papers inside them. Somebody definitely went through the drawers and tried to make it look like they hadn't. I have no idea if they found something or what that something was. Nothing jumped out at me as being missing."

"Either they didn't find what they were looking for, or they found it and it made getting rid of you that much more urgent." Patrick scowled. "Besides recipes, what kinds of files do you keep?"

"My utility bills. My health records, lab results— that kind of thing. My receipts for items purchased. My medical insurance. The common charges for my condo."

"You're one organized lady. Although I can't imagine any of those things being of interest to our offender. Still, you never know. One restaurant receipt, one item purchased…" Patrick loosened his tie and rolled up his shirtsleeves. "Time for me to get started. Let's see if we can figure out what you have that's worth killing for."

Marc gave Hero more exercise than the bloodhound was used to.

During the extralong walk around Tribeca, Hero's ears were flapping in the crisp breeze, his paws crunching in piles of leaves, as Marc strode along at a speedier pace than usual.

All was forgiven, however, when Hero saw where Marc was finishing up their jaunt—at the dog park, which was alive with bright autumn colors and some fellow canines. Marc closed the gate and removed Hero's leash, letting him run off and have some playtime with his peers.

Walk or no walk, Marc hadn't worked one drop of tension out of his body, nor had he unwound even the slightest bit. He sank down on a park bench, keeping an eye on Hero and wishing he could spend the entire afternoon at the gym, rather than going back to the brownstone. He needed to expend some serious energy.

"Hi." A pretty blonde woman, about thirty years old with a black Labrador retriever tugging at his leash, stopped next to Marc. "Which dog is yours?" she asked, giving Marc a flirtatious smile as she tucked a strand of blowing hair behind her ear.

Marc had been hunched over, elbows on his knees, gaze fixed on Hero. Now he sat up, giving the woman a cordial but reserved smile and folding his arms across his chest. He knew his body language was less than welcoming. In fact, it was closing him off. Normally he'd enjoy passing the time here with an attractive woman. But not today. Today he needed to be alone.

"The bloodhound." He pointed, simultaneously pulling out his iPhone as if he was about to start some major project. "And between watching him and getting my work done, I'm going crazy."

The woman's face fell. "I guess that means you're not in the mood for a conversation break."

Marc's expression softened a bit. After all, it wasn't this woman's fault that his head was messed up today. "Oh, I'm in the mood for one. Unfortunately, I can't do it. Not today. My boss would kill me. I should have done this research on my office laptop, but I opted for a walk instead. So I'm stuck looking at a tiny screen, reading detailed legal documents."

"Say no more. I understand." The blonde, who looked like a professional herself, extended her hand. "I'm Robin."

"Marc." He shook her hand, fully aware of the intentionally warm grasp of her fingers. "Can I take a rain check?"

"No problem." Her tone perked up. "Dash and I stop by the park every day at lunchtime. He gets a walk and I get a break. I'm surprised I haven't seen you here before."

"I usually take Hero's evening shift. My colleague takes the one midday. I'm beginning to understand why." Marc mustered a grin. "Maybe I can make some schedule changes. I'll certainly try."

"Hero?" Awareness dawned in Robin's eyes. "Then Ryan is your colleague. I should have guessed. Why is it that all the hot guys band together?"

Marc had to laugh at that one. "I'll duck that question and just say thanks for the compliment."

Robin fumbled in her purse and pulled out a piece of paper, scribbling down her phone number. "Call me—Marc." She stuffed the piece of paper in his hand. "Maybe we can coordinate dog park visits."

"Maybe we can." Marc pocketed the slip of paper and lifted his hand in a wave as Robin strolled off to join some of the women across the way. Judging from her friendly demeanor, she knew them. Dog park buddies. A nice way to pass the lunch hour.

Marc continued to stare at his iPhone, not even seeing it.

All he could see was Maddy.

How long had it been? Nine years? No, ten.

A lifetime. And a heartbeat.

They'd met in the hospital cafeteria. Maddy's eight-hour nursing shift had just ended, and she was grabbing a cup of coffee and a crumb bun to tide her over until she could get a decent meal. Marc had recently gotten back from an overseas mission to the Middle East, and he was at Bethesda for a routine physical, which he'd just passed with flying colors.

They'd bumped into each other on the cafeteria line—literally.

As she'd juggled to balance her tray, Maddy had pivoted, walked smack into Marc and knocked the cup of hot coffee he'd been holding all over him.

She'd been totally mortified. He'd been totally amused. Yeah, the hot liquid stung, but he'd gotten a kick out of the way she took care of the problem, folding and applying napkins to his shirt as if she was dressing a wound.

Chewing her lip, deep in concentration, she'd been so serious about the task at hand that it had taken a good five minutes before she spotted the twinkle in Marc's eyes.

Then she'd risen to her feet, tossed down the napkins and, without a single word, went over and bought Marc another cup of coffee.

"Here you go." She'd handed it to him. "I'd say we're even."

His grin had turned into a deep-throated chuckle, and his gaze had scrutinized her from head to toe. "Not unless you sit down and share a cup with me. *Then* we'll be even."

She had. And that's when and where it had begun.

Marc didn't open up easily. He was reserved by nature—a trait which had been accentuated by his covert role as a navy SEAL. Yet with Maddy, he was relaxed, comfortable. She was easy to talk to. She didn't pry and she didn't pursue any subject he chose to avoid. She was open about her own life—a small-town girl who'd read six biographies on Florence Nightingale and had always wanted to be a nurse. ROTC had paid her scholarship to college, and she'd gone on to be a navy nurse, stationed here in Bethesda Medical Center. From the additional info Marc had made sure to dig up, Maddy had completely undersold herself. It was no wonder she'd become an E.R. nurse. She had an incredible gift. There were military guys in the hospital who, by all rights, should have died from their injuries, but hadn't—thanks to Madeline. She wasn't beautiful, but there was something incredibly sexy and stunning about her. Dark hair, big brown eyes, delicate features and a body to kill for, she possessed a certain warmth and style that was impossible to miss.

The sexual pull between them had been instant and overwhelming. Even that first evening, when Marc had done nothing more than walk her to her door and kiss her good-night, they'd both felt the burn. It had taken all Marc's self-control not to back her into the apartment, tear off her clothes and bury himself inside her until neither of them could breathe.

Maddy had felt the same. He saw it in her eyes when his lips left hers—the wonder, the astonishment, the desire. And her heart had been racing; he could see the rapid rise and fall of her chest.

All from one kiss.

One kiss that had led to another date, and then another.

By that third date, Marc's iron control snapped.

He was barely able to get through dinner before he tossed down his napkin and stared straight into Maddy's eyes.

"I can't do coffee and dessert," he said bluntly. "I've got to get inside you."

Maddy didn't bat a lash. She folded her napkin neatly, placed it beside her half-eaten meal and rose.

"I'll get my coat. You get the check. I'll meet you outside in five minutes," she replied.

It took Marc three.

They sat apart in the taxi, not even daring to touch each other. They both knew that once they did, it would be all over. But the sexual tension in the backseat was so thick it was suffocating.

By the time Marc kicked her apartment door shut and reached behind him to flip the lock, Maddy was unbuttoning his shirt. Marc finished the job for her, shrugging out of the shirt and tossing it aside.

Then he reached for her, pulling her against him.

He took her mouth in a devouring kiss that nearly brought them to their knees. Maddy pressed herself against him, and Marc backed her toward the bedroom, never breaking the kiss. He pulled off her clothes as they staggered down the short hall and into her room.

They were naked when they hit the bed.

Neither of them could withstand the preliminaries— not this first time. There were no gentle strokes, no soft words, no tender touches. It was fast, and it was hot and it was primal.

Afterward, Marc collapsed on top of her. Never in his life had he lost control like that, coming with the urgency and explosiveness of a teenager. He'd barely been able to hold back long enough to feel Maddy unravel beneath him, pulse all around him, cry out his name.

He knew he'd shouted hers, as well. And he knew he was lost.

"Shit," he'd muttered.

A soft laugh had shimmered through Maddy's body. "Nice. Just the thing a girl wants to hear after...*this*."

With the greatest of efforts, Marc had propped himself on his elbows, gazing down into Maddy's deep, dark eyes.

"Did you feel it, too?" he asked bluntly.

A soft smile through kiss-swollen lips. "Yes," she whispered, tracing his jaw with her fingertip. "I felt it. I've never felt anything like it before. But you knew that."

"I knew it because it was the same with me." Marc shut his eyes, pressed his forehead to hers. "Shit," he said again.

Maddy was silent for a moment. "We don't have to give this a name or overanalyze it, Marc," she murmured. "We can just enjoy it—whatever *it* is and whatever *it* becomes."

"We both know that's a cop-out, Maddy. The name is hanging out there, whether or not the words are said. The feelings are real and they're off the charts. I'm already in so deep I can't get through a meeting without thinking about this." He pushed his hips gently against hers. "And that was *before* it happened. Now I'll probably walk around with a 24/7 hard-on."

Maddy began to laugh. "I like that image. Very SEAL-like." Her fingertips caressed his back, and her breath caught as she felt him harden inside her. "Let's not talk. For now—I'm here." She wrapped her legs around him. "Right here."

Right here had gone on for months—the most emotionally consuming months of Marc's life.

And emotionally consuming was not the mindset of a navy SEAL. It couldn't be.

An outburst of barks, followed by Hero slamming his full weight against Marc's legs, snapped Marc out of his trip down memory lane in a hurry. Hero jumped up, scrambling, without much success, to get his beefy body onto Marc's lap.

"Down," Marc commanded, snapping his fingers.

Instantly Hero obeyed.

"Sit."

Hero's bottom hit the ground and he gazed at Marc, waiting for his reward.

"Very subtle." Marc reached in his pocket for one of the organic carrots Claire had cut up this morning. "Good boy." He extended his hand and gave Hero what he was waiting for.

As Hero chomped down the carrot, Marc rose, now very much in the present. "I take it you've had enough playtime with your buddies and are ready to head back. So am I."

Robin waved at Marc as he leashed Hero, and he grinned and waved back. She brought her hand to her ear in a gesture that said *Call me.* Marc nodded. He wished he was in the market for a hookup that would be that simple.

But simple had never been his forte.

Feeling restless and in a foul mood, Marc walked Hero briskly back to work.

"Have a good outing?" Casey asked as he passed by her office.

"Hero got some exercise and I got hit on. So I'd say, yeah, it was a good outing."

Casey glanced up and watched the tension in his broad-shouldered body as he continued on his way.

"I'd try the gym," she called after him. "It's probably better for what ails you."

5

Casey arrived at Madeline's apartment at 11:00 a.m. sharp, the time Emma had confirmed with her first thing that morning.

"Hey, John," Casey greeted the security guard at the door. John Nickels was one of Patrick's best and sharpest.

"Casey—hi." John gave her a professional smile. He was well over six feet, with the body of a linebacker. He'd served the NYPD in the homicide department for twenty-five years. No one was getting by him, that was for damned sure.

Now he stepped aside for Casey to ring the bell. The doorman had already announced her and gotten Madeline's okay to send her up. "Everything here's been quiet," he said.

"Good." Casey rang the bell. "That's how I like it."

Madeline opened the door. She was wearing jeans and a pale yellow sweater. Again, expensive but understated.

She was still moving stiffly as she showed Casey in, urging her to make herself comfortable on the living room's deep-cushioned, pebble-brown club chair, which was positioned diagonally across from the sofa.

"Don't even offer to get me anything." Casey cut off what she saw was coming, hanging her coat on one of the polished brass hooks adjacent to the door. "Just sit down on that sofa and relax. We'll talk."

"I feel like a ridiculous invalid," Madeline said, lowering herself to the sofa with a grimace. "I'm sitting in the exact same spot as I was yesterday when Patrick was checking out my apartment. Other than showering, eating and creeping in and out of my bed, I've done very little but lie here and read."

"You're healing," Casey replied. "You need the rest."

"I haven't slept well since the break-in, and certainly not since the attempt on my life," Madeline admitted. "I wouldn't have shut an eye if John hadn't been outside my door all night. I can't thank you or Patrick enough for arranging security for me."

"We protect our clients." Casey was adamant. "Nothing is going to happen to you. Not on our watch. You can count on it."

"I am." Madeline folded her hands in her lap. "Go ahead. Ask me whatever you'd like."

Casey held up her iPhone with a questioning look. "All right if I tape the convo? I want to concentrate without taking notes." A grin. "And unfortunately, Yoda isn't transportable."

Madeline chuckled, waved her hand to indicate that Casey should go ahead. "Record away."

Casey pressed the appropriate button and set the iPhone on the coffee table. She sat back, crossing one leg over the other. "Let's review potential suspects. Starting with Conrad."

Madeline inclined her head in surprise. "Conrad? Isn't that a reach? I mean, I know the spouse is always number one on the list, but under the circumstances, my ex is in no position to try to run me down."

"Your ex is a rich man with lots of connections and pull. He's in a health care facility, not a prison. He could have hired someone to do his dirty work." Casey propped her elbow on her knee and leaned forward, her chin resting on her hand. "You said your divorce was amicable, but it was still a divorce. Were you seeing someone else? Was there a dispute over money? Did you get anything in the settlement that Conrad badly wanted to keep?"

Casey stopped her litany of questions to ask the most important one. "Was Conrad unstable enough to let any one of those things push him over the edge?"

"And hire a hit man to kill me?" Madeline's tone was filled with disbelief. "Absolutely not. He's severely depressed and in a very dark place. But his anger is all aimed inward. Our conversations have been few, but they've all been civil, even friendly. And no, I wasn't and am not seeing anyone else. Nor did I demand anything in the divorce. Conrad was more than generous. I really think you're barking up the wrong tree."

"Maybe. Maybe not." Casey intentionally kept her posture relaxed. She was easing the conversation in a strategic direction that could possibly put Madeline on the defensive—especially since she'd just written her ex-husband off as a suspect. "Would you object if I were to drive up and have a talk with Conrad?"

Madeline's eyes widened, more in surprise than in defensiveness.

"Just being thorough," Casey added lightly.

After considering that for a moment, Madeline shrugged. "I guess not," she said. "The truth is, Conrad and I may be divorced, but I still care about him. I have no idea what his current state of mind is, and I don't want to cause a setback. So let's talk to his doctor first and get her opinion. Her name is Dr. Marie Oberlin. I'll call her before you leave. If she gives us her okay, I'll text you all her contact info, and you can make the trip up to Danbury."

"That would be great."

Madeline's eyes narrowed quizzically. "I wasn't expecting you to take such an aggressive stance when it came to Conrad. You weren't that way yesterday. What changed? Did you dig up something I should know about?"

"No." Casey was blunt. "What changed is that you and I are now alone and Marc isn't in the room."

A flush stained Madeline's cheeks, and she dropped her gaze. "How much did Marc tell you?" she asked.

"Marc doesn't share. Not his personal life. But I'm sure that comes as no surprise to you."

"It doesn't."

"Is there anything *you'd* like to share?"

Madeline's hesitation was brief. "I guess I came to Forensic Instincts because of and in spite of Marc. Your company's reputation is stellar. I also know how extraordinary Marc is at everything he does. *Failure's* not in his vocabulary. But I didn't expect to react so powerfully to seeing him again. It's been ten years. Maybe I made a mistake coming to you."

"You didn't. We just need to work this through." Casey wasn't surprised by anything Madeline had just said. "Here's what I know. You two met in Bethesda during Marc's navy SEAL days. I gather you had a relationship—a pretty intense one, judging from both your reactions. I won't pry. But you have to take the lead with me on this one. How much do you want Marc to be included in or excluded from? How hard will it be to separate business from personal? I'll handle this any way you want me to. And it *can* be handled. But you have to tell me what you want—Marc's expertise or his absence. Either can be arranged."

There was a long silence—one that Casey had anticipated. She just sat quietly, watching Madeline pick at a fingernail and waiting for her response.

"I trust Marc with my life," she said at last. "I'd be an idiot to exclude him. We're both adults. We'll have to get past our residual feelings—that is, unless Marc's indicated otherwise."

"To the contrary, Marc is his usual proactive self, ready to take on and solve the case. But *you're* our client. You have to be at ease."

"What I have to be is *alive,*" Madeline responded. "So yes, please include Marc in your investigation."

"Fine." Casey nodded. "Next question. I'd like to take Marc with me when I visit Conrad. I rely on his intuition and his strategies. Does Conrad know about Marc?"

"He knows I was involved with someone in Bethesda years ago. He's not privy to the details. And I didn't exactly leave photos lying around. So he wouldn't recognize Marc or his name."

"Good." Again, Casey nodded. "So you'll call Dr. Oberlin before I leave. If all goes as planned, Marc and I will visit Crest Haven Residential Treatment Center. Agreed?"

"Agreed."

"Let's move on, then. I'll need a list of all your friends, supposed friends and associates, both inside and outside the hospital—everything from Ronald Lexington's wife, to his professional successor, to your coffee or lunch buddies, to your dentist and hair stylist. Start composing it as soon as I leave. I'll need it ASAP."

"Wow." Madeline rubbed a hand across her brow. "That's going to be quite a challenge."

"I'm sure. But it has to be done." Casey could see that Madeline's strength was waning. "One more thing and then I'll let you make that phone call and we'll call it a morning. What's changed in your life—either personal or professional—over the past few weeks or months? Anything at all that comes to mind?"

"The merger," Madeline replied without missing a beat.

"Yes, the hospital merger." Casey wasn't surprised that Madeline responded so quickly and went straight to that particular subject. Based on Ryan's preliminary research, the health care industry was abuzz with news of the merger between Manhattan Memorial Hospital—the hospital where Madeline and Conrad worked—and New York Medical Center.

"Ryan did some digging," Casey said. "According to him, the merger you're describing recently went from being a dead issue to a done deal. I understand why the hospital board put it on hold—Ronald Lexington's death. I also understand that he's been gone for several months. What rekindled the interest in the merger now?"

"Profitability did," Madeline replied. "Our hospital was in turmoil after Ronald's death. It took a while, but now it's running smoothly again, thanks to our interim hospital administrator—who's adamantly in favor of the merger, by the way. The board was waiting for him to be brought up to speed to consummate a deal."

"Interesting. You said that Ronald was just as adamantly opposed." Casey processed that. "Where did Conrad fit into this?"

"Oh, he was a major advocate. And, in the interest of full disclosure, his pro stance wasn't entirely altruistic. Part of the reason he was so eager for the merger to happen is that he was being offered the position of chief of surgery of the new conglomerate."

"I see." Actually, Casey already knew that. But it was important that Madeline trusted her enough to tell her everything.

"Personally, Ronald thought that was wonderful for Conrad. But he was opposed to expanding the hospital into a huge, impersonal entity—and to having to eliminate staff in the process."

"That was then. Let's talk about now."

"As I said, the merger was just announced," Madeline replied. "Rumors are flying everywhere. The entire hospital chats about little else. There are a lot of people freaking out—not that I blame them. People are worried about losing their jobs, about pay cuts, about resource cuts, about increased responsibilities and fewer staff members to fulfill them. And the whole process is in everyone's face, so the stress is through the roof. Due diligence has already started. There are accountants and lawyers meeting with Jacob Casper every day."

"Jacob Casper," Casey repeated, referring to the interim hospital administrator. "Tell me about him."

"He was one of a dozen potential candidates, from what I understand. The board thought the world of him. They interviewed like crazy, but Jacob was appointed at Manhattan Memorial less than a month after Ronald's passing."

"And the general consensus on him?"

"He's a good man for the job," Madeline replied. "He was one of Ron's key people, although they didn't see eye-to-eye on many things. He's well-respected, if not particularly well-liked. Ron was a real person. Jacob is a corporate guy."

"And he's pushing for the merger." Casey tapped her index finger against her lips. "Do you have any idea what his inclinations are where it comes to Conrad? Does he endorse his becoming chief of surgery? Is he open-minded about his return? Or has he temporarily— or permanently—written him off?"

Madeline turned up her palms. "I have no idea. As Conrad's ex, all I hear about him is gossip—nothing I'd place any stock in. And even before the divorce, no one in the hospital would have discussed Conrad with me. That would be unethical and unprofessional."

Casey processed that with a nod. "We can find a way into the hospital to conduct some interviews, including Jacob Casper. But some of what we need access to requires a more delicate approach."

A hint of a smile curved Madeline's lips. "I think the detective shows call that infiltrating the place."

"I call it getting what's necessary to keep you safe." Casey paused, recalling a tidbit of information that Ryan had run by her earlier. "Ryan caught a brief internet post on the hospital's website—something about a courtyard dedication to Ronald Lexington?"

"Yes," Madeline replied. "After Ronald's death, donors contributed money to the hospital in his name. Ronald loved the outdoors, so all the donations went toward building a small courtyard near the administrative wing.

It was just completed. There's going to be a dedication ceremony next week."

"Perfect," Casey said. "How small and private is the ceremony?"

"Anyone employed by the hospital is free to come. And it's not high security or anything, so I'm sure you could find your way in."

"We'd do better as invited guests—invited and accompanied by a respected hospital staff member."

Madeline's brows rose. "Me?"

"Will you be up to it?"

"If you think it will help, I'll make myself be up to it."

"Good," Casey replied. "That's just what I wanted to hear."

6

Crest Haven Residential Treatment Center looked more like a posh and well-manicured country club than it did a health care facility—right down to the sprawling grounds and cast-iron entrance gates.

Casey drove the FI van up to the security booth, and provided the guard with both hers and Marc's names and P.I. identification cards. The thin-lipped man with the balding head peered inside the car at the two of them, checked their IDs and finally made a brief phone call while squinting at his visitors' list. Whatever he was told evidently satisfied him, because he pressed a button that made the heavy iron gates swing open.

"The visitors' lot is at the far right of the grounds," he said in a flat monotone. "Follow the signs. Avoid the handicapped spots. Enter the main building through the front doors. You'll be met at the reception desk just inside. Do not proceed farther or you will be stopped and escorted out."

"Thank you." Casey shifted the van back into Drive and moved through the open gates and along the winding driveway.

"What a charmer," Marc muttered. "He must attract women like a magnet."

Casey smiled. "At least Dr. Oberlin left the right instructions about our visit. Otherwise, I think Mr. Charmer would be cuffing us right about now."

"That still might happen. We'd better not put a toe beyond the reception desk or the fires of hell will swallow us up."

Chuckling, Casey headed to the far right grounds and followed the signs to the visitors' lot. She and Marc drove by a golf course, two tennis courts and an Olympic-size swimming pool.

"Nice accommodations," Marc commented. "Certainly conducive to recovery."

"*If* the patient has the mind-set to utilize the facilities. Severe depression puts a damper on all facets of life."

"I know," Marc answered quietly. "I've seen the results firsthand."

Casey nodded. She couldn't even begin to imagine the posttraumatic stress disorder and deep, dark depressions Marc had seen during his navy SEAL days.

"Madeline made it sound like Conrad was in bad shape," she commented instead.

"Yeah, well, being a top-notch surgeon and having your best friend die on your operating table is pretty traumatic, especially after he begged you to do the surgery even though there was way too personal a connection for that to happen. Clearly Ronald Lexington had complete faith in Conrad."

"And in Conrad's eyes, he broke that faith in the most horrifying way possible." Casey pulled into a parking spot and flipped off the ignition, then turned to face Marc. "Let's see what we've got."

* * *

The security at the facility was every bit as tight as Mr. Charmer had implied. The doorman checked their IDs against a list he had, and then gestured for them to approach the white marble semicircular reception desk—an exquisite piece of furniture in an equally exquisite waiting room filled with mauve leather chairs and a gray-and-white marble floor.

A toned middle-aged woman with short salon-styled hair and a designer pantsuit looked up as they stopped in front of her.

"Yes?" she inquired.

For what seemed like the twentieth time, Casey and Marc presented their private investigator IDs and an explanation about Dr. Oberlin expecting them. Yet again, the woman checked out their story, this time on her computer, where she typed in their information with manicured fingernails.

"I'll let Dr. Oberlin know you're here," she informed them. "Have a seat."

Not a surprise that the seats she indicated were located in the front reception alcove. The guardian of the gates. No one would get by her, that was for sure.

"It's easier to get into an FBI field office than it is to get in here," Marc muttered. "The only difference is that here I'm allowed to keep my driver's license and cell phone." He glanced up as a male nurse headed in their direction. "Correction. The system here is a helluva lot faster than the Bureau's."

Casey didn't have time to answer before a young man in a blue uniform approached them. His name tag read William Cook, RN.

"Ms. Woods? Mr. Devereaux?" he asked. Seeing their

nods, he continued, "Dr. Oberlin is expecting you. Please follow me."

He escorted them to the elevators, where he waited for them to precede him. He then pressed the third-floor button and stood, hands clasped behind him, as the doors shut.

"I'll be taking you directly to Dr. Oberlin's office," he informed them. "She'll have a brief meeting with you and then take you to see the patient you've requested to see—Dr. Westfield. He has a time limit on his visitations, so you'll be allowed only a designated amount of time with him."

"We understand." Casey exchanged a quick glance with Marc. It felt like they were in the friggin' military rather than a recuperation center.

The elevator doors opened on the third floor, and Nurse Cook led them down a few corridors until he reached an office whose gold plaque read Marie Oberlin, M.D.

He knocked.

"Yes?" came a crisp female voice from inside.

The RN opened the door partway. "Ms. Woods and Mr. Devereaux are here."

There was the sound of a chair being rolled back, and then the click of heels on the floor. A tall, slim, middle-aged woman with chin-length dark hair and an understated pantsuit opened the door the rest of the way and gave them a professional smile. "Come in," she said, gesturing. She shot a quick glance at the nurse, who was making his exit. "Thanks, Bill," she added.

She shut the door, turned and shook Casey's and Marc's hands. "I'm Marie Oberlin, Dr. Westfield's primary attending physician."

"Nice to meet you, Dr. Oberlin," Casey replied. She quickly scanned the office—lovely and elegant, but as understated as Dr. Oberlin herself, with rich walnut rather than stark, in-your-face marble furnishings. "We thank you for your time," Casey added. "We realize it's valuable."

"Not as valuable as my patients." Dr. Oberlin spoke with candor rather than arrogance. "I'm a little uncomfortable having private investigators as visitors. This isn't exactly a social call, and I don't want Dr. Westfield to suffer any setbacks. He's here to recover, not to be agitated."

"We understand that." Casey nodded. "I'm sure Madeline Westfield explained the nature of our visit. We only want to ask her ex-husband a few questions as this involves her life and her safety."

"She did explain that, which is why I'm permitting this visit. The stipulations are that I be present during the interview, and that when I say it's over, it's over."

Casey wasn't happy, but she wasn't surprised, either. Conrad Westfield was a psychiatric patient. His physician wasn't about to let him feel vulnerable and alone while being grilled by two P.I.s.

"Fair enough," Casey responded. "And just so Marc and I know what to expect, could you summarize Dr. Westfield's current mental state without compromising doctor-patient confidentiality? We know he had a psychotic break after the loss of his friend and that he came here in a severely depressive state. Is he clearheaded?"

Dr. Oberlin looked a little put off by the question. "If you're asking if Dr. Westfield is in his right mind, the answer is yes. He's depressed, not unaware. If his condition were more severe, or if he were unable to understand or answer your questions, I wouldn't permit this visit, regardless of how dire the circumstances. In addition, he's expecting you. I don't surprise my patients. The final decision of who they do or don't see is theirs. Dr. Westfield chose to have you here."

"I understand—and we're very appreciative." Casey cautioned herself to tread lightly. The last thing she wanted to do was to offend the woman they needed as their ally. "I certainly wasn't questioning your judgment. I only wanted to know what to expect so that Marc and I can accomplish what we need to as quickly and easily as possible. We're not here to upset your patient, Dr. Oberlin. You have my word."

That seemed to relax the psychiatrist a bit. "All right, then." She scooped up a file and gestured toward the door. "Let's go."

"Just one more question." Casey held up her palm for an instant. "How much did you tell Conrad Westfield about his ex-wife? Does he know she was burglarized? Almost hit by a car?"

"He knows both," Dr. Oberlin replied. "And he's very concerned."

"Good." Casey nodded. "Then we're ready for our interview."

From a rear view, Conrad Westfield looked like any successful middle-aged man standing in his living room on a day off from work.

He was at the room's bay window, back turned toward them, gazing outside. Dressed in designer sweats, he was tall, broad-shouldered and tan, with a full head of salt-and-pepper hair. He looked strong and healthy, and not at all bent and broken.

Casey and Marc exchanged glances.

Dr. Oberlin intercepted the look. "Appearances are often deceiving," she murmured. "At the same time, any manifestation of normal behavior is a positive sign." Aloud, she said, "Conrad, your visitors are here."

Conrad Westfield turned around. He was a handsome man, but instantly, Casey could see that Dr. Oberlin was right. Put together or not, Conrad's face was drawn and his eyes were hollow and faraway.

"Dr. Westfield, thank you for seeing us." Casey stepped forward and extended her hand. "I'm Casey Woods, and this is my associate, Marc Devereaux."

"Ms. Woods. Mr. Devereaux." Conrad shook both their hands. There was no reaction at all when he said Marc's name or met his gaze—again, not a surprise since Madeline had told them she'd never mentioned Marc's name to her ex. But Marc indiscernibly tensed up, and his stare intensified, however subtly, as he scrutinized the man who'd been married to his former lover.

Casey knew Conrad wouldn't notice, but she certainly did. And it concerned her. She intended to watch Marc like a hawk. If he couldn't keep his personal feelings in check for this interview, then he was being relegated to the background on this case. No second chances. No questions asked.

Marc must have sensed his boss's thought process, because he settled into his usual professional self ASAP.

"Please, sit down," Conrad said, gesturing at the high-backed chairs on either side of a matching sofa, complete with coffee table. He glanced at Dr. Oberlin. "Are you staying?"

"Yes, unless you would prefer I didn't," she replied.

He made an offhand gesture. "I have no problem

either way. I just don't want Ms. Woods and Mr. Devereaux to feel they can't be open and honest." A wry
smile. "Or to think they're dealing with a crazy person."

"That thought never occurred to us," Casey said.
"And Dr. Oberlin is more than welcome to stay. We
won't take up much of your time."

That comment made Conrad's smile widen. "Time is
one thing I have an infinite amount of."

The group of them sat down, Conrad on one end of
the curved sofa, his physician on the other. This way she
had a full view of him and his reactions.

Conrad opened the conversation right away. "How
is Madeline?"

"Understandably anxious and upset," Casey replied.
"And still in pain. She took a nasty fall when she tried
to avoid that SUV."

Worry, not guilt, furrowed Conrad's brow.

"I don't understand it," he said. "Why would someone want to hurt Madeline? She doesn't have an enemy
in the world."

"Clearly that's not true." Marc spoke up for the first
time, and he was all business, without a trace of personal involvement. "Our best guess is that the offender
thinks she knows something incriminating, and that she
has proof of it in her possession."

"I don't understand. Did she witness a crime?"

"Not that we know of," Marc replied. "So far we
haven't found the offender's trigger. But we will."

"The police don't have the manpower to do anything
without solid evidence of our theory," Casey added. "But
Forensic Instincts does, which is why Madeline hired
us."

"I'm grateful." Again, Conrad looked and sounded

genuine. "And please, whatever extra funds need to be spent, I'm more than happy to cover them. Just keep her safe."

"That's the plan," Casey said. "Which is why we wanted to ask you a few questions."

"Starting with, did I hire someone to try to kill my ex-wife." Conrad spoke very matter-of-factly. He waved away any forthcoming clarification from Casey. "I'm not mentally healthy right now. But I do have my full wits about me. The husband—or former husband, in this case—is always the first suspect. The answer is no, I most certainly did not try to harm Madeline. Do whatever you need to do, look into whatever phone records you'd like—anything required to back up my claim. You have carte blanche to dig into my life—or whatever's left of it."

"Thank you." Casey was wary about how *extremely* forthcoming Conrad was being. It could be that his complete and open honesty was real, and based only upon his fondness for his ex-wife. On the other hand, it could be that he was trying to throw them off track.

Either way, his cooperation made things a hell of a lot easier.

"You asked if Madeline witnessed a crime," Casey said aloud. "As Marc told you, the answer is no—nothing overt. Can you think of any situation she might be overlooking that would make her a target?"

Conrad spread his palms wide. "No, but I'm at a distinct disadvantage. I haven't seen my ex-wife in months, and my exposure to her life, most especially to her work, is nil." He paused. "My former place of employment is not a topic that's introduced to me unless I bring it up in a session."

"Your *former* place of employment?" Marc responded to that one. "I was under the impression that you planned to return to your previous position—or your new one, when the hospital merger goes through."

"You don't have to discuss this if you'd rather not, Conrad," Dr. Oberlin was quick to point out.

Conrad stared down at the carpet for a moment, then lifted his gaze—that sad, hollow gaze. "That's all right. I'm just not sure how to answer your question. Whether or not the position is still open to me isn't the primary issue. The truth is, I don't know if I'll ever be capable of performing surgery again. I'm not even sure how I'd react to walking into an operating room."

Casey couldn't help but feel pity. The man was visibly suffering. A huge portion of his life and his identity were gone.

"I'm very sorry about Ronald Lexington," she said quietly but directly. "I can't imagine how painful his loss has been for you. But from what I understand, you're a brilliant surgeon. Hundreds of people could benefit from your skills. Life happens. That doesn't make it your fault."

"We're not here to analyze Dr. Westfield or to discuss his ghosts," Dr. Oberlin interrupted. "Do you have any other questions for him—ones that relate to his former wife's predicament?"

Casey took the hint, and fast. She backed off from any reference to Ronald Lexington or to Conrad's state of mind. "We won't keep you." She rose and handed Conrad a business card. "If you could make arrangements for us to do the necessary background check that you so kindly offered, that would be great. Also if you think of anything—however small—that might give us a lead, please call Forensic Instincts anytime, day or night."

"Of course." Conrad took her card and came to his feet, as well. His forehead was still creased. "Is Madeline being protected?"

"She has 24/7 security detail," Marc stated flatly. He was letting Conrad know that if he was concerned about Madeline, he had nothing to worry about. And if he wasn't—if it was access to his ex-wife he was looking for—that wouldn't be happening. "No one is going to reach Madeline again, much less harm her. We've made sure of that."

"Thank God." Again, relief—genuine or otherwise—swept Conrad's face. "I realize we're divorced, but I still care deeply for her. Madeline is a wonderful and special woman who places everyone's needs above her own. I want her kept safe, regardless of the cost."

"She will be." Marc's tone was still firm, his expression still impersonal. Whatever he was feeling, he was keeping it under control.

"I'd appreciate if you'd keep me posted," Conrad added. "I'll arrange with Dr. Oberlin for your phone calls to be put through to me immediately."

Marc stared out the window as Casey steered the van up the winding driveway leading to the iron gates.

She edged him a sidelong glance. He looked tense and introspective. "Brooding?" she asked.

"Aren't you subtle," Marc returned drily. "No, I'm not brooding. I'm thinking. Westfield is either a decent guy and the best ex-husband any woman could hope for, or a consummate actor and con artist…and an attempted murderer." A pregnant pause. "And yes, I'm being objective."

"Actually, I think you are." Casey's eyes were back on the road as she slowed down at the gates and signaled the guard that they were leaving. "I also think you're purposely avoiding stating the obvious, because you think I'll call you on it. Well, I won't. Because I see the same thing. Conrad Westfield still has feelings for his ex-wife." She paused. "Feelings that Madeline is totally unaware of and that she doesn't return."

Marc grunted. "I wonder how that factors into this little equation."

The iron gates swung open, and Casey steered the van onto the main road.

"It could exacerbate it. And it could mean nothing. But you're right," Casey continued. "The depression is real, and it's deep. So is the self-blame. But Conrad is very intelligent and very aware. Could he have orchestrated the attacks on Madeline—out of pain, spite, whatever? Cognitively, yes."

"So now we check out his phone records, which are going to be squeaky-clean or he wouldn't have offered them up. Then what?"

"Then we have Ryan dig deeper. Figure out if Conrad has a burner phone or some other means of communication. Find out if he has any seedy connections inside the facility who might be willing to do his dirty work for him. Conrad's rich and well-connected. This meeting we just had is only step one where it comes to Madeline's ex." Casey frowned. "My concern is the long list of hospital employees Madeline gave me, every one of whom is a potential suspect until we figure out the assailant's motive."

"Some of them will talk to us willingly," Marc said.

"And some won't. Plus, who knows who'll be lying and why? Between the skills you learned from your days at the FBI's Behavioral Analysis Unit and my psychological training, we'll be able to do a pretty good job of figuring out who's lying. But their motives? That's another story entirely. We've got to find a nonconfrontational way into that hospital to get a thorough take on the names on Madeline's list. We have to plan our approach carefully. We'll only get one chance at this before we lose the chance to keep our role in Madeline's life a secret."

"The dedication ceremony to Ronald Lexington is our best shot at doing that," Marc replied. Casey had told him about the hospital courtyard ceremony on the drive to Connecticut.

"Exactly." Casey nodded. "But we can't just walk in there. We'll need to go as Madeline's guests. Just a few of us, not the whole team."

"That few will include me."

The emphatic tone of Marc's response wasn't lost on Casey.

"Do you think that's a good idea?" she asked.

Marc pivoted to face her. "Look, Casey. You and I agreed that I was going to assume my usual role in this investigation. I haven't given you any reason to doubt that I can. So keeping me away from Madeline is ridiculous. I'm the most qualified person on the team to protect her, while simultaneously scrutinizing and assessing the attendees. I think it should be you, me and Claire who go."

"And Emma," Casey surprised him by saying.

"Emma?"

"Uh-huh. Let's go back to the office. I have a plan that I think will work."

7

The hospital courtyard was lovely, and not just from the natural beauty of the red, orange and gold trees around it. The area was lined with miniature boxwoods and colorful, manicured plants, and surrounded by an iron fence that gave the entire area a close, intimate feel, despite being surrounded by tall hospital buildings. There were several benches situated around the courtyard's periphery, so that employees could sit and enjoy the view. And, most impressive of all, there was a brass plate planted in the grassy entranceway that was engraved In Honor of Ronald Lexington.

Casey glanced around as the small group of FI team members and Madeline approached the site, noting that there were already so many attendees they were barely able to be contained within the courtyard itself and were spilling over onto the hospital grounds.

"Clearly Ronald Lexington was a well-respected man," Casey murmured.

"Or everyone is just kissing the necessary asses," Emma responded under her breath.

Claire bit her lip to keep from laughing. "Such a cynic."

"She's probably right," Marc said. "For the most part, this is a political event, not a lovefest."

"Shhh." Madeline put her finger to her lips as a few people spotted her and started to walk over. "We're on."

"Wait." Casey touched Madeline's arm, then pointed at an attractive, middle-aged woman with frosted blond hair who was flanked on either side by a young woman and a young man. Given the resemblance, it wasn't a long shot to guess that those were her kids. All three of them were surrounded by attendees. There was an air of importance about her as if she was central to the occasion, and Casey could guess why.

"Is that Ronald Lexington's widow?" she asked Madeline.

"Nancy Lexington, yes," Madeline confirmed. "Those are her two children, Ron and Felicia. Not really children anymore. I think Ron is twenty-five and Felicia twenty-four."

Casey took all that in. "I'll need to meet the three of them later when the masses have left their sides."

"No problem. I'll make it happen."

The next half hour was spent with Madeline introducing her "friends" and discussing her accident with what seemed to be an endless flow of people. Casey had suggested that Madeline get as many introductions as possible out of the way before the ceremony, so that the FI team could mingle comfortably and do their own behavioral analysis as the event unfolded, while Madeline paid the appropriate respect to Ronald Lexington's memory. There was no point in arousing any suspicions of her motives for being here.

On the other hand, Casey had also instructed Madeline to be up front about who her FI "plus-ones" were.

Much to their chagrin, Forensic Instincts team members had been interviewed too many times by TV media sources to assume that no one would recognize them. Candor was their best defense.

"If you tell the truth, you don't have to remember anything," Casey said, quoting Mark Twain. "In this case, you'll just tweak the truth to make it work for us. Explain that while you were a nurse in Bethesda, you treated Marc for an injury he sustained, and that, ironically, you ran into each other again in New York. And tell them that Claire and I were both recently patients in this hospital. We received excellent care and wanted to support the facility with a donation." Casey stopped right there. The reasons for hers and Claire's hospital admission were not things she wanted to discuss, nor did she need to. The details were no secret. The media had made sure of that.

"As for Emma," Casey had concluded, "she's fascinated by the medical field, and she loves helping people. She was hoping that by meeting someone in hospital administration, she could land a candy-striper job."

Emma hadn't blinked. She knew her dual roles in today's visit.

Madeline didn't, but she'd accepted Casey's strategy at face value. "So, when you heard Marc was coming, you all opted to join him, each for your own reasons."

"Exactly. We gave you a call, you offered to bring us as your guests, and that's that."

"Okay. That works."

And it had. No matter how fascinating Forensic Instincts was, the crowd of hospital employees was far more interested in hearing about Madeline's misfortunes and the severity of her injuries.

That gave the FI team the access they needed.

Their agendas had been laid out by Casey.

Emma headed off to begin her search for the right target.

Claire, keeping a low profile, moved about and stopped here and there to hover near clusters of people. Sipping her sparkling water, she listened, seeing if she picked up any negative energy. There was plenty to be had.

Casey noted the same thing as she chatted with the various employees. She listened to their feelings about Ronald Lexington, watching their body language as they spoke and assessing who was disingenuous and who was for real. The gist of what she heard was positive, and it was obvious that Lexington had been an affable guy whose only flaw was that he liked women just a tad too much for a happily married man. But if you played into his charm, all would be cool.

There was an entirely different vibe that came through when people talked about Jacob Casper. No matter how diplomatically people spoke, it was clear that there was no love lost between the staff and their interim hospital administrator. Listening to what *wasn't* said as well as to what *was,* it was obvious that the hospital employees felt that Casper's interests were totally self-centered, and that he didn't give a damn about anything but money and power.

Casey wanted to form her own opinion. The employees were hardly unbiased at this particularly vulnerable time. There were anxious whispered conversations about the hospital merger—fears of job loss, reduced benefits, staff cuts and the resulting overwork for those who remained. The lack of job security and fear for financial survival was crushing—and naturally, those feelings were directly aimed at Jacob Casper. So Casey would have to meet him and decipher what he was for herself.

Multitasking as always, Casey glanced around, her expert gaze seeking and finding the specific individuals Madeline had named and provided physical descriptions of as being those who'd been closest—either in a professional or a personal capacity—to Ronald Lexington. She'd find a way to talk to all of them after the formalities were complete. She wanted to get a feel for who might have it in for Madeline.

Marc, for his part, was keeping a close watch on Madeline.

Periodically Casey would make sure to look around and check on the progress her team members were making. Everyone seemed to be gleaning something from their efforts. When her gaze found Emma, it took enormous restraint not to smile. Emma was busy chatting up the most stereotypical IT guy she could find in the group. He was tall, skinny and definitely dorky looking, with eyeglasses he kept shoving up on his nose and a tendency to blink furiously. Clearly he was awkward around people and, Casey suspected, far more at home hiding behind a computer monitor and a keyboard. On the other hand, he was over the moon about Emma's interest in him, visibly entranced by her vivacious personality and her California-girl looks. As for Emma, she was standing close to him, head cocked as she hung on to his every word, asking question after question about his fascinating job. The more questions she asked, the more enthusiastic he got—and the more distracted.

Good girl, Casey thought. She'd been dead-on right to bring Emma here. If Emma ultimately accomplished her two goals, Forensic Instincts would have a clear shot at getting what they needed here.

The next step would be for Madeline to introduce Casey to Jacob Casper so that Casey could get an actual read on him. He represented the new regime, and talking to him was crucial, especially in light of how edgy the staff was around him, and how overall their dislike for him was. That could simply be the fear of losing their jobs, given that Casper was so pro-merger and would work hard to see the due diligence process succeed, or it could be more. As a necessary bonus, Casey would have Madeline introduce Emma to him—and put in a good word for her as a potential candy striper. That was going to have to happen fast to make Casey's plan work.

Jacob Casper was a cut-to-the-chase kind of guy, solidly built and all about the bottom line. He was pleasant enough, but Casey could tell that affability didn't come easily to him. He was trying to make people like him to ease his way, but doing that took a great effort on his part. His mind was on money, not relationship-building.

Casey let him chat with Madeline for a few minutes while she observed. Bottom line or not, he seemed genuinely saddened by Ronald Lexington's passing and equally saddened by the effect it had had on Conrad.

"My greatest pleasure will be to see Conrad walk back through those doors and resume doing what he does best," Casper told Madeline. "That man is a surgical genius."

"I agree on both counts," Madeline said.

So Casper was aware that Madeline and her ex-husband had an amicable relationship. Nice point of interest.

"Would chief of surgery still be in the cards for

Conrad if he returned after the hospital merger goes through?" Casey asked.

Casper looked a little surprised that Casey was so plugged into the goings-on at the hospital. His eyes flickered from Casey to Madeline and back.

"I see that Madeline had filled you in on the offer that was on the table during the original negotiations," he replied. "I don't know how things will play out this time. But if I have any say, Conrad will be my first choice for the position."

"*If* he's up for it," Madeline said softly.

"Yes, of course. I didn't mean to imply otherwise," Casper amended. His jaw tightened just a fraction. "I'd never put pressure on him. But I remain optimistic."

"We all do."

Casey noted the subtle change in Casper's body language, and his quick response to Madeline's qualification. It might mean nothing more than that the interim hospital administrator was stressed out by the time pressure involved in getting Conrad back before the high-level position was filled by someone else. Then again, it might mean more.

"It was a pleasure meeting you, Mr. Casper," Casey said, extending her hand.

"Please, call me Jacob." He met Casey's grasp, the tension easing from his body. "It was great meeting you, as well. I've heard and read so much about the Forensic Instincts team." A smile. "You're like the avengers of evil."

Casey laughed. "I like that image. I'll pass it on to the rest of the team." She paused, just long enough for impact. "But today I'm here as a grateful former patient. Forensic Instincts would like to make a donation to the hospital. Can we wire it directly to the administrative office?"

Genuine gratitude flickered across Jacob Casper's face. "That would be wonderful. We appreciate your generosity."

"And *we* appreciate the health care services you provide." Casey was ready to mingle with more of the crowd. She had no worries about leaving Madeline alone with Jacob. Casey could feel Marc's presence nearby, and his trained gaze fixed on their client. Plus, she wanted to give Madeline time alone with Jacob so she could put in a good word for Emma as a potential—and immediate—candy striper. What better time than when FI had just pledged a nice donation to the hospital?

"I think I'll get a cup of coffee." Casey left the matter in Madeline's hands. She knew what she had to do. "Madeline told me you'd be making a short speech in a few minutes. I'm looking forward to it."

"Thank you. I appreciate that," Jacob replied.

Casey headed toward the beverage station, leaving Madeline to her task and filing away the conversation she'd just had for later analysis.

"How did things go with Jacob Casper?" Claire murmured, joining Casey at the coffee urn.

"Interesting. More later. How about you? Any strong energy?"

"A few individuals stand out. Especially when Madeline is near them."

"Then we'll have lots to discuss at the office."

Claire edged a glance to her right and laughed softly. "Emma is really working this. You've got to give the girl credit. She's a talented little thing."

"Yeah, like the Artful Dodger." Casey followed

Claire's line of vision, and chuckled as she watched Emma ease a bit closer to her enamored target. "I think the guy is going to come in his pants."

"I hope not. That might kill the objective."

Their conversation was interrupted as Jacob made his way to the platform and tapped the mike that had been set up for him.

"Good morning, everyone," he began. "We're all here for the same reason—to honor the memory of Ronald Lexington. Ronald was an exceptional man, an exceptional husband and father and an exceptional hospital administrator. He had a way with people that drew them to him, including our patients, whom he cared deeply about. He wanted nothing more than to see people heal and our hospital to thrive."

Jacob cleared his throat, his gaze flitting about with obvious discomfort. "This is a very difficult time at Manhattan Memorial. The upcoming merger is a bit unsettling. I know that Ronald had his reservations about it, and I respected those. But the realities of the health care industry have changed significantly since his death, and I feel certain that, at this point in time, he would have supported this merger for the benefit of all. As we move forward, we will keep his spirit alive. The combined strengths of Manhattan Memorial Hospital and New York Medical Center will be more profitable than the sum of its parts. We'll be able to serve more patients faster and with better outcomes. All of that would mean the world to Ronald. I'm proud to have known and worked with him, and I'm proud to dedicate this beautiful courtyard in his name. Thank you."

Jacob's brow was dotted with sweat as he left the podium.

For a brief instant, there was dead silence. Then came a round of robotic applause—accompanied by drawn expressions, furrowed brows and frightened gazes.

"The negative energy here just went through the roof," Claire said, stating the obvious as she clapped politely.

"I don't blame these people," Casey replied quietly. "That was more of a campaign speech than a heartfelt dedication. I'm sure Ronald Lexington was not a fan of Casper's, nor would he be any more pro-merger now then he was three months ago. This situation is ugly."

As she spoke, Casey caught Emma's eye. A quick nod told Casey that part one of Emma's job was done. Now their new team member was heading toward Madeline, who was beckoning her over to meet Jacob Casper.

Smooth sailing for their plan.

On to meeting Nancy Lexington and her kids. Then it would be chat time with the three people on Casey's list.

Casey caught Madeline's gaze, and Madeline nodded, excusing herself from the group of nurses she'd been chatting with—one gray-haired, seasoned-looking woman in her early sixties, one petite, dark-haired girl who didn't look much older than Emma and one round-faced, smiling guy in his mid-thirties. Beneath their jackets, they were all in their uniforms and all in deep conversation.

"What's the topic being discussed in that group?" Casey asked Madeline, once she'd made her way over. "It seems intense."

"More of the same," Madeline replied. "Fears about the merger. Everyone's very anxious." She sighed. "Dan and his wife are expecting a baby. Carolyn is a couple of years away from retirement and is terrified of being forced into it prematurely. And Diana is a young, fairly new hire, who figures she'll be one of the first to go."

"I feel for them."

"So do I." Madeline winced a bit. "The anticipation is deadly."

"Do you need to leave?" Casey asked quickly. "You look like you're in pain."

"I'll manage. I want you to meet Nancy, her kids and the three people I mentioned in our earlier conversation and put on my list—Dr. Sharon Gilding, Dr. Doug Wilton and Janet Moss."

"I'm ready. But first, I have to ask you again—is there anyone here that you have problems with? Anyone who might have a motive to hurt you?"

A rueful smile. "I don't know about hurting me. But you're about to meet someone who dislikes me intensely."

8

"Nancy Lexington?" Casey looked surprised.

"None other. She still blames Conrad for Ronald's death. She's never let it go. And maybe because we socialized together as couples or because of some other reason I don't know about, she sees me as an extension of my ex-husband."

"So she hates you, too. Interesting. I'm more eager than ever to have this introduction."

"Let's go."

They walked up to the Lexington family, who were now standing alone in a unified group, in quiet discussion.

"Hello, Nancy." Madeline's smile was cordial but tight.

Nancy froze the instant she saw who was addressing her. "Madeline," she said. "I'm surprised to see you attending the dedication ceremony."

"I was very fond of Ronald, both personally and professionally. His presence in the hospital is deeply missed."

"I agree. He had a great deal of life left to live. Unfortunately, it was cut short." Nancy's gaze flickered to Casey. "And you are…?"

"Casey Woods." Casey extended her hand. "I asked Madeline to introduce us. She and I met through one of my business associates."

Casey's statement was a purposeful attempt to separate herself from Madeline so as to nip any guilt-by-association in the bud. The best way to behaviorally assess Nancy was to make sure their meeting was on unbiased terms. It would only cloud the process by having Nancy dislike her from the get-go.

"I'm a former patient and small benefactor of the hospital," Casey said. "This was all fairly recent, so I didn't know your husband. But from everything I've learned, he was a special man. I wanted to extend my belated condolences and to tell you how lovely the courtyard garden is."

Nancy's expression altered completely, and she shook Casey's hand. Her grip was friendly, but her gaze kept edging toward Madeline, a bitter look in her eyes. "Thank you. Ronald was totally devoted to this hospital. It's not the same here—or at home—without him." She turned to gesture at her children. "These are my children, Ron and Felicia."

"It's nice to meet you." Casey turned from one to the other. "My condolences to you both, as well."

"We appreciate that," Felicia said. Her words were directed at Casey, but both she and her brother were eyeballing Madeline. They looked almost as thrilled to see her as their mother did. "We're grateful for today's overwhelming turnout. Our father was an extraordinary man. We miss him every day."

"I'm sure you do." Casey took a step backward. "I don't want to intrude or to take up any more of your time. I just wanted to meet you, to pay my respects and

to offer my gratitude. I received excellent, compassionate care at Manhattan Memorial."

"That's good to hear," Nancy replied. "It was lovely
to meet you."

Not a word to or a glance at Madeline.

"Wow," Casey murmured, giving a low whistle as
she and Madeline retraced their steps. "That woman de-
spises you. She bears looking into, as do her kids. Any
other enemies you failed to mention?"

For the umpteenth time, Madeline searched the sea
of faces.

"No one I can pick out," she said truthfully. "If someone out there hates me, I don't know about it."

"Then that's up to us to find out. In the meantime,
let's go meet Gilding, Wilton and Moss."

Jacob Casper had separated himself from the crowd
to scrutinize the scene between Nancy Lexington and
Madeline Westfield. Now he scowled. This wasn't a
good sign.

He made his way over to Dr. Harold Majors, who was
head of Manhattan Memorial's psychiatric department.

"I was hoping this ceremony would appease her,"
Jacob murmured, "but that doesn't seem to be happening. I need to know how bad she is and how far she'd go
to hurt the hospital."

"As I've said, she's not my patient, Jacob. All I can
give you is an informal evaluation," Majors replied.

"That's all I need. Go over and chat with her. Figure out if she's just stuck in the anger phase of mourn-
ing, or if she's going off the deep end and becoming a
major threat."

Majors nodded. Waiting for the right time, he walked over to offer his condolences to Nancy Lexington.

Dr. Sharon Gilding was a piece of work, Casey noted. Attractive, blonde and as cold as her icy-blue eyes, she was in her mid-forties and reputed to be the best neuro-surgeon in the hospital—and next in line for Conrad's position if he weren't able to fill it. She was also, like Conrad, a close friend of Ronald Lexington's—although what he saw in her, Casey couldn't fathom. No, that wasn't true. If Ronald liked women as much as Casey had been hearing, then she could see him going after Sharon Gilding. Her looks were striking, and her figure was great. But her arrogance? Her haughtiness? Maybe Ronald liked a challenge.

Sharon Gilding's arctic stare moved from Madeline to Casey as Madeline introduced them. Her eyes shot daggers at Madeline, but she inquired politely about her health, and then turned and shook Casey's hand.

"I've seen news flashes about Forensic Instincts on TV," she said. "Congratulations on your well-earned success."

"Thank you." Casey could feel Sharon's dislike for Madeline even when she wasn't addressing her. "From what I understand, neurosurgery is one of the most complex areas of medicine. You must be very talented."

"My career is my life. And yes, I'm exceptional at what I do. The human brain is the most fascinating organ in the body. It controls every nerve and motor function." A tight smile. "I could go on, but the complexity of it would probably bore you."

Wow, did this woman come on strong. Then why did Casey sense that she was protecting herself in some way?

"I hear you're second in line for chief of surgery." Casey went for blunt and fast, wanting to see Sharon Gilding's undisguised reaction. "What happens if Conrad Westfield comes back and accepts the job?"

Surprise mingled with something else shot across the neurosurgeon's face. "Then I continue doing what I'm doing," she responded, schooling her features. "Conrad is a genius in his field. He deserves the position as much as I do."

"That's very magnanimous of you." Casey softened her words with a smile. "Clearly you respect talent in all areas of the medical field."

"I do."

"Were you and Ronald Lexington friends?"

Sharon's shoulders lifted. "We were good colleagues. Ronald discussed administrative issues with me, and I kept him up to date on surgical issues. He was fascinated by every aspect of this hospital, medical or otherwise. I admired his commitment. So yes, we spent time together—as much time as I could spare." She glanced at her watch. "Speaking of which, I really have to be going. I have to be in surgery in an hour."

"Of course." Casey nodded. "It was a pleasure to meet you."

"Likewise." She was already walking away.

"That was interesting," Casey murmured.

"Yes, Sharon is never one for diplomacy," Madeline replied.

"She dislikes you."

"She dislikes everyone."

Casey stifled a grin. "Who's next on the list?"

"Doug Wilton. He's in cardio with Conrad, although he's a cardiologist, not a surgeon. He was one of Conrad's and Ronald's golfing buddies. He's pretty plugged into what goes on at the hospital, but he's also a good guy."

"I could use a good guy after Dr. Gilding."

As it turned out, Madeline was right. Doug Wilton was a good guy. He chatted with them about both Ronald and Conrad, and told funny stories about their golfing excursions.

"Ron and I didn't spend much time together at the hospital. But we had a hell of a good time outside these walls. He had a big heart. I miss him. As for Conrad..." He paused, visibly upset. "I consulted with him on almost every one of my cases. He was an invaluable asset, to me and to the hospital. I can't tell you how much I hope he'll be back. Losing Ron was personally painful for me. Losing Conrad would be devastating."

"I hope it won't come to that," Madeline said.

"So do I," Doug responded. He didn't look surprised by Madeline's compassion for her ex. Casey wondered how much he and Conrad had discussed Madeline—*and* if Doug had any reason to dislike her.

Casey tucked that thought into the bears-further-investigation category.

Once that conversation was over, Madeline led Casey over to Janet Moss, who was the assistant to the hospital administrator, and probably a walking wealth of information.

"Janet has been here for years," Madeline confirmed in a whisper as they neared her. "She worked closely with Ronald, and she works closely with Jacob. She knows everything that goes on in the administrative offices."

"A good person to talk to." Casey gave Janet Moss a

quick once-over. About average height. Slender. Chest-nut-brown hair worn in a simple chignon—one that might look too dressy for work on most women, but one that Janet pulled off with utter grace. High-styled eye-glasses that said designer. Not a lot of makeup, but well-applied and far from cheap. A put-together, professional woman who'd clearly worked her way up to making a decent salary, consistent with Madeline's description.

"Madeline, hi." Janet caught a glimpse of her out of her peripheral vision and turned away from the group of people she'd been talking to so that she could speak to her. "How are you feeling?"

Her tone and expression were concerned. She did shoot a curious glance at Casey, but that was to be expected. Janet was a woman who knew everyone in her hospital, and Casey was not one of those people.

"I'm on the mend," Madeline was replying with a small smile. Actually, Casey noted, Madeline looked as though her energy level was fading. Just this one meeting, then Casey was taking her home.

"Thank you again for the beautiful floral arrangement," Madeline continued. "Just looking at all those vivid colors made lying on the sofa, doing nothing, more pleasant."

"I'm so glad you liked them," Janet replied. "I wish I could have done more."

"It's not necessary. I'm really fine." Having caught Janet's second questioning glance in Casey's direction, Madeline turned and made the introductions.

"No wonder you look familiar." Janet was visibly impressed as she shook Casey's hand. "Your picture's been in the newspapers and on TV. Your investigative firm—Forensic Instincts, right?—has been in the lime-light. Wow. It's good to meet you."

"Good to meet you, too." Casey smiled. "I hear you hold the administrative wing of the hospital together."

Janet chuckled. "I wouldn't go that far. But I've been in the administrative wing for nineteen years. Before that, I did clerical work for four different departments in the hospital. I hate to say it because it ages me, but I've worked at Manhattan Memorial for twenty-six years." A teasing grin. "Since I was twelve."

Casey laughed with her. "Well, if it matters, you certainly don't look old enough to have worked anywhere for that long."

"Makeup is magic."

"How true." Casey was ready to get down to business. "Jacob Casper seems, in a very short time, to have a firm grip on his job and on the upcoming merger. That's pretty impressive, considering the big shoes he had to fill. You worked for both him and Ronald Lexington. Is there a big difference in their styles?"

Janet looked a little wary, as well she should. Casey was asking an inside question.

"They each have their own strengths," she answered diplomatically. "Jacob is the hospital's future. But Ronald cared equally as much. Both men are and were totally committed to their jobs and powerful advocates for the hospital." She steered the conversation to safer ground. "I do have a soft spot for Ronald. He gave my daughter a job here. She had several offers, but selfishly, I love having her close by."

"I don't think I met your daughter," Casey replied.

"She's over there." Janet pointed at the group Madeline had been chatting with earlier. "Diana."

"Oh." Casey remembered the pretty young woman. Madeline had said she was a fairly new hire, and afraid of losing her job once the merger was finalized.

"She's a circulating nurse," Janet said. "She graduated at the top of her class, specialized in surgical nursing and then earned her registered nurse license and her operating-room nurse certification at a ridiculously young age. Ronald hired her about six months before he passed away. He felt strongly about that decision—even more so as Diana proved herself. Jacob feels the same way. Diana is a very talented young woman—and I'm not just saying that because she's my daughter."

"Diana really is exceptional," Madeline agreed. "The entire surgical staff has nothing but praise for her. Conrad often requested her to be his circulating nurse."

"Which is high praise, coming from Conrad." Janet beamed. "He's a genius."

Casey tilted her head quizzically. "What exactly is a circulating nurse?" she asked.

"Basically she's in charge of everything in the operating room, from setup to the surgical procedure, to reorganizing things afterward." Janet paused, looking a bit embarrassed. "I don't mean she performs the surgery itself. Obviously that's the surgeon's job. But she makes sure everything is running smoothly and that all the necessary instruments are ready. She moves around the O.R. throughout the surgery, overseeing the staff and the procedure."

"And that's where the term *circulating nurse* comes from," Casey concluded.

"Exactly."

"That sounds like quite a job." Casey's wheels were turning. She didn't doubt that Diana was outstanding, but that wasn't what was on her mind now. What was on her mind was Janet. She was someone Casey needed to spend more time with. Her inside knowledge—personal and professional—of everything and everyone at the hospital might shed some light on who would want Madeline eliminated. The question was how to take the next step without arousing Janet's suspicions.

Janet solved that problem for her.

"Enough about me. I'm boring compared to you." She turned to Madeline. "How do you know people at Forensic Instincts? You never mentioned having famous friends."

Madeline played her part well. "Actually, Casey and I just met recently. The person I know is Marc Devereaux." She pointed in Marc's direction. "I knew him long before Forensic Instincts even existed. I was his attending nurse during my time in Bethesda. He was a navy SEAL in those days. I ran into him in New York. He's the one who told me that some of his team members at Forensic Instincts wanted to make a donation to our hospital, so I invited them here today to meet Jacob and our wonderful staff."

Janet looked enthralled, like a teenager who'd just met a rock star. "I love crime investigation TV shows."

Casey saw an "in" and grabbed it. "So do I, although they tend to stretch the truth or sometimes distort it. Real-life investigations are very different."

"How so?" Janet leaned in to hear more.

With a rueful expression, Casey glanced over at Madeline. "I'd love to explain all this to you, but I think Madeline is tiring. She did us a huge favor by letting us share in this day. I don't want to tax her any more than necessary."

"Of course." All Janet's excitement was extinguished in the blink of an eye.

Casey chewed her lip in alleged contemplation. Then she pulled out her iPhone. "Give me your cell phone number. I'll text you my contact information. Maybe we can get together for lunch."

"Really?" That excitement was back.

Casey's thumb was poised and ready on her keypad. "Of course. As I said, this hospital—and Madeline—have been very good to us. If I can return the favor in any way, I'd be delighted."

Janet rattled off her cell number in about ten seconds.

Casey added it to her contacts, then forwarded her own information to Janet. A trill of tones told her the text had been received.

"It's here," Janet confirmed. She gave Casey a radiant smile. "May I text you later today?"

"No problem. Just give me a sense of your schedule. I'll look at my calendar. We'll have lunch either this week or next."

"Wonderful."

"Let's get going, Madeline." Casey's concern was real as she saw how peaked Madeline had become. "We'll drop you off at home so you can rest."

Madeline nodded. "Thank you."

"It was great meeting you, Janet." Casey shook her hand.

"You, too. I can't wait for our lunch." The instant Janet released Casey's grip, she began scanning her electronic calendar. Good. The sooner this lunch happened, the better.

In the meantime, Casey's work here was done.

She made eye contact with each member of her team.

They all got the message and gave quick nods, telling Casey that they were wrapping up whatever they were involved in and then making their way to the van.

Time to get the investigation moving.

9

The Forensic Instincts team gathered around the oval conference table. Hero padded in to join them, stretching out in his usual spot beside Casey, looking comfortable but attentive. He seemed to know that this room meant serious business, so he never romped or slobbered on his beloved team members during meetings here.

Casey set down her cup of coffee, and took her regular seat at the head of the table, pausing only to lean over and scratch Hero's floppy ears. She then crossed her legs, interlaced her fingers on the table and leaned forward.

"First, those of us who attended Ronald Lexington's dedication ceremony will go around the table and share impressions," she began. "Then we'll move on to any information Ryan and Patrick have to share." She paused. "Yoda, please record this meeting and project any necessary documents on the screen."

"I'm fully prepared, Casey," Yoda replied. "I've already activated the record function. And I'll be on alert until you need me."

"Thank you." Casey glanced around the table, her gaze settling on Emma. "Good news for you, newbie. You charmed Jacob Casper with your earnest desire to help people and your bubbly personality. Madeline sealed the deal by pitching your abilities. You're in. You'll fill out the necessary paperwork, attend the requisite class and start next week as a candy striper."

"Class?" Emma sat up in her seat. "No one said anything about school. I suck at school. If there's a test, I'll fail it. Also, what do you mean I'll *start* as a candy striper? I thought this was a one-shot deal."

Casey's lips twitched. "You'll do just fine. As for candy striping, it would look awfully suspicious if you checked in, worked for a day and then vanished. You're supposed to be committed to this. Plus, you working at the hospital will give me a viable reason for visiting— which I need to do to chat up potential suspects. Do it for a few weeks. Then I'll come up with a reason why you're needed here full-time, and you'll get a reprieve. Consider it a character-building experience."

Sulky and irked, Emma propped her chin on her palm and muttered, "I consider it a pain in the ass."

"You'll live," Ryan assured her with a broad grin.

"Unlikely."

"Pardon me for interrupting," Yoda said. "But I can tutor Emma in what she needs to know. There is extensive information available on how to be a candy striper."

"Good idea, Yoda," Casey replied. "Please start right after the meeting."

"Are you kidding me?" Emma had had it. "That artificial intelligence know-it-all lectures me all day long. Now he's going to be my teacher, too?"

Ryan threw back his head and burst out laughing. "Take it in stride, spitfire," he advised her. "Yoda is brilliant. Just look at who created him."

"I'm going to puke," Claire said under her breath.

"So am I," Emma echoed. "It's bad enough I had to suck up to that loser, Roger the IT guy. Now I have to do all *this?*"

"You're just spoiled." Ryan continued to tease her. "You're used to me—an IT genius *and* a hunk. You don't get all that in one package. I'm one of a kind."

Claire shoved back her chair and rose. "I need a cup of herbal tea—or something stronger."

"What's the matter, Clairevoyant? Is it something I said?"

"I'm just thirsty." Claire shot Ryan a look. "A cup of chamomile tea and honey is just what I need. It's the perfect way to quell a wave of nausea."

Ryan had opened his mouth to taunt Claire further when Patrick interrupted.

"Enough, kiddies. Let's save the playground behavior for later." As always, Patrick was the stabilizing force of the group. "As for the candy-striping, we all have to suck it up sometimes. This time it's you, Emma. Now let's move on."

"I couldn't have said it better." Casey nodded gratefully in Patrick's direction. There was a steady, no-bullshit quality about him. It was innate, but definitely enhanced by the thirty-plus years he'd spent working Violent Crimes at the Bureau. He was like the father of the FI team, and they all respected him when he spoke up.

"Back to the subject at hand," Casey continued. "I had the chance to meet Ronald Lexington's widow and children, as well as to chat with a half dozen doctors and nurses—a few of which are standouts—not to mention Jacob Casper and his administrative assistant.

"Let's start with Nancy Lexington." Casey frowned. "Boy, does she detest Madeline. Her anger is off the charts. And I'm not sure it's solely because Madeline was married to Conrad. I think there's more to it, maybe even more to her. Just a gut feeling I have. Her kids dislike Madeline, too, but it's not the same. Still, I wouldn't write them off as suspects, or maybe accomplices."

"Interesting." Ryan pursed his lips. "I'll have to dig into those three."

"Do that."

"On to Casper. He's a piece of work," Marc said. "Tries to come off like Ronald Lexington's legacy and falls short."

"Do you think he's full of it?"

"I think he's a politician soliciting votes. Becoming hospital administrator of a massive institution like the one the merger would create would open *huge* doors for him. Whether or not it goes deeper than that, I'd need time to figure out." Marc glanced down at his notes. "Dr. Sharon Gilding stuck out, as well. She's definitely got a bug up her ass. She looks at Madeline with extreme resentment, and glares at her whenever she thinks no one's watching."

"I caught that, too," Casey said. "She's also in competition with Conrad to become the chief of surgery of the combined hospital entity. She claims to be fine with that and to respect the hell out of him. I don't believe her. And the cake topper is that she was tight with Ronald Lexington. She played down the relationship, but where there's smoke, there's usually fire. Frankly I just don't trust her."

"Nor do I." Claire contributed her thoughts on the matter. "There was negative energy all around her. It increased when she looked at or addressed Madeline."

"Then we'd better dig deeper and find out more about

her," Casey concluded. "We'll start by talking to Madeline tomorrow."

"I can tell you now that she'd be a close second to Conrad in securing that chief of surgery position." Ryan glanced down at his printouts. He'd done a cursory job of researching every employee at the hospital. More in-depth analysis was in the works. "She a world-class neurosurgeon. Great educational pedigree and flawless professional history. She could definitely give Conrad a run for his money, especially if his mental state keeps him from performing the way he did before Lexington's death."

"Or if he doesn't come back at all." Casey gestured at Ryan's notes. "Find out more."

"Already working on it, boss."

"I've got more names on my list," Marc continued. "A few employees—or their spouses—who attended the dedication and whose behavior toward Madeline seemed off."

"I wonder how many of those names match the ones I compiled," Claire said, reseating herself with her cup of herbal tea.

"I've got a couple of names myself," Emma surprised them by saying. "When I wasn't pretending to hook up with Mr. IT Loser, I did some glancing around." Her brows arched when she saw the team's surprised reaction. "Don't look so shocked. How do you think I used to pick my marks? I checked them out. Not the way you do, but my way. So I can tell you that there were at least three women at that ceremony who hate Madeline's guts. I don't know their names, but I can describe them. I can also tell you why they hate her. They're dowdy, with knockoff clothes and purses, along with costume jewelry. Madeline is rich and pretty. She dresses expensively, but everything's understated. She's divorced, free to live her own life any way she wants to and is loaded to boot. That's a lot of reasons for the average woman to detest someone."

Casey's lips twitched again. "Ah, Emma, you're so young to be such a cynic."

"Young but smart. You know that everything I just said is right."

"Yes, I do." Casey took out her file and opened it to review her own notes and take new ones. "Let's go over each of our lists. I'm curious to see how many matches we have." She glanced up. "Oh, and by the way, I'm scheduling a lunch with Janet Moss. She's been the hospital administrator's assistant for years. She's the go-to person, in my opinion—the information hub of the hospital."

"Yeah, she wields a fair amount of power." Ryan was scanning his notes again. "She moved up the ranks quickly, and kept in close contact with everyone she worked with along the way. They're all still chummy with her, if you read her personal emails. Which, of course, I did. I'll know more after I gain access to the hospital computer system. As a side note, Ronald Lexington relied heavily upon her."

"Any sign of a romantic link?"

"None that I've seen yet. Then again, it would be like looking for a needle in a haystack, especially if they were discreet. My male radar says that Lexington slept with a quarter of the female hospital staff and hit on the rest." Ryan saw Casey's expression and modified his statement. "Okay, I'm exaggerating. But when people call him a player, they're not lying. I can't wait to read his email exchanges."

"Till then, let's get started compiling our lists." Casey looked up. "Yoda, I need a whiteboard, with half a dozen headings and lots of space underneath each of them."

"Done, Casey." The virtual whiteboard appeared on the long wall behind Casey.

It suddenly occurred to her that Patrick had been unusually quiet during this meeting.

"Patrick?" A questioning look. "Anything to share before we start our analysis?"

Patrick was tapping his pen on the table. "I'm working on a different lead. Hero and I took a walk around Madeline's apartment building while you were at the ceremony. I brought the scent pads you made from Madeline's scarf."

He was referring to the special gauze pads Casey used, along with what Ryan called "her canine vacuum," to make scent pads from the personal belongings of their clients. Sniffing out people or items those people had been in contact with was Hero's specialty.

"Hero went straight to the obvious places," Patrick continued. "The walkway to Madeline's building. The front door. But he also came to a dead halt and started barking near a low window in back of the building. I let him do his thing. He unearthed a file folder, an empty one, unfortunately. But it was labeled Conrad, Personal.

"Really." Claire leaned forward. "I'd like to hold that folder, if it's okay with you. I might pick up on something."

"After I dust it for prints," Patrick replied. "I used gloves to retrieve it, and I put it in a Ziploc." A corner of his mouth lifted. "Old habits die hard. I guess I'll always be a dinosaur FBI agent."

"You're no dinosaur," Marc assured him. "You're just damned thorough. That's an asset." A pensive pause. "What did the intruder hope to find in that file folder?"

"And did he get what he was looking for?" Ryan asked. "The file folder was empty. So the perp obviously took the contents. Did those contents contain something that would make getting rid of Madeline necessary? Did he think she'd read something that made her a threat?"

"Or were the contents a waste of time, and he thinks there's something more Madeline has or knows?" Marc frowned. "Why do I feel as if we're going around in circles?"

"Maybe because we are." Casey tapped her pen in irritation. "Let's make our whiteboard lists—suspects' names, jobs and possible motives. We'll move on from there."

Casey couldn't sleep.

She tossed and turned until two in the morning and then finally gave up, reaching over to turn on her lamp.

Hero, who had been snoozing in his comfy bed just beside Casey's, lifted his head and looked quizzically up at his mistress.

"No problems, boy," she assured him. "Go back to sleep."

The soothing tone of Casey's voice was enough to make the bloodhound put his head down and doze off again.

Casey glanced at her iPad. She'd just downloaded a new book, but she didn't feel like reading. She looked at the pile of pages fanned out across her bed. The case was bugging her; however, her brain was on overload and she wouldn't be effective if she tried to review the dozens of minute details that she and her team had brought to the table for discussion.

She reached for her cell phone. Yeah, it was the middle of the night, but Hutch's hours were crazy.

He answered on the second ring. "Hey, you. I can't sleep, either. Good that you called. Even better if it's for phone sex."

Casey began to laugh. "I miss you, too. We've got to carve out a few days—even if we meet in a motel halfway between Manhattan and D.C."

"I must be desperate. Even that sounds good to me. It's been six weeks."

"I know. I've been counting, too."

Hutch—or Supervisory Special Agent Kyle Hutchinson—was with the FBI's Behavioral Analysis Unit in Quantico. He was also Casey's one-and-only. The problem was that each of them had insane jobs and schedules, not to mention the fact that they were separated by two hundred and seventy miles and four and a half hours—all of which meant that it took major planning to see each other. Even so, they made it work. Love was a strong motivator.

"You've got something on your mind," Hutch stated flatly. "I can hear it in your voice. So let's talk first. Then we'll get to the phone sex. It'll give me the incentive I need to listen."

That was a joke coming from Hutch. He was one of the best listeners Casey had ever met. His job required it.

"You read me too well," she said with a sigh. "I'd really prefer the phone sex."

"All in good time. What's going on in the Big Apple?"

"First tell me about you. Anything you're working on that you can discuss?"

"Nope. But I'm on a plane for Munich tomorrow. I'll be gone for a few days. That takes care of me. On to you. What's the case you're working on that's creating the tension in your voice?"

"A client dealing with attempted murder and a long list of suspects." Casey stopped there. That was all she could say. As always, she was dying to ask Hutch's opinion, but she valued the confidentiality she promised her clients.

"If you need to run theoretical scenarios by me, I'm here."

"I know. I guess I just wanted to hear the sound of your voice." Casey paused. "Actually, I didn't promise confidentiality on a personal angle that I picked up on by myself. Not that it was a reach. But it might be a complication. And it's definitely a first."

"Go on."

Casey knew that anything she ran by Hutch would stay with him.

"Our client was once—not to sound corny—the love of Marc's life. He nearly lost it when she walked into the room."

"That *is* a first. I never knew Marc was that close to anyone."

"It was years ago, during his navy SEAL days. But his reaction told me he never got over her."

"Is he able to be objective?"

"That's the problem. I don't know. He's adamant that he can and will be. But that's his brain talking."

"Yup. His heart and his dick are another story."

Blunt and direct. That was Hutch.

"Exactly." Casey rubbed her temples, feeling the beginnings of a lack-of-sleep headache.

"Keep an eye on him. I should know. I've had my ass reamed out more than once for pushing the boundaries of my job because of my feelings for you. It's a rough role to balance. And it usually sucks."

"I know. And I am."

Casey's call-waiting buzz sounded. She glanced at her iPhone screen. Madeline. At 2:15 in the morning? That couldn't be good.

"Hutch, I gotta go. My client's on the other line. Rain check on the phone sex?"

"Okay." He sounded about as thrilled as a kid who'd gotten his privileges revoked. "Take the call from your client. *I'm* taking a cold shower."

"I wish I could take it with you."

"Then I wouldn't need it."

Casey smiled. "Call me from Munich. We'll have international phone sex."

"Done."

Casey punched off and answered Madeline's call.

"Madeline? What's the matter?"

"I'm sorry to call you in the middle of the night." Madeline's voice was trembling violently. "But Conrad is in the E.R. Patrick and I are about ten minutes away."

Casey sat straight up. "What happened?"

"An overdose. The doctors are calling it attempted suicide."

"And you?"

"I'm calling it attempted murder."

10

Casey sped up to Danbury Hospital, getting there in under an hour. It was still pitch-dark out, without a sign of dawn's arrival, and a fine mist of rain was falling, making the roads slick with water and dampening leaves, and the visibility crappy.

With a quick glance at the clock on her dashboard, Casey realized it was 4:00 a.m. She hadn't even been aware of the time. She just wanted to get to Madeline ASAP.

Thank God Patrick had been on security detail at Madeline's apartment. No one was as good as he was. If anyone else had been on duty, Madeline would probably have found a way to give her guard the slip, made the drive alone—and risked her life in the process.

After locking the car, Casey rushed through the front doors of the hospital. Madeline was pacing in the lobby waiting for her. Her face was drawn, and she'd obviously been crying. Patrick was standing close by her side. He and Casey exchanged quick glances. Patrick looked troubled and suspicious.

"How's Conrad?" Casey asked.

"He's alive and his vitals are weak but steady." Madeline didn't sound any better than she had on the phone. She looked like hell, white as a sheet, her face streaked with tears.

"If an aide hadn't found him when she did…" She stopped, and averted her head.

"So he's going to make it."

"I think so, yes."

Casey blew out a relieved breath, and then looked at Patrick. "What facts do we have?"

"Conrad was prescribed a cocktail for his depression and anxiety," Madeline replied before Patrick could speak.

"A cocktail?"

"Several different psychiatric medications given together. They were prescribed by Dr. Oberlin, and divvied out to Conrad each day, a few of them two to four times a day. The pills and dosages were strictly administered by licensed nurses. Medication was never left in his room."

"Okay." Casey digested that information, and then turned her gaze, once again, to Patrick. "So the police think he did what—chose not to take the medication until he'd stored up enough to kill himself?"

"That's about the size of it."

"No." Madeline dragged a hand through her hair. "Conrad would *never* take his own life. He spent too much time saving others. Life was precious to him. Besides, he was doing better. I saw him right after Ronald was pronounced dead. He was shattered. If he was going to do something stupid, he would have done it then. He didn't. As for now, there were absolutely no signs of this. Dr. Oberlin adamantly agrees."

"So do I, for what it's worth," Casey said. "I'm just

a layperson, but when I met with Conrad, I didn't see a man on the verge of suicide. I saw someone who was trying to reconcile himself to the past and move on." She frowned. "The problem is, the police will never believe that someone got past the security at Crest Haven. That residential treatment center is like Sing Sing."

"I know."

Patrick cleared his throat. "It may be Sing Sing, but it's also a hospital. So is Manhattan Memorial, which is filled with professionals who know just what types and dosages of medication are prescribed for Conrad's condition."

"And how much it would take to kill him," Casey finished for him. "So if this was attempted murder, our killer could be a doctor or nurse who found a way to get through security and blend in."

"Or pay off a Crest Haven employee. That might be an easier in."

Madeline pressed her palms to her face. "In which case, whoever broke into my apartment and then tried to kill me could be the same person who tried to kill Conrad. And that person works at my hospital."

"We have no concrete evidence to go on, but my gut instincts say yes, that's where we'll find our perp," Casey said. She glanced at her watch again—4:20 a.m. "Is there any chance that I'll be able to talk to Conrad?"

"No." Madeline shook her head hard. "Even if he wakes up soon, he'll be too groggy to talk. It'll be a while. Plus, he shouldn't be overtaxed. Not until it's absolutely necessary."

"I'd like to talk to his doctor. Who's Conrad's health care proxy?"

"That would still be me. We never had the opportunity or the reason to change it."

"Then would you authorize my speaking with Dr....?"

"Geraldine Lacy," Madeline filled in. "And yes, I'll authorize you to speak with her."

Casey emerged from the meeting not knowing much more than she had earlier. Conrad had overdosed on antidepressants, mood stabilizers and antianxiety medication. Fortunately, an aide had discovered him unconscious soon enough to take instant emergency action, which had probably saved his life. Dr. Lacy had looked blankly at Casey when she'd asked if there was a way to tell if someone else had administered those meds to Conrad, or dissolved them in a liquid he'd consumed.

"Are you actually suggesting foul play? In an institution like Crest Haven?" The doctor had sounded as taken aback as if someone had just told her she had a marmoset on her head.

"Not suggesting. Just asking," Casey had qualified. "I'm an investigator. I'm just doing my job."

Dr. Lacy had shaken her head. "The medical staff—including myself—concur with local law enforcement that this was an attempted suicide. There is absolutely no evidence that someone forced these meds on Dr. Westfield. They were all prescribed specifically for him, and administered directly to him."

"Thank you." Casey paused. "Do you have any idea when Dr. Westfield will be awake?"

"I'm not certain." This time Dr. Lacy had stared Casey down. "And when he does awaken, I won't be allowing him outside visitors, particularly those who want to interrogate him."

Casey shut her mouth and left. There was no point in shoving harder against a brick wall. Only Conrad could supply the answers they were looking for.

As Casey headed to the elevators, she got a text from Madeline saying that she and Patrick were now in the waiting area near Conrad's room. Meet us on the fourth floor. Make a right-hand turn from the elevators and walk down that corridor.

Casey complied. When she reached the waiting room, she saw Madeline fidgeting in a chair, and Patrick standing beside her, scrutinizing the area attentively.

Madeline's head came up as Casey approached. "Well?"

"I learned nothing," Casey replied. "Other than the fact that if I show up in the hallway down there—" she pointed to the corridor "—I'll probably be tossed out on my ass." Casey's sigh was filled with frustration. "I'm not going to be stonc walled."

"You won't be," Patrick said. "But you're not going to accomplish anything here, either. It's after five. We don't know when Conrad is going to wake up and be ready to talk. You've been banned from seeing him, anyway. But I haven't."

Casey inclined her head. "They don't know you're with Forensic Instincts?"

"Nope. They only know I brought Madeline here. So you go back to the city, catch a few hours' sleep and then interview whomever you need to. I'll stay here with Madeline and talk to Conrad when the time is right."

Relieved, Casey made eye contact with Patrick. She knew exactly what he was thinking—that he'd also be keeping a close watch on Madeline in case the killer was hanging around to see the results of his handiwork. He'd guard Madeline with his life.

"We'll stay right here," he continued, giving Casey a meaningful look that said that no one would be getting near Conrad, either. "This way, Madeline can be close by when Conrad wakes up."

"Good." Casey turned back to Madeline. "Do you happen to know what arrangements Conrad made for his apartment while he was away?"

"He's not subletting, if that's what you mean," Madeline replied. "He has a service that checks it out weekly. Why?"

"Do you know the name of that service?"

"Yes." Brow furrowed, Madeline took out a scrap of paper and scribbled a company name on it. "What are you thinking?"

"I'm thinking that you should leave the investigating to us." Casey squeezed Madeline's arm. "We're going to find whoever's targeting you and Conrad. I promise."

"I hope so." Madeline was still a wreck and rightfully so. "I'm even more terrified now, for Conrad and for me. Where are we safe? Not at work. Not at home. And obviously not at Crest Haven, either."

"I'll see what I can do about arranging for additional security for Conrad," Casey said. "Although I'm guessing the staff there, who all believe this was a suicide attempt, will be watching him like a hawk to make sure he doesn't try anything again. I'll talk to Dr. Oberlin and the facilities administrator and see if I can arrange for a couple of Patrick's people to take shifts and post themselves outside Conrad's door." Casey gave an irritated wave of her arm. "Crest Haven will probably vet

Patrick's guys back to their elementary school days, but I'm guessing the powers-that-be will finally agree."

"Thank you," Madeline managed. "I seem to be saying that to you a lot."

"Don't. We're doing our job. Just stay close to Patrick." Casey's gaze flickered to Patrick. "And keep me posted."

"Will do."

Marc called Casey on her cell about five minutes into her drive home. Not a surprise. She'd texted him when she left the hospital.

"What the hell happened?" he asked, his voice gravelly with sleep. "Why are you in Danbury?"

Calmly, Casey explained to him what had happened and what was going on.

"Is Maddy all right?" The question slipped out before Marc could censor it.

"She's fine. Just very shaken and upset, but fine." Casey didn't fault Marc for his concern. This life-or-death situation was expanding. "Patrick is with her. They're waiting for Conrad to wake up."

Marc made a disgusted sound. "You know damned well that when he does wake up, he's going to confirm what we already know—that there was no suicide attempt involved. Someone wants him and Madeline gone."

"I know. What we still *don't* know is why. What we *do* know is that we've been concentrating on Conrad as a possible perp. Now I'm shifting him to the victim category. Which means we have to add another component to our investigation."

"You want me to break into Conrad's penthouse,"

Marc said without missing a beat. "See if it's been trashed and what the visitor might have been looking for."

It was never a surprise to Casey when Marc's mind and hers were in sync. They had different histories, strengths and personalities, but their brains operated on the same wavelength. "Yes. We don't have time to wait for Conrad to be conscious and capable of processing everything, so asking him for a key is out of the question."

"Agreed."

"I need you to do it tonight—after I call the security company that's supposed to be keeping an eye on it."

"If someone wanted in, they could have easily canceled those security visits on Conrad's behalf."

"That's what I'm thinking," Casey said. "So while I'm checking it out, get Ryan to do some techno hocuspocus so that the cameras can't ID you. Then do your thing tonight. Conrad's apartment hasn't been lived in for three months. It could be pristine…"

"Or it could be ransacked," Marc finished for her. "I'll take care of it."

"You'll call Ryan?"

"Yeah, right—in a few hours. You know how Sleeping Beauty gets if he's sleep deprived. Plus, knowing him, he'll have some contraption built by noon."

Casey smiled. "Good point. I'm heading back to catch a few hours of sleep. Then I'm calling Nancy Lexington and seeing if I can set up an appointment to explore the idea of donating additional funds to Manhattan Memorial."

"Gotcha. Good luck."

"You, too."

11

Madeline jumped up from her chair in the hospital waiting area the instant a young female intern emerged. The intern scanned the empty room until her gaze finally settled on Madeline.

"Mrs. Westfield?"

"Yes." Madeline and Patrick were already in motion.

"Dr. Westfield is up to having visitors." She stared at her clipboard with a frown. "Dr. Lacy asked about family. I realize you're his health care proxy, but you're also divorced. Is there someone we should notify?"

"I've already called Conrad's father and his brother," Madeline replied. "His father is frail and elderly, and not up to making the trip from Arizona. His brother and his family are out of the country on vacation. Each of them is waiting to hear from me. You can contact them directly if you'd rather." Madeline's features tightened in concern. "Why? Is something wrong? Have there been complications?"

"No, nothing like that." The intern brushed an arm across her forehead. She looked tired, cranky and exhausted. "Dr. Lacy just likes to follow protocol. I'll get those names and phone numbers from you after your visit." A quick glance at Patrick. "And you are…?"

"Patrick Lynch." Patrick knew exactly what he had to convey. "I'm a close family friend of the Westfields. Madeline called me immediately after you called her. We drove up here together. I'd like to go with her to see Conrad, if Dr. Lacy has no issue with that."

The intern almost flinched at the sound of Dr. Lacy's name, and based on what Casey had reported about her "talk" with the good doctor, Patrick suspected that Lacy was a slave driver.

"It's no problem," the intern assured him. "Follow me."

They headed down the corridor and paused outside Room 43. The intern gestured for them to go in.

So this was Conrad Westfield, Patrick thought silently as they entered the room. Or at least Westfield on a bad day.

The man in the hospital gown, propped up on pillows, and with his headboard raised, looked as if he were normally strong and physically fit. Salt-and-pepper hair. Sharp features. Half-open eyes that were a keen blue in color, although slightly glazed right now. Lines of stress were visible on his forehead and around his lips. Calm, given what he had been through. Yup, the description matched what Patrick had expected.

There was an IV bag beside Conrad that was dripping fluids into his body to restore his strength and to replenish whatever nutrients he'd lost. There were also a couple of other monitors attached to him, blinking steadily and beeping in a regular rhythm.

Despite how tired and weak he was, Conrad gave a slight smile when he saw his ex-wife.

"Madeline." He reached out a hand. "Thank you for driving all the way up here." His voice was raspy from the endotracheal tube that had been put down his throat during the stomach-pumping process.

"I came as soon as I heard." She took his hand, simultaneously dragging a chair closer to the bed and sitting down. "How do you feel?"

"Like I was run over by a truck. But thankfully, none of my organ systems was affected. The ambulance got me here in time." Conrad's gaze flickered to Patrick. "I'm sorry, have we met?"

"Not yet." Patrick stayed back, not wanting to crowd Conrad. "I'm Patrick Lynch. I work at Forensic Instincts with Casey Woods and Marc Devereaux."

"Ah." Conrad nodded. "And you drove Madeline up here to safeguard her and to keep her from making this ridiculously long drive alone. I'm glad. Thank you."

"It looks like you're going to need some safeguarding, too," Madeline said anxiously.

Before Conrad could reply, Patrick hit him with the unspoken question. It had to be now, before the conversation veered off in a different direction.

"Did you try to take your own life, Dr. Westfield?"

The start of surprise Conrad gave, the pained widening of his eyes and his hoarse *"What?"* told Patrick what he needed to know.

Conrad was still staring. "Is that what they're saying?" he asked. "That I tried to kill myself?" He broke off with a bitter laugh. "Of course they are. Crest Haven is protecting itself and its employees. A murder attempt wouldn't do much for their image. Plus, I might initiate a lawsuit. Bad for them, either way."

"I told Forensic Instincts that you'd never do such a thing," Madeline said. "Casey agreed with me."

"I'm glad to hear someone has the ability to read people." Conrad rubbed a hand over his jaw. "I've been severely depressed—I've never denied that—but suicide? Never."

Patrick pulled a chair to the foot of the bed and sat down. "What sequence of events do you remember?"

Conrad grew thoughtful. "Nothing out of the ordinary. I watched a movie in my room. My aide brought me my nighttime meds, which I counted and identified, as always. I took them with the glass of water on my nightstand. Now that I think about it, I became very groggy very quickly, but that didn't raise any red flags for me. I haven't been sleeping well, so Dr. Oberlin has increased my bedtime dosage. That's all I recall."

Patrick processed that. "The water itself—did the aide bring it in or was a pitcher of it already on your nightstand?"

"He poured me a glass. That and the pitcher were already on my nightstand." Conrad paused, abruptly meeting Patrick's gaze. "I remember that the pitcher had been refilled when I returned to my room."

"When was that?"

"A little after ten, when I got ready for bed. I'd been playing cards with a group of men." His expression turned grim. "Are you thinking that someone spiked my water pitcher with additional drugs?"

"That's exactly what I'm thinking," Patrick replied. "Which means that whoever wants to kill Madeline, wants to kill you, too."

* * *

Marc was in the office by 6:00 a.m.

He waited until a little before seven, and then called Ryan.

"Hey." Ryan sounded wide-awake and a little breathless.

"Did I interrupt something?" Marc asked drily. "You sound winded."

"No, smart-ass. I just ran five miles. If you were 'interrupting' something, I would have let your call go to voice mail."

"Nice to know." Marc poured himself a second cup of coffee. "So I need your help."

"Shoot."

Marc explained the whole situation.

"Piece of cake," Ryan replied. "I'll jump in the shower, and then head right over to the office." He paused, and then went for it. "You hanging in?"

"Why wouldn't I be?"

"Come on, Marc, I'm not an asshole. You've got some major history with our client. I'm not asking for sordid details. I'm just checking on you."

"I'm fine."

"Wanna talk about it?"

"Not even a little."

"Okay." Ryan didn't seem the least bit surprised by Marc's answer. Marc was Marc. "If you change your mind—"

"I'll let you know," Marc interrupted. "Now get moving. I've got a long night to plan for."

"The shower's already on."

"Good. Hey, Ryan?"

"What?"

"Thanks."

* * *

The alarm on Casey's nightstand went off.

Rolling over in bed, she groped around until she found the off button and slapped her palm on it. She felt as if she could sleep another half day, but it was time to get her ass in gear. It was a quarter to ten—plenty late enough to put in a phone call to Nancy Lexington.

Ronald's widow answered on the third ring. "Hello?"

"Hello, Mrs. Lexington, this is Casey Woods. We met yesterday at the dedication ceremony for your husband."

A thoughtful pause. "Oh, yes, I remember. Madeline Westfield introduced you."

Not a good sign. Casey had to steer the conversation away from Madeline—for now.

"Yes, she did. I wanted to offer my condolences and to speak to you about donating money to the hospital in your husband's name." A bit of an exaggeration, but close enough to ring true.

"Of course." Fascinating how a person's tone could make such a rapid one-eighty. "How can I help you?"

"Would it be possible for me to drop by today? I'd love to get your opinion on my donation."

Nancy hesitated. "My children are still in town," she said.

Perfect. Ideal. Couldn't be better.

"I completely understand. It's just that it's nearing the end of my company's fiscal year, and if we want to make a charitable donation…"

"I see. Then that's fine. Why don't you join Felicia, Ron and I for a light lunch, say, at twelve-thirty. We can eat and talk at the same time."

Bull's-eye.

"That sounds perfect." Casey grabbed a pen and paper. "What's your address?"

Nancy lived in Yorkville, which was on the Upper East Side, while FI was in Tribeca, at the opposite end of Manhattan. Casey would have to allow herself about forty-five minutes to dash to the subway station, hop on and change over to the Lexington line before arriving in Yorkville and sprinting to the Lexington apartment. She'd better get moving—a quick cup of coffee, a shower and enough time to get dressed and put on some makeup.

She'd be there.

"I look forward to it, Mrs. Lexington," she said.

It was just after noon, and Ryan's lair was even more chaotic than usual.

Oblivious to the mess, Ryan narrowed his eyes in concentration, leaning over his worktable to epoxy another LED to the black wool face mask.

The door creaked open, and Claire stepped into the room, shutting the door behind her. "Hi."

"Hi, yourself." Ryan shot her a quick, dazzling grin— one he reserved for the times when the two of them were alone. "If you're here to have your way with me, it'll have to wait just a little while. I'm on high alert here." Another grin. "Can you hold out?"

Claire walked over and punched his arm. "Asshole."

"Careful," he said with a chuckle. "I need to have steady hands for this creation."

"*That's* why I came down here," Claire said. "Sorry to burst your egocentric bubble, but I was dying of curiosity. Marc is in his intense mood, waiting for something from you. His energy is so palpable that I had to see for myself what was going on." She peered over Ryan's shoulder. "What is that?"

"Insurance that Marc will remain unrecognizable to prying cameras when he breaks into Conrad Westfield's apartment tonight."

"Ah." Claire understood immediately. Marc had filled her and Patrick in on Conrad's overdose. It wasn't a jump to figure out what was coming next. "How does your contraption work?"

Ryan was bent over the table again. "I'm gluing enough LEDs and mirrors to this mask to blind anyone. If the security tapes are reviewed, all that will be visible is a blinding light on top of a blurred black blob, that blob being Marc. No face. No mask. Just a miniature version of the Times Square ball on New Year's Eve."

"Very smart," Claire had to grudgingly admit. "What about whoever's manning the lobby?"

"That's my job. I'll take care of him." Ryan winked. "A man needs some secrets. I'll tell you about it afterward." With careful precision, he put down the mask and his tools. "Maybe I could take a short break." He tunneled his fingers through Claire's hair. "What would you think about a quickie?"

Her eyes twinkled, although their light blue color darkened a bit. "I'd prefer a long-ie." She ran her palms up and down the front of Ryan's sweater. "I'm free tonight after your escapade. Wanna drop by?"

Instantly Ryan's body reacted. This unprecedented weakness he had for this woman—a woman who was his total opposite—was maddening. It was the same way for Claire. Neither of them understood the powerful sexual and emotional cravings that drove them into each other's arms, but neither of them was denying it anymore. It was what it was.

"I'm not dropping by," Ryan replied. "I'm staying the night." He tilted back her head and kissed her. "I'll be late," he said against her mouth. "But I'll make it up to you. Don't expect to sleep."

"I'm flattered." Her palms slid under his sweater and rested on his chest. "You'd give up a night's sleep for me?"

"I've done it before, remember?" Another kiss, this one deeper than the last.

"I remember." Reluctantly, Claire stepped back. "We'd better stop now, before things get out of hand." She adjusted Ryan's sweater.

"Yeah," Ryan agreed, scowling. "We'd better." He turned back to the ski mask. "Tell Marc I'm almost done and he can come down for his fitting."

Claire laughed. "I will." She headed for the door, then paused with her hand on the knob. "Tonight—be careful."

"Always am."

12

Nancy Lexington opened the door and greeted Casey. "Ms. Woods. Come in."

"Please, call me Casey." Stepping into the foyer, Casey shrugged out of her coat.

Strains of a violin bathed the apartment in acoustical warmth. As Casey moved farther inside, the music got richer and more embracing.

"I've never heard the *Pachelbel Canon* sound so vibrant," she said. "It feels as if there's a live orchestra playing here."

"Ronald was an audiophile," Nancy replied. "He was constantly buying new equipment and tinkering with it to get the best sound possible. This version of the *Pachelbel* was his favorite." Her eyes misted. "Listening to it makes me feel closer to my husband."

"I understand." Casey felt a twinge of pity, despite the reason for her being here.

"I doubt that, but thank you."

The twinge of pity was rapidly extinguished. This woman certainly didn't inspire compassion.

Casey glanced around. The Lexington apartment was much as she'd imagined—tasteful but not over the top.

The polished oak floors matched the furnishings, which were carved oak with burgundy and gold accents. The floor plan was open, and there were expansive bay windows in the living room and dining room. Down the hall, there appeared to be a bathroom and two bedrooms, while the master bedroom was off the foyer.

Lovely, cozy, definitely not inexpensive, but not a multimillion-dollar penthouse, either. Ronald had made an excellent salary as the hospital administrator, but he wasn't rolling in money, the way an eminent specialty surgeon like Conrad was.

"I appreciate your seeing me on such short notice," Casey said, following Nancy into the living room. There was a tray of tea sandwiches and a steaming carafe set up on the coffee table. China, silver and burgundy cloth napkins were laid out beside their lunch. And in the matching wingback chairs sat Felicia and Ron like two sentries guarding their mother.

Nancy picked up a remote control and lowered the music. "You remember my children," she said more than asked.

"Of course—Felicia, Ron, nice to see you again."

Felicia's smile was polite. "You, too."

Ron said nothing. He merely studied Casey as if assessing whether she was friend or foe. Clearly the connection to Madeline in conjunction with the "Forensic Instincts factor" was still resounding with him. Not a stupid guy. Also, not a problem. Casey would be speaking directly to his questions.

Nancy's children ate in silence, while Casey and their mother discussed a substantial contribution to the hospital in Ronald's name.

"I'm very grateful," Nancy said, sipping at her coffee. "But I have to ask, why are you doing this? I know you said that you had a positive experience at Manhattan Memorial, and I'm pleased to hear that, but there are hundreds of organizations you could be donating to. Why the hospital? And why in Ronald's name?"

"Honestly? Two reasons—one altruistic and one not. You have no idea what a bad state I was in when I was admitted to the hospital. The details are very personal, and I'd prefer not to discuss them, but I was badly in need of the services I was offered—and they were offered with compassion and delivered with excellence. Your husband was running the hospital at that time. I feel a kinship and the need to give back."

"That's a lovely altruistic reason." Nancy set down her cup. "And the not-so-lovely reason?"

Casey met her gaze head-on. "The hospital merger is a fait accompli. I believe it will result in medical care second to none. Meanwhile, news of it is dominating the media. Linking Forensic Instincts' name with it is a wise idea."

"Ah, good press for your company."

"Exactly."

Nancy leaned forward, her fingers linked tightly in her lap. "You know, of course, that Ronald was adamantly against the merger?"

Casey brows rose in feigned surprise. "I thought that had changed. Jacob Casper said—"

"I don't give a damn what Jacob said." Nancy's eyes flashed. "Ronald would never have changed his mind. He cared about his employees and the quality of his hospital's medical care, not creating a medical empire."

"I see." Casey fell silent for an instant. "Would you prefer I not make the donation? I wanted to honor your husband's name, not to offend you. Madeline Westfield spoke so highly of him. She never mentioned—"

"Madeline Westfield?" Nancy spoke her name with venom. "She's hardly a reliable source."

"I'm sorry." Casey spread her hands wide in apparent confusion. "I was under the impression that you and your husband were close friends of the Westfields."

"According to whom?" Nancy was visibly fighting to keep her anger in check.

"Madeline. The hospital staff. Everyone I spoke to."

"They were wrong." There was a heartbeat of a pause before Nancy blurted out, "Conrad is the reason Ronald is dead. And Madeline's reputed magical nursing skills did nothing to save my husband. They *were* our friends. Now they're my enemies."

"Mother," Ron spoke up, a meaningful note in his voice. "Don't."

"Ron's right," Felicia added quickly. "You'll only upset yourself."

Nancy's children were obviously protecting her. But from what? Saying something that might upset her or that might incriminate her? And how the hell did Madeline factor into Ronald's death?

"I'm fine." Nancy waved off her children. "I just want Ms. Woods to know with whom she's dealing."

"I barely know Madeline," Casey admitted. "I have no idea what you're talking about. I heard that Conrad Westfield was your husband's surgeon and that he couldn't save him. That's all I know."

"Conrad was brilliant. He didn't make mistakes. But suddenly, with a merger in the works that would have made Conrad everything he always wanted to be, he lets his closest friend bleed out—a friend who might get in the way of his promotion? That was no accident. And his dear wife failed to do the job she always excelled at and save my husband—a coincidence? Not in this lifetime."

Baffled, Casey shook her head. "You think Conrad *intentionally* let Ronald die?"

"Mother." This time Ron's tone was firm. "Stop this."

Nancy nodded, getting herself in check. "I can't know what was in Conrad's mind," she said. "Or Madeline's."

"How does Madeline factor into this?" Casey asked. "She's an E.R. nurse, isn't she? How would that relate to your husband's surgery?"

"Because Madeline was on call that day. She was part of the code team."

"Code team?"

"I'm not surprised she didn't mention it. She can't be proud of her failure." Nancy's lip thinned. "Each day the hospital assigns a different team to respond to codes. The team consists of an anesthesiologist—who's usually a resident—a respiratory therapist and three nurses, all of whom carry pagers."

Tears filled Nancy's eyes. "I was in the waiting room. Conrad came out to talk to me after the surgery. He was reassuring me that all was well when the Code Blue alert blasted over the PA system. It was Conrad's name and operating room they were saying, summoning him back in and paging the code team."

"Madeline was part of the team that day?" This time Casey didn't have to feign her surprise.

"Indeed she was. Once she heard the announcement, she knew exactly who and where the Code Blue was. She and the others rushed down a minute after Conrad flew back into the O.R."

"I don't understand. What was happening? What does the code team do?"

"Ronald started bleeding out after Conrad had closed him up. That's the point where the code team does its job. CPR, intubation, arrhythmia treatment—whatever. Once the patient is reopened, their job is done and they all leave. Only Madeline didn't leave. She stayed on and watched while my husband died. She did nothing. And Conrad didn't do enough. That's why I loathe them both. I'll never forgive them. They deserve—"

"Mother!" Felicia was on her feet, going over to stand beside Nancy and squeezing her arm. "I don't want you reliving this again." She turned to Casey. "I don't mean to be impolite, but I think it's best that you leave. This is a very difficult subject for my mother. I want her to take a sedative and lie down."

"Of course." Casey rose, setting down her plate of un-eaten tea sandwiches. "I'm terribly sorry if I upset her."

"You had no way of knowing."

"I apologize, Ms. Woods." At Felicia's urging, Nancy stood up shakily. "I didn't mean to draw you into my grief and anger. I appreciate your donation. Ronald would have, too. Now please excuse me."

She left the room with Felicia's arm wrapped around her shoulders.

"I'll show you out." Ron got up and gestured toward the foyer. "I'm sorry for the family drama," he said as he led Casey to the front door. "Our father's death hit us very hard. My mother is still reeling from the shock."

"I understand." Casey shook Ron's hand. "Thank you for having me."

Casey did nothing until she was heading out of the

elevator on the ground floor. Then she whipped out her iPhone and called Madeline.

"I need to see you now. I'm on my way."

Joseph Buzak, another of Patrick's security team, opened the door for Casey.

"Hi, Joe," she greeted him. "It's good to see you."

"You, too." He was a tall, husky man who'd retired from the Secret Service a few years back, and who'd known Patrick for ages.

"Casey." Madeline appeared almost instantly, her brow furrowed with concern. "You sounded urgent. What's wrong?"

"You tell me." Casey didn't even take off her coat. She just strode into the living room and sat down, pointedly waiting for Madeline to join her.

Madeline complied, walking into the room and perching nervously at the edge of a chair. "You're clearly angry at me. What did I do?"

"You failed to mention to me that you were in the O.R. when Ronald Lexington died."

Madeline still looked blank. "I was part of the code team that day. I frequently am, as are anesthesiologists, respiratory therapists and most of the nursing staff. It's routine. So yes, I was there along with the others. But we didn't—couldn't—do anything. Conrad had already opened Ronald up again and was trying to stop the bleeding. Once the patient has been reopened, the code team leaves. I stayed behind because I was praying that the expression on Conrad's face didn't mean what I thought it meant. Unfortunately, it did." She made a wide gesture, using both hands. "I'm still not sure why that makes you so angry."

"Because it goes to motive." The tension eased a bit from Casey's body. Okay, so Madeline's omission had been based on foolishness, not deception. That, Casey could handle.

"Someone is trying to kill you," she said. "They're also now trying to kill Conrad. The FI team is searching for any common link. That's a big one, especially given the meeting I just had with Nancy Lexington."

"You met with Nancy?" Madeline's eyes widened, more in curiosity than discomfort. "What happened?"

"She spewed a lot of pertinent rage."

"I told you that Nancy blames me, in some misguided way, for Ronald's death."

"Yes, but you didn't tell me why."

"It's because I was in the O.R.?" Genuine surprise laced Madeline's tone. "Are you serious?"

"You bet. You have no idea how deep Nancy's hatred runs. It would have helped if I hadn't been blindsided by what she told me. She laid out the whole Code Blue scenario, with you as the villainess who did nothing to keep her husband from dying."

"I'm so sorry," Madeline responded, visibly shocked by what she was hearing. "I knew that Nancy tied me to Conrad and, as a result, to Ronald's death. But I'm an E.R. nurse, not a surgical one. I wasn't part of the operation. The code team never had the opportunity to lay a hand on Ronald. Nancy knew that."

"That doesn't mean she's rational about it."

With that, Casey rose and began pacing around, thinking aloud. "It's the intensity of her anger and blame that concerns me. Also, her children concern me. They were *very* present at the luncheon. They sat by their mother's side like two guard dogs."

"And said what?" Madeline asked.

"Almost nothing—except when Nancy's anger started spiraling out of control. Then they quickly interceded and calmed her down, finally cutting the luncheon short and leading her away to 'rest.' It seemed as if they knew she might say something incriminating, and they were trying to protect her. Or maybe it's not just her they're trying to protect. Maybe themselves, as well. If Nancy is guilty, I wouldn't be surprised if her kids were in on this with her."

Madeline gasped, her hand flying to her mouth.

Casey continued relaying the necessary information to her client. "I saw the distaste in Felicia's and Ron's eyes, both at the ceremony when they looked at you and in their mother's home when we talked about you. And Nancy's loathing of you is over the top. That living room was so rife with anger and resentment it was suffocating."

Madeline was visibly struggling to deal with the implications of what Casey was saying. "What are you going to do next?"

"Have my team dig. Find out the whereabouts of all the Lexingtons on the night that SUV almost killed you and on the night your place was trashed. We'll be checking out Conrad's place, too. I want to know if it was also ransacked. If it was—and I suspect it was—I want to know what was disturbed and what was taken."

"I told you, Conrad had a security service...."

"A security service that, according to our findings, was canceled by 'a representative of Dr. Westfield's' over a month ago," Casey finished for her.

"Oh, my God. But there was never a report of a break-in." Madeline paused. "Then again, why would there be? Conrad hasn't lived there in three months."

"Exactly."

Abruptly Madeline gripped the edges of her chair, and looked at Casey. "You're not involving the police. So that means you're sending Marc in."

"There's no one better. Clearly you know that."

"Will he be safe?" Madeline dismissed her own question. "Forget I asked that. Marc can handle himself."

"He certainly can." Casey paused, then threw caution to the wind and spoke her mind. "When Marc heard about the attempt on Conrad's life, you're the first one he asked about, too. Madeline, I never get personally involved in my client's lives, but I'm going to make an exception—for your sake and for Marc's."

"All right."

"In a nutshell, neither of you has gotten over the other. When this investigation is successfully behind us and the attempted murderer is locked away, I suggest you revisit your relationship. It's none of my business, of course, and Marc would kill me if he knew I was discussing this with you, but he's my right hand. I hold him in the highest regard. If you're the one to make him happy, just get over yourself and do it."

Casey's diatribe made Madeline's lips twitch. "You certainly don't mince words, do you? It's refreshing, after all the years I've spent being politically correct." She glanced away, then looked back. "Since you prefer candor, I'll give it to you. I never stopped loving Marc. What he and I had was a once-in-a-lifetime connection. Maybe that's why my marriage to Conrad didn't stand a chance, no matter how hard I tried to make it work. There was always Marc, right there between us."

"Well, you're divorced now, Marc is single, and he's not a navy SEAL anymore. So there's nothing to stand in your way. Don't wait for him to make the first move. He won't. God forbid he shows a crack in his armor. He might appear to be weak." Casey rose. "I've got to get back to the office and get to work. I'll be in touch."

13

Conrad lived in a multimillion dollar duplex at Seventy-Second Street and York.

The building itself was old and architecturally beautiful, located in a pricey Upper East Side neighborhood. And the security guy manning the front desk was keeping himself awake with a cup of black coffee.

That's just what Ryan had been counting on when he chose 10:00 p.m. for his delivery.

Dressed as generically as possible—jeans, a navy T-shirt and a well-worn army jacket with a navy Yankees cap he wore backward—Ryan looked less than memorable. The two boxes of a dozen doughnuts apiece that he carried would be the focus, not him.

Sure enough, the guard's head came up when Ryan walked in.

"Can I help you?" he asked, eyeing the boxes.

"Actually, I'm the one helping you." Ryan chuckled, placing the doughnuts on the front desk, in between the guard and his coffee. "Some of the tenants had these sent over as a thank-you for all your hard work."

"Which tenants?" The guard was already tipping open the cover of the top box.

"Don't know. The service doesn't tell me anything. I just make the deliveries." Ryan's right hand slipped into his coat pocket and extracted a vial of liquid. With one twist of his fingers, he opened it, then quickly poured it into the guard's coffee before stuffing the empty vial back in his pocket.

"Anyway," he continued without missing a beat. "I do know that it was from a bunch of tenants. I guess they like you."

"I guess so." The guard was grinning as he helped himself to a powdered jelly doughnut. "I'm here every night, all night long. It's good to know someone appreciates it."

"Well, they do." Ryan held up a palm, declining the dollar bill the guard offered him. "Nah. We working guys have to stick together." He snapped off a salute. "Enjoy."

With that, he turned and walked out of the lobby and into the windy autumn night.

Two hours later, Ryan strolled by the building, glancing briefly inside. As expected, the guard was slumped in his chair at the front desk.

"You're cool," he told Marc through the mike of his specially designed bike helmet.

"Good." Marc turned on the lights of his LED mask, feeling like one of the character's walking in Disney's Main Street Electrical Parade. He then pulled down the mask and yanked on his gloves. "Going in the service entrance."

"Going to the coffee shop down the street," Ryan responded. "Check in when you need me." He kept walking, jacket collar turned up.

Marc glanced around briefly before tackling his job. He'd had a bad feeling about a young guy who was hanging around on the street corner. The kid appeared to be harmless enough—early twenties, fleece jacket, dark green backpack, talking on his cell phone and smoking a cigarette. He shouldn't be raising any red flags—but he was.

Marc made a mental note to check him out once he'd done what he came here to do.

Turning to the task at hand, Marc made quick work of the back door lock. Three minutes later, he was in. He veered to the staircase door directly on the right. Conrad's duplex was twenty floors up.

Marc loped up the steps, rounded landings and continued ascending the stairs. He saw a video camera positioned in the upper corner of every landing, but Ryan's LEDs would blind the cameras to anything except a moving figure in black. No one would have reason to review the footage, anyway. Why would they when there'd be no intrusion reported? And the security guy, who was snoozing at his desk, certainly wouldn't be sharing news of his catnap without provocation.

Marc reached the twentieth floor, and turned off the LEDs. Pulling up the mask, he angled his head and looked through the glass pane on the door, checking up and down the short hall several times.

It was deserted.

Marc slipped out and walked swiftly to Conrad's apartment.

A standard lock. Dead bolt not thrown. Piece of cake.

Again, just a few tools needed from his tool kit, and Marc was inside the apartment, door shut behind him.

He flipped on the light in the foyer, and almost tripped over an overturned decorative urn.

Talk about trashed.

The entire duplex looked as if an army squad had raided the room and cleared it of terrorists, leaving nothing unturned in their wake. There were items everywhere—lamps, books, papers, shattered glass—and that was only the part of the duplex that was visible from the foyer.

Too bad, Marc thought, taking in the scene so he could decide where to begin. It was a hell of a nice place. Polished oak floors. A glass-enclosed winding staircase leading up to the second floor. An open floor plan, making it easy for Marc to scan level one. It consisted of a living room, dining room, state-of-the-art kitchen, art gallery lined with expensive paintings, study and master bedroom suite.

Interesting, Marc noted, his gaze fixing on the art gallery. The paintings, all pricey and by noted artists, had been shoved aside so the intruder could see what was behind them. But none of those authentic paintings had been taken. And back in the kitchen, the floor was strewn with expensive sterling silverware and fine china—that latter of which was now smashed into pieces. Again, broken but not taken. So whoever had bulldozed their way through the place wasn't there to burglarize it. They were clearly looking for something—just like they had been in Madeline's apartment. With the blatant disregard for what they broke, it seemed not only intentional but malicious.

That thought in mind, Marc went straight for the study. The cabinet drawers were all pulled open, and loose papers and empty file folders were strewn around the room—under the desk, chairs, sofa and coffee table.

The first thing Marc did was squat down and sort through everything, using his iPhone to snap pictures as he went. Both the file folders and the loose papers appeared to be personal. Then again, very few professionals kept records in paper format anymore. Conrad probably stored anything of importance on his computer.

Marc rose and scrutinized every inch of the room. No computer, only a rectangular mark on the desk where a laptop had been. But the laptop hadn't been stolen. Marc remembered seeing it in Conrad's room at Crest Haven.

This study was way too generic.

Frowning, Marc considered the options, then headed into the master bedroom suite to see if Conrad had a workstation set up there.

The damned suite could easily house a small family, Marc thought, taking stock of his surroundings. His chest tightened as he saw little touches that he knew were Maddy's—the soft lavender walls, the cream-and-lavender drapes and matching bedspread. For a nanosecond, Marc pictured Maddy lying in this bed with Conrad, and then forced away the thought—along with the knot in his stomach triggered by the image. This wasn't about Maddy's marriage; it was about saving her life.

He searched the entire bedroom and found nothing of substance. Yes, the contents of Conrad's nightstand had been emptied on the floor, but there was little to speak of—mostly cuff link and wristwatch boxes and a pile of rubber-banded business cards. Maddy's nightstand was open but empty, since she'd obviously taken all her things when she moved out. Nope, the bedroom was a total bust.

Time to go upstairs.

On the second floor, there was a huge media room, which had been ransacked in much the same way as Patrick had described Maddy's place. CDs, DVDs, electronic components toppled everywhere, but nothing obvious that was missing.

Again, Marc took pictures.

Then he prowled around some more.

Right outside the media room, before the hall that led down to the guest bedrooms and baths, was another smaller study. It had the kind of intimate feel that convinced Marc this was Conrad's *real* study—the place he felt connected to when he was at home.

Sure enough, there was an imposing Mac Pro desktop computer at his workstation—an industrial size and strength desktop—the kind that could hold a tremendous amount of graphics and data. That would make sense for a surgeon who stored hundreds of intricate images, articles and videos relating to his field.

Marc walked up to the computer, wishing Ryan were here. Hacking wasn't exactly his thing. He took some photos and was about to call Ryan for ideas when he noticed something that seemed wrong.

One end of a small black cable was connected to the computer. But the other end was just hanging there, dangling alone, attached to nothing.

Marc squatted down, took a few detailed close-ups and then texted them to Ryan. He waited a minute before calling.

"I got them," Ryan responded.

"And?"

"And it looks to me like it's a USB hard drive with the hard drive itself missing."

"Are you sure?"

"Yeah. The hard drive is a solid rectangular box just bigger than a pack of playing cards. It belongs at the other end of that cable wire."

"So someone stole it."

"Seems that way. But whether that someone knew or just guessed that the drive held the information they wanted so badly—that, I don't know."

"My guess is that Conrad's place was the first target," Marc said, still rummaging through loose papers. "So, if they did get something here, it wasn't enough. Not if they still tore Madeline's place apart."

"True." Ryan made a disgusted sound. "Man, do I wish I could get my hands on that hard drive."

Marc frowned as he continued to find no other leads in any of the strewn file folders, most of which were labeled with technical medical names.

He straightened, knowing in his gut that he'd done all he could at Conrad's place.

"The only thing we have in our favor is knowing that they probably haven't found the information they're looking for," he told Ryan. "We've got to find it ourselves before they do. Meanwhile, I've got a quick matter to take care of before I head back."

"What kind of matter?"

"When I got here, I saw this kid down the block who gave me a bad feeling. I doubt it has anything to do with us, but I'm going to check him out."

"Okay." Ryan sounded puzzled, but he accepted Marc's gut instincts without further question. "Do what you have to. Then go home and chill out."

Marc left the building the same way he'd come in. He unzipped his duffel bag, stuffed the mask inside and pulled out his parka. Once that was on, he looked like everyone else on the street—just not as classy.

He slung his duffel bag onto his shoulder and strolled along the sidewalk, turning in the direction where the kid had been standing before.

Sure enough, he was still there. Only this time, he was poised like a predator, staring intently across the street. There was a switchblade clutched in his hand.

Marc's gaze shifted to follow the hoodlum's view. There was a thirtysomething woman standing at the corner, waiting to cross the street. Dark hair, slim—she had the same body type and coloring as Madeline. She was texting somebody, and her handbag was swinging freely, half-open, on her shoulder.

The kid's hand tightened on his blade handle, waiting for the woman to cross. He was clearly ready to be as violent as necessary to get his hands on that purse.

Something inside Marc snapped.

He reached the kid in a heartbeat, before the traffic light had time to change.

Accosting him from behind, Marc locked an arm around his neck, squeezing until the kid was gasping for air and struggling to free himself.

"Drop it," Marc commanded quietly.

The switchblade clattered to the ground.

"I suggest you get the hell out of here now." Marc's arm squeezed tighter, and the guy whimpered in pain and fear. "If I ever see you around here again, I'm going to break your neck. Are we clear?"

Against the inside of Marc's elbow, the kid nodded.

"Good. Now go." Marc practically flung the kid into the street.

Scrambling to his feet, the kid took off like a gunshot. He never once looked back. Marc scooped up the switchblade and pocketed it.

The traffic light changed.

The woman stopped texting and crossed the street, passing right in front of Marc, without the slightest idea of what he'd just saved her from.

Turning up the collar of his parka, Marc walked off in the darkness.

Casey was waiting up, pacing in the conference room, when Marc got back. He didn't look the slightest bit surprised to see her up and at 'em at midnight.

"Hey," he greeted her, tossing his jacket and duffel bag onto a chair. "Where's Hero?"

"Sleeping on my bed. What did you find?"

"Conrad's place was tossed like a salad." He scowled. "Other than that, not a fucking thing. On the plus side, it's what I didn't find that might mean something."

He went on to explain what Ryan had told him about the Mac Pro and the missing hard drive.

"Dammit." Casey sank down into a chair, crossing one leg angrily over the other. "We've got to find out who has that hard drive and what's on it."

"They themselves might not even know. It could be that they can't crack it, or that they don't understand what they're looking at."

"Either way, they're still trying to kill Madeline and Conrad. So we have zip."

"We have suspects," Marc reminded her. "Now we need to explore them. Want me to take a look at Nancy Lexington's apartment?"

Casey shook her head. "Not yet. If Nancy's at the helm, the hard drive could be at either of her children's apartments as well as her own. We're not about to break into one place after another."

Marc shrugged. "I'm game."

"I'm sure you are. But there are other suspects we need to follow up on. In the meantime, I'll have Patrick put a tail on each of the Lexingtons. We'll know every move they make."

"Ryan can up that security," Marc said. "He can bug their phones and put tracking devices on their cars. That way we'll also know who they visit and who they call—which could include the person or persons they employ to do their dirty work."

"Smart idea." Casey glanced at her watch. "It's pretty late—but Ryan's a night owl. I'll give him a call."

"Uh, unless it's an emergency, I'd give him the rest of the night off. I think he has plans."

Casey's lips twitched. "I hear you. It can wait until morning."

Marc nodded. "Anything else before I take off?"

"Hmm?" Casey's wheels were still turning. "No, you go catch some sleep. I have some strategizing to do. Dr. Sharon Gilding is still bugging me."

"Yeah, well, that neurosurgeon is a bitch. There's also something going on beneath the surface. I sense it, too."

"I have to decide which member of the FI team can get the most information out of her. I'm thinking Claire. She's the softest and least threatening of us. Plus, she a woman. I don't think Bitch Doctor likes men."

"Particularly her chief competitor."

"Conrad."

Marc nodded. "My thoughts exactly. I don't care what she says, Gilding resents the hell out of him for being

Ronald's and Casper's first choice to be chief of surgery—a job she thinks rightfully belongs to her."

"Maybe Claire can zero in on how deep that anger and resentment go if she's with Gilding one-on-one, without the distractions she had to deal with at the dedication ceremony."

"What 'in' would Claire use to set up a meeting with Gilding?"

Casey arched a brow. "She'd appeal to Bitch Doctor's ego. She'd tell her that all she heard at the dedication ceremony was that Gilding was the best neurosurgeon ever. She'd ask for a half hour of her time to better understand the human brain. It would help her get a grip on her psychic abilities, to understand whether or not they're real or even plausible."

Marc chuckled. "I can hardly wait to hear Claire's reaction to that."

"She'll hate it. But if it helps solve the case, she'll do it. The plan needs fine-tuning to make it convincing. That's what I'll be doing while you're sleeping and Ryan is enjoying his 'plans.'" She paused. "And in the morning, I'll be calling 'Information Central.'"

"Janet Moss."

"Uh-huh. It's time that she and I set up a firm lunch date."

Fonextricity or "Trix"—the nickname chosen by the MixMasters, an online group of hard-core audiophiles—refilled a goblet with zinfandel to ease the daily stress away. The first glass had taken the edge off. The next one would do the trick.

For the past month, Trix had been asking for advice about synthesizers from fellow MixMasters. A decision about which one to purchase had been made, and Trix was vibrating from excitement at the thought of using the Roland Jupiter-80 synthesizer that had just been delivered. The Sam Ash salesman had promised that this was a big step up from the Juno that Trix was currently using. The online advice and reviews were compelling. The eager salesman threw in a one-year warranty on the gently used Jupiter. So, it was bye-bye, Juno, hello, Jupiter.

The question was: What song to try on the new Roland?

The wine helped the answer surface. A perfect choice. The first track to be laid down would be the violins... the most important instrumental voices in the whole endeavor.

Beginning the process, Trix's left hand glided over the keys to get a feel for the new synthesizer. Right hand unplugged the USB drive from the MacBook Pro. A frown. The drive looked funny—a white cable paired with a black drive. Looked like a mutant black rat with a white tail. Well, waste not, want not. Might as well reuse the drive even if the color scheme didn't match. The damned thing hadn't contained the desired information, anyway.

Pivoting around on the swivel chair, Trix reached for the masking tape and a black Sharpie in the desk drawer, and then swiveled back. Ripping off a two-inch piece of tape, Trix slapped it on the small drive, clicked the retractable Sharpie and wrote in bold block letters "November 5, 2014—Pachelbel."

14

Casey tossed and turned all night.

She felt as if she and her team were running down a dozen labyrinthine paths, but there was no central focus to their investigation.

Someone wanted Madeline and Conrad dead. It could be for information, but that wouldn't apply if the killers were Nancy and/or her children. Their motive would be revenge, in which case, the hard drive would be superfluous. Or would it? Had they trashed Conrad's and Madeline's apartments and stolen the hard drive looking for evidence—evidence that documented Conrad's guilt, whether accidental or premeditated, in Ronald's death? Which begged the question: Why the hell would Conrad deliberately kill his best friend—over a potential merger that would offer him a prestigious position and lots of money?

It didn't fit. Even if it did, how could Conrad intentionally screw up a surgery without one of his crackerjack surgical team members spotting it? Further, if they did notice it, how did Conrad keep them quiet? Pay them off to keep their mouths shut?

With a disgusted sound, Casey threw off the covers and got up. It was five in the morning and still dark outside. A November wind was blowing piles of leaves around, leaving shadows on the windowpane and a chill in the air. It was the perfect time to snuggle back under the covers and doze.

Not happening. Casey was already reaching for her robe.

Hero's head popped up in surprise.

"It's okay, boy," Casey reassured him. "I'm just making a cup of coffee and getting some files. I'll be back in a minute. You rest."

Hero gave her one of his astute brown-eyed stares. Then he put his head down between his front paws. He didn't shut his eyes, though, and Casey knew he wouldn't—not until she was back in the room.

Five minutes later, she walked back in, smiling as Hero spotted her, after which he closed his eyes and settled into his doggy sofa for more sleep. Casey envied him.

Accepting that her own restless night's sleep was over, she placed her coffee cup on the nightstand, and plopped the file folders near her pillow. She picked up her backrest and positioned it at the head of the bed. Then she switched on her lamp, and crawled into the bed, settling herself to do some work.

She reviewed everything she had, and the frustration she felt kept growing. Even the empty file folder labeled "Conrad, Personal" that Hero had sniffed out for Patrick had been a dead end. No prints other than Madeline's. And to the best of Madeline's recollection, there had been nothing inside the folder but the scorecard from Conrad's best round of golf, World Series ticket stubs and a photo of him, Ronald and Doug Wilton looking like the Three Musketeers. Memorable but meaningless to FI's investigation.

Claire had sensed lots of negative energy on the folder, but none that translated into a name or a person.

Tons of theories, no resolutions.

Opening the Ronald Lexington file, Casey reread the facts she already knew. Well-liked and well-respected hospital administrator. Family consists of blah, blah, blah. Charismatic and charming, with a reputation for liking the ladies—maybe a bit too much.

Rereading those facts again, two thoughts popped into Casey's head. One, did Nancy know about her husband's philandering? Two, why was there no information in this file about Ronald's surgery?

The answer to the first question was obvious in Casey's mind now that she'd spent time with Nancy Lexington. The woman was smart. Casey doubted there was anything about Ronald she didn't know. If he was cheating on her, she knew it, and she'd know with whom and how many paramours there were.

How she reacted to that knowledge was another story entirely. It was definitely worth finding out once Ryan's tools were in place. And definitely worth the FI team finding out who those ladies were and if any of them had a grudge against Conrad.

The first question led directly into the second. The reason the FI team hadn't gathered more information on Ronald's surgery or his personal life was because his death had never been a focus in this investigation. Now that Conrad had become a target and Madeline was not only his ex-wife, but a member of the code team who'd been present in the O.R. when Ronald died, everything had changed. Conrad's credibility as a surgeon and his motives regarding Ronald's survival were all of a sudden in question.

The first person to shed light on this new investigative angle was Conrad himself.

Casey knew he'd been released from Danbury Hospital. She had to get Conrad's consent to interview him at Crest Haven without having his psychiatrist perched by his side.

That shouldn't be a problem. When she and Marc had visited him at Crest Haven last time, he'd indicated that he was amenable to talking to them without Dr. Oberlin present. Casey doubted he'd changed his mind, especially now that his own life was also at stake.

But Dr. Oberlin wasn't the only obstacle. The facility believed Conrad had tried to commit suicide, which meant that the Crest Haven staff would be watching his every move.

Conrad had given Casey his direct number. She'd call him first and get him on board. After that, she'd need Madeline to make the official phone call to initiate the process, and hopefully get past the suicide patrol.

Taking a sip of coffee, Casey drew up her knees, holding the mug with one hand and drumming her fingers on it with the other. She'd shower, get dressed and grab something quick to eat. Then she'd take Hero for a long walk.

By that time it would be late enough to make her phone calls.

Emma had only been candy-striping for a few days, but already she was bored and restless. That was *her* problem. Casey had been hard as nails when she'd reiterated her expectations. And the truth was, Emma was kind of loving her job at Forensic Instincts, sans Yoda, whom she wished she could smack. But in spite of his pain-in-the-ass lectures on the proper roles and responsibilities of candy-striping, she didn't want to screw up this job. Soon a month of her probation period would be over. Two more months and she'd be official. She'd get a Forensic Instincts employee ID card, the pass code to the Hirsch pad and maybe even some cool business cards to show off.

So she'd put up with Yoda, stick around this antiseptic place that had all the excitement of a high school library and give Casey the information and the access she needed. To do that, she'd keep her eyes and ears open. Most important, she'd flirt with that IT loser, Roger, until she'd gotten what she needed from him.

That part would be like old times, only easier, since Roger spent most of his time gawking at her face and body, making his awareness of anything else zero. Casey had given her free rein to pick the right opportunity to go for it. Piece of cake. Once she'd finished her job, the team would act, deciding where to concentrate their efforts in the hospital's internal data system before kicking their plan into motion. Emma couldn't wait. How awesome was that going to be? Not to mention that she could get the hell out of here and rejoin the team.

With that motivation, she headed over to a chattering group of candy stripers to see if there was any new gossip she'd missed.

Ryan almost collided with Casey and Hero in the doorway of the brownstone.

His head came up, and his brows rose in surprise. "Hey. You guys are out walking early. Something up?"

Casey arched a brow. "An interesting choice of words. It's the reason Marc talked me out of calling you last night. Have fun?"

A corner of Ryan's mouth lifted, and he leaned over to scratch Hero's ears. "Is nothing sacred anymore?"

"Oh, please." Casey rolled her eyes. "Your life is about as private as a celebrity's."

"Touché. Okay, I had a great night. Now, what were you going to call me about?"

Casey filled him in on what he needed to do regarding the Lexingtons.

"It'll be in place this morning. What else?"

"Morning." Marc strolled over, interrupting them and glancing at Ryan. "Did you do the gym today, or were you too wiped out?"

"I don't get wiped out." Ryan didn't even blink. "Just recharged. I'll go for a run later and the gym tonight. Okay by you?"

Marc chuckled.

"What happened with that sleazy kid you were eyeballing last night?" Ryan asked.

"What sleazy kid?" Casey turned to Marc.

"There was a young guy hanging out near Conrad's place," Marc replied briefly. "I got a bad feeling from him. Turns out he was about to mug a woman and snatch her purse. I took care of him."

"What do you mean, you took care of him?" Casey knew there was something missing. She just didn't know what. And she wasn't happy with the expression on Marc's face. It was too intense. He looked…emotionally involved.

"I roughed him up a little. Scared him a lot. Ended the problem."

That definitely was an understatement. When Marc spoke in short, terse phrases like that, the situation was worse than he was saying.

"Did you do any permanent damage?" she asked, folding her arms across her chest.

Marc shrugged. "Maybe I choked him a little too hard. He'll live."

"What did this woman look like?"

"Is this an interrogation?" Marc asked. "She was a woman. Mid-thirties, dark hair—I couldn't make out her taste in clothing in the dark."

That description was enough. And it explained why Marc had gone overboard in his actions.

Now was not the time to get into this.

"Getting back to what we were discussing, I was just filling Ryan in," Casey said instead. "I'm about to call Conrad and then Madeline. Time to make the necessary arrangements to set up a meeting with Conrad. We need to know more about what happened during Ronald's surgery to understand whether that could be a motive for targeting Conrad." She gave Marc a questioning look. "Wanna drive up to Crest Haven with me?"

"Absolutely." He didn't hesitate for an instant.

"Good. Also, I'll be making that phone call to Janet Moss. Hopefully our lunch will happen in a day or two."

"What about Bitch Doctor?"

Ryan blinked. "Bitch Doctor? Ah, you must mean the charming Sharon Gilding."

"None other. Marc will explain my plan to you. It involves Claire. I need to talk to her." Another pointed look at Ryan. "Any idea when she'll be coming in?"

"I'm here." Claire walked over and joined the group,

looking puzzled. "Why are we meeting on the sidewalk?"

"Good point." Casey punched in the alarm code and opened the front door. "Let's go up to the conference room." She walked past Emma's empty desk and headed for the stairs. The other team members followed suit.

"This will be a quick update to get us all on the same page," Casey said as they rounded the landing. "Followed by a one-on-one between Claire and me."

"Good morning, Casey, Marc, Ryan, Claire and Hero," Yoda greeted them politely as they opened the conference room door. "The room is set at seventy-two degrees. Is that sufficient?"

"Perfect, Yoda."

"Will Patrick be joining you?"

"He's finishing up a night shift at Madeline's," Casey replied. "My guess is that he'll swing by here in a while, but I'll conference him in on my iPad."

"I'll connect FaceTime for you while you get settled."

"Great, Yoda, thanks."

Once inside, everyone settled down, and Patrick's face appeared on Casey's screen. Despite having put in a long overnight shift, he looked totally awake and ready to go.

"Good morning," he said.

"Good morning." Casey shook her head in admiration. "You're unbelievable. If it weren't for your five-o'clock shadow, I'd never know you worked all night."

Patrick gave a half grin. "Maybe I'm getting older but better. Plus, Madeline made me a terrific dinner and an equally terrific breakfast. A meat loaf that rivals my wife's and a Western omelet. Tons of protein, flavor and energy."

Casey smiled back. "I'm beginning to wish *I'd* done security duty there last night." She paused. "Patrick, after I bring you up to speed and we have our meeting, could you put Madeline on the screen?"

"Sure. Right now she's calling her doctor to see when she can go back to work."

"Isn't it too soon?" Claire asked.

He shrugged. "That's her doctor's decision, not ours. She seems to be coming back to herself pretty quickly." Patrick leaned forward. "Bring me up to date."

Casey did just that, filling in details for Ryan and Claire, as well. Marc knew more than the others, since he'd been at the office when Casey was rolling out theories and strategies. The only part he wasn't aware of was her early morning thinking and the conclusions that had arisen from that.

"I convinced Crest Haven to allow one of my security guys to stand outside Conrad's room," Patrick informed Casey. "He has to be invisible and agree not to interfere with any of the treatment center's schedules or procedures. But they *do not* want a lawsuit. So, since it's costing them nothing, they'll accept the added protection—just in the event that Conrad didn't try to kill himself, but someone else did."

"How magnanimous of them," Casey said drily. "They should be thanking you."

"That'll never happen. I'm just glad Conrad will be protected. Whatever the hell is going on here, he's as much at risk as Madeline."

Casey nodded, and then glanced around the room. "So, is everyone good?"

"One more thing," Ryan said. "I've run a thorough background check on every single name on that personal list Madeline gave us. The combined stories read like a soap opera, but individually each of them is a Boy or Girl Scout. There isn't a shred of evidence to suggest motivation for murder. It's time we kissed this angle goodbye."

"Then it's time to set Emma into motion, and have her do what we put her in that hospital to do," Casey replied, speaking directly to Ryan. "She'll steal the access card so that you can dig into the hospital computer systems."

"Yes." Ryan pumped his fist in the air. "Finally. A real challenge."

"I'm still in the dark," Claire chimed in. "I have no idea what you want me to do."

"We'll take care of that now." Casey looked back at Patrick's face on her screen. "Now that you're current on everything, you don't have to stop by the office before heading home. Get some sleep. We'll talk later today. Maybe we'll have updates for you by then."

"Thanks." Patrick stifled a yawn. "Dave is due here in about forty minutes. Then I'll head home to catch some sleep and to see if Adele remembers me."

"Your wife is a sweetheart, and you guys are great together," Casey replied. "She won't be forgetting you anytime soon."

"I'll tell her that when she's pissed at me." Patrick glanced over his shoulder. "I think Madeline just hung up. You want me to get her?"

"Please." Casey nodded.

A minute later, Madeline's face appeared on the screen. She looked better but annoyed. "Hi."

"Let me guess," Casey said. "The doctor didn't give you the go-ahead to resume your E.R. duties."

"It's ridiculous," Madeline responded, running her fingers through her hair. "I feel fine. I'm a little sore. I won't lift anything heavy, but I'm perfectly capable of doing my job."

"How much longer does he want you to wait?" Claire asked.

"He wants to examine me next week. Then he'll make a decision." Madeline glanced around the group. Her gaze lingered on Marc for a second, and Casey remembered that—not counting the dedication ceremony, among throngs of people—they hadn't seen each other since the day she'd walked into the brownstone.

"I apologize," Madeline said with a rueful smile. "Good morning to you all. Pay no attention to me. I'm just cranky from being idle."

"We're workaholics ourselves," Ryan replied. "No apologies necessary."

Madeline's expression grew quizzical. "Patrick said you wanted to speak with me?"

"Yes." Casey leaned forward. "I have to meet with Conrad—*alone*—and I need your help." She went on to explain her reasoning, during which time Madeline nodded.

"I'm on the same page as you," she replied. "And I agree that Conrad would never refuse you. Let me know once you've reached him, then I'll call Crest Haven myself and set the wheels in motion. Between the two of us, we'll get you in."

"Great. Give me an hour. I'll be getting back to you."

Casey closed FaceTime, and turned to the group. "Questions?"

"Nope. Actions." Marc rose. "I'll feed Hero and get things together for our trip up to Danbury." It never occurred to him that Casey wouldn't make the trip happen. He unhooked Hero's leash and snapped his fingers. "C'mon, boy. Chow time."

"I'm off, too." Ryan jumped up. "The Lexingtons can say goodbye to their private chitchats and visits. And Emma can say hello to Hacking 101."

The meeting room emptied out except for Casey and Claire.

Claire's soft blue eyes searched Casey's face, and she waited, interlacing her fingers on the desk. "I'm ready."

Casey explained the idea she'd had last night.

"None of us, including you, trust Dr. Gilding," she concluded. "But we're not sure why. You're the team member with the necessary skills to get a solid handle on her. And I know you. One-on-one is the best method with the least distractions. Do you think you can pull it off?"

"I'll make it my business to," Claire replied. She inhaled deeply, then exhaled. "I just need to prepare myself. You know what a miserable liar I am. Also how hard it is for me to minimize the importance of my gift. But I'll find the ability to do both. I only hope it's enough to convince Dr. Gilding to meet with me. She's big on announcing how crushing her schedule is."

Casey smiled. "But you represent such a challenge. How can she resist? Pitch it that way. Believe me, it'll work."

"I'll head upstairs to my yoga room." Claire slid back her chair and rose. "If anything can infuse me with the necessary energy, yoga can."

"Let me know once you've made the appointment."

"I will."

Claire shut the door behind her, and headed straight for the stairs and up to the small room on the third floor that Casey had helped her set up as her personal space/ yoga quarters.

It was pretty ironic actually, Casey thought as she stared at the closed door. She owned the brownstone outright, thanks to an inheritance from her grandfather, and it was an ideal building for the FI team's needs. Every single room on three of the four floors was used for some designated purpose.

Then there was the fourth floor—Casey's apartment, laid out specifically for her. Those were the rooms that got the least use of all. She passed out on the conference room sofa as often as she slept in her bed, and she lived on takeout, almost never making a meal in her kitchen. On the plus side, Hero was a big fan of her bed, and Casey was a big fan of her shower. Otherwise, with the exception of when Hutch was visiting, the apartment was a convenience rather than a home. Yet the brownstone, in its entirety, still felt like home.

It was an interesting reality, Casey thought as she picked up her iPhone. She, like all the other FI members, lived a very different life than the rest of the world. And she wouldn't change it for anything.

She took out the slip of paper Conrad had given her, and punched in his direct room number.

15

An hour and a half later, Marc and Casey were on the road, driving up to Danbury.

"I'm having lunch with Janet Moss tomorrow," Casey said, settling into the passenger seat of their van. She was exhausted, and relieved as hell that Marc had offered to drive.

"I never doubted it." Marc swung into the stream of traffic, and began snaking his way through Manhattan toward the West Side Highway. "Do you want to brainstorm while we drive? We can cover our strategy with Conrad and yours with Janet."

"Good idea. But let's grab a sandwich and a cup of coffee first. I'm starving."

"Me, too. We'll take them on the road. This way we can talk and think without starving to death."

Casey and Marc covered a lot of verbal territory by the time they pulled into Crest Haven's gated entranceway. They were ready for their direct approach with Conrad, and Casey had jotted down a long list of leading questions to steer Janet in the direction she wanted when they had lunch.

They went through the tedious security process, parked the van and headed inside.

Their visit this time was completely different. They were welcomed as guests, given visitors' tags and were cordially escorted upstairs to Conrad's room.

Casey glanced at Marc as they walked down the hallway, several steps ahead of the nurse. "They really are worried about the fallout from this," she said quietly.

"Um-hum." He nodded. "Whether it's a lawsuit or just bad press that hurts their reputation, they want this to go away."

There were two guys standing outside Conrad's door. One, Casey recognized as Hank McCloud, one of Patrick's men, and the other, who was dressed in a blue uniform, was obviously a Crest Haven aide or orderly or someone posted there to ensure that Conrad didn't pull a repeat performance.

"Hey, Hank," Casey greeted the security guard as they reached the door.

"Hey, Casey, Marc," he replied. He shot a quick sideways glance at the orderly beside him and rolled his eyes.

Casey stifled a grin, waiting as the nurse knocked on the door and poked her head in. "Dr. Westfield? Your guests are here. Shall I show them in?"

"Yes." Conrad's voice sounded strong. Good. The better shape he was in, the more effective this meeting would go.

The nurse opened the door wide, and gestured for Casey and Marc to go in. "Please don't tire him," was all she said before leaving, shutting the door behind her.

"Ms. Woods, Mr. Devereaux, it's good to see you." Conrad was up and dressed in jeans and a navy polo fleece shirt. He was a little pale, but steady on his feet, and with no signs of upset at their visit.

"I can't tell you how much I appreciate the security you're providing," he said, shaking their hands. "I'm still pretty thrown by what happened. First Madeline, now me...this is a nightmare."

"We're as relieved as you are that Crest Haven agreed to our guards being outside your room," Casey replied. "We want you and Madeline kept safe. And by the way, it's Casey and Marc. We're not big on formalities."

He acknowledged that with a nod. "Nor am I. Please call me Conrad." A shadow crossed his face. "The term *doctor* sounds somehow disingenuous these past months."

"That's something we need to talk about." Marc gestured toward the sitting area. "Can we sit while we talk?"

"Of course. Would you like anything—coffee? Tea? I can request either or both."

"Nothing, thanks."

Casey took a seat in the same chair she'd used last time. Marc followed suit, settling himself in the matching chair. Conrad sank down on the sofa, leaning forward so he could meet their gazes.

"You said on the phone that there were several things you wanted to discuss in person. Shoot."

"Your apartment was trashed." Casey didn't mince any words.

Conrad blinked. "What?"

"It occurred to us that if someone was targeting you the way they're targeting Madeline, they might have broken into your place, as well. So we took a look."

"But I have a service that—"

"It was canceled, supposedly on your authority," Casey told him.

"Someone wanted to get in. And they did." Conrad ran his fingers through his hair. He didn't ask how Forensic Instincts had managed to "take a look," nor did he seem to care. He just looked as though he was trying to process this.

"What did they take? How bad is the apartment?"

"It's wrecked," Marc responded, going on to elaborate everything he'd found. "As for what they took, it's hard to tell. The one thing that was definitely missing was a USB drive that should have been attached to your Mac Pro. Do you have it?"

Conrad shook his head. "The only computer I have here is my laptop—and no accessories."

"What was on that hard drive?"

Conrad spread his arms wide in noncomprehension. "Just professional material. Certainly nothing of value or importance to anyone but me. And *definitely* nothing to kill for."

"Can you guess what they might have thought was on there?"

"Not a clue."

"Did you keep personal memos or documentation of any kind?"

"Emails. Abstracts. Articles. Videos of cutting-edge surgeries." He paused. "I can make a full list for you. I'm upset that the material is gone, just as any professional would be. But I don't feel threatened in any way—not by this."

"Please make us as comprehensive a list as you can," Casey said. "Think about it carefully, come up with anything that occurs to you and email us."

"No problem. I'll do it as soon as you leave."

"Good."

Even more agitated than he'd been before, Conrad propped his elbows on his knees, interlaced his fingers and rested his chin on them. Tension rippled through him like an electric current.

"Also, when we talked on the phone earlier, you asked if I was strong enough to talk about Ronald's surgery. I am. I discuss it frequently in therapy. I think I can handle talking about it with people who are trying to save my life." His head inclined slightly. "I'm just not sure how it relates to your investigation. Then again, I'm not sure of anything anymore."

Casey waved away his confusion. "We didn't think it related to our investigation, either. But now, we're wondering if whoever is trying to kill you and Madeline might be motivated by revenge." She proceeded to fill him in on the situation with Nancy Lexington and her children.

Conrad blinked in momentary shock, and then his shoulders sagged. "I wouldn't think Nancy, Felicia or Ron were capable of murder. But I saw how they were after I lost Ronald. They were furious. I don't blame them. But Madeline? She played no part in the surgery, other than just being there at the very end."

"That doesn't seem to make her less guilty in Nancy's mind." Casey stared straight at Conrad, never pausing or averting her gaze. "We need to discuss the surgery itself, and why anyone would believe that a cardiothoracic surgeon of your caliber would unexpectedly lose a patient—particularly *this* patient."

"Unexpectedly? Or on purpose?" Conrad asked the obvious question. "I swear to you that I would never intentionally harm any patient. I took an oath to save lives, and that was always my goal when I walked into the O.R. As for Ronald, he was my closest friend. The only reason I agreed to operate on him, despite our personal relationship, is that I knew I was the best surgeon to perform the surgery. Intent isn't even in the room, in this case, no matter what anyone believes."

Casey never doubted the sincerity in Conrad's tone or body language. He was innocent of any wrongdoing. The idea of killing his friend because he was an obstacle to a hospital merger was preposterous.

"I believe you," Casey said. "But we need to discuss the unintentional. What went wrong with the surgery and why?"

Conrad sighed, a sigh that rippled through his whole body. "That question haunts me every day. I wish I had an answer for you. The surgery went well. It was a very delicate procedure, which is why Ronald came to me to begin with. He was suffering from aortic valve and ascending aorta disease." Conrad glanced from Casey to Marc. "I don't know how familiar either of you is with that disease or with the Bentall procedure."

"Not a clue on either." Casey answered for both of them. "All I know is that the aorta is the large artery that leads from the heart."

"Correct." Conrad snapped into surgeon mode. "The Bentall procedure involves replacing the aortic valve, the aortic root and the ascending aorta. Ronald was at a crisis point, and needed the surgery done immediately. He insisted that I be the one to perform it. My success rate is over ninety-nine percent," Conrad stated the last without arrogance, only the factual, statistical reality.

"What happened this time?"

"I honestly don't know. The surgery itself went flawlessly—everything from dilating the diseased aorta to replacing that diseased section with a Dacron graft. I finished up, and attached the right and left coronary buttons without incident. To be even more cautious, I reinforced the sutures with tissue sealant. Everything looked hemostatic, so we took Ronald off the cardiopulmonary bypass."

"Which is?"

"Sorry. The CPB is the heart-lung machine. I closed up his chest. Everything looked fine, so I went out to give Nancy the good news, leaving the surgical team to put in the final skin sutures. While I was gone, there was an abrupt drop in Ronald's blood pressure and massive bleeding from his chest tubes. A Code Blue was announced, and I rushed back to the O.R. We emergently opened the chest."

"And?"

"And I couldn't control the bleeding that was coming from the aortic root. By this time, Ronald's blood pressure had been low for a prolonged period of time, so we had to put him back on the CPB machine. There was massive bleeding from both the coronary buttons. I removed the sealant to visualize the anastomosis, which I then redid. Things got worse, not better. The bleeding was now more diffuse. We were losing him and I knew it. We rushed him to the ICU with his chest open, held together with a vacuum dressing. We did an EEG and a CT scan, both of which confirmed brain death."

Conrad's pain echoed from deep inside him. "So the patient—*my* patient—was declared. I couldn't believe it. I still can't. There were absolutely no indications that this would happen."

"When did Madeline factor in?" Marc asked.

"When the Code Blue was announced. She rushed in, as did the rest of the code team. It was already too late. I'd reopened Ronald and was trying to repair the damage. The code team left the O.R. Madeline stayed. I believe she was in the ICU, as well, but I was concentrating only on Ronald. He was gone. I don't recall what Madeline did after that."

Conrad dropped his head into his hands. "I constantly relive this surgery. I ask myself, did I tie the knots too tightly, causing the sutures to break? Did I tie the knots too loosely, resulting in the bleed-out? Should I not have used glue to clog the needle holes at all? I just don't know. And I never will."

For the first time, Casey understood the enormity of the burden Conrad was carrying. To tell him that he'd done everything he could would be patronizing and useless. So she said the only sincere thing she could say. "I'm sorry you have to live with this. I'm also sorry we had to dredge it all up again."

"Don't be sorry." Conrad raised his head. "You're not dredging up anything that doesn't haunt me every day. As for Nancy and her kids—I don't know what to think. I used to have an intuitive feel for people. I seem to have lost that completely. So pursue this in any way you need to." He gave them a quizzical look. "Is it time for another payment? I can have it wired directly to your account."

"We're fine," Casey assured him. "Madeline paid us well." She paused for a minute. "I have one more question to ask you before we go. It's not a particularly comfortable one, but I have to ask it, anyway."

"Go ahead."

"What's your relationship with Sharon Gilding?"

Conrad looked surprised, as if that was the last question he'd been expecting. "Relationship? Do you mean professional or personal?"

"Both."

"Professionally, we respect each other's expertise. Sharon is a brilliant neurosurgeon. Yes, I know she's my competition for the job of chief of surgery. That seemed to bother her a lot more than it did me. She's a very high achiever. I can't fault her for that."

"You didn't answer the personal part."

"Sharon isn't my favorite person," Conrad admitted. "She's cold and self-centered. She's short on compassion for her patients. We've argued about that. We have different styles."

"But you aren't or weren't sleeping together?"

"What?" Conrad's head shot up. "Absolutely not. Why would you think that?"

"We weren't sure. Now we are." Casey paused again. "What about Ronald Lexington? Was she sleeping with him?"

This time, Conrad squirmed a bit. "I don't think so. But I don't know."

"Go on." Casey knew there was more, and she wasn't letting Conrad off the hook. "We need you to be totally candid with us."

There was a hint of a pause. "This is an uncomfortable subject for me. But fine. In the interest of full disclosure, Ronald liked women, and they liked him. He made it no secret to me that he had extramarital affairs. Some of those were with hospital personnel, and some were with women he met elsewhere. He wasn't particularly discreet, at least not to my way of thinking. I called him out on it more than once, especially when a few of his paramours' hospital work suffered so much from the affairs with Ronald that they had to be fired. But he couldn't help it—he charmed every attractive young female who walked through the hospital doors. I called it the Bill Clinton effect."

"Can you give us any names?"

Conrad's forehead creased as he thought for a moment. Then he gave a rueful shrug. "I wish I could. The truth is, I was obsessed with my work. I lived and breathed it. I can tell you minute details of any of my surgeries, but I can't give you the names of half my patients, much less the names of Ronald's lovers. In both cases, there were so many." A wry smile. "That should tell you how vast his sexual adventures were."

Marc made a disgusted sound.

"I understand your distaste for the situation," Conrad responded. "It wasn't one of Ronald's finer qualities. But he was a good man and a good friend. So Doug and I put up with his weekly sexual updates, and focused on our weekly golf games."

Doug Wilton. Casey remembered him well from the dedication ceremony.

"Doug spoke very highly of you," she said. "As he did of Ronald. But in your case, he was pretty devastated that you might not come back. He respects you enormously as a surgeon."

This time Conrad's smile was genuine. "Doug is a great cardiologist and a great guy. We worked well together, and we were friends outside the hospital. I didn't socialize much, since I spent most of my life in the O.R. But Doug, Ronald and I were pretty tight."

Casey exchanged a quick glance with Marc. He un-

derstood. Her next job would be to talk to Janet. His
would be to talk to Doug.

"One last question, and then we'll let you get some
rest," she said. "Did Nancy Lexington know about her
husband's indiscretions?"

"Can I swear to it?" Conrad replied. "No. But Nancy
is a very shrewd woman. She'd have to be very naive—
which she's not—to be totally unaware of Ronald's sexual liaisons. When Madeline and I went out to dinner
with them or socialized with them in any way, Nancy
kept a tight watch on her husband. So I'd have to say
yes, Nancy knew Ronald had a roving eye."

"Thank you." Casey rose. "We've tired you out
enough. We'll get back to work and let you lie down."

"Did Ronald hit on Madeline?" Marc's question came
out of nowhere.

Conrad's head shake was adamant. "Absolutely not.
Ronald was a loyal friend. He would never do that to
me. Plus, Madeline would have told me. She was not a
fan of Ronald's behavior."

"Okay, then that's a dead end," Marc replied. "There's
no one who would be jealous of Madeline, at least not
for that."

"No."

"This whole case could have nothing to do with Ronald Lexington," Casey said. "But we have to check every
angle, which we are. In fact, I'm going to lunch with
Janet Moss tomorrow to see what I can learn."

Conrad chuckled. "You're going to the right source.
No one sneezes in Manhattan Memorial without Janet
knowing about it."

"Then she might be a gold mine. By your own account, you practically lived at that hospital. And Mad-

eline's life is pretty tied up there, too. Not to mention the fact that whoever tried to kill you managed to be at Crest Haven and also knew what combination of meds would cause a massive overdose. So it's probable that the perp works in your hospital or possibly even here."

Conrad's lips thinned into a grim line. "I know. That's why I'm so grateful for the security you're providing."

"Don't be grateful. Just let our security guys do their job. And make us the list of what might have been on that external hard drive. It's possible we'll spot something you're missing."

16

Casey edged a look at Marc as he drove out of the Crest Haven gates.

"Careful, navy SEAL. Your personal feelings are starting to show again."

Marc's jaw tightened. "The question was a legitimate one, and had nothing to do with personal feelings. I was trying to find a common motive that would explain why the killer wants to get rid of both Madeline and Conrad."

"I get it. But you don't usually ask questions with such passion."

"Stop looking for things that aren't there, Casey. I'm just doing my job."

"Uh-huh." Casey dropped the subject. She'd made her point.

"You'll set up a meeting with Doug Wilton?" she asked.

"Yup. ASAP. Followed by Jacob Casper." Marc frowned. "But when I talk with them, I'm going to concentrate on Conrad and Madeline, not just Ronald. I feel as if we're forgetting who the intended victims are. Lexington is dead. He's not a victim or a suspect. It's a shame he died, but Conrad didn't murder him. Nor did Madeline."

"I agree." Casey pursed her lips. "So you think we're getting off track?"

"Unless the killers are the Lexingtons, yes. It's been three months since Lexington's death. Only his family could be so affected by his loss for their pain to fester and grow until it exploded into revenge against the people they hold responsible. Even then, Madeline's guilt in the failed surgery is weak. Add up the pieces and the only people who fit the guilty bill are Nancy and her kids. And Ryan's already all over that angle. So it's time we spread our investigative wings and look elsewhere."

"You're right," Casey agreed. "And I plan to do exactly that with Janet Moss. Tomorrow's lunch will be very interesting."

The next morning at 10:00 a.m. Casey's cell phone rang.

Her heart sank when she saw Janet's number. Dammit. The woman was probably canceling.

"Hi, Janet. What's up?" She could hear the bustling hum of the hospital in the background.

"My schedule, that's what's up." Janet sounded frazzled and upset. "I can't get away at noon. I can take a one o'clock break, but probably only for forty-five minutes. I know this is a tacky thing to ask, but would you mind meeting me at the first-floor Au Bon Pain? I so don't want to cancel, but unfortunately, convenience has to trump a good meal."

How much more perfect could it get? Access to Janet and the hospital staff all at once.

"Of course I don't mind," Casey replied. "I'll meet you outside the entrance at one."

"Oh, thank you." Janet sounded as relieved as Casey felt. "I want to hear all about you and Forensic Instincts."

"And you will. I'll see you at one."

It was astonishing how "cafeterias" in hospitals had changed—at least this one, Casey noted, standing outside Au Bon Pain at 12:55 p.m. Gone was the old-fashioned institutional cafeteria. In its place was one of several small but modern, well-known eateries scattered throughout the hospital. Space-efficient and a lot more pleasing to the palette.

Scanning the busy first floor, Casey was pleased to see that the people passing through the corridor were either arriving visitors or destination-oriented personnel. The restaurant followed suit: its patrons were mostly those who were grabbing a quick cup of coffee or a light meal to take with them.

That meant that the little round tables and matching white chairs were almost completely empty. Casey suspected that the upper-level eateries had a lot more sit-down traffic, but this was the in-and-out level.

Maybe that's why Janet had picked it.

At that moment, Janet appeared, weaving hurriedly between the passersby until she reached Casey's side.

"I got here the moment I could," she said breathlessly.

"I was early. You're more than on time." Casey extended her hand. "It's good to see you again."

"I'm thrilled." Janet's handshake was firm and friendly. "I can't thank you enough for taking the time to talk with me." She gestured at the restaurant. "Let's get our food. The farthest table on the right is empty and the longest distance from the corridor. We'll have some privacy to talk."

"Great," Casey replied. "You sound like you've done this before."

"For more private conversations, yes." Janet smiled. "After twenty-six years of working here, I'd better have picked up a few tricks. Otherwise, I'd be a complete idiot."

The two women got their salads and coffee and sat down at the table Janet had indicated.

Casey glanced at her watch. Forty minutes to go. She'd spend fifteen of those minutes telling Janet the most exciting aspects of Forensic Instincts, and then shift the conversation where she wanted it—on Conrad, Madeline, Ronald and other hospital personnel.

Janet pushed aside her salad, propped her elbows on the table and leaned forward.

"So what's it like running Forensic Instincts? Is it similar to what you see on *Criminal Minds?* You're an expert in human behavior. That's kind of like what they are on that show. It's scary and riveting all at once."

Casey had heard that question a dozen times.

"It's a lot less Hollywood, but no less exciting," she replied, giving Janet a mixture of the truth and the answer she wanted to hear. "We catch all kinds of criminals, from kidnappers, to money launderers, to rapists and murderers."

Janet's eyes grew huge. "I read all about your last case. You were the target. How terrifying. What happened when—?"

"Janet." Casey held up her palm. There was no acting involved here. "I can't talk about that case. It's still too raw."

"I understand." She nodded sagely. "Can you tell me about your team? How did you put it together?"

That was a far easier question, one that Casey explained candidly. She was damned proud of the FI team, and tooting their horns was something she did without hesitation.

She gave Janet a few more highlights, then took a bite of her salad.

"I know you need to get back soon," she said. "You must have a very significant job here."

Janet puffed up a bit. "I started at the bottom. Twenty-six years later, I run the administrative wing. All the staff members there report to me."

"Pretty impressive. I don't know how you keep it all straight."

"I have an unbelievable memory. I remember everything, not only about my staff but about everything that goes on in this hospital. Of course, I was outclassed by Ronald." She smiled fondly. "He had a photographic memory. There was nothing he couldn't recall. It was sometimes frustrating as hell to work with him."

"I can imagine. But Jacob Casper must really appreciate you."

"He does." Janet sounded less than enthusiastic. "And he runs a very tight, by-the-book department. Truthfully, it was more interesting when Ronald was in charge."

"Yes, from what I'm hearing he was a very charismatic man," Casey said carefully. It was too soon to tread on Janet's toes.

Janet picked up on the inference, anyway. It was written all over her face.

"Ronald was good, not only at his job but to his employees," she replied. Her tone was politically correct.

But it was also sincere. "He made them want to work there. The atmosphere was much more relaxed and friendly when he was at the helm."

"I see." Casey allowed a brief silence, hoping Janet would fill it.

She wasn't disappointed.

"By *charismatic* I assume you're referring to Ronald's personal life."

"Am I prying?"

Janet shrugged. "It's hardly a secret. Ronald loved women and they loved him. But it was always mutual. No lines were crossed…except a few hospital lines."

"No harm, no foul," Casey responded. "If the women were willing and their work didn't suffer—"

"I didn't say that," Janet interrupted. She lowered her voice to a whisper. "There was an incident some months back. Ronald was sleeping with two women in our department—Valerie Pintar and Francine Ryder. Each knew about the other, and there was genuine hatred between them. Their work went down the tubes. I had no choice but to go to Ronald with the problem. Both women had to be dismissed."

"But there was no disciplinary action taken against Ronald?"

Janet shifted uncomfortably. "We kept Ronald's name out of the report—although I think some people thought we should do otherwise."

"Which people?"

"Conrad and Madeline Westfield."

Casey blinked. "But they were close friends."

"That's why I think they backed down in the end," Janet replied, picking at her salad. "Conrad had a huge argument with Ronald. I could hear it through the wall that connected our offices. He told Ronald bluntly that he couldn't go on mixing personal and professional. He said he was uncomfortable looking the other way. Ronald was sheepish and admitted that he'd been wrong. I guess Conrad felt placated. Their voices had quieted before Conrad left the office."

"What about Madeline? Where did she factor into it?"

"She went to Ronald separately," Janet said. "Their conversation wasn't as heated, but she was pretty firm. Ronald said he'd already talked to Conrad and he'd be changing his behavior. That's all I could overhear."

Casey went for it. "Is there any chance that Nancy Lexington knew about the affairs or the confrontations between her husband and the Westfields?"

Janet contemplated answering. Then she said, "You're a private investigator so I know this will stay between us. Nancy was in the administrative wing that day. She was helping out since we were short staffed. I can't be sure, but Conrad and Ronald were pretty loud. It's very possible she overheard them. And she definitely saw Madeline go in there. She was right outside the door during that argument."

More motive stacked up against Nancy Lexington.

"Wow," Casey replied. "That must have been a tough one for a wife to swallow. I don't envy her."

"She knew who she was married to."

"I suppose." Enough on that subject. "But I hardly think there'd be any hard feelings when it came to Madeline. She's such a warm, likable person."

"Yes, she is," Janet confirmed. "Everyone in the hospital adores her. When Diana first came to work here, Madeline mentored her in so many ways, so I'm biased. But I'm far from alone. When Conrad and Madeline's divorce was final, a slew of people stood behind Madeline and offered their help and support. Conrad didn't have nearly that big a fan club. Then again, he didn't interact much with the staff. He was either in the O.R. or reviewing his own work."

"So he was disliked?"

Another shrug. "I don't think anyone was close enough to him to dislike him. He was resented, mostly by jealous staff members. Personable or not, his talent was unquestionable. But when the merger first came up, there were definite rumblings. Many people thought he was secretly cutthroat about getting that new job."

"What about Sharon Gilding?"

Janet made a face. "She's *always* cutthroat. And about being chief of surgery? I think she'd do anything short of killing someone for that position. Conrad is the front-runner, but she's right on his heels. God help him if he gets that job—even though I truly believe he deserves it more. He's been with the hospital longer, and his techniques in cardiothoracic surgery have been published everywhere. Plus, Sharon would run the surgical unit like a dictator. Everyone already hates her—that would put the icing on the cake. An atmosphere like that can't help but breed negativity and lackluster performance."

"So there's no love lost between Sharon and Conrad."

"None, at least from her perspective. I'm not even sure Conrad is aware of how deep her competitive instincts run."

"And Madeline? Is she impacted by Dr. Gilding's personality—more than the rest of the staff, I mean?"

Janet sighed. "Madeline is such a kind soul, I don't think she realizes that people like Sharon think of her and Conrad as a package deal. I know they're divorced, but that's a moot point since they've been living apart for ages. The fact is, they began as friends and they're still friends. They're each other's strongest advocates. From what I've heard through the neurology department's grapevine, Sharon thinks of Madeline as an asset to Conrad that she wishes would go away."

Casey was about to open her mouth when a tentative female voice interrupted her.

"Hi, Mom."

Glancing up, Casey recognized the dark-haired young woman who was standing there holding a tray as Janet's daughter, Diana.

"Well, hi, honey." Janet went for surprise and failed miserably. "What brings you to this neck of the woods?"

Diana surprised Casey by answering honestly. "You don't have to pretend on my account. We talked about this. I've seen Forensic Instincts on the news and online. I wanted to meet Ms. Woods. Having her here is the most exciting thing I can remember happening at the hospital."

"I agree." Janet shot Casey an apologetic look. "Do you mind if Diana joins us? I have to run in a few minutes, anyway, and I know she also wants to hear about you and your team."

"Of course not." Casey gestured for Diana to pull up a chair. This unexpected development had its benefits. Casey had gotten some good preliminary info from Janet. Maybe Diana could give her another point of view. She might not be a gossipmonger like her mother, but she was a nurse—right in the trenches.

"Thank you." Diana slid into a chair and placed her tray, which contained a bowl of soup and a piece of French bread, on the table.

Janet glanced at her watch and rolled her eyes. "Five more minutes, max, or Jacob will have my head." A hopeful look at Casey. "Maybe you and I could have dinner one evening after work so we can talk more about your exciting life at a time when I don't have to cut things short and make you eat shrink-wrapped food."

Casey chuckled. "I didn't mind. It was nice getting to know you better. Sure, let's check our schedules and set up a dinner."

"Wonderful," Janet said, looking once again like a kid in a candy store.

The next five minutes Casey spent recapping a lot of the same FI specifics that she had with Janet. Diana was quieter than her mother, but her listening skills were better. Her eyes stayed glued to Casey, wide and interested. She ate her soup on autopilot, not even seeming to notice it.

"So you don't all move together as a unit all the time?" she asked when Casey paused to take a breath. "Each team member acts on his or her skill set?"

"Yup." Casey nodded. "Sometimes we all move in tandem. Sometimes we divvy up responsibilities. The individual talents of my team are varied but unbeatable, especially when you add them all up. They're simply the best of the best." A wry grin. "No bias on my part, of course."

"I know you have a bloodhound," Diana said. "Hero. I saw him in an article I read about your company."

Casey frowned. "We try to avoid publicity. Unfortunately, it finds us."

"Well, Hero looks magnificent."

"Hero is nothing if not photogenic," Casey responded. "He's also an amazing human-scent evidence dog."

"Bloodhounds have a keen sense of smell." Diana took a quick bite of bread. "Why did Hero leave the FBI?"

"Okay, that's my cue to get back to work." Janet rose, taking a last gulp of coffee and leaving most of her salad untouched. "Diana is now going to bombard you with questions about Hero. She's a dog worshipper and knows trivia I doubt most veterinarians do." Janet extended her hand to Casey. "Thank you for seeing me. If it's okay, I'll text you about that dinner."

"Please do," Casey replied.

Janet blew her daughter a kiss. "Have fun, ladies." She took her tray to the trash and recycling area, and then hurried off.

"Do you mind my curiosity over Hero?" Diana asked.

"Of course not." Casey took a bite of her salad. "You're talking about the guy I sleep with every night."

That made Diana laugh. She was pretty when she laughed—young and free and not so closed-off and serious.

Then again, if Casey were clinging to a job that might be snatched away at any moment, she'd be pretty strained, too.

She told Diana all about Hero's background and that he'd been at the top of his class. The problem was that he'd been a poor traveler, which made it impossible for him to stay with the canine unit.

"And the FBI's loss was our gain," Casey concluded. "Hero can pick up scents from miles away, and he's as loyal as they come. Like the rest of us, he'd give his life for the team. No one could ask for more." She grinned. "Plus, I'm crazy about him. He and I have become a tight twosome."

"Do you live at your brownstone?"

Casey nodded. "The top level is my apartment. Hero spends more time sleeping there than I do."

"You work long hours. I can relate to that." Diana fiddled with her bread. "Do you think I could meet Hero sometime?"

She sounded so wistful that it tugged at Casey's heart. This was one lonely young woman.

"Sure," she told Diana. "We'll work it out."

"Oh, thank you." There was that hint of youthful joy again. Diana resembled Janet around the nose and mouth, but her eyes were set wide apart, and they were deep brown and very expressive.

"Diana, it's my turn to overstep," Casey said. "The couple of times I've seen you, you look so sober. Your mother told me all about your exceptional skills as a circulating nurse. Is the hospital merger threatening your job?"

Diana turned up her palms. "I don't know. I've only been here a year. That makes me vulnerable. On the other hand, my reviews have been really positive, so I'm hoping my skills are enough to convince the people integrating the two hospitals to keep me on."

"Which translates into long work hours and no social life. I hear you." Casey took another bite of salad, then offhandedly asked, "Do you at least hang out with some of the hospital employees?"

"Yes." Diana tore off another piece of bread and nibbled on it. "Manhattan Memorial has some gifted, warmhearted people who work here. We tend to bond because we dedicate so much of our lives to our careers. That bonding is even more accentuated now since we're all kind of free-falling and nervous."

"I get it."

Diana's expression brightened. "I've chatted with that young candy striper you recommended—Emma. She's smart as a whip and very feisty. She definitely speaks her mind."

"That's Emma," Casey said dryly.

"Does she work with your team?"

Casey answered very carefully. "She's our part-time receptionist. She files and answers phones, that kind of thing. She's really leaning toward a career in nursing, but in the meantime, her job at FI means she can pay the bills."

"She said that Madeline Westfield helped her get the job by speaking to Mr. Casper."

Smart, Emma, Casey thought.

"She did." Casey ran with Emma's entrée. "That was very nice of Madeline, considering we hardly know her. But as a friend of Marc's, she agreed to pitch Emma. Marc's judgment is spot-on, and Madeline knows it. So she did Emma an enormous favor."

"That's typical Madeline," Diana replied. "We call her Florence Nightingale. She's constantly helping and healing. She's pretty inspirational. And I *am* biased. She taught me the ropes when I first came to Manhattan Memorial. She's an E.R. nurse, so she's seen just about everything. And she was married to a surgeon, so she knew a lot about being a circulating nurse. Most of all, she brought me into the fold, so to speak. She introduced me around and made it easier for me to make friends. I'll always be grateful."

Diana pressed her lips together for a minute. "I know it sounds silly since I'm a trained professional, but I was very relieved that she was on the code team the day Ronald Lexington died. It was a horrible loss, and it was my first. Madeline, of course, was devastated. But just her presence helped me get through it."

Casey's fork stopped on its way to her salad. "You were the circulating nurse during Ronald Lexington's surgery?"

"Yes." Diana looked puzzled at Casey's reaction. "Why? Is that significant in some way?" She paled. "Do you think the hospital will count that against me when they're making their decision?"

"No, no, of course not." Casey chastised herself for showing any reaction. It wasn't like her to slip up like that, but she'd truly been shocked. She wasn't even sure why. It's just that it seemed that everything about Ronald Lexington's surgery was cast in shadows. It was like an onion being peeled away one layer at a time.

"I guess after that beautiful dedication ceremony, I'm surprised no one mentioned that you were in the O.R. when Ronald passed away and how traumatized you must have been," she said, trying to continue the conversation without making Diana suspicious.

Diana sighed, taking the bait. "Most people are more stoic than I am. Besides, my mother worked hard to shield me—harder than she should have. I've got to toughen up. I can handle pretty much anything—except losing a patient. I'm still grappling with that one. And I'd better hurry up and get over it because it's a factor in a circulating nurse's life, even if it is a rare occurrence. Also, Mr. Lexington's death truly came out of nowhere. One minute he was fine, the next he was bleeding out. We never expected such a successful surgery to reverse itself so abruptly."

"I agree." Casey frowned. "At the dedication ceremony, I heard so much gossip and speculation about that surgery. People were whispering. Some of them even blamed Conrad Westfield."

"I know." A spark of anger flashed in Diana's eyes. "And it's horrible and untrue. Dr. Westfield did everything—and then some—to save Mr. Lexington's life. He called on every one of us to assist him. I was running back and forth bringing instruments and sponges. The surgical nurses did everything he needed and responded to his every command. And afterward…" Diana's voice trembled a bit. "Both he and Madeline were devastated. Dr. Westfield was white as a sheet and there were tears in his eyes. Anyone who blames him is cruel and dead wrong."

Casey saw how upset Diana was getting. She clearly regarded herself as one of the team—a team that had lost someone of great significance.

"Were you there the whole time?" Casey asked.

She nodded. "The circulating nurse is the first one in the O.R. and the last one out. I make sure the O.R. is fully ready for the incoming surgery—from the operating table to the surgical instruments. I assist the anesthesiologist in positioning the patients. I monitor lights, adjust equipment and assist with the final sponge and instrument count. I could go on and on, but I don't want to bore you."

"I'm not bored. I find medicine fascinating." Casey ate some of her salad, reestablishing the calm that had been lost. "I'm sorry you had to go through such a trauma. But I'm also impressed. I'm sure Conrad used the A-team for that surgery. He must think a lot of you."

"Thank you," Diana said sincerely. "I respect him

tremendously. Watching him operate is seeing a natural gift unfold. He's a genius."

"I believe you." Casey picked up her napkin and dabbed at her mouth. It was time to leave. Too many more questions and her interest in all this would become suspicious. There'd be other occasions—like dinner with Janet—to dig some more.

"I'm so sorry, Diana, but I have to get going." Casey placed a hand on the girl's shoulder.

It was rigid.

"Have your mother send me your cell number," she said. "We'll make an appointment for you to come by the office and meet Hero."

Diana relaxed, a smile spreading across her face. "I would love that."

"So will he."

Casey whipped out her cell phone the minute she got in the car, and punched the Ryan button.

"Yes, chief," he answered.

"Anything on Nancy or her kids?"

"Nope. Just the usual bullshit. Nothing incriminating—at least not yet."

"Damn," Casey muttered. "I know you're getting ready for your excursion with Emma, but later on, would you get me the full list of names of the staff that was present during Ronald Lexington's surgery? All friggin' roads seem to lead back to him."

She paused. "I have a funny feeling. As the operating surgeon, Conrad picked his team. Which is fine, except that everyone I talk to, including our client, seems to have been around when Lexington died."

"I'll be able to get you any information your heart desires in a few hours," Ryan assured her. "Just hang in there while I work my magic."

17

Emma found her guy without much trouble.

Roger Lewis—or Loser, as Emma called him—was either locked in the IT section of the hospital or glued to her side, looking like a lovesick teenager.

This time he was on his way back to work, but taking a route that was out of his way to find her.

Perfect, she thought as she saw him coming. It was time for their tête-à-tête.

She'd already scouted out every floor of the hospital so she was ready when the opportunity presented itself. The third-floor bathrooms were right around the bend in a tiny, isolated alcove—ideal for what she had in mind. It was dead quiet.

Score.

Waiting until she was sure Roger had spotted her, Emma yanked on a pair of latex hospital gloves—as if she'd just come from seeing a patient—and strode across the hospital floor. She paused as she turned toward the bathroom.

"Hi." There was that puppy-dog voice, coming up behind her. She couldn't wait to never hear it again.

She turned around. "Roger." She gave him a brilliant smile. "I haven't seen you all day."

He scowled. "I've been tied up working on this new database to help the data integration of both hospitals." He proceeded to ramble on in computer-ese until Emma could barely keep her eyes open.

"I can't get over how brilliant you are," she said, choking back a gag. "It's so cool how you handle software and computer programs I've never even heard of."

Roger puffed up. "That's my job."

"Well, you're awesome at it." Emma leaned a little closer than usual and laid a light hand on his shirt. "I'm sure you're amazing at everything you do."

He looked as if he was going to pee his pants.

"I..." He turned beet-red. "Maybe we could have a drink sometime," he blurted out.

"I'd like that." Emma's nod was eager. "But right now, I have to get to the ladies' room ASAP. I've been waiting to go for a half hour."

"Sure. Yeah. Of course." Roger stepped aside. "I'll talk to you later."

"Can't wait." Emma hurried into the ladies' room, shut the door and shuddered. Remembering her end goal, she glanced down at her tightly fisted gloved hand. *Good girl,* she congratulated herself. *You haven't lost your touch.*

Twenty minutes later, Emma headed down to the basement. She had to be careful, since this was where the IT department was. But it was also the least bustling place in the hospital. So she stopped short of where Roger's office was, made a quick left turn and, as planned, headed toward the custodial closet.

She surveyed the corridor as she approached. A thin flow of people. That was the best it would be.

She cleared her throat when she was two steps from the closet.

The door opened, and the man in the janitor's uniform collided with Emma in the hallway.

"Oh, excuse me," Ryan said, shifting the mop he was carrying to block the front of his uniform from view.

"No problem."

Emma bent down as if to pick up something she'd dropped. Using her gloved hand, she adeptly reached into her candy-striper frock, retrieved the hospital ID badge she had just pickpocketed from poor, unsuspecting Roger and slipped it into Ryan's jacket pocket.

"You look soooo hot," she muttered in a teasing voice. "Good luck."

With that, she continued down the hall.

Ryan rolled his eyes. Then he turned to do his job. He walked over to the locked door of the first office in the ramshackle hall. He knocked. No answer. He knocked again. Nothing.

Convinced that Emma was right about this office being virtually unoccupied, he held the ID card up to the proximity reader with a gloved hand and waited for the loud "clunk" as the bolt retracted, unlocking the door.

The office looked like a storage room, but it contained the one piece of equipment Ryan needed—a computer.

He shut the door behind him, heard the lock reengage and went straight to the desk. Seated behind the computer, Ryan removed the stolen badge carefully, pulled a special fingerprint kit from his other pocket and proceeded to "lift" the IT guy's prints from the ID badge. He then transferred the index finger print to a flexible plastic strip and punched the button that woke up the computer.

Pressing Ctrl-Alt-Del, the screen whirred to life and waited for authentication. Ryan took the plastic strip, slid it carefully across the fingerprint reader and smiled as the system recognized him as Roger Lewis, Systems Administrator, with access to all resources.

Ryan navigated through the maze of drives and folders, until he came across one named "rlexington." He expanded the menu to show file permissions and attributes and saw that one directory called "personal" had every file inside encrypted with a password.

Realizing this would take too long to break, he reached into his pocket for an empty USB drive, inserted it into the computer and initiated the replication of the entire contents of the "rlexington" folder.

But that wasn't enough. The next order of business was to create a new administrative account for himself, with full remote access so he could obtain everything else he needed in the future. He worked quickly.

Done.

He then inserted a different USB drive and installed a spyware program of his own design that would allow him to access the hospital network via the internet, all without detection by antivirus and intrusion protection software—just in case the extra administrative account was found and expunged.

Eliminating any sign of his being here, Ryan packed up his gear and waited for the computer workstation to go back into sleep mode. He pocketed the ID badge to drop off just outside the IT offices. By now, the panicked Roger Lewis would be looking everywhere for his badge. Some pal of his would have let him in—but camaraderie like that wouldn't last for long. Lewis would be frantic. Eventually he—or his irate boss—would find the badge in the niche between the door and the wall, and Roger would think it had accidentally unclipped from his belt and fallen off when he pushed through the door. Little did he know...

Ryan dumped his mop and uniform in the custodial closet and retraced his steps through the basement. As he walked, he removed the latex gloves he was wearing, and dropped them in the garbage just before he left the hospital.

Janet was entering some administrative data into her computer when her office door abruptly opened.

Nancy Lexington strode inside, her coat billowing out around her as she turned to shut the door. She whipped around, taking a few steps toward Janet's desk. Her eyes were blazing, and anger emanated from her.

Clearly this wasn't a friendly social visit.

"Hello, Nancy," Janet said carefully. Ronald might be dead, but his wife still commanded some respect in this neck of the woods. "What can I do for you?"

"You can tell me why you were meeting with Casey Woods."

Janet's jaw dropped. That news had traveled fast, even for Manhattan Memorial.

"Who told you that?" she asked.

"Does it matter? It's true, isn't it?"

Janet rose from behind her desk. At least this way she could address Nancy on equal footing.

"Casey Woods and I had a quick lunch together," she replied. "I wanted to learn more about Forensic Instincts. I find what they do fascinating. Is there a problem with that?"

"There's a problem with the assumptions people make when they see you lunching with a well-known private investigator."

Janet was starting to get angry. "And what would those assumptions be?"

Nancy closed the distance between herself and the desk, placing her palms flat on top of it. "Don't play stupid games with me," Nancy replied. "You know damned well what I'm talking about. You knew everything about Ronald—including his extracurricular activities. I don't want that smut reaching my children's ears."

Janet couldn't keep herself from laughing. "You're kidding, right? *Everyone* knew about Ronald's 'extracurricular activities.' Half of the hospital's female population gossiped about it, and the rest were eager participants. As for your children, they're not kids anymore. I'm quite sure they know who—and what—their father was."

Nancy's face had reddened. "That doesn't mean they should have their noses rubbed in it. So keep your mouth shut and make different friends."

"Or what?" Janet's control snapped. "You'll have me disposed of? I'm not afraid of you, Nancy, even if you are one step away from insane. So stop strutting around like you own this place. You're nothing but a pathetic widow who couldn't hold on to her husband when she had him. Maybe if you'd been a better wife, Ronald wouldn't have spent so much time in other women's beds."

Nancy slapped Janet across the face so hard that the impact propelled her back a few steps. "You bitch," she grated.

Janet pressed her palm to her cheek, which was already swelling with Nancy's finger marks.

"You really are crazy." Janet's voice trembled with suppressed rage. "Not only that, but you're delusional. You've actually conjured up some distorted image of your husband—heroic and monogamous to the end, despite a hospital filled with sluts who were throwing themselves at him. A noble man who was killed by a conniving surgeon, aided by his wife. Pull your head out of the sand and get some professional help. Concentrate on dealing with your grief and stop lashing out. Or is it too late? Are you already way past the lashing-out stage?"

Nancy's eyes narrowed. "What are you implying?"

"I'm not implying. I'm stating facts. You blame Conrad, Madeline and God knows who else for Ronald's death. Ronald's heart condition was bad. He didn't make it. Accept that."

Now it was Janet's turn to lean forward, gripping the edge of her desk with whitened knuckles. "And if you have any thoughts of broadening your retaliatory actions to include the rest of the surgical team—such as my daughter—forget them now. You think you love your children? You have no idea. If you so much as lay a finger on Diana, I'll take a page right out of your book. I'll kill you."

Nancy had grown ashen long before Janet's threat. "What retaliatory actions? What gossip are you spreading now?"

"I'm not spreading a goddamned thing. There are all kinds of rumors flying around this hospital about the extent to which you've gone to avenge Ronald's death."

"And you passed those rumors on to Casey Woods?"

"My, aren't we paranoid for a woman who claims to know nothing of what I'm saying. As for Casey Woods, I asked her to lunch to discuss Forensic Instincts. Period. Any other conversations we had were superfluous—unless, of course, you have something to hide."

Nancy looked positively ill. "Don't invite Ms. Woods to this hospital again, or I'll use my influence with the board to have you both thrown out."

She stalked out of the office, slamming the door behind her.

Janet stared after her, a pensive expression on her face.

18

Ryan was in his lair with the encrypted files he'd stolen. He was at his desk, about to start working on trying to crack the encryption process, when Claire knocked and walked in.

"Bad time?" she asked.

"Good time," Ryan replied, swiveling his chair around to face her. "I was just about to get into these files I took from the hospital." He waved the USB drive at her. "But I haven't shoved this baby in yet, so I'm all yours." He frowned, seeing the upset expression on Claire's face. "What's wrong?"

"I just spent fifteen minutes with Dr. Gilding—which was all she would grant me. Sort of like a follow-up visit for a patient with a cold."

"What did Bitch Doctor say?" Ryan asked. He could see that Claire was more than upset. She was pissed.

"Bitch Doctor is right." Claire folded her arms across her chest. "I've met more than my share of nonbelievers. It's a downside of my talent, and I accept that. But Sharon Gilding wasn't just a nonbeliever. She went out of her way to insult me. And not just me. She covered the gamut, tearing apart the very idea of claircognizance, clairvoyance, clairsentience, clairaudience, clair—"

"Okay, I get it," Ryan interrupted. "She beat the shit out of every clair in existence. Does that really surprise you?"

"Actually, yes." Claire inhaled deeply, and then blew out her breath to calm herself. "Not her disbelief, but her scathing comments. I've never met a professional who was quite so vicious and denigrating."

"Yeah, that is kind of extreme. So I assume that all you got out of this meeting was that Bitch Doctor lives up to her nickname, and that she gave off tons of negative energy about your skills."

"Untrue." Claire shook her head. "I picked up on lots of things. I'm on my way upstairs to see if Casey is here so I can to talk to her. Sorry I interrupted your computer hacking. I just needed to blow off steam."

Ryan stood up, and walked over to Claire. He tipped up her chin, lowered his head and kissed her. "Don't let Sharon Gilding get to you. She probably needs to get laid."

"Oh, no, she doesn't. She's getting plenty of that already. I just need to figure out by whom."

"Wow." A corner of Ryan's mouth lifted. "Poor guy, whoever he is. Now you've really piqued my interest. I'd come up with you to see Casey and hear all the sordid details, but I've got to get started on these files. It could take a long time to crack."

"Then get started." Claire reached up and brushed her lips against Ryan's. "I'll fill you in later."

"I'm holding you to that."

Casey was in the conference room having a heated negotiation with Emma when Claire walked in.

"Oh, come on, Casey," Emma was saying, sitting

across from her boss at the conference table and leaning forward as she pled her case. "I did everything you
asked me to do and more. I sucked up to that loser forever, and I got Ryan what he needs. Why can't I come
back here now?"

Casey crossed one leg over the other, looking as if
she were lecturing a petulant teenager.

"First of all, it was a week, Emma, not forever. And
yes, you did a great job. I'm proud of you." Casey held
up a palm to silence Emma's next outburst. She shot a
quick look at Claire. "Urgent?"

"It can wait a few minutes. Do you want me to leave?"

"No," Emma said. "I could use some support."

"You're not getting any," Casey replied. "Let's clarify
the situation. I didn't say you couldn't come back to FI.
I said you can't come back *yet*."

"Why?"

Emma's youth was showing, Claire thought. She had
yet to learn patience and to sacrifice immediate grati-
fication for the big picture. But she'd get there. Then
she'd really shine. There was no doubt in Claire's—or
any of the other team members' minds—that Emma was
a natural addition to their team.

Two more months and it would be official.

"Because," Casey was explaining, "it would be glar-
ingly obvious that I'd put you there as a plant."

Emma chewed her lip. She couldn't argue with that
one.

"That would undo everything the team did to work
the hospital system," Emma admitted grudgingly. "Yeah,
I get it." She gave Casey a measured look, and asked the
dreaded question. "How long do I have to stay in that

hellhole, changing bed pans and smiling as if I love doing it?"

Casey couldn't stifle a smile. Neither could Claire, who was still hovering in the doorway. There was something very refreshing about Emma's direct honesty.

"How about a business workweek—five days." Casey wasn't really asking. She was coming to a decision, one that would be nonnegotiable. "Five days would be long enough for me to come to the realization that our clerical system was getting out of hand and we needed our receptionist back without raising any red flags. I'll explain the dilemma to Jacob Casper, and I'll assure him that as soon as we get ourselves up to speed, you can resume candy striping."

"What?" Emma shot up like a rocket.

"Calm down. You won't be going back. I'll work that angle when the time comes. Right now your job is to continue working at the hospital."

"What about Loser? He asked me out for a drink." Emma groaned. "And I said yes. What am I supposed to do about that?"

"Go."

"You're kidding," Emma said.

"No, I'm not. You agreed to join him for a drink. If you blow him off now, he'll have all kinds of questions. We can't have that. Keep up the charm for another five days." Casey grinned at Emma's nauseated expression. "You don't have to sleep with the guy. He's too awkward to ask you to, anyway. So set the date for three days from now, and you'll already have one foot out of the hospital door."

"Fine. I'll do it. But only because I want in on this team." Emma pushed back her chair and rose. "When you said probation, you really meant it. Is there anything else? Want me to fall on a sword?"

"I want you to watch your mouth. I seem to remember mentioning respect when we first talked."

A reluctant nod. "You're right. I apologize. I'll go back to Manhattan Memorial tomorrow."

"Good. Then we're all set." Casey's words brought the conversation to a close.

Emma took the hint and headed for the door. "Good luck," she murmured to Claire.

The minute the door shut, Claire began to laugh. "She's a handful."

"Tell me about it." Casey's lips were twitching, too. "I feel like I'm negotiating with the rebellious teenage daughter I never had. But the truth is, her personality is working for us. She's managed to piss off everyone at the hospital. They see her as a typical immature young woman—a kid who romanticized being a nurse and is now finding out the truth. Nursing means hard work, compassion that's hard to muster under pressure and being up to your neck in bodily fluids. Given Emma's attitude, no one would ever suspect that she's a plant."

"Obviously that's true," Claire agreed. "Because Ryan's downstairs already trying to get into whatever is on that flash drive."

"Good. I hope he deciphers it quickly. The clock is working against us. It's only a matter of time before the killer decides to try again. You and I both know that security can only go so far. If someone wants Madeline and Conrad dead badly enough, they'll find a way to breach our security team."

"We can't let that happen."

"I know." Casey took in Claire's tone and body language, not to mention the pissed-off look on her face. "What happened with Sharon Gilding?"

"Nothing good." Claire explained Gilding's reaction to her talent and that she'd all but thrown her out after fifteen minutes.

"Nice," Casey said drily. "She's even more obnoxious than we thought."

"That's not all." Claire walked over, poured herself a glass of water and took a seat. "The negative energy that emanates from that woman is overwhelming. She's arrogant, she's bitter and she's having a torrid affair with someone—someone who could help her climb the ladder. I'm not even sure if she gives a damn about the guy, only that she's using him for her own purposes."

"She wants the chief of surgery job that Conrad is the frontrunner for."

"She more than wants it. She's obsessed with it. She'd go to scary lengths to ensure that she's the next chief of surgery."

"Scary? You mean like murder?"

"I think she's capable of it. I just can't figure out if she's tried it."

Casey processed that. "You have no idea who her lover is?"

Claire frowned. "I tried. The images of what was going on were very graphic. Truthfully I wanted to throw up. But all I could make out was Gilding and the silhouette of a guy going at it like two rutting animals. Judging from his physique, I'd say he's not tall and not thin. He's got a solid build with that slight middle-aged paunch. But his face..." Claire made a fist and brought it down on the table. "Dammit. I just can't make it out."

"You've done a hell of a job already." Casey's mind

was working. "I can think of one guy who has that type of build and who'd be instrumental in getting Gilding that job. And it's someone who's not too popular with the hospital staff right now, but holds its future—and the future of the chief of surgery—in his hands."

"Jacob Casper," Claire filled in.

"You bet." She paused. "Marc is going to be meeting with Casper. Talk to Marc and figure out a way that you can go together. I want to know how strong an energy you pick up there—and if it matches whatever you got from Bitch Doctor."

A Starbucks was just three blocks from the hospital. One venti Americano and blueberry scone later, Trix sat down at the round table in the middle of the café. Trix put down the snack and pulled out a digital recorder, turning it on and placing it on the table.

It was time to collect a sample to test the capabilities of Audio Detracktor. Trix needed to know just how accurate the app would be in separating and enhancing even the most insignificant of sounds. It would be interesting to hear what noise would be the Starbucks equivalent of a guitar pick bouncing off the stage, just as the *Sound on Sound* review had described.

All the sounds of Starbucks filled the café. The squeal of the steam wands. The rush of hot coffee being poured from urns. The beep of the oven popping out freshly warmed pastries. The whirring of blenders mixing frappuccinos for the local teenagers.

Two such teens were at the next table over, taking selfies and shrieking at their iPhones as friends sent them photos via Snapchat. The recorder captured the girls' conversation—something about their plans over the holiday break. Two more girls joined them at the table carrying bright pink blended beverages—cotton candy frappuccinos OMG—and Trix heard the sound of their tall green straws as the girls slurped up the diabetes-inducing liquid. Talk about a sugar rush. Trix pitied their parents. But the straw sounds were perfect for the audio test.

Satisfied that there was enough material captured, Trix finished the scone, packed up the recorder and began the walk to the subway, Americano in hand.

It was November, so darkness fell early. Cold. Windy. Naked trees casting shadows everywhere. And not even a sliver of moonlight to lessen the creepiness of the night.

Madeline rubbed her arms to warm the internal chill that pervaded her body. Then she looked out her bedroom window and down at the street for the fifth time in the past hour.

The same car was there, parked by the curb. A black sedan—maybe a Mercedes or a BMW. Madeline couldn't make it out in the blackness, nor see how many occupants were inside. But the vehicle had been in the same spot for several hours now, right next to a fire hydrant. Once, a police car had made its rounds, turning down the street. Clearly having spotted the officers, the driver of the sedan had eased away, heading smoothly down the block.

Ten minutes later, it was back.

It couldn't be a coincidence. The driver of that car was watching her apartment. Watching her.

Trembling violently, Madeline turned away, trying to be rational. So a car was parked outside. It could be an airport service picking up a passenger. It could be someone who was waiting for a friend and didn't want to go to a parking garage.

Or it could be someone scrutinizing her apartment and her.

She drew the blinds, telling herself that she was being paranoid. Why would someone be watching her apartment?

Because they were trying to figure out the logistics of what was going on inside. They were trying to discern if there was a guard stationed in the apartment. And they were trying to determine how to get inside and finish what they started.

Was someone planning to kill her right here in her apartment?

Panic rising inside her, Madeline walked back to the window like a child who was terrified of a movie, but had to peek through their fingers to see what was happening, anyway. She shifted the blinds aside and pressed close to the window, squinting as she desperately tried to make out the driver or the license plate or something that could help her identify who and why the driver was there.

Abruptly the car headlights came on, as if they'd spotted her and were zeroing in on her.

Freezing in place, Madeline lost it entirely.

She rushed to the bedroom door, yanked it open and hurried into the foyer.

John was posted near the door, sitting on a folding chair and reading something on his iPad.

"Ms. Westfield?" He stood up, seeing her ashen coloring. "Is everything okay?"

"I don't know." Madeline was still rubbing her arms,

more vigorously now. "There's a car outside. It's been sitting there for hours in direct view of my apartment."

John went straight to Madeline's bedroom, and moved the curtain at her window ever so slightly. "The black sedan?"

"Yes."

"I'll call Patrick. He'll cruise by and see what's up. I'll stay here with you." He'd already punched on his phone.

"No. Wait." Madeline had no idea what she was doing. She only knew she was doing it. "Before you call Patrick, I want to call another member of the FI team. He can stay with me while you and Patrick go out together."

John shook his head as he headed back out to the foyer. "You call whomever you want to. I'm contacting Patrick."

Madeline didn't argue further. She just walked over to her bedside where her handbag was sitting. She picked it up and opened it, groping inside until she found what she wanted—the agreement she'd signed with Forensic Instincts. She unfolded it and turned to the last page. As she recalled, all their cell numbers were listed at the bottom.

For a long moment, she stared at the sheet of paper.

Then she did what she'd wanted to do since she'd hired the team.

She called the person who had prompted her to seek out Forensic Instincts to begin with—the person she trusted most with her life.

The phone rang three times before he answered.

"Devereaux."

"Marc, it's me."

"Maddy? What's wrong?" He sounded worried.

She told him what was going on.

"John is calling Patrick," she said. "But I'd feel better if you were here. I'm scared. I need someone I…" She paused. "I need you."

"I'm on my way."

19

Marc and Patrick reached Madeline's building at the same time. Patrick had driven his car over, and Marc had grabbed a taxi, paying him double to get him to East Eighty-Second in record time.

Patrick was talking to the doorman, flashing his P.I. credentials and asking the uniformed man to watch his car, when Marc's cab came screeching up to the curb.

Marc jumped out, threw a bunch of bills at the driver and almost collided with Patrick in the doorway.

"Hey." Patrick's brows rose in surprise. "I didn't know you were coming."

"Madeline called me," Marc said simply. "You check down by First Avenue. I think that's where the car must be parked because Madeline's apartment faces that side. I'll go upstairs."

Patrick didn't ask any more questions. He simply nodded.

Marc flashed his ID as he blew by the doorman. Three minutes later, he was standing in front of Madeline's apartment.

He knocked, and waited while John checked him out through the peephole.

The door opened. "Hey, Marc." John stepped aside so he could enter. "Madeline mentioned that she was calling someone at FI. I think she's overreacting. We've got things under control. I'm here with her, and Patrick is outside. He just texted me. If there's someone watching this apartment, we'll find out who it is and why they're here."

"Go help Patrick. I'll watch Madeline." Marc tossed his coat on the side table. "Where is she?"

"I'm right here." Madeline walked out, having heard Marc's voice. "Thank you for coming."

Marc's gut twisted. It wasn't just seeing Maddy again. It was seeing her like this, still bruised, pale and thin and, despite the cashmere turtleneck she was wearing, shaking violently. He wanted to kill the perp himself.

John had already put on his jacket. "I'll join Patrick and get going on this."

The front door shut behind him.

With obvious effort, Madeline met Marc's gaze and forced herself to speak candidly. "Whether or not I'm overreacting, this whole nightmare has become too much. So I don't want a stranger sitting with me while we find out if a killer is parked outside my door, ready to finish what he started. I want the man who led me to Forensic Instincts to begin with." She paused, wet her lips with the tip of her tongue. "As I said on the phone, I want you."

Marc's jaw tightened. "This is a mistake. I heard your voice and I just reacted. Old habits die hard. I'll leave when John gets back."

"No. You won't. Nor do you want to." Madeline didn't back down. "You're putting up that wall of yours again.

Don't. You've never been a coward. Don't become one now."

"This isn't about what I want. It's about keeping you safe."

"It's about both." Madeline walked over until she was standing right in front of him. "It's about wanting to keep me safe, and it's about wanting me." She flattened her palms on his chest, easing them slowly up and down over the wool of his sweater. "I want you, too," she whispered.

Marc made a strangled sound. He was fighting with all his emotional strength. But despite everything he was capable of, everything he'd been and done, he couldn't fight these feelings. When Madeline tilted back her head and gazed up at him with those incredible eyes, he was lost.

Slowly he raised his arms and threaded his fingers through her hair. "Maddy," he murmured. "Dammit, Maddy."

He wasn't sure who moved first. He only knew that Madeline was flush against his body, her arms wrapped around his neck, and that their mouths were fused, devouring each other's. It was Maddy who backed them into her bedroom, Maddy who turned the lock. But it was Marc who pulled away long enough to strip her sweater over her head, unhook her bra and tug off the rest of her clothes.

She was as breathtaking as ever.

Madeline stood still for an instant and let Marc's hungry gaze rake her. Then she walked over to the bed, slid between the sheets and reached out her hand. "Hurry."

That's all Marc had to hear. He was naked in under a minute and in her bed in less than that.

He groaned aloud at the feel of her body against his—

it was like coming home and coming back to life all at once. He didn't think, didn't care, didn't listen to the voice of reason in his head.

He just made love to her, caressing her skin, inhaling her fragrance. He kissed the fading bruises on her face and the dark splotches of purple on her ribs.

Madeline shivered with each touch, moaning aloud when they became more intimate. "I can't wait," she managed.

"Neither can I." Marc eased his body over hers, careful not to give her his full weight. "Tell me if I'm hurting you."

"The only way you could hurt me is by stopping. Don't."

"I can't," he replied in a husky voice filled with desire. "It's way too late for that."

There were no more words, just the sound of their rough breathing as Marc eased himself between her thighs. He shuddered as she wrapped her legs around his waist.

"Okay?" he asked, needing to make sure she wasn't in pain.

"No, not okay," Madeline answered breathlessly. "Not yet." Lifting her hips, she urged him inside her.

Marc lost it completely.

Pushing all the way in, he braced himself on his elbows, holding himself that way until the muscles in his arms were bulging. He gritted his teeth, felt sweat dripping down his spine and fought for control.

"No." Madeline pulled at his biceps. "Let go. I want to feel all of you on me and in me." Her arms and legs urged him down to her.

When Maddy began to shift under him, begging him

to give her everything, Marc gave it up. He lowered his body onto hers, pushing even farther inside her. He savored the feel of her and started to move, slowly at first, and then faster, more urgently. Maddy arched into each thrust, moaning aloud and drawing him deeper and deeper inside her.

Time suspended as their bodies became one, moving in perfect unison.

Then the world blew apart, all in one exquisite, poignant moment.

Maddy came all around Marc, crying out his name and raking her fingernails down his back. He let out a guttural shout, grabbing hold of the headboard bars and pouring himself into her.

Time passed.

Then slowly, gingerly, Marc released his death grip on the headboard and gave Maddy all his weight, pressing her into the mattress.

"Shit," he muttered.

Madeline began to laugh. "That's what you said the first time. History repeats itself."

"In more ways than one." Marc tried to move and failed. "I should get up. I'm probably hurting you."

"If you dare move an inch, I'll hit you."

Marc chuckled. "You've become more volatile since the last time."

"The last time," Madeline murmured. "That was a lifetime ago." Her voice quavered. "Is this really happening?"

"It already did. It still is." Marc was done lying to himself and to her. There was no escaping the enormity of what was occurring, what had never stopped occurring. He didn't even want to try.

"I love you," he said, his lips against her ear.

At that, Madeline began to cry. "I love you, too," she got out. "Then. Now. Always."

Marc rose up on his elbows again, staring directly into her eyes. "We have a lot to work out, a lot to talk about. But I'm not letting go of this—not like the last time."

"I wouldn't let you."

They both heard the front door open, and Marc jumped up, simultaneously reaching for his clothes and offering Madeline a hand to hasten her out of bed.

They dressed frantically, and Madeline ran a brush through her hair while Marc rearranged the bed, which was in shambles.

Hearing John walk into the apartment right behind Patrick, Marc and Madeline looked at each other and began to laugh.

"By the skin of our teeth," Madeline said, smoothing Marc's hair off his face.

As if to support her statement, they heard Patrick call out, "Madeline? Marc?"

"Coming." Marc was already halfway to the door. He turned around to look at Madeline. "To be continued," he said.

"I'm counting on it."

Marc strode into the foyer. "What did you find?"

"Nothing." Patrick looked disgusted. "I drove all the way down East Eighty-Second, and John did the same on First Avenue. There wasn't a suspicious car to be found."

"They must have seen us pull up," Marc said, "and got the hell away as soon as they did."

"If someone's watching Madeline's place, we've got

to get the make, model and license plate number of the car."

"Yeah, and we have to increase her security." Marc met Patrick's gaze. "I'm going to be around a lot more often. I'll double-up with you and your security guys."

Patrick glanced from Marc to Madeline and back. "Okay. Just run it by Casey."

"I'm going to the brownstone right now to do just that."

Marc went straight to the second-floor conference room when he arrived. He heard Ryan cursing all the way from the basement, but he didn't care to see what was going on. He had to get this confrontation with Casey over with.

She was sitting at the table, files spread out all around her, talking on the phone. Marc knew immediately from her soft tone of voice that it was Hutch.

He halted in the doorway, just as she looked up and saw him.

"C'mon in, Marc. I'm just hanging up."

"Say hi to Hutch for me," he said as he waited politely for her to finish.

"Marc says hi," Casey repeated into the phone. "He looks like hell."

A second later, she started to laugh. "Hutch says hi back, and it must be a woman since nothing in the world rattles you."

Marc's lips thinned, and he didn't smile.

Casey took note of that. "Be safe," she said into the phone. "And call me as soon as you can." A pause. "I miss you, too." She dropped her voice. "I love you."

She disconnected the call.

"What's wrong?" she asked Marc. "I know that Patrick flew over to Madeline's to check out a suspicious-looking car. Did he text you?"

"He didn't have to. I was there."

Casey studied his face. "Why don't you take a seat?"

Marc crossed over, pulled out the chair next to Casey's and sat, leaning forward in his more aggressive stance.

"The car took off before Patrick and John could track it down."

"Patrick and John," Casey repeated. "Does that mean you stayed with Madeline?"

"Yeah, it does." Marc never hedged. "She called and asked me to come. So I went." He put his hands on his knees. "Look, Casey, let's not play twenty questions. I'll save you the trouble. Things have changed between Madeline and me."

"What a surprise," came Casey's dry response.

Marc ignored the sarcasm. "The point is, things also have to change on this case. I want to keep an eye on Madeline. If the killer is aggressively moving in, one security guard's not enough." He held up his palm. "And before you ask, no, that second somebody won't be Patrick. It'll be me."

Casey fiddled with her pen for a long time.

"I told you what would happen if you let your personal feelings take over this investigation," she said at last. "I tried to give you the benefit of the doubt, even after you practically broke a kid's neck because he was about to mug someone who looked like Madeline. But I can't ignore the obvious any longer—especially not after what you just said."

"Meaning?"

"I'm going to have to ask you to take a backseat.

Interview Casper with Claire, and then stick with be-hind-the-scenes work. We've got a couple of new cases on the horizon. Get involved with those. But there's no way you're going to be clearheaded enough to safeguard Madeline. You're off this one, Marc."

"The hell I am." Marc's eyes blazed and a muscle worked in his jaw. "I love Madeline. Her life's in dan-ger. I'm not working on some bullshit case because you're overreacting to my abilities to deal with this. I'm damned good at what I do. There'd be a huge hole in the investigation if I wasn't a part of it. Forget it, Casey, I'm not going anywhere."

"Excuse me?" Casey rose, her own eyes fiery. "That's not your call. It's mine. And I've made it."

"And I've ignored it."

"This is a team, Marc, but it's not a democracy. *I* make the final decisions here. And I've given you mine. I didn't ask if you agreed with it. I gave you a direct order."

"I don't take direct orders. My military days are be-hind me. I respect the fact that you run this company, but this is one time I won't let it stop me. Fire me if you want to. That's your right. I'll still do what I have to do to keep Madeline safe. You can't prevent that."

The words *fire me* crackled between them like a lit fuse.

"Is that an ultimatum?" Casey demanded. "Because if it is—"

"Aren't you being a total hypocrite?" Marc inter-rupted what he knew was coming. His stare went straight through her. "Hutch was so emotionally involved in a couple of recent cases where your life was in jeopardy, he was practically part of the FI team."

"That's irrelevant," Casey shot back. "Hutch doesn't work for me. You do—at least for now. His conflict of interests affected the FBI, and that was his challenge to deal with. This is strictly a Forensic Instincts matter. I need my team sharp and with no emotional ties to our clients. You tried that path. It didn't work. As you said, you're in love with Madeline. You always have been. But you kept things in check. That's no longer the case."

"This sucks, Casey." Marc stood up and began pacing around the room. "I wanted to do this aboveboard. I could have gone on with this relationship and said nothing to you. But I wouldn't insult you like that."

"But you'd insult me by refusing to respect my decision?"

"It wasn't meant as an insult." Marc stopped pacing and turned to face her. "Can we take this down a notch?"

Casey nodded, looking as trapped by the predicament as Marc did.

"I don't want to leave Forensic Instincts. It's where I belong, and this team means a lot to me. I'm sorry I was insubordinate. You know that's not my style. So let's put it differently. I've never asked you for special consideration, but I'm asking now. I believe I can be even more effective because of my feelings for Madeline. I know what I have to do. Will you please trust me to do it?"

Casey drew a harsh breath, and dragged her hand through her hair. "Goddammit, Marc," she said finally. "You're putting me in a shitty situation, and you know it. If you screw up because of your feelings for Madeline..."

"I won't. You have my word."

There was never a doubt about Marc's word, not to Casey. He kept it, no matter what.

"Don't make me regret this," she replied. "But all

right. Do what you have to. Just keep me posted every step of the way."

"I will." Marc walked over and touched her sleeve. "Thank you for trusting me—and for not kicking my ass out of here. It would have been justified. By the way, just so you know, I'm going to follow up on every single angle we discussed."

"I expected no less."

"We should talk to Patrick and put extra security on Conrad, too. If Madeline's in greater danger, then so is he."

"Point taken. I'll handle it."

Marc held out his hand. "Truce?"

"Truce." Casey shook his hand, and then leaned up to hug him. "Now that we've killed each other, I want you to know how happy for you I am. You and Madeline are the real deal. Hold on to it."

"After losing it once? You bet your ass I will."

20

If you tell the truth, you don't have to remember anything.

Mark Twain's words. Casey's favorite quote.

Marc adhered to it when he set up the appointment with Jacob Casper. And he and Claire fully intended to follow through on it during that meeting.

"How did Casper react when you said this meeting pertained to Conrad Westfield?" Claire asked as they headed from the subway to Manhattan Memorial.

"First, he was dead quiet, like I'd punched him in the gut," Marc replied. "Then he wanted details. I told him I'd rather discuss them in person."

"That must have freaked him out."

"Sure did." Marc's smile was tight. "Anything that rocks the boat now will freak him out. He sees the brass ring just ahead. Once the merger is finalized, he'll be the man."

"So the question is, is he nervous about this meeting because it might put a chink in his plans to become hospital administrator of the new megahospital, or is it because he's guilty of going after Conrad and Madeline?"

"Either way, I'm going to find out. That's my job."

Marc shot Claire a look. "Your job is to find out if he's doing Sharon Gilding, and if they might have joined forces to get rid of the threats."

Claire nodded, slowing down as they neared the hospital doors. "Let's go for it."

Jacob Casper was in his office when they arrived.

Despite there being a perfectly good and available receptionist at her desk in the entrance of the administrative wing, Janet Moss came out to greet them. She was wearing black slacks and a red blazer, but her hair was down this time, straight and simple as it framed her face.

"Hello." She shook their hands. "Mr. Devereaux and Ms. Hedgleigh, right?"

It was a perfunctory question, one that Janet obviously knew the answer to, but both Marc and Claire nodded.

"I realize you're here to see Jacob, but I had to come out and meet the two of you. I've talked with Casey Woods, who told me so many fascinating stories about Forensic Instincts, and I'm now meeting two of her team members. It's really exciting for me. I've read so much about your cases and the roles each of you have played. I've seen you interviewed on TV and online. You're really impressive."

"Thank you." Claire answered quickly, before Marc could make some blunt statement that blew off the compliment. "We appreciate your support. We love what we do, and we're grateful when we're able to help our clients."

Marc was on the verge of bringing the conversation to a close when Jacob Casper's door opened, and he walked stiffly out to greet them. He didn't look too happy.

"Ms. Hedgleigh, Mr. Devereaux, please come in."

"It was so nice to meet you." Janet smiled, stepped aside and crossed over to talk to the receptionist.

As they started following Casper, Claire murmured to Marc, "Overapplied makeup. Hair down. Check out her left cheek. Someone hit her."

"I know," Marc replied. "I saw."

"File it away for later so we can talk."

"Done."

Casper led them into his office, which was a lot less antiseptic than the rest of the hospital and a whole lot nicer than either Marc or Claire had expected.

Across from the door, there was a walnut desk, kitty-cornered by a fully equipped computer table. Across the top of the office periphery was a semicircle of matching walnut overhead cabinets. Casper's desk was neat as a pin with only a telephone, a family photo, some office supplies and a neatly stacked bunch of files on it. The walls were clean and sparse, as well, with a few scattered paintings and a hospital calendar hanging on them.

Across from the desk were two chairs, which Casper now gestured toward.

"Please sit." He settled himself behind his desk, hands folded in front of him.

Defensive, Marc thought. Placing a definitive barrier between them. His stance was rigid, like a watchful German shepherd who'd heard an intruder come in.

"Can I have my receptionist bring you anything? Coffee? Tea? Water?" Jacob asked.

"Thank you, no," Claire replied. "We're fine. And we don't want to take up too much of your time."

"Then why don't you tell me what this is about? Why do you want to talk about Conrad Westfield? What is there about him that concerns you?" He cleared his throat. "And forgive me for being rude, but how do you even know him?"

Both Marc and Claire had expected just those questions. And as they'd decided, Marc took the lead.

"We don't know him, not personally," he said. "But his wife, Madeline, and I go back to her days in Bethesda and my days as a navy SEAL. She was an excellent nurse when I needed one. So when I ran into her in New York, we caught up. I also introduced her to the rest of the Forensic Instincts team."

"So I understand." Jacob nodded. "That's why you all came with her to Ronald's dedication ceremony."

"That and to make a substantial donation," Marc reminded him. "Claire and Casey were both patients at Manhattan Memorial. They had excellent care. Our company wanted to contribute a generous sum as our thanks."

"And we appreciate that," Jacob responded as if he were waiting for the other shoe to drop.

"Madeline and I really hit it off." Claire stepped in where she was supposed to. "We talked quite a bit. She's terribly upset about the rumors that are circulating about her ex-husband."

Jacob stiffened even more. "What rumors?"

"Rumors that Conrad was somehow responsible for Ronald Lexington's death."

Sweat broke out on Jacob's brow. "I've heard no such rumors. And they'd be preposterous. Conrad is one of the top cardiothoracic surgeons in the world. He tried everything to save Ronald, but to no avail. It was a horrible, tragic loss. But Conrad's skill was never in question."

"Perhaps not to you, but others apparently felt differently—some who went so far as to blame Madeline, as well, just because she was in the ICU when Ronald died."

"What?" That one seemed to genuinely take Jacob aback. "That's beyond absurd. Madeline was on the code team that day. She never laid a finger on Ronald. How could she be blamed for his death?"

"I can't answer that. But the rumors are very real and very hurtful," Claire told him.

"And completely uncalled for." Jacob was adamant on that score. "There are no two people I respect more than Conrad and Madeline."

Now that might or might not be true.

"So you really meant it when you said you'd use your influence to recommend Conrad for chief of surgery once the merger is complete?" Marc asked.

"Of course." There was an uncomfortable pause. "If he's able and wants the position, I'll do what I can to make sure he gets it."

"You mean if he gets out of Crest Haven," Marc said.

Jacob looked like he was going to fall through the floor. "Madeline told you about that?"

"She was upset," Claire replied. "She needed someone to talk to—I'm a very good listener. The important thing is that you believe in Conrad and have faith that he'll be up to assuming such a significant position. That will ease Madeline's mind. She and her ex are still very good friends. They stay in touch. The fact that anyone would question his integrity really threw her."

"Why didn't she come to me herself?" Jacob asked.

"Because she's proud. Because she wanted the truth, and she wasn't sure you'd say it straight to her face. And since we happen to be an investigative firm, she thought we'd be the best intermediaries to pursue this on her behalf."

"I see." It didn't take a professional to see that Jacob was really shaken up by this meeting. "I didn't know about this gossip, but I'll find out who's spreading it and put an end to it. Please tell that to Madeline. And tell her I plan on speaking to her myself, to reiterate my personal commitment to Conrad."

"We certainly will." Claire gave a bright smile. "From what Madeline has told me, Conrad's doctors feel he's improving rapidly. By the time your due diligence is done, he should be able to return and lead the combined surgical staff of the new entity."

"I'm so glad to hear that."

Yeah, right, Marc thought. *You sound about as happy as a kid who's getting detention.*

"Thank you for seeing us, Mr. Casper," Claire said. "We won't take up any more of your time. And we'll convey your support to Madeline right away."

"Please do," Jacob replied. "I want this cleared up as soon as possible."

He stared after Claire and Marc as they left his office and made a left turn toward the elevators.

The minute they disappeared, he shut the door and picked up the phone.

"You know he's calling someone by now," Marc commented as they exited the hospital. "The question is, who?"

"Sharon Gilding," Claire supplied. "They're sleeping together. She's using him to get the chief of surgery job. And he's an idiot who thinks she's really into him."

"Sounds right."

Claire gave a shudder. "This is one of those times I wish I could wash my mind out with soap. The two of them together...yuck."

A chuckle. "Kinky stuff?"

"Let's drop it. I might puke."

"Okay, then let's take this in another direction." As he spoke, Marc and Claire veered toward the subway station. "I'm sure you agree with me that Casper knew about the rumors."

"Definitely."

"And he's not shutting down because he doesn't want to air the hospital's dirty laundry in front of me. From what you just told me, I'd say he's being led around by his dick."

"He is." Claire nodded. "The feeling of manipulation, greed and determination to get what they want at all costs came through loud and clear. But murder? I couldn't get a handle on that. I'm just not sure. There was darkness and there was ugliness. If I'd only picked up on pure evil, it would have been easier. But this was murkier. I'm not sure why."

"From a behavioral standpoint, Casper was a wreck. He emanated guilt and deception. The question is, was that simply because he's afraid Bitch Doctor will dump him if he doesn't deliver her the job she wants? Or was it because he thought we were onto them for something a lot bigger than sex and political bullshit." Marc frowned. "He's a guilty man. I just don't know how guilty. So we definitely can't scratch him or Gilding off our list of suspects. The motive and the body tells are there."

Claire nodded again, taking longer strides to keep up with Marc.

"Anything else in the claircognizant realm?" Marc asked.

"As a matter of fact, yes," Claire replied. "I got some different kind of harsh vibes from Janet Moss. That bruise of hers—I kept getting flashes of a major altercation and a severe threat. Whoever smacked her was female and in quite the rage. Plus, I kept getting a sense of Casey—as if she was right between them. Not physically but spiritually. Her presence was strong."

"You think they fought about her?"

"Yes, I do. I wish I knew why."

Marc was quiet for a moment. "That bruise wasn't fresh. It could have happened a few days ago."

Claire understood where he was going with this. "Such as right after Casey had lunch with Janet."

"Yup. Maybe that lunch pissed someone off—someone who didn't want Casey plying these hallowed halls, where she might learn something they would prefer remained hidden."

Claire and Marc slowed down as they reached the subway stop and hurried down the steps to catch the next train.

"Janet has no intention of staying away from Casey," Claire stated, keeping her voice as low as she could for Marc to hear her over the throngs of people moving with them. "She's scheduling a dinner with Casey. Plus, she was superfriendly to us, too. Clearly whoever struck her didn't scare her off."

"That doesn't mean she shouldn't have. Janet could be grossly underestimating her enemy."

Something about Marc's words gave Claire a dark feeling. "I'm afraid you're right."

21

The FI team was, yet again, gathered around the conference table, reviewing all the updated information that Marc and Claire's outing had yielded. Patrick had rejoined them, after arranging for both John and Dave to safeguard Madeline and doubling up security for Conrad at Crest Haven.

Ryan was conspicuously absent.

"What's the deal with Ryan?" Marc asked. "I heard him cursing all the way from the basement. What's he up to?"

"Playing with his toys," Claire supplied.

No one even blinked. They all knew that when Ryan was überfrustrated or pissed, he went to the robot section of his lair and tried out some of his new techno creations.

Patrick scowled. "Does that mean he's having trouble cracking the encrypted files?"

"Yup," Claire replied. "And I wouldn't go down there if you paid me."

"Well, I want an update, good or bad," Casey said. "So I'm not going down there, but he's coming up here. Yoda," she called out. "Please tell Ryan I want him to report to the conference room now with whatever data he has."

"Immediately, Casey," Yoda replied.

"This should be fun," Emma commented, not looking particularly worried. To the contrary, she looked like the cat who swallowed the canary since Casey had invited her to sit in on this meeting—her very first meeting in the "Oval Office," as she called it. Hell, it had been worth her morning candy striping shift to do this.

"Yeah, take cover," Marc said drily.

A few minutes later, Ryan strode into the room, a pile of printouts in his hand, and shut the door. He walked over to the table, plopped his paperwork down and dropped into a chair.

"I'm here," he announced, looking and sounding like a petulant child.

"Are we going to throw a temper tantrum?" Casey inquired. "Because if we are, don't break anything."

Ryan shot her a look. "I'm frustrated as hell. See all this crap?" He pointed at the papers strewn across the table in front of him. "It's all my attempts to crack Lexington's encryption key. And I came up empty. Here's the list of file names and the key phrases I tried—every fucking password I could think of. His birthday. His kids' names. His wife's name. His anniversary…"

Casey sat up straighter. "What list?"

Ryan shoved a sheet of paper toward her. "File names, none of which I can get into. Each one of them is a number, and they're not sequential. Some have two digits, some have three or four, and there's no pattern."

Casey glanced at the page. "We have no way of knowing why Ronald chose those numbers or what they connect to." She frowned. "What we do know is that whatever this list represents, it's pretty important. Otherwise, he wouldn't go to such great lengths to protect its contents."

"Which doesn't do a damned thing for us unless I can hack into those files," Ryan replied. "I've been on this since Emma and I did our thing and I brought home the USB drive. I'm hitting one brick wall after another. And I *don't* hit brick walls. It's just not who I am."

Emma lowered her head to stifle a smile.

"You need help," Casey stated factually. "From a person who specializes in cracking encrypted data."

"Yeah, and who would that be?"

Casey's gaze flickered to Marc.

He nodded. "I'll call Aidan."

"Who the hell is Aidan?" Patrick asked.

"My brother."

Claire's head came up. "You have a brother?"

A corner of Marc's mouth lifted. "I'm not an alien, Claire. I have a life and a family outside of Forensic Instincts."

"Yeah, but you never mentioned him," Patrick said, and then waved away his own comment. "Forget I said that. Need to know. Special Ops. I get it."

Claire was eyeing Ryan, who clearly liked this idea enough to calm him down. Actually, he was more than calm; he was nodding his approval. "Why don't you look surprised?" she asked.

"You know why." Casey interlaced her fingers on the table. "Because Ryan hacked everyone's file and read up on all of you."

"Yup." Ryan grinned. "Like Yoda, I'm omniscient." He turned to Marc. "Do you think Aidan would do it?"

"If I ask him like a respectful younger brother, then

yeah, I think he'd do it. That is if he's in New York and not traveling God knows where."

Claire looked quizzical, although Marc's comment made her smile. "Can I ask for details about this mysterious brother of yours, now that he's been revealed?"

"Sure." Marc gave an offhand shrug. "Aidan's three years older than I am. We went to the Naval Academy at Annapolis at the same time—he was a senior when I was a freshman. Not a lot of fun for me. He went on to the marines and became a hybrid intelligence officer and communications officer. In English, that means he thinks like an intel officer and acts like a communications officer. Among his achievements, he breezed right through an intensive Cryptological Divisions Officers Course."

"That's how he can help us," Claire murmured.

"Uh-huh." Marc went on. "I can't tell you much more because everything he did in the military was classified, so I'm in the dark as much as you are. But once he moved on to civilian life, he went to work as a troubleshooter for Heckman Flax. He's been there since."

"You said New York—do you mean he works right here in the city?" Patrick, along with Claire and Emma, looked startled.

"Yup."

"Jesus, Marc, Heckman Flax isn't just an investment bank. It's like a hub for the financial geniuses of the world."

"True. And Aidan is responsible for all their trading platforms worldwide. He travels everywhere at a moment's notice to put out fires. And there you have the story of my brother. Happy?"

"Is he hot?" Emma asked.

Marc rolled his eyes. "He's old enough to be your father."

"If he got someone pregnant when he was in his teens, I guess that's true," Emma acknowledged. "But ick, I wasn't thinking of him *that* way. I just wanted to know if he had your cool French-Asian looks." She paused. "Although you really don't have too much of the Asian on your mother's side, except the slight slant of your eyes. Mostly there's steamy European blood."

Marc was having trouble not laughing at Emma's physical analysis. "Since you're so into genetics and physical characteristics, I'll let you meet Aidan and judge for yourself. How's that?"

"Cool."

Marc took out his cell phone and made the call.

"Hey," he greeted his brother. "Are you in New York?" A pause. "Good. My team's in a bind here. We need your expertise....Yeah, some files that have to be decrypted....Yesterday, if possible." Another pause. "Yeah, yeah, I know—marines rule. How fast can you get here?... That's no problem—just bring her. She'll have plenty of people to entertain her....Great. Thanks. See you."

He hung up. "Aidan will be here in about an hour."

"Who's *she?*" Claire asked. "Who is it that we'll be entertaining?"

"Abby. Aidan's daughter. The nanny's sick so he's on babysitting duty, and that's harder than all our jobs combined. Abby is three and she's a real operator. I'm afraid she's going to grow up to be Emma."

"Hey," Emma protested. "That's a good thing."

"If you say so."

"It's a moot point, anyway." Casey had started to laugh. "With a military father and uncle? No way."

"How about Mrs. Aidan?" Emma asked.

"There is none. Never was," Marc answered. "Aidan was pretty heavily involved with someone in France. They reconnected in the U.S., and then eventually broke it off. She died in a car crash. He never even knew she was pregnant until social services showed up on his doorstep with Abby in their arms."

"Poor baby," Claire murmured.

"You won't think so after she's trashed your yoga room." Marc's words of warning were belied by the tender note in his voice. "She's a pistol but she's a heartbreaker. She has my tough brother wrapped around her tiny little finger."

"It sounds like she's got her navy SEAL uncle wrapped that way, too," Claire said.

"Guilty as charged. I'm crazy about the little brat."

"This should be fun," Emma said brightly.

"It's not about fun, Emma. It's about work." Casey brought her receptionist back to earth. "Aidan is coming here to help Ryan. But since you're so psyched about this, you can be the chief babysitter. How's that?"

"Sure. Aidan can play with Ryan. I'm sure I can teach Abby a trick or two about torturing the Devereaux men."

22

An hour and a half later, Emma wasn't so sure.

Aidan had arrived promptly like any respectable former marine. Emma had flown to the front door, leaving her chair swiveling around wildly from the motion.

She punched in the dummy code and opened the door.

Outside stood a tall, serious-looking man, with Marc's straight black hair and broad shoulders. But Aidan's eyes were navy blue and rounder, his forehead was high and his nose was more patrician than Marc's. In his open cashmere coat and rock-hard build, he came across as even more intimidating than Marc—if that was possible.

Beside him, jumping up and down and saying, "Daddy, is this where Uncle Marc works?" was an adorable little girl with a mop of dark hair and her father's blue eyes and stubborn chin.

"Yes, Abby, and we're going to leave it in one piece," Aidan said in a deep, loving voice. He glanced up at Emma and held out his hand. "I'm Aidan Devereaux. This is my daughter, Abby."

"Hi. We've been expecting you both. Come in." Emma squatted down at once so she could meet Abby at eye level. "Hi, Abby, I'm Emma. Do you like cupcakes?"

"Yes!" Abby exclaimed, her face lighting up.

"Good, because I bought way too many, and I need help eating them." Emma glanced up. "Is it okay with your daddy?"

"It's fine." Aidan was hanging up his coat, revealing a navy sweater and jeans. "Just not too many. She's already bouncing off the walls. More sugar will turn her into the Energizer Bunny."

Abby was poking Emma's arm persistently. "I like shawclate better than vanela."

"Well, we have both. So chocolate it is." Emma rose and extended her hand to Abby. "Come on. I'll take you to the kitchen."

"'Kay." Abby gripped Emma's fingers tightly. "Bye, Daddy."

Aidan's lips twitched. "Bye, princess." He mouthed the words *thank you* to Emma.

She smiled and called out, "Yoda, please summon the team and tell them Aidan's here."

"No need, Yoda," Casey said as the whole team descended the steps into the foyer. "We're already here."

"Uncle Marc!" Abby broke away from Emma to rush over and propel herself into Marc's arms.

"Hey, you." Marc caught her and gave her a huge bear hug. "Wow, you got heavy." He pretended to drop her. "Did you get way taller since I saw you?"

Abby laughed. "No, silly. You just sawed me..." She screwed up her face. "Friday."

"You know, you're right. I must be getting weaker or something."

"No, you're not. You're strong. Like Daddy. 'Cuz you're brudders."

"You were right the first time, princess," Aidan said.

"Uncle Marc must be getting weaker. He doesn't work out as much as Daddy."

Marc shot him a look. "Where are you headed?" he asked Abby, tousling her hair.

"That lady—" Abby pointed at Emma "—said she has cupcakes. I'm gonna help her eat them."

"Well, I won't keep you, then." Marc set her on her feet. "Just leave a couple for me, okay? Vanilla is fine. You can eat all the chocolate."

"Gee, thanks," Aidan muttered.

"Anytime," Marc said with a grin.

"Bye, Uncle Marc. See ya later." Abby took off and eagerly grabbed Emma's hand. "Let's go."

They all watched her drag Emma along, until Emma told her the kitchen was a few floors up. Then she reversed her steps, pulling Emma toward the staircase. Her little legs pumped as she climbed up with Emma following behind.

"She's precious." Casey extended her hand. "I'm Casey Woods. It's a pleasure to meet you."

"And you, as well," Aidan replied.

The rest of the team followed suit, shaking Aidan's hand and introducing themselves. Hero went up to sniff Aidan out. He seemed especially intrigued by Aidan's jeans pocket.

"Sorry, Hero, I almost forgot." He pulled a sizable dog biscuit out of his pocket. "This is for you."

Hero barked, snatched the bone and veered into the first office to enjoy his treat in private.

"Did you just check out our website or hack into our files so you'd be up to speed on all our team members?" Ryan asked.

A corner of Aidan's mouth lifted. "Let's just say there

won't be any surprises. Now you and I should get to work."

"Great. Let's go down to my lair. I'm all set up for you."

By the time Ryan and Aidan were reviewing what Ryan had tackled thus far, Abby had polished off a chunk of three separate chocolate cupcakes—mostly the top parts that had the icing. Her face and hands were covered with chocolate, and before Emma could wash them, Abby had bolted out of the kitchen and raced to the main conference room.

"Wow. This is big!" she exclaimed. She went over to the table that held all the tech equipment and began fiddling with the buttons, leaving chocolate marks everywhere. "Where's the TV?" she asked as Emma rushed in behind her. "Does this one change the channels?"

"Warning, an unauthorized intruder!" Yoda's voice filled the room. "No access granted!"

"Who's that?" Rather than being terrified, Abby looked intrigued. Her blue eyes swept the office as she tried to place where the sound was coming from. "Is that the Wizard of Oz?"

Emma started to laugh. "Kind of, yes." She raised her head. "It's okay, Yoda. Abby is with me."

"It is most definitely not okay, Emma," Yoda responded. "You have no authorization to allow visitors. You yourself are still within your probationary period for another fifty-five days."

"Then check with Casey," Emma snapped, trying to deal with Yoda and keep an eye on Abby at the same time. One was a friggin' dictator, the other was the Roadrunner.

"I most definitely shall, immediately. And tell that small person to stop touching the equipment."

"I'll try, Yoda." Emma couldn't wait for him to summon Casey. She was at her wit's end.

Meanwhile, Abby had already gotten bored with the conversation. She was now swiveling around and around in Casey's chair, leaving more chocolate stains on the leather and on the polished wood table.

"Whee! This is fun! A big chair like Daddy's!" She wiped her mouth with the back of her hand, leaving splotches of chocolate in both places.

"What are these?" Abby reached for the pile of papers stacked neatly in front of her. "Can I color?" She turned the first page over, picked up a pen and began scribbling. "Do you have crayons? This color is ugly."

"Please, Abby, don't do that," she repeated.

"'Kay." Abby climbed onto the table, stood up and slid her feet around on the polished surface. "Look! I'm a ice skater in the 'lympics!"

"Come down, Abby. You're going to hurt yourself." Emma lunged for her, catching her around the waist.

Abby yelped in protest.

"Warning. Stack overflow error. Kernel panic imminent," Yoda announced. "Shut down sequence initiated. Restart in ten seconds. Goodbye."

Panicked, Emma pressed Marc's intercom button.

"Problem, Emma?" he asked drily, having answered on the first ring.

"Marc, *do* something!" she pleaded. "She's going to kill us both!"

He chuckled. "Where are you?"

"In what's left of the conference room."

Three minutes later, Marc strode into the disaster of a conference room.

He was greeted by the sight of a panic-stricken Emma standing on the conference table, clutching his chocolate-covered, desk-skating niece. Glancing around the ravaged room and taking in the total picture, Marc had to stifle his laughter.

"What's going on here?" he asked, keeping his voice stern.

"Uncle Marc!" Abby promptly broke away from Emma and jumped off the table.

Emma cried out in alarm.

Long before Abby hit the floor, Marc caught her in one arm. His other arm was filled with art supplies.

Completely unshaken by her near-collision with the floor, Abby gave Emma a puzzled look. "Why is Imma yelling, Uncle Marc? Is she hurt?"

"No, I'm fine, sweetheart." Emma was shaking as she got down from the table. "I was a little afraid on the ice without you."

"Oh." Abby nodded sagely. "It's 'kay. Daddy says if you do sumpthing a lot, you get good at it. You need to—" Abby searched for the right word "—pwactice. I'll help you." Her little face lit up with a smile.

This time Marc chuckled aloud. "I think you scared Emma. Let's let her go get a snack and lie down for a nap."

Another sage nod. "She didn't even finish one cupcake," Abby reported. "She's pwobably hungry."

"I'm probably dying," Emma muttered as she headed for the door. "I'm not having kids till I'm forty."

"What's that, Uncle Marc?" Emma heard Abby say as she left the room.

"That, my little tyrant, is a whole bunch of paper and three markers. Claire went out to get you a big box of crayons with lots of colors."

"Thank you!" Abby lowered her voice to a loud whisper. "I hated that pen. It was ugly and it only made black. But I like Imma. She's nice."

Marc sat down at the conference table with Abby on his lap. "We can draw with these until Claire gets here. Make me a picture."

"Of what?"

"Of the cupcakes you ate."

"'Kay." Abby started drawing.

She'd finished drawing what appeared to be two yellow blobs with black tops and some dots of red all over them when Claire walked in.

She glanced around the conference room, and her lips twitched.

"One superthick coloring book and a humongous box of crayons," she announced, waving them in the air.

"Yay!" Abby bounced up and down on Marc's lap. "Thank you." A tiny terror, but always polite, Marc thought. That was one thing Aidan insisted on.

Eagerly, Abby took the coloring book and box of crayons. "You're nice, too. What's your name?"

"Claire."

Abby's face fell. "Daddy uses that word when he's mad. He says, 'Is that clear?'" On the last part, Abby lowered her voice to as deep a sound as she could muster in an attempt to imitate her father.

Without allowing herself to smile, Claire nodded. "My daddy used to say that a lot to me, too. The good news is, my name's not *Clear,* it's *Claire.* It rhymes with *hair.*"

"Oh." Abby digested that. "Claire," she repeated. "I like that name. And you have nice hair. It's yellow and straight. Mine's black and has waves like the ocean. That's what Daddy says."

"Your daddy is right. You have beautiful hair. Maybe we can brush it later—after we do some somersaults on my special mat. I have a room here with lots of mats and balls in it."

"Really?" Abby's eyes had grown round. "Can we go now?"

"Of course we can—under one condition."

"What?"

"That we stop at the bathroom and get all washed up."

"'Kay," Abby said again.

"Great. Let's go, then." Claire held out her hand.

Jumping off Marc's lap, Abby asked him, "It's 'kay, right, Uncle Marc? Claire's not a stranger, she's your friend."

"It's absolutely 'kay," Marc assured her. "Happy somersaulting."

Marc was scrubbing the knobs on the equipment and there was a pile of brown paper towels on the floor beside him when Aidan and Casey walked in.

"I'm afraid to ask," Aidan said, surveying the room.

There was an overturned chair, papers strewn everywhere and footprints on the expensive oval table. The wall above the tech table was smeared with chocolate, and there were crayons scattered on the table and on Casey's tilted chair. Her monogrammed pen was a brown-frosting mess on the floor.

"You don't need to ask," Marc replied. "You already know. The miniature cyclone was here."

Aidan turned to Casey. "I apologize. I'll have a cleaning crew sent over immediately to restore this place to normal."

Casey grinned. "Oh, I don't know. I think your brother is doing a great job."

Marc scowled in her direction. "He can't afford my rates."

"Where's Abby now?" Aidan asked tentatively.

"Doing somersaults with Claire—or on Claire—in the yoga room."

"Oh, God." Aidan squeezed his eyes shut. "I'd better rescue poor Claire and get out of here before Abby wrecks the whole place."

At that moment, Ryan came in, scanning some of the printouts he and Aidan had made of their work.

"Thanks, Aidan," Ryan was saying. "I…" He halted in his tracks. "What the hell happened in here? And why is Marc fiddling with my equipment?"

"Abby had a little fun," Casey explained. She patted Ryan's arm. "Not to worry. We'll restore everything to its original state under Yoda's guidance."

"If Yoda hasn't croaked by now," Marc said, finishing up his task. "Last I heard, he wasn't feeling too well."

"Who blames him?"

"Sorry, Ryan," Aidan said. "But take it from one who knows, the equipment will be okay. Abby has applied every known substance to every knob and dial at my place."

"Okay." Ryan looked dubious.

"So what's the verdict with the decryption process?" Marc asked.

Aidan held up the USB drive that Ryan had given

him. "I'm taking this with me, and continuing our efforts at home."

"Yeah." Ryan perked right up. "Aidan designed a special computer strictly for decryption purposes. The man's a genius. He bought off-the-shelf GPUs and assembled them into a killer computer optimized for decryption. I can't wait to see what this baby can do."

"The problem with the decryption process is that you never know how long it'll take," Aidan reminded him. "We could have an answer in hours or we could never have an answer."

"Don't I know it." Ryan rubbed the back of his neck. "To further complicate things, Ronald Lexington had a photographic memory. Janet Moss told Casey that at their lunch. So while most people have a problem remembering a couple of short passwords, this guy would have no trouble devising and remembering a long and complex encryption key that would make most of us cringe."

"Let's be optimistic," Casey said. "We won't know if we don't try."

"Yup." Aidan turned around. "So let me collect my daughter and get home to get started."

23

Sharon Gilding was entering the ladies' room, just as Janet Moss was coming out. They each nodded hello, but before the neurosurgeon had continued on her way, Janet's eagle eye did a quick once-over.

Sharon's skirt was askew, her lipstick was smeared and her overall appearance was ruffled.

Dr. Sharon Gilding was never ruffled. Well, *almost* never.

Janet smiled to herself. At least her boss would be in a good mood this afternoon. Sex always put men in a good mood. Unless, of course, it was one of *those* times. Times when Sharon was angry and pissy about the damned chief of surgery job she wanted. Then Jacob would have had to listen to her rant about how she'd done everything and more to ensure that it was she, and not Conrad Westfield, who got that job, and how Jacob had better make it happen.

If that's how their afternoon delight had ended, Jacob would be cranky and snappish—and less than cheerful.

Janet had prepared herself for that, but not for the explosion that ensued when she returned from the ladies' room.

She'd just opened the door into the executive offices when Jacob came sputtering out of his office, red as a beet. He saw Janet and shouted, "Get me Stephen Diamond on the phone. *Now.*"

Each sputter was accentuated by the pile of legal papers Jacob was waving furiously in the air.

Janet raced into her office and straight to her desk and took care of calling the hospital chief counsel. She'd never seen Jacob Casper so out of control.

About an hour later, Stephen Diamond, Esq.—a lanky, stony-faced man of about forty-five—appeared in the executive offices and was ushered immediately into Jacob's office.

Through the walls of her own office, Janet could hear the agitated conversation, which was punctuated repeatedly by Jacob screaming, "That fucking bitch!" She was seriously considering going out to his door and blatantly listening in when the door flew open.

Jacob stomped out and stalked straight into her office.

"Stop whatever you're doing," he demanded.

She dropped her paperwork without a sound.

"The chairman of the hospital board is calling an emergency board meeting. At eight-thirty *tonight,*" Jacob informed her. "I have instructions for you to follow—*now!*"

He barely waited for Janet to grab a pad and pen before continuing. "Notify every board member of the meeting and confirm his or her attendance. Anyone who's traveling must tie in by video or audio conference. No exceptions."

Janet finished scribbling, and then put down her pad and took her life in her hands. "What happened, Jacob? What's going on?"

"What's going on?" Jacob snapped. "Ronald Lexington's fucking widow, Nancy, has reached new heights of insanity and revenge. She's decided to sue us for medical malpractice wrongful death. And by 'us' I mean the hospital. She's not only going after Conrad for Ronald's death. She's going after the whole cardiac and surgical team, plus the hospital itself, claiming incompetence and neglect resulting in her loss."

"Medical malpractice…?" Janet paled. "Oh, my God, I never thought… Ronald loved this hospital so much. How can his wife…?" She broke off, seeing the apoplectic look on her boss's face. "I'll take care of it immediately."

Ryan strode into the conference room, where Casey was working.

"Something is going on with the Lexington clan," he announced. "Nancy went to see her lawyer today. And Ron and Felicia were at the apartment when she left. They were discussing how worried they were about their mother, about how she was in denial over who their father really was and how out of control she was in what she was planning."

Casey put down her work and stared at Ryan. "Were those their exact words—'out of control in what she was planning'?"

"Pretty much, yeah." Ryan held up his device. "I'll let you listen to the recording. They've been playing along with their mother's repeated claim that Ronald was faithful, even though they knew he was anything but—and they're convinced that she knew it, too. At one point, Felicia asked Ron if he thought their father had been sleeping with Madeline Westfield. He said he wasn't sure, but judging from their mother's hatred toward her and the extent to which she was carrying that hatred, it was a distinct possibility."

"But why did she go to see her lawyer?" Casey gave a puzzled frown. "Do you think she's making provisions for her kids in case anything happens to her?"

"Good thought. Especially if she's going into battle to kill."

"Marc is over at Madeline's on guard duty now. Let's listen to this recording, then call him. We might need him to pay a visit to the lawyer's secretary tomorrow, disguised as whoever the hell you two decide, and charm her a bit to find out what that meeting was about."

Marc and Madeline were having dinner in her apartment when her phone rang.

She glanced down at the caller ID. "It's Crest Haven," she said, the color draining from her face.

"Answer it," Marc instructed. "And don't jump to conclusions."

She nodded and picked up the phone. "Hello?"

"Madeline? It's Conrad."

She heard the panic in his voice. "Conrad. What is it? What's the matter?"

"You'll never believe this," he replied. "Nancy Lexington is suing me and Manhattan Memorial for medical malpractice wrongful death—Ronald's death. I'm in shock."

Madeline recoiled, as well. "My God. How do you know this?"

"Because I was just served."

"All right." Madeline fought for and found some composure. "I don't want you to worry about this. I'll get Ed on the phone. He'll know who to reach out for."

"I appreciate that. But, Madeline, please don't placate me. Keep me fully informed. I'm strong, and I don't shrink away from my problems anymore. I'm fully aware of what kind of Pandora's box this is going to open. Stop worrying about my mental health. I have to face this."

Madeline nodded at the phone. "I'll get back to you as soon as I've spoken to Ed."

"Thank you."

"Who's Ed and what's going on?" Marc demanded once Madeline had hung up.

"He's our attorney. This is bad, Marc." She told Marc exactly what Conrad had told her.

"It's bad, but it can be dealt with." Marc squeezed her hand. "You call your attorney. I'm calling the office."

Ryan beat him to the punch.

Marc's phone began vibrating just as he reached for it.

The meeting didn't end until after midnight.

The end result was ugly but expected. The board instructed Jacob and Manhattan Memorial's team of lawyers to settle the lawsuit. They authorized up to five million dollars to make this go away. Their reasoning was sound. With a major lawsuit pending and the plaintiff's attorney having a reputation as a media hound, it was going to be a PR nightmare that everyone wanted to avoid—especially with the hospital merger under way.

The Board of New York Medical Center would have to be notified of this material event immediately. Jacob had cringed at that thought. His only hope was that he could communicate the lawsuit and an agreement to settle in principle at the same time.

He didn't want to go home after that meeting. He went straight to the nearest bar to drink himself into oblivion.

The entire FI team met in the living room at Madeline's apartment. It was easier that way since Madeline was an integral part of the conversation and Marc was already there. In addition, Patrick was on his way to do his overnight security shift, and Casey and Ryan were already together. So Casey just called Claire and had her meet them at Madeline's ASAP. Only Hero stayed home, stretched out on Casey's bed, happy to be relaxing.

"So now we know why Nancy was consulting with her lawyer," Casey said. "No need to dig. But why the lawsuit? Why now?"

"Because she's a nutcase? Because she tried breaking and entering and attempted murder, and neither of them has worked," Ryan suggested. "So she's going after Madeline and Conrad in another life-destroying way."

Casey looked dubious. "I don't doubt that this reaction of hers is a vindictive woman's attempt at revenge, but there's a piece still missing. Either Conrad or Madeline—or both—have something the killer wants."

"Maybe Nancy figures it'll come out in discovery," Patrick said. "The Lexingtons' attorney will demand every record, abstract, file folder and medical document in Madeline's and Conrad's possession."

Marc frowned. "The profile is off, though. Attempted murder doesn't get tossed in helter-skelter. It's either the first and only thing attempted, or it's the culmination of rage and frustration when other methods don't work. Why would Nancy's fury escalate to the point of trying to kill Madeline and Conrad, and then suddenly become subdued enough for her to just sue them?"

"A guns-blazing lawsuit isn't exactly rational," Ryan said.

"Compared to murder, it is."

"This is unbearable." Madeline rubbed her head. "I feel like I'm living in someone else's nightmare. It just keeps getting worse and worse."

"Emma needs to keep candy striping at the hospital for longer than she's planned," Claire interrupted. "I know she'll probably kill me, but I feel it's necessary. Partly because she'll be on the inside when word of this lawsuit starts spreading and people start reacting. And partly because my instincts are telling me so. I'm not sure why."

"Done," Casey replied. "How long?"

"Just an extra week or two. At least, I think so." Claire's tone was rueful. "I really feel bad about this. Emma is counting the days to get out of Manhattan Memorial and return to FI."

"She'll live," Ryan replied. "This is important. Meanwhile, I have to keep a close monitoring ear on every conversation the Lexingtons have and every place they go. I don't know how deep Ron and Felicia's involvement in this is, and I don't know how far Nancy's already gone. But I will."

Abby was finally asleep, and Aidan used that time to sit down at his decryption computer and check on the files he had been given by Forensic Instincts.

With what Marc had relayed to him a little while ago about the hospital lawsuit, it was more important than ever that he crack the key.

Aidan had repeated Ryan's efforts first, this time using special decryption algorithms. He started his efforts with seed words based on Ronald's life, hoping for an early win. Family members. Pets' names. Favorite sports teams. Hobbies. Alma maters. All the personal information that he and Ryan had dug up and that formed many people's core passwords and even encryption keys.

Aidan's computer had quickly analyzed the millions of permutations and rejected all of them. Now it was going to take brute force techniques to break the encryption key. Billions of attempts. Billions of failures.

Hunched over the computer, Aidan responded to Ryan's earlier text with a simple but accurate answer. Not yet.

24

Word of the lawsuit spread through Manhattan Memorial like wildfire.

The staff was shocked and terrified as their worlds were thrown totally into chaos. The potential fallout from the hospital merger became secondary compared to this. Even the *possibility* of a lawsuit of this magnitude could impact the entire hospital.

The atmosphere within the walls was grim, the silence and whispered conversations permeating everything, compromising the fine work that had always been associated with Manhattan Memorial.

Jacob Casper was locked in his office with counsel almost around the clock, desperately working to stop this avalanche before it took on a life of its own.

Janet had no time for anything, much less a dinner with Casey. She was expected to be in on all the meetings with Jacob, taking notes, following up on instructions. For once, she was too overworked and exhausted to be plugged into her gossip line. Besides, there was nothing to gossip about other than what was happening here. And she was in the inner loop, bound by confidentiality. There was nothing she could do to calm the frenzied staff.

This was just an overwhelming nightmare.

During the limited time Janet had to run to the ladies' room and buy a bite to eat, she did, and then hurried back to her office to eat in privacy. To hang out at Au Bon Pain would mean to answer a million questions—none of which she could, or was permitted to, answer. Plus, she didn't want to be bombarded. To say what? That no one's job was secure? That no one's future was a fait accompli? That no one even knew if the hospital would survive this unless the lawsuit was settled quickly and quietly?

Solitude was the only solution. That, and a lot of strong black coffee.

During one of those brief, solo meals, Diana knocked on her door.

Janet looked up, and then gave a faint smile when she saw who it was. "Come in, sweetheart."

Diana poked her head in and waved a brown paper bag. "I thought you might like some company for lunch—company who loves you and has no desire to pump you for information."

"That sounds wonderful." Janet gave a weary sigh. "Pull up a chair and join me. I apologize in advance. I'm lousy company."

"No apology necessary. You're going through hell." Diana settled herself, placed her lunch on the desk and glanced at the small fruit salad her mother was picking at.

"Mom, you have to eat." She pulled out the turkey sandwich she'd brought from home and placed half of it in front of her mother. "You're going to get yourself sick. Nothing is worth that."

Janet stared down at the sandwich, and then lifted her gaze. "Thank you. I'm trying to keep it together. But sitting in that conference room, hour upon hour, hearing the same ominous predictions—it really gets to me. This is *my* hospital, too. I've worked here forever. And that bitch, Nancy Lexington, wants nothing more than to destroy it. For what? It won't bring Ronald back."

"Yeah. I know." Diana swallowed hard. "And selfishly, I'm hysterical, Mom. My job was in flux before. Now? What am I going to do if they cut me loose?"

"We'll fix it the way we fix everything," Janet replied. "But right now, we don't even know if there's going to be a job to fight for, or a Manhattan Memorial to practice in."

"What are the odds that Nancy Lexington will settle?"

Janet shrugged, trying to choke down a bite of sandwich. "It depends. The woman who burst in here last week, threatened me and slapped me across the face was definitely irrational and paranoid. Maybe she's really lost it and she went over the edge for good. I don't know. But if she won't accept the millions we're offering her, we're in deep trouble."

Diana munched on a carrot stick, her own mind working. "If she doesn't give a damn about the money for herself, you'd think she'd care about it for her children—the children who she so loves and shields."

"Shhh," Janet said. "You're not supposed to know about what she's shielding them from."

"I've never repeated anything you told me, and I never will," Diana replied. "I'm just talking to you. We're alone, and the door is locked. But I don't know what more that woman wants other than what she already has—and now, what she's being offered. FYI, I doubt her children are in the dark about anything their father did. He wasn't exactly discreet—even if he thought he was."

"I'm not sure how much Nancy wants or what would be enough for her to settle. But I have a feeling we'll be finding out very soon."

"Soon" came even sooner than Janet had expected.

At eight o'clock, with Janet sitting at her desk wondering if she'd be needed any more that day, Jacob burst through the administrative doors and into Janet's office.

"We had our settlement conference."

"Already?" Janet was surprised. "That wasn't supposed to take place until tomorrow."

"Well, Nancy Lexington's attorney summoned us. So counsel and I went."

Janet didn't have to ask. She could tell that the conference had gone horribly just by looking at Jacob. He was positively gray, and he looked as rattled as the rest of the staff. The only difference was he also looked livid.

"Get the board chairman on the phone now," he commanded.

She nodded. "I can see that you're furious. May I ask what happened?"

"No settlement. Nancy Lexington was there, and she wouldn't budge. She doesn't want money, she wants revenge. She wants everyone's head. Conrad's. Madeline's. Manhattan Memorial. The entire world, all of whom she holds responsible for Ronald's death. The woman is certifiable."

"Are those demands her attorney's or hers?"

"If they were the attorney's, we'd stand half a chance," Jacob snapped, running a shaky hand through his hair. "But no, those are Nancy's own demands. Actually, her attorney had begged her to accept the more than generous offer. He continued to urge her to do so throughout the meeting. And she continued to refuse."

A dark pause, during which Jacob lowered his head. "I even followed the board's instructions and offered to fire Conrad and Madeline. She didn't give a damn. That wasn't enough. She wants a court of law to find them responsible for Ronald's death. Once that judgment is entered, they'll be ruined. She wants no part of settlements wrapped in confidentiality agreements to protect the guilty parties' reputations. She wants them and their reputations destroyed, personally and financially. Her goal is to have the Westfields unemployable, except for flipping burgers in a fast-food restaurant, and if the hospital goes down with them, so be it."

"Oh, my God." That was worse than Janet had expected. Without pursuing it further, she reached for the phone. "I'll get the board chairman right now."

Ryan sat down at the computer desk in his lair. He had to listen to the recording of the latest conversation that had taken place at Nancy Lexington's house—courtesy of the bug he'd planted there when no one was home. He was really psyched, not about the content, but about how he was going to listen to it.

He'd been looking for the right opportunity to test Audio Detracktor, the new app he'd downloaded to his iPad, and this Lexington family conversation would be perfect for the task at hand.

"Yoda, please upload the Lexington audio file to my iPad Dropbox account," he said.

Mere seconds passed. "Your request has been completed," Yoda responded.

"Excellent." Ryan launched the app, selected the file and tapped the analyze button on his screen.

The app displayed "Working," together with a swirling icon, as it crunched through the audio, attempting to separate similar sounds into layers. Each layer appeared as a horizontal band, stacked one on top of another, down the screen. They were arranged in descending order based on average decibel, the intensity of the sound isolated by the software.

Ryan tapped the play icon on the first and loudest layer. After a few seconds of silence, he heard some harsh words from Ron Lexington. Then more silence. Ryan tapped Stop, and moved onto the second layer. The voice he heard was Nancy Lexington's, angry and irrational. A quick pause and then more of Nancy, petering down into silence.

Time to move on to the next layer.

This time it was Felicia, who sounded no less pissed off than her brother.

Cool.

The app had detected the pattern of each of their voices and separated each of them from the other as well as from the other sounds in the room.

Felicia's words ended. Curious, Ryan played the next layer in the sequence. A honking horn from the traffic in the street below. The rumble of a truck's diesel engine lumbering down the street. Then the *click-click-click* of high heels on a wooden floor, followed by the springs of a sofa as someone either sat or stood. And finally, *tick-tick-tick,* the telltale sound of expanding metal radiators as the heat kicked on inside the room. Ryan was beginning to wonder if he'd be able to hear the room's occupants breathing.

His excitement over this new toy was abruptly halted when his mind reassembled the pieces of this audio puzzle, and he realized that the conversation in its entirety was important.

Time to actually listen.

"Yoda, please shut down the app," he said.

"Of course, Ryan." An instant later it had been done.

Now Ryan played the audio file using the standard music app so he could concentrate on the conversation itself.

Evidently Nancy had recently arrived home to find her children waiting.

"Mom, what did you do at that meeting?" Ron demanded.

"Exactly what I said I was going to do." Nancy sounded completely unhinged. "I turned down their offer and insisted on going to trial."

Felicia groaned. "Didn't you hear a word we said?" she asked. "This witch hunt of yours is going to drag Dad's name through the mud. The media will have a field day with what the hospital leaks. They're going to go for the jugular, not just sit back and let you destroy Manhattan Memorial and its staff members. They're going to come at you with all they've got."

"Really?" Nancy gave a triumphant laugh. "Let them. They're desperate. I already got them to offer to fire both Conrad and Madeline. Quite a coup, wouldn't you say?"

"Are you kidding?" Ron sounded flabbergasted. "Isn't that enough? What more do you want? Conrad and Madeline will be disgraced, jobless and punished for the crime you're convinced they committed. Take the money and their offer to kick the Westfields out of Manhattan Memorial and walk away."

"Never."

"Mother." Felicia was clearly about to go for her mother's Achilles' heel. "The hospital is going to uncover every sordid affair that Dad ever had. Every woman he ever slept with. Every employee he crossed the line with and then lied about. Every hospital employee he got fired to keep them from talking about their trysts. The media will gobble up every word—and magnify and sensationalize it. Dad's reputation will be shattered. And our lives will be ruined."

"Don't ever speak of your father like that!" Nancy screamed. "He was a good man. An honorable man. He loved all of us. And he loved his job. There's nothing they can say that will undermine that!"

"They're not trying to undermine him," Ron said. "They're trying to destroy him. They want popular opinion to shift to the Westfields as victims in all this. You'll be labeled jealous and crazy, and we'll be penniless. If you accept the settlement, Dad's good name will remain as such, and we'll be as rich as kings. Isn't that the ultimate revenge?"

"No. And I'm not discussing this anymore. You should both be ashamed of yourself, disrespecting your father like this. I'm disgusted by your lack of support. Now get out! I don't want to look at either of you!"

After that, there was nothing more than the sound of a door slamming—Ryan would guess the door to Nancy's bedroom—and the rustling of coats being donned.

"She's lost it, Ron," Felicia murmured. "We have to do something."

"We will," he replied.

Marc lay quietly, holding Madeline in his arms. The one pillow that was still left on the bed he'd propped under his head, and the one section of bedcovers that wasn't crumpled on the floor he'd pulled over them when Maddy started shivering in the aftermath of their love-making.

Despite the crises that were going on around them, they were still reveling in the wonder of their reunion. Quite frankly, Marc couldn't get enough of Maddy, nor she of him.

Now she shifted a little, draping one leg over Marc's.

"I wish we could stay at your place," she murmured. "I hate that I'm trapped inside these walls ninety per-cent of the time. And yet I'm scared to death about what Nancy Lexington has in store for me."

Cradling her closer, Marc stared at the ceiling, his jaw hard. "I'm more worried about when and how the perp will strike next."

Madeline tilted her head back and gazed up at Marc. "You're still not convinced that Nancy is the one trying to kill Conrad and me."

"Less and less so every day," he replied. "She's cer-tainly not keeping a low profile with this lawsuit. Kill-ers don't usually wave red flags saying they're crazed with rage and on the warpath. Plus, how does she think that winning her lawsuit will eliminate whatever in-criminating evidence or knowledge you and/or Conrad must have? Sure, she'd discredit the two of you, maybe even destroy your careers, but you'd still be walking around. So how does that satisfy her needs? Why would she go backward in her attempts to wipe you both out as threats?"

Madeline considered that for a moment. "I can't dispute any of what you said. But if you're right, it scares me even more. My killer is still a nameless, faceless enemy at large. How can I combat that?"

"That's FI's job," Marc responded. "We'll keep you safe. And we'll find the son of a bitch who's going after you."

Madeline shut her eyes, wishing she could shut out everything outside this bed with it. "I believe you. I just wish I could *do* something. Much as I love you, I'm not the type to sit around like a damsel in distress."

Marc's lips twitched. "Yeah, I know. You're the type to spill coffee on an unarmed man."

He was rewarded with a playful punch in the arm. "You'll never let me live that down, will you?"

"Nope."

Madeline was silent for a moment, then said, "I have to talk to you about something."

"Uh-oh. I know that tone. I'm not going to like what you're about to say, am I?"

"Probably not. But it's not up for debate. As I just said, I hate being trapped in this apartment. And as I also said, I'm not the type to sit around doing nothing. So I pushed up the appointment I had for a recheck with my doctor. I went early this morning."

Marc did *not* like what he was hearing. "Why didn't I know about this doctor's appointment? Who went with you?"

"Patrick did. And before you call and ream him out, it's my fault that he didn't tell you. I made him promise not to. Our deal was that I had to tell you myself by the end of the day, or he'd go to you. I'm living up to my end of the bargain, so cut the poor guy some slack. I didn't ask his opinion. I announced that I was going with or without him. He just did his job."

"Son of a bitch," Marc muttered. "How is it that I know what's coming next?"

"Because you know me." Madeline propped herself on an elbow and gazed down at Marc. "I'm going back to work tomorrow—*with* my doctor's approval. My ribs are sore but healing, and my concussion is long gone. I'm not allowed to lift heavy objects, and my initial shifts have to be shortened. But I'll be back at Manhattan Memorial."

Marc's entire body was tense, and his stare bore through her. "This is the wrong time for this, Maddy. Even if you are feeling stronger. You're in the middle of a lawsuit that will probably go to trial, making you a prime target for the media, for hospital staff members and for anyone else who wants a piece of you. Conrad's not back, so you'll be standing in for him, too. Don't do this. It's a bad idea."

"I'm not afraid of emotional backlash. If I walk back into that hospital with my head held high, it says I have nothing to feel guilty about. Hiding suggests guilt."

"You're not hiding. You're recuperating." Marc frowned. "Also, have you given any thought to your security? How the hell can we watch you at work? Follow you around like puppies?"

Madeline's lips twitched. "Somehow I find it hard to think of you as a puppy. But yes, I've thought of that. I'll be among people every minute. I won't even go to the ladies' room alone. You and FI can post security guards at every hospital entrance I use. You can even make periodic strolls through the halls and watch me. Marc, I will *not* be a prisoner forever. Who knows when this ordeal will be over? I can't live like a princess in a tower anymore. Of course I'm scared. I already told you that. But work will take my mind off my fear. I'll be busy, and I'll be helping people. That's what I was trained to do."

With that, her chin came up like a warrior entering battle. "I'll be reporting for my shift at 8:00 a.m. Patrick is arranging the necessary security as we speak. They'll be discreet, so no one will know I'm being guarded. As for Jacob, I've already notified him. He's less than thrilled, but he has no basis to prevent me from returning. So that's that."

Marc had to smile. She looked so damned cute when she was dictatorial. And yeah, he was pissed, but he had to admire her determination. He also had to admit to himself that, were he in her shoes, he'd do the same thing.

His knuckles caressed her cheek. "You're a pain in the ass, do you know that?"

"Then we're well-matched," she replied. "Because so are you."

"You know I'll be living at that hospital whenever you're working."

"I never doubted it." Madeline relaxed and slid her body over his. "I think we've argued enough for now."

"I agree." He pulled her more firmly over him. "Let's make up."

25

It was predawn the next morning when Aidan's software broke the encryption code for 266.

The contents were labeled Valerie Pintar. It provided her full name, address, contact information, position at Manhattan Memorial, date of employment, date of termination of employment, yada, yada, yada.

Aidan skipped down past the basic specs, and he rolled his eyes when he saw that the entire top section of her file was a sexual performance evaluation. The second section was an explicit physical description of Valerie naked, including a couple of photos. Next came a list of all the dates of her and Ronald's liaisons. There were quite a few. The guy was obviously a busy boy.

The file went on to do a comprehensive write-up of Ronald's sexual fantasies with regard to Valerie and what she did to satisfy them.

And last and finally somewhat interesting was a summary of the steps Ronald had taken to end the affair, together with a payout schedule of the hospital money he'd been availing himself of to ensure Valerie's silence.

"So much for true love," Aidan muttered under his breath. He was more amused than anything else. He'd seen it all, decrypted international secrets that could make or break empires. The sex life of Ronald Lexington was less than exciting—although he was sure that Forensic Instincts would care about the embezzling part.

The other annoying factor here, given that only Valerie's file had been decrypted, was that Lexington had clearly set up different encryption keys for each file. That was going to make this process more time-consuming and a bigger pain in the ass than Aidan had hoped. And Jesus, he hoped it was worth it and the jerk hadn't just done repeats of his sexual exploits, assigning a different encryption key to each woman he'd screwed.

"Daddy, I'm up. Don't work." Abby ran into the room, and scrambled onto her father's lap. "Can we play?"

"At 5:00 a.m.? Sure, imp. I'd love nothing better," Aidan replied.

Quickly, he texted Ryan, and then emailed everything to him.

Then he went off to do the Barbie thing with Abby.

Ryan liked his sleep.

But when he was in the middle of a case, that went by the wayside.

He heard his cell phone bing, followed by a trilling sound from his email.

Rolling over, he reached for his iPhone. He scanned Aidan's text and then opened the email, scanning its contents.

"Holy shit," he muttered. "Smut and stealing all at once."

Jumping out of bed, Ryan headed for the shower. Simultaneously he called Casey. He knew her well enough to know that he'd be expected in the office, armed with info, yesterday.

Twenty minutes later, he was on his way.

Casey was a busy woman that morning.

When Ryan came in, Marc was already perched at the conference room table. He'd just told her that Madeline was headed back to work in a few hours, and she'd responded by telling him that Casper had offered to fire Conrad and Madeline to settle the lawsuit.

"Shit," Marc had said. "How do you know?"

"The bug in Nancy Lexington's house. Ryan listened to the conversation. She boasted about it to her kids."

"Shit," he said again. "Madeline is walking into a hornet's nest."

"I've got news," Ryan announced, interrupting the conversation. "I got a text from Aidan." He handed Casey the pages he'd printed out. "One file. One woman. One unique encryption key. That part sucks. This, on the other hand, makes for fascinating reading."

"A naked woman in erotic positions?" Casey commented drily as she scanned the first few pages. "Porn isn't usually your style, Ryan."

"Keep reading."

Marc had gone around behind Casey to read over her shoulder.

"Valerie Pintar. That's one of the names Janet mentioned—an employee who slept with Ronald and got fired for it," Casey said, reading on.

"Now this is interesting," Marc commented, pointing as they got to the embezzlement part. "Far from shocking, but interesting. So Ronald Lexington wasn't just a womanizer. He was a thief."

Casey looked up. "What did you mean when you said, 'That sucks'?"

"Aidan is telling us that he only cracked this one numerical file. That means that Ronald has a different encryption key for each file, which makes his and our jobs that much harder."

"Each encryption key has to be broken separately," Marc murmured.

"Exactly. And who knows how the hell long that will take?"

"You're right," Casey said. "That sucks. We have no time for a setback." Her eyes rose to meet Ryan's. "I want you to access the human resources database at the hospital. Search every bit of material available for Valerie Pintar. See if you can find any connection between her and the number 266—her birthday, social security number—anything."

"Already under way," Ryan replied. "But this could well be a dead end. The numbers could be random or they could be things the records would never show—like Valerie and Ronald's first date, the hotel room number from their first night together, their first-month anniversary...."

"I get it, but try. In the meantime, it's my turn. I don't give a damn how much turmoil the hospital's in. I'm scheduling that dinner with Janet Moss. I want to pump her for information about any more of Ronald's paramours she knows of. I want to hear the ideas she might have regarding personal vendettas these women could have concerning Ronald's death."

"This might blow your cover," Marc pointed out.

"It might. But I'll try to elicit her help as an ally. We'll see how that flies."

* * *

Emergency board meetings were becoming a regular part of hospital procedure, Janet thought as she filed into the conference room.

This time the meeting was a tactical one since Nancy's lawsuit was going to trial. Jacob and the team of lawyers were instructed by the board to start the legal process of discovery.

Every one of Conrad's surgeries would be peer-reviewed by experts using a fine-tooth comb. The hospital's surgical procedures, safety records, health code violations, etc., were all fair game. If Ronald Lexington's widow wouldn't settle, then Manhattan Memorial would prove beyond a shadow of a doubt that Lexington's death was not the hospital's fault.

The lawyers were instructed by the board to throw anyone they needed to under the bus—Conrad, Madeline, any one of their employees who could be personally blamed for Ronald's death. Whatever was necessary for the hospital to avoid responsibility. The sooner this went to trial, the better.

Janet was ordered to call an urgent management team meeting to alert them to what was about to occur and how it should be handled.

She got on it the instant the board meeting broke up.

Two hours later, Janet and Jacob closeted themselves in a smaller conference room, this time with the entire hospital management team. It was standing room only. Jacob explained the details of the situation to them and demanded their cooperation. The hospital would stand unified in its efforts to defend its stellar reputation.

Every department was given its role.

Sharon Gilding, the hastily appointed temporary chief of surgery, was told to make sure personally that everything in her department was double-and triple-checked. No lapses in paperwork. They would be under a continuous microscope until the lawsuit was over.

The head of security was instructed to hire a private investigator to delve into Ronald Lexington and his entire family, gathering anything that could undermine Nancy Lexington's lawsuit. Jacob stressed that he and the hospital's legal team would expect daily briefings.

The IT director was told to assign someone to work with the legal team—someone who was qualified enough to give them free access and get them everything they asked for.

The most qualified person was selected for the job.

Roger Lewis.

Patrick was stationed right outside the main hospital entrance.

Madeline walked past him as if she didn't know him and pushed the hospital's revolving doors, stepping inside and circling around until she entered the building.

For a long moment, she just stood there, absorbing the feeling of being back where she belonged. It had only been a couple of weeks, but it had felt like an eternity. The antiseptic smell. The fast-paced activity. The constant paging of doctors and surgeons over the PA system.

Manhattan Memorial was like her second home.

It didn't feel that way for long.

Madeline had barely crossed the lobby floor when staff members began coming to a halt and staring at her. She smiled and said hello, and was greeted with stony silence. No welcome-backs. No how-do-you-feels. No smiles or waves. Just icy glares and silence.

Feeling a chill creep up her spine, Madeline walked to the elevators and pressed the button for the E.R., one level up from the main lobby. There were a handful of people already waiting in the elevator corridor.

Everyone except the visitors shut down the second she arrived, silently staring at her with those cold looks before turning to whisper among themselves.

Taking the stairs seemed suddenly more appealing.

Madeline's gut twisted as she climbed to the second floor. She'd expected tons of questions, even more anxiety and maybe some resentment. But this total snubbing? This leashed anger that every staff member seemed to share?

And it wasn't just the lobby. Nor was it just the nurses.

The E.R. doctors were terse and frosty, speaking to her only as necessary and giving her as little to do as possible. The mixed group of employees who'd always been her friends—from surgeons to candy stripers and everyone in between—wanted nothing to do with her. Even the friggin' receptionists gave her dismissive looks and went back to work.

What in God's name had Jacob Casper told them? Madeline wondered later as she sat alone in the break room for a cup of coffee, and staff members strolled in and out, glancing at her and then quickly looking away. She felt like a pariah, isolated and invisible in her own workplace.

Not really invisible, not to everyone. There was definite anger in many of their faces, bitter conversation and eyes shooting daggers in her direction.

Clearly she'd been set up to take the fall, being

blamed as the culprit for the predicament the hospital was in. And with Conrad away, she was taking that fall all by herself.

No way.

Madeline set down her unfinished cup of coffee and took her tray to the trash and recyclable area. Her shock and hurt had started to ebb and transform into anger. This was ridiculous. If Jacob thought she was going to slink off like some guilty child who'd broken a family heirloom, he had something else coming.

She marched into the administrative wing and through the doors that led to the executive offices.

Sue, the receptionist, was cataloging some data sheets.

"May I help you?" she asked without looking up.

"Yes, Sue, you can." Madeline waited until the receptionist's head had popped up, an awkward expression crossing her face.

"Madeline."

"It's nice to know someone remembers my name," Madeline said. "Good to see you. Now I'd like to see Jacob."

Sue fidgeted in her seat. "He has back-to-back meetings all day long."

"Fine." Madeline walked over and sank down into one of the waiting area chairs. She crossed her legs and picked up a magazine. "I'll wait." A pointed pause. "For as long as I have to." She turned to the magazine's table of contents.

"But..." Sue was clearly out of her depth. She picked up the phone and pressed an extension, speaking quietly to the person at the other end.

Madeline didn't need to guess who that person was.

Sure enough, the door next to Jacob's opened, and Janet walked out.

"Madeline," she said cordially. "I didn't think you had healed enough to come back yet."

"Yet? Or at all?" Madeline gave her a bright smile. "There have certainly been some changes since I left."

Janet's expression was frosty. "Well, as you know, we're in the middle of a crisis."

"I'm very well aware of that." Madeline rose. "I'd like to discuss that very crisis with Jacob. And he must be between meetings because I distinctly heard his voice through the office door. He must be on the phone."

"If he is, then he's far too busy to see you."

"Let's ask him ourselves."

Before Janet could stop her, Madeline strode over to Jacob's closed door. She skipped knocking and just turned the knob and pushed open the door.

She stepped inside, Janet hot on her heels.

"What is it?" Jacob snapped without looking up.

"It's me, Jacob," Madeline replied. "It's time that you and I had a little talk."

26

Jacob's head came up, and he stared at Madeline warily.

"It's your first day back, Madeline," he said, recovering his authoritative demeanor. "I assumed you'd be busy reacquainting yourself with the E.R. patients and with your responsibilities. Besides, we have nothing to talk about." He shot Janet a dark look. "Please show Madeline out. And I'd appreciate if you and Sue would do a better job of screening my visitors."

Madeline shook off Janet's hand as soon as it touched her arm. She was getting angrier and angrier as the moments passed.

"No one is escorting me anywhere," she informed Jacob. "I'm not leaving this office until we've spoken. How long that takes to accomplish is up to you." She turned to Janet. "You can leave now."

Uncertainty flashed across Janet's face. She glanced from Madeline to Jacob.

"Go." Jacob waved her away. "And shut the door behind you. I'll handle this. The last thing this hospital needs is another scene."

Reluctantly, Janet did as she was told—although Madeline was quite certain that the gossipmonger was standing outside with her ear pressed tightly against the door.

"Sit down, Madeline," Jacob said.

He reached into his drawer and pulled out a hand-size digital recorder, showing it to her and then turning it on. He placed it in the center of his desk. "I'm taping this conversation. Our lawyers would recommend it."

"Record away," Madeline replied, waving her arm. She pulled out the chair directly across from Jacob's desk and sat stiffly at the edge.

"What is it you want?"

"To know what you relayed to the entire hospital staff about me. Because whatever that was, it's succeeded in alienating me to the point where no one will even look at me except with resentment. Did you tell them I'm the entire reason that Nancy Lexington initiated a lawsuit?"

"I told them the truth."

"And what truth is that? That you offered to unload Conrad and me as a settlement prize?"

He started. "Who told you that?"

"Does it matter? I know. Or are you denying it?"

"I'm denying nothing. I did what I had to do to save this hospital."

"You mean to preserve your future." Madeline's eyes blazed. "Why didn't the offer to kick Conrad and me out work, Jacob? Wasn't it enough? Did Nancy Lexington want more—like a larger fortune and the total ruin of the hospital—on top of having Conrad's and my heads?"

Jacob was clearly thrown by how much Madeline knew. He swiveled around to his computer and punched some buttons. A few seconds later, his printer fired up and printed a two-page memo.

"This is the entirety of what's been shared with the

staff." He handed the memo to Madeline. "You can call it up on your own computer, but here it is in black-and-white. Now you'll be fully informed and you can leave my office."

Madeline glanced down and scanned the memo.

It began by informing the staff that Manhattan Memorial was the target of a medical malpractice wrongful death lawsuit, initiated by Nancy Lexington. No details were disclosed, except the names of the accused. That list was several lines long, including the whole cardiac unit as well as the whole surgical team.

But Conrad's and Madeline's names stood out, like blazing neon signs. The description of their involvement was so heavily weighted that it stopped just short of accusing them of negligence and sloppy surgical work and naming them the root cause of Ronald Lexington's death.

The memo closed by assuring the entire staff that everything was being handled professionally and ethically to make the lawsuit go away as soon as possible, and that Manhattan Memorial should continue to operate business as usual.

Madeline looked up, her eyes narrow and her lips tight with anger. "You bastard," she said, shredding the memo and tossing the pieces on the floor. "You're saving face by throwing Conrad and me under the bus. If that's the way you and your attorneys want to play it, I'll be contacting ours. I'm sure we'll be filing defamation of character lawsuits. You know damned well that neither Conrad nor I was responsible for Ronald's death. I never laid a finger on him, and Conrad sweated bullets to save his life."

Madeline rose. "And here's more news for you and your recorder. If you think I'm going away, I'm not. This is where I work. I plan to come in for every one of my shifts—regardless of how few you give me—and do the best job I can, even if my coworkers refuse to speak to me. What you've done is despicable. And I'm not going down quietly."

Gesturing at the small box on Jacob's desk, Madeline informed him, "You can turn that thing off now. I've said everything I plan to say."

She stalked to the door and called out, "Back off, Janet. Eavesdropping time is over. I'm about to fling open this door so hard it will knock you on your ass."

A brief flurry of activity from the other side of the door preceded Madeline's exit by a split second.

She strode past Janet and the receptionist and headed back to the emergency room.

Madeline called their attorney, Edward Markham, the moment her shift was over, explaining exactly what was taking place. "I printed another copy of the memo I tore up as soon as I left Jacob's office," she told him, "so we have that damning email in our possession."

"I'll contact the hospital lawyers and get copies of everything, including the summons and complaint," Markham said. "It's interesting that Conrad was served and you weren't. That means they have no basis for their accusations against you and can only subpoena you as a material witness. I'll begin drafting a summons and complaint. Leave this to me."

The next call Madeline made was to Marc.

"I'm not surprised," Marc responded. "This is why I suggested you stay home a little longer."

"I'm not backing down," Madeline informed him. "If anything, I'm more determined than ever to show up at that hospital and act like everything is normal. And maybe, just maybe, I'll find out I still have a few friends there."

Marc chuckled. "Are you planning on softening a few hearts?"

"No. Just finding out who has one."

Roger was utterly exhausted.

He turned the key to the front door of his Brooklyn apartment, kicked the door shut behind him and pulled off his wrinkled clothes as he walked toward the bathroom.

A minute later, he was standing under a steaming shower.

He hadn't been home in three days.

All he'd done was stare at the computer screen for hours at a time, running one query after another on several hospital databases and providing a bunch of pompous, pain-in-the-ass lawyers with the information they wanted.

Frankly he was losing patience. He didn't care about the lawsuit. He didn't even care if the hospital went down and he wound up losing his job. Talent like his would be appreciated elsewhere.

The only reason he was working so hard to stick around Manhattan Memorial was Emma.

Roger's heart beat faster just thinking about her. She was funny and beautiful, and she listened to him like he was important. He'd never known a girl like her.

Hunger started to swell up inside him, and his hand slid down his body to relieve the painful longing.

Soon he wouldn't have to do this.

Soon he'd have the real thing.

* * *

Sleep wasn't coming to him that night, regardless of his exhaustion. His body was tense from stress and from sexual need. They'd be going out on their first date soon. He'd get up the guts to do something then. He had to believe she'd be receptive. Maybe she even wanted him as much as he wanted her. If not, he'd convince her.

He couldn't take lying there anymore. He turned on the lamp next to his bed and squinted at the clock— 2:00 a.m.

He wondered what she was doing now. Probably sleeping, that luscious blond hair spread out across her pillow. And then she'd wake up, open those gorgeous eyes, flash that beautiful smile and brush that incredible hair.

It was unearthly, fit for a princess.

But like any true hero, Roger knew he had to earn his princess.

Groping on his nightstand, he found and put on his glasses and grabbed his favorite toy: a Nintendo 3DS. It was a portable three-dimensional gaming system capable of transporting him to many different worlds, whenever he wanted.

And right now all Roger wanted was to save his magnificent blonde princess.

Popping in the cartridge, Roger entered the world of Zelda. In that moment, Roger became Link, the brave warrior fighting to save his Princess Zelda. The game started from his last save, where he was ready to enter Hyrule Castle.

Once inside, Link had to defeat the dozens of guards blocking his path. Cycling between weapons, Link destroyed every guard, statue and enemy in his quest to save the princess. Weaving his way up staircases and down long hallways and killing guards along the way, Link finally made it to the top level of the castle. There she was! The beautiful Princess Zelda was once again being held captive by the evil Yuga. To Link's horror, Yuga used his black magic to transform her into a stunning portrait. She was trapped. Link knew he had to defeat Yuga. He chased the evil sorcerer through the castle—and the Boss Battle began.

Dozens of sword-slashes later, Link won the battle. But Yuga escaped again with the princess trapped in the portrait. Link followed, and suddenly found himself sucked into another world: Lorule. Dark and scary though it was, Link didn't care. He would follow Princess Zelda to the end of time and earn her love by becoming the hero she needed.

Sighing, Roger saved his game and powered off the 3DS. If only he had Link's courage and confidence. Then he would win Emma for sure.

It was now 4:00 a.m. He had to be back at work in two hours. Time to try sleeping again.

He turned the lamp off and started to doze. Images of blonde princesses flashed through his head, and he finally fell asleep with a smile on his face.

27

If Madeline thought things were going to get better, she was wrong.

The more days that passed, and the more visible the attorneys and accountants were within the hospital walls, the more hostile her work environment became. Even the people she'd counted on to reach out to her were too angry or too afraid of the ramifications to do so. Once in a while, she'd see one of her colleague friends gazing in her direction, as if they wanted to say something reassuring, but then thought better of it and hurried on their way.

Madeline was totally shocked and devastated.

The only two people at Manhattan Memorial with whom she ever really spoke were Emma, who didn't give a damn what anyone thought of her, and Doug Wilton, who, fortunately, hadn't been Ronald's cardiologist and was therefore unnamed in the lawsuit.

Doug was a true friend, and not just to Conrad, but to her. Because of his loyalty to them both, he cared more about preserving the friendships than he did about whatever revenge Jacob Casper would take if he knew that Doug had "broken the rules." The injustice of the lawsuit pissed him off. He was a top cardiologist with credentials to match. He could get a job anywhere.

Still, Madeline didn't want to jeopardize Doug's career. So the two of them talked only in private—in Doug's office with the door shut. He kept her apprised of any memos he received or gossip he overheard, and he listened when she needed to vent.

Because Madeline and Conrad had been advised by their attorney to make no contact with each other, Doug filled Madeline in on Conrad's end of things. As Madeline already knew from Casey, Conrad had released himself from Crest Haven several days ago and was back in his own apartment under a psychiatrist's care. He and his lawyer would be meeting with Manhattan Memorial and their counsel to answer whatever questions Ed agreed to let Conrad address. If no meeting of the minds took place, Ed would be preparing papers to serve the hospital on behalf of both Conrad and Madeline, and yet more lawsuits would commence.

The whole situation was spinning out of control.

Sometimes, when Madeline finished up a particularly painful shift, she'd leave the hospital—always with her head held high—go straight home and weep. She was a strong woman, but even she had her limits. She felt like Hester Prynne straight out of *The Scarlet Letter.*

With one wonderful difference—she had Marc.

Marc always seemed to know when she needed him because he'd show up at her door with sandwiches or Chinese food or her favorite cinnamon buns from the bakery around the corner. They'd eat and talk and inevitably wind up in bed, which was the only time Madeline's mind was truly free, filled only with Marc and her love for him.

"We're going to get through this," he told her repeatedly. "This bullshit lawsuit is going to be a thing of the past. More important, you're going to be safe. Whoever's trying to kill you will be thrown in jail to rot. And you and I can start to build the life together that we should have started ten years ago."

Those words got Madeline through the worst of the days.

But the stress of it all was wearing her down more and more each day.

Emma marched into the FI conference room, tossed down her tote bag and threw herself into a chair.

"This sucks," she said.

Casey put down the attachment Patrick had emailed her, outlining the security detail now firmly posted inside Conrad's apartment. The agreement they had with Conrad was that thcy supplied the security and he supplied updates on what was happening at his end. It was a win-win arrangement for all of them—although Conrad insisted on paying them a substantial fee, as well.

Now Casey shot an impatient look at Emma.

"Are we talking about your candy striping again?"

"No." Emma straightened up in her chair. "I can handle that. I'm even having a drink with Roger the loser later this week. What sucks is the way everyone is treating Madeline. She's such a good person, she hasn't done anything wrong and they're treating her like crap."

"I agree." Casey was surprised and touched by Emma's concern. The cocky little girl who'd walked in here a month and a half ago, thinking only of herself, had matured into a young woman who was showing compassion—and grit for sticking out her responsibility to Forensic Instincts.

One step closer to being an FI team member.

"I just don't understand it," Emma continued. "Madeline was barely in the O.R. when Ronald Lexington died. Why is she being named in this lawsuit? And why is the hospital dumping on her?"

Ryan walked in in time to hear Emma's last comment and to respond to it. "Because Nancy Lexington is a vindictive bitch and because Jacob Casper is throwing everyone he can under the bus to save his ambitious ass."

"Well, his ambitious ass is screwing Sharon Gilding," Emma informed him. "She's now the temporary chief of surgery. You should hear what the staff thinks about that."

"I can imagine." Casey was unsurprised by Emma's announcement. Based on what Claire had sensed, she'd long suspected that the man having sex with Sharon Gilding was Jacob Casper. And Madeline had already told her about Bitch Doctor's "temporary" promotion. It wasn't hard to figure out what had precipitated that.

"She's got him by the balls. No surprise there." Ryan plopped a pile of printouts in front of Casey and Emma, all articles from the current online editions of tristate area newspapers.

"The media must have missed that hookup. But they didn't miss much. Take a look at these," he said.

Both women leaned over and read Patients Spooked by Rumors of Malpractice at Manhattan Memorial, Hospital Kills One of Its Own and Surgical Sloppiness at Manhattan Memorial.

"None of this is exactly a shock," Casey said, frowning. "The media got wind of what's going on and they're running with it. They're probably interviewing every staff member who'll talk and every patient going in and out of the hospital."

She turned to Emma. "What's the inside scoop?"

"Nothing good," Emma stated flatly. "I listen and I ask questions. The bottom line is that patients are canceling elective surgeries. The surgical suites, which are normally SRO, are half-empty. Surgeons who have multiple hospital affiliations are opting to do their surgeries at other facilities—at the request of their patients."

Ryan nodded. "From what I'm seeing from the internal emails shooting back and forth is that the hospital board has told inside and outside counsel to work faster. More lawyers. More paralegals. Everyone's hours are being cut back to save money, which is scaring the shit out of staff members already afraid of losing their jobs. The surgical nurses are especially hard hit because that department is limping due to the effects of the lawsuit and the ensuing media feeding frenzy."

"Yeah, and candy stripers are being asked to do more and more work," Emma added, rolling her eyes. "There's nothing like using slave labor to save money."

"And Madeline is right in the middle of this." Casey ran a frustrated hand through her hair. "Not only is she being treated like a pariah, she's less safe than she was at home. No matter how thorough Patrick's security is, Madeline is a sitting duck throughout her entire shift. I don't like it any more than Marc does."

"Would it help if I knew exactly what information the hospital was trying to dig up?" Ryan asked.

"Absolutely. What did you have in mind?"

"I can deploy keystroke logging software on all the major players' computers. They won't have any idea what's going on, and by knowing every key that they press, we'll be able to see what information they're compiling against Madeline and Conrad."

Casey gave an emphatic nod. "Do it."

"Done. When is Conrad being questioned?" Ryan asked.

"Yeah," Emma echoed. "Isn't it time he gets his share of the heat?"

"It'll be soon. But his lawyer is delaying that as long as possible," Casey replied. "The Westfields' attorney is still gathering ammo to initiate defamation of character lawsuits. He needs to find a way to subpoena that audio file Jacob Casper made when Madeline took him on. There's verbal confirmation on that recorder. And there's verbal confirmation Ryan has on the audio recording of Nancy's voice, but she's hardly a reliable source."

"Why don't you let Marc loose to get a copy of what's on that digital recorder?" Ryan asked.

"If it comes down to it, I will. I'm just buying time."

"Yeah, well, time is one thing we're running out of."

Trix was thinking much the same thing.

The walls were starting to close in. Once the next steps were taken, it was only a matter of days, maybe hours.

If only there was a strategy guide to life. The anticipation was lethal, knowing that it could be Game Over any second. The odds were stacked in this Boss Battle—and not in Trix's favor. Which meant that the likelihood of victory was slim, and there were no extra lives, no second chances. Trix needed some Jack, hold the Coke.

Time to abort mission.

Time for a Hail Mary.

Trix fired up the Tor Browser. No cookies. No browsing history on the computer. Trix was too smart and too careful to leave electronic footprints.

Anonymity was now ensured. No one could know about this. No one would be able to trace this. Not ever.

The worst was about to become reality. An emergency exit was needed.

Six words were typed into the start page search bar: *Criminal Defense Attorney, New York City.*

28

Days had passed. Janet was worn out and disgusted.

This damned lawsuit was dominating every minute of her time. And it had yet to go to court. By the time this bloodbath was over, Nancy Lexington would be dead of old age and unable to reap the joys of her revenge.

And Madeline was a new thorn in Janet's side, insisting on reporting for all her shifts and intensifying the tension throughout the hospital—especially with Jacob. Couldn't she have just stayed home and out of the way?

Then Janet had her daughter to worry about. Because of the escalating tension, Diana was a nervous wreck. Worse than that, Diana felt compassion for Madeline, who'd been such a mentor to her, so kind and helpful— those were feelings that Janet had to nip in the bud. Diana was young, vulnerable and compassionate. But now was not the time to align herself with a liability. Janet explained that to Diana over and over again. So far, Diana had listened, quite simply out of fear of the ramifications of standing up for Madeline.

Things had to be brought under control. And Janet had no clue of how to do that. All she knew was that she was about to explode.

So when Casey Woods called and asked her to dinner, Janet was thrilled for the chance to get away from the hospital, the lawsuit and the weight of the burden on her shoulders. She was flattered that Casey had sought her out, rather than the other way around. And she was more than eager to talk about the adventures and procedures of Forensic Instincts rather than the lawsuit threatening Manhattan Memorial's very existence.

Casey had another agenda in mind.

The two women met at Lusardi's, a lovely, gracious Italian restaurant on Second Avenue.

"I've never been here before," Janet said after they'd both checked their coats and been escorted to their seats at a small square table near the back.

"It's one of my favorite restaurants in this part of Manhattan," Casey said. "I don't get here often, but I'm never disappointed when I do."

Janet nodded, smoothing her hair and looking around. "A combination of elegant and rustic. I really like it."

"Wait till you taste the food," Casey replied with a smile. "You'll be back again before you know it."

"I hope that's true." The upbeat tone of Janet's voice took a distinctively downward turn. "Right now, I seem to be trapped in the hospital 24/7."

"Really?" Casey gestured for the waiter. "You'll have to tell me about it."

That took a while. Their appetizers came and went. Their main courses arrived and were delicious. All the while, Janet was asking questions about Forensic Instincts—from the cases they'd worked on to the techniques they used to solve their cases. It was almost as if she were going to start her own investigation company.

Casey's antennae went up. This was no longer the interest of a fan. This was someone probing for information. Had Jacob Casper sent Janet to figure out if FI's acquaintanceship with Madeline went deeper than that?

If so, he was about to get his answer.

"I've done enough talking," she said. "Tell me more about the lawsuit going on at Manhattan Memorial. Is there any chance of settling, or is Nancy Lexington going for blood?"

As Casey had expected, Janet became immediately guarded, slowly sipping her glass of merlot and watching every word that came out of her mouth.

"I'm not sure how this is going to play out," she said. "All I'm sure of is that preparations for the legal battle ahead are dominating all the hospital resources, creating a media frenzy and making it increasingly difficult for the staff to do the exemplary jobs they've always done."

"Does that include Madeline Westfield?"

"Pardon me?" Clearly that question caught Janet off guard.

"From what I understand, Madeline is being ostracized to the point where doing her job is a virtual impossibility."

Janet's eyes narrowed. "I assume you heard that from Madeline's friend Marc?"

"Actually, I heard it from Madeline herself." Casey didn't even pretend to lie. The only thing she kept carefully hidden was the fact that she knew about the animosity that had developed between Janet and Madeline. That was imperative to what Casey intended to accomplish here.

"We've all become very fond of Madeline, and we're all concerned," Casey continued. "She's told us that Conrad is specifically named in the medical malpractice wrongful death suit and that she's been linked with it, as well. That means, at the very least, that she'll be deposed. She's frightened, so she came to us for help. I know how friendly you and Madeline are, so I'm hoping you can assist us with some information we're trying to get at."

Janet's expression was carefully blank. She'd taken Casey's bait—hook, line and sinker.

"What kind of information?" Janet asked. "I hope you're not asking me to spy on the hospital, because—"

"No, of course not," Casey interrupted. "Nothing illegal. Just data that might ring a bell for you, given your long-term affiliation with Ronald Lexington and your steel-trap mind."

"Ronald? What does he have to do with this?"

"He *is* the object of the lawsuit. And Madeline and Conrad have to protect themselves in whatever way possible."

"All right." Janet sounded as if she were balancing on a tightrope.

Casey pulled the folded list of numbers out of her purse. She unfolded the page, smoothed it out and handed it to Janet.

"What is this?" Janet asked, scanning the page.

"Numerical data from one of Ronald's files, given to us by a source I'm not at liberty to name. Unfortunately, it seems to be encrypted. We're trying to figure out why Ronald would encrypt it and what the contents are."

"All I see are random numbers."

"That's just it. We don't think they're random. We were able to decipher number 266, which is the sixth number down." Casey leaned forward and pointed. "It's a complete file on Valerie Pintar."

"Valerie Pintar?" Janet looked shocked. "Why?"

"We're not sure. But we're wondering if each of these numbers corresponds to a woman Ronald was sexually involved with over the years. You worked with him for a long time and knew him better than anyone—maybe even his own wife."

"Why do you need this information? How will it help Madeline?"

"We want to interview all these women. Maybe one of them knows something about Ronald's health—his irresponsible use of medication, his overactive physical activity—anything that might have contributed to his death. That would help cast reasonable doubt, should things progress that far."

Janet looked back down at the list. "So Ronald encrypted the entire file?"

"Yes."

Biting her lip, Janet continued to stare at the numbers. "Do you know the encryption key? Maybe if I think about it, I could see a relationship between Valerie, the number 266 and the encryption key that could help you crack the other files much faster. Would that help?"

"More than you know." Casey had already whipped out her iPhone and was busily texting Aidan. "I'll get you the encryption key now."

She pressed Send, and waited.

A minute later, Aidan's reply arrived: veaLmarsalA$ 187.56penneputtanescacannoli.

"Here you go." Casey texted the information on to Janet, carefully leaving Aidan's name and information out of the text.

Janet's phone went *bing,* and she looked down at it. Her eyes were huge. "I feel as if I'm being disloyal to Ronald."

"How?" Casey asked. "It's not as if it isn't common knowledge that Ronald's charisma resulted in a lot of sexual affairs. But if anything, or anyone, other than fate was responsible for his death, doesn't that deserve to be known? Shouldn't the right person be punished?"

Nodding slowly, Janet replied, "Yes."

"So then you'll help us?"

"I'll do everything I can."

Emma was in the largest of the FI bathrooms with her makeup case spread out across the countertop.

She brushed on two coats of mascara, smoothed on her glossy lip stain and then stood back to check out the total effect.

Nice job, she congratulated herself. Too bad she was wasting it on Roger.

She'd made sure to pick out a party dress. After all, she wasn't going to some sleazy bar. Thanks to Ryan's influence, she was meeting Roger at a hopping Tribeca club—one she'd actually been dying to try. So her outfit had to be up to the decor.

And it was.

Her sapphire-blue minidress was formfitting with a keyhole cutout in the sheer illusion neckline that showed off the top of her cleavage. The back was also sheer, plunging down to the small of her back. Sexy but not slutty. Her legs were bare, showing a good amount of thigh. Completing her look were four-inch stiletto, open-toe strappy silver sandals and a blinged-out statement necklace with matching drop earrings. Her hair was down, arranged around her shoulders in loose curls.

The total package would turn the loser on like a light-bulb.

And hey, you never knew. Maybe some hunk would sidle over and ask for her phone number, which she could give him on the sly. That way the evening wouldn't be a total bust.

Emma packed up her makeup case, stacked everything neatly next to her folded sweater and jeans, picked up her purse and headed out of the bathroom.

She walked past Ryan and Claire, who were chatting in the hallway.

Ryan did a double take. "Wow. You clean up nice. No more little brat girl."

Emma made a face at him.

"Ah, I stand corrected," he said. "Still little brat girl, only in supermodel disguise."

Claire poked him in the ribs. "What Ryan is trying to say is that you look beautiful. Roger won't know what hit him."

"Speaking of hitting him, you're wearing the long-range transmitter I gave you, right?" Ryan asked. "Just in case Roger gets too friendly?"

"Yes, Dad, I'm wearing it." Emma patted the upper edge of her dress. "And if you think it was easy to clip that thing on this skimpy little backless bra I bought, think again. I practically had to tape it to my boobs."

"TMI," Ryan replied, shaking his head. "As long as you're wearing it, that's all I need to know."

Emma rolled her eyes. "Remember my juvie roots. I've dealt with a whole lot worse than Mr. Virgin. Believe me, I can handle him." She grimaced. "But after this, I'm done. If Casey wants me to go on a second date, one of you is going."

She shot Ryan a mischievous look. "I'll loan you my dress. You'd look so hot in it—almost as hot as you looked in a custodian's uniform."

Claire's laughter drowned out whatever nasty retort Ryan muttered under his breath.

29

Emma walked the three blocks to the club. She stopped when she reached the line outside the door. She could hear the pounding music and see the flashing lights even from here.

It was showtime.

She scanned the crowd of people, searching for Roger.

She spotted him without any trouble. Talk about finding your mark. He stuck out like a box of prunes in the candy aisle.

His pants were about two inches too short, his sweater was from the dark ages and his sports jacket had more wrinkles in it than the prunes themselves. But he broke into a broad smile when he saw her, waving frantically as if she might miss him.

No chance of that.

She walked over, relishing the admiring stares of the other guys in line. Hey, she could still get lucky for another night.

"Y-you look incredible," Roger stammered, shoving his glasses back on his nose. Doubtful they would stay put, given the fine sheen of nervous perspiration on his nose and forehead.

Emma gave him a charming smile. "Thank you."

"I guess you hear that all the time."

"Not nearly enough. You'd be surprised." Emma glanced around. She was already impatient. She couldn't deal with the throngs of vapid girls, fixing one another's hair and makeup and chattering nonstop about meaningless gossip.

Grabbing Roger's hand, she pushed her way to the front of the line. Roger looked positively green with anxiety. Emma ignored the nasty comments and slurs being thrown her way. Too bad. Those slutty bitches could suck it. She was on a mission.

When they reached the bouncer at the door, Emma gave him their names. Never changing his expression, the bouncer robotically asked for their IDs. Emma whipped hers out while Roger fumbled with his wallet. The bouncer glanced down at their licenses. No problem, thanks to Ryan—he'd hacked into the club's server and gotten their names added to the guest list.

Awesome—now they wouldn't even have to pay the cover charge.

Still running the show, Emma didn't wait for Roger to get the door. Flinging it open, she absorbed everything: the pumping music, flashing lights, dancing crowds. This was amazing. Except for one thing: someone was wearing way too much cheap perfume. It mingled with the smell of sweat and alcohol. Emma felt nauseous.

Snatching Roger's clammy hand again, she practically dragged him to the enormous bar set up in the back of the club. It was time to catch up—time to drink. While Roger looked around with huge owlish eyes, Emma scanned for a bartender, preferably young, male and straight so she could get her drinks ASAP. Her eyes narrowed as she honed in on a bartender who met her specifications. Putting on her most seductive smile, she headed in his direction.

"Are we getting drinks now?" Roger asked.

Shit. Emma had forgotten about the little worm.

"Yes. What would you like to drink, Roger?" Emma's voice was pure honey.

Roger began stammering so hard at this point, she almost felt bad. Almost.

"Um, whatever y-you're h-having?" It was a question, not a statement.

Emma grinned and turned back toward the bar. She reached her bartender of choice and waved her arm to get his attention. It must have been her natural blond hair coupled with the amazing dress. The bartender came over right away.

"How can I help *you?*" The guy was practically oozing testosterone through his fake tan and tattoos.

Choking back vomit, Emma ordered two Long Island iced teas, then winked at the bartender. Hopefully that would motivate him to move faster. Less than a minute later, the two beverages were waiting for her. The bartender seemed quite pleased with himself.

Emma handed him two twenties. "Keep the change," she cooed. The bartender flashed a grin, even more excited by the generous tip than by Emma's flirting.

Drinks in hand, Emma walked back to where Roger was awkwardly standing. She handed him a glass. He eyed it nervously, like a parakeet inspecting a pretty new toy.

Amateur. Emma almost said the word out loud. Catching herself in time, she instead explained, "Long Island iced teas. They guarantee us a good time!" She flashed a persuasive grin.

Not wanting to displease her, Roger grabbed one of the drinks and pretended to be enthused.

Emma almost started to laugh. Not only did Roger have no idea what an LIT was, he'd probably never had a drink in his life that didn't come with a little umbrella in it.

The two of them searched around for a bit, finally finding a table in a quieter section of the club. Emma plopped down on one of the cushy couches, putting her drink on the low table just in front of it. She patted the seat right next to her, indicating that Roger should sit. He eased down onto the couch.

"You know they have speakers in the walls?" Roger was vibrating with excitement. "They conduct the vibrations so that the thumping bass you feel resonates through the whole club."

Frankly, Emma couldn't care less, but nodded appreciatively as she downed her drink. Even with the multiple types of liquor in it, the LIT still didn't have enough alcohol to make this pasty loser seem tolerable.

As if he sensed her boredom, Roger sheepishly admitted, "I'm sorry for going on about the speakers. It's just that anything technological like video games and sound systems gets me excited."

Figures he would be a gamer, Emma thought in disgust.

"Drink up," she encouraged him.

They sat for a good thirty minutes, drinking their beverages, while Roger droned on endlessly about technology, superheroes and video games. He kept mumbling about some blonde princess named Zelda. Whoever she was, Emma felt sorry for her.

Time to regroup. She was about ten seconds away from punching Roger in the face, glasses and all.

"Let's dance." Emma snatched both of Roger's hands and pulled him to the dance floor, which had now taken over the entire club. Moving with the massive crowd, she let the beat guide her. Roger was not that coordinated. He stumbled around the dance floor, waving his arms like a deflated puppet.

Roger didn't even notice. Clearly the alcohol had kicked in. As the bass thumped louder, Roger waved his arms more violently and started shrieking something about techno music and how much he loved it. Emma couldn't wait for the night to end. Talk about a terrible waste of an awesome club. Maybe Ryan could get her back in some other time so she could actually enjoy herself.

Roger was completely oblivious to Emma's inner monologue. Still stumbling around like a seasick sailor, he stopped right in front of her.

Uh-oh, Emma thought. *Liquid courage. This was going to be bad.*

"You're so unbelievably beautiful," Roger slurred. "My princess…" And in one quick motion, he wrapped his arms around her and rested his wormy hands on her ass. Before Emma could register this invasion, he squeezed her—hard—and lowered his head, attempting to stick his tongue down her throat.

"Let go of me." Emma struggled to get free.

When he showed no signs of doing so, she yanked out of his grasp and slapped him across the face with all her strength. The force of this motion, coupled with the alcohol and his lack of coordination, sent Roger reeling back a few steps.

Angry red fingerprints marred his face. He looked stunned.

That's it. Emma was done. Bad enough that she'd wasted her entire night out with this sketchy loser, but she didn't need him groping her ass, looking for a hookup, too.

Furious, she stalked out of the club, slamming down those four-inch stilettos with every step. She pushed past the sweaty, drunk people congregating around the door and made her way outside.

Instead of taking the hint, Roger weaved his way out of the club, as well, grabbing Emma's arm just as she was taking off.

"What the hell?" he slurred. "Where are you going?"

"Far away from you." She tried to shake off his iron grip. "We came here to get to know each other, not to screw on the dance floor. Get your fucking hands off me." She pushed him away with her other hand.

"You bitch." His grip didn't loosen. "You've been coming on to me for weeks. Now you take me to this sexy club and wear a dress that makes every guy in the place get hard. But you wore it for me. I'm just taking what you offered."

He pulled her against him, kissing her with wet, drunken lips and groping at her breast with his free hand.

Fortunately, he missed her transmitter by about two inches.

Emma was about to slam her knee into his groin when a familiar voice interrupted her.

"Emma? Hey." Ryan stopped beside them, a leashed

Hero sitting obediently beside him. "Sorry to break this up, but I've been calling you for weeks. Too busy to meet with an old friend?" He winked at her.

"Ryan." Emma moved away from Roger—whose hand had dropped and who looked totally stupefied—and stepped closer to Ryan. "You know I'm never too busy for you." She gave him a suggestive, intimate smile. "Work and school have just been crazy. This is my first night out in ages."

She squatted down and stroked Hero's head. "How are you, boy?" she murmured. "Have you and your daddy been playing tug-of-war with that stuffed snake I got you?"

"Nonstop," Ryan assured her. "He won't put it down." Another wink. "I know the feeling."

Emma turned to Roger, whose face was bright red now—either with embarrassment or anger, Emma wasn't sure. Nor did she care.

"Roger, you and I are finished here, anyway," she informed him in an icy voice. "I'm going to take off with my friend. See you at work."

She linked her arm through Ryan's and, without a backward glance, walked away with him and Hero.

"Thanks," she muttered. "I appreciate the reinforcements. Although I was kind of looking forward to kneeing his balls through his nose."

Ryan grinned. "An interesting image. Think I'll erase it." He gave her that big-brotherly glance. "You okay?"

"Other than the fact that I can't wait to take a shower and wash his slimy hands and mouth off me, yes." She leaned over to pat Hero again. "You did a great job, Hero. You and Ryan probably kept me out of jail for assault charges."

"That's a plus. By the way, I'd suggest you come back to the office with me and change your clothes," Ryan said. "Riding the subway in that outfit? Not a good idea."

"Agreed." Emma sighed. "I hope Casey's not pissed, but my romance with Loser is over."

"She won't be pissed. You strung Roger along for more than enough time. We're now into diminishing marginal returns. It's not worth putting you through this charade any longer. Now he can go home and puke up his LIT."

30

It was the middle of the night.

Janet was standing like a sentry at her window, watching the traffic thin down to near-nothing and the sidewalks become empty of pedestrians.

She checked her watch—again: 2:05 a.m.

It was time.

She turned away from the window and went to gather her things. She'd prepped in every way she could. She'd stopped at Nuthouse Hardware on her way home from Lusardi's to pick up what she needed. Fortunately, she'd driven her car to the restaurant. She didn't like riding subways at night. She'd rather deal with traffic and pay for parking. Besides, she was already on the East Side, so it wasn't a major hassle.

As luck would have it, she didn't have to pay a dime or go to a parking garage when she reached home. There was an unoccupied parking space on the street diagonally across from her apartment.

Janet had parked her sedan and carried everything up to her apartment. There'd be no leaving her purchases in the car. It was way too risky. Plus, everything needed repacking—in the unlikely event that someone saw her in her travels.

Upstairs in her apartment, she'd placed all her purchases in a proper tote bag that she'd sling over her arm.

And then, she'd begun waiting.

Twice, she'd unfolded the sheet of paper Casey had given her and read the encryption key she'd jotted down at the top of the page. A shiver had run up her spine. Oh, she could crack this all right. And she knew what she'd find. But that obstacle would have to wait till later. Tonight a more urgent situation required her attention.

She'd tucked the paper away.

Now she took the essentials out of her purse—her wallet, key ring and cell phone—and slipped them in the front pocket of her tote bag. Then she hooked the bag over her shoulder and hurried out of the apartment, locking the door behind her.

It was a very long drive. She had to be back in time to shower, change and be at her desk at 9:00 a.m. She'd make it. She'd take care of everything.

She always did.

Roger was still shaking as he paced around his apartment. He was totally devastated. How could Emma do this to him? Lead him on, then break his heart? She was just like all the other girls—fake, superficial and shallow.

Why had he fallen for it, thought she was truly interested in him, opened himself up? For what? Rejection as usual. No girls ever wanted him for anything more than fixing their computers. He was just a techie to them, only good for servicing their needs, and then they dismissed him like the loser he was. He was going to die alone, surrounded by the comic books and collectible figurines he found on eBay.

Time passed. Self-deprecation and depression slowly turned to anger. This wasn't his fault. It was Emma's. She was the two-faced bitch who left him the minute a better option came up. What did she see in that arrogant prick—*Ryan*—anyway? He was just a typical juicer, a glorified superhero wannabe. Totally plastic. And clearly not new-in-box, not with that kind of charm. This guy had had more women than Steven Tyler. And Emma had fallen for it like a goddamn brainwashed Barbie doll. More plastic.

What a slut.

As always, when real life let him down—which was often—Roger turned to his virtual world. Powering up his gaming station, he waited for the familiar green Sims logo to appear on his twenty-seven-inch LED HD monitor. Here he could do anything and everything he wanted.

And what he wanted to do now was put that bitch in her place.

Selecting the story of Roger Lewis, created around the avatar in his likeness, he zoomed into his Sims house. Unlike Roger's own shit hole, this house was huge and totally pimped out. He'd spent quite a bit of his paycheck on SimPoints to get the latest and greatest content for his avatar's lifestyle. He might as well be a baller in the Sims world since he'd always be a loser in real life.

Roger's Sim ate a snack, then hit up the cell phone of Emma's Sim. He'd created her the day he met the real Emma. She was totally perfect: blonde and thin with huge boobs, a tight dress and heels—every bit the woman of his dreams.

And *this* Emma always listened to him. Over the past few weeks, he'd been courting her. In the Sims world, they hung out and watched TV at his place, took long walks together and met up for dinner. When they'd finished dinner last night, she'd let him hold her hand. It was the best part of his day. His Sim had gone home totally love struck, with a little heart icon marking his thumbnail on the toolbar.

He was in love.

But now all that was ruined. Roger furiously clicked on his computer mouse. Emma was destroying him and she had to pay. Sim Emma picked up her cell and agreed to come over to his place. Roger waited. His anger was escalating. When Emma's Sim walked through the door, she gave him a big hug.

Liar. Liar. Liar.

The word kept pounding through Roger's head. Time to get forceful.

Roger walked his Sim up to hers and gave her a kiss on the lips. Just like the real Emma, her Sim shook him off, and their Relationship Bar dropped. The whole relationship he'd built was spiraling downward, fast.

In a last-ditch attempt to repair the damage, Roger had his Sim grab Emma's and plant another huge kiss on her lips. This time, she struggled free and slapped him across the face. She was good at that.

Rage exploded through Roger's head, adrenaline kicking in.

How dare she?

After all the courting he'd done, she had the nerve

to reject him—and in the most insulting way possible. Well, now she'd learn some consequences.

With the click of a few mouse buttons, Roger compelled his Sim to angrily poke Emma's Sim in the chest, screaming at her and rocking her back with the violent motion. In return, she started waving her hands in the air and yelling back.

Their Relationship Bar dropped again. It was red now, in the negatives. Roger had nothing to lose. He started shoving her, getting in her face and raging with all the anger he'd been holding inside. She tried to protest, but he was done with her excuses. He started hitting her, over and over. Before she could defend herself, Roger started beating Emma, engaging in a fight.

His superior strength—at least in the Sims world—was no match for hers. He destroyed her.

Slapping Emma one more time, Roger felt some of his anger dissipate. His heart was racing. He'd certainly taught her a lesson. He was *not* someone to be toyed with. Now she knew better.

Emma's Sim called a cab and crawled off in defeat. Good. The bitch had gotten what she deserved. And who knew? Maybe tomorrow night he'd start courting her again, repair their relationship, only to smack her around once more. He'd lead her on, just to crush her... the same way she'd done to him. This could give him hours of entertainment.

That gave Roger an idea. His heart started pumping with more adrenaline, and his mind started racing. It would be a shame if Emma's Sims house burned to the ground. Grease fires were so lethal...an oven could go up in smoke in mere minutes. And if he took away the windows and doors, she would have no escape. She'd be totally helpless, dependent on him to save her very life.

The very princess he'd rescued would meet destruction by his hands. Well, that's what happened to plastic people.

They melted.

Ironically, the Sims world wasn't that different from real life.

Thinking about the task at hand, Janet pressed down on the gas pedal and accelerated a bit. Most New Yorkers hated driving. Not her. Under normal conditions, she actually enjoyed driving her Lincoln Town Car. When Dr. Safron had offered to sell it to her at a bargain price, she'd jumped at the opportunity. It was more luxurious than she could have afforded new, and she loved the way it floated on the highway. She also enjoyed the respect it commanded from onlookers, who assumed she was a person of some means.

If only they knew the truth.

She'd been driving for over an hour and a half when she pulled off the thruway at Exit 19, Kingston. Normally she would have used her E-ZPass, but tonight she pulled a ticket upon entering the thruway and paid cash upon leaving. She headed west on Onteora Trail toward the Ashokan Reservoir and Belleayre Ski Center.

Another twenty minutes and she'd be there.

Janet arrived at the tiny ski lodge cabin at 3:45 a.m.

She turned off her headlights and drove all the way down the gravel driveway until her car was no longer visible from the dirt road. The closest neighbor was twenty acres away, so no one would see her.

She took her tote bag and let herself in through the back door.

The same warm, fuzzy feeling as always greeted Janet as she came in. She loved this place. It might be owned by a corporation, but in all ways that mattered, it was hers.

Given how long it had been since someone had lived here, the place should smell musty. It didn't. Janet prided herself on her biweekly visits, when she scrubbed the cabin from top to bottom, left it smelling fresh as pine trees, after which she spent one nostalgic night in the master bed.

Alone with her memories.

Now she shut the back door behind her, put down her tote and flipped on the low light over the kitchen stove. The cabin went from blackness to twilight. There was something very fitting about the aura it created—a melancholy ache that permeated the few small rooms. A galley kitchen, a cozy den with a fireplace and a bathroom between two bedrooms.

Janet walked around the cabin, looking at each room and remembering. She ran her hand over the rustic wooden furniture in the kitchen and den. She stood in the doorway of the smaller bedroom—taking in all the pinks and whites she remembered so well, with stuffed animals still sitting on the bed.

Then she turned to the master bedroom, hovering in the doorway and gazing at the bed.

Waves of memory flooded her.

Weekends of passionate lovemaking with Ronald. The final months of pregnancy living here all alone. The joy of giving birth to Diana within these very walls, assisted only by a local midwife. The mania of being a new mother. The joy of watching Diana grow from an infant into a little girl. Occasional ski weekends when Diana would sleep over at one of Janet's local friends— just so the ski weekend could be only her and Ronald. Promises that Ronald made and never kept. Janet's loneliness without companionship. Diana's desperate need for a father that she never knew.

It was time to bring this chapter of their lives to a close—before Forensic Instincts closed it for them.

Returning to the kitchen, Janet opened her tote bag and removed the purchases she'd made at Nuthouse Hardware.

First, she placed the large cast-iron skillet on the propane stove and lit the burner. She waited until the pan was blazing hot. Then she removed the bacon from its package and dropped it into the skillet. The meat and fat hissed angrily in the skillet as it started to smoke. She reached up, opened a nearby cabinet and took out the bottle of Jack Daniel's she kept there. Unscrewing the cap, she carelessly spilled the whiskey all over the counter, stove and skillet.

Instantly the amber liquid exploded in flames, quickly engulfing the counter and the nearby oven mitts. The flames traveled up the greasy backsplash and licked at the wooden cabinets. Rapidly the fire spread to adjacent walls, then to the ceiling.

Tears rolled down Janet's cheeks as her eyes were accosted by the smoke. But the sobs escaping her were not caused by the smoke. This was emotional agony in its basest sense.

Squeezing her eyes shut to block out the scene, she turned, walked to the back door and opened it. The rush of fresh air added a burst of energy to the raging inferno behind her. She walked outside numbly, turning only when she reached her car.

Taking one last look, she saw sparks flying everywhere as the roof collapsed into the fiery pile of wood that was once her home.

31

Roger was in a crappy mood when he went to work the next day. Not only had he been humiliated, degraded and dumped, he'd spent half the night puking up those Long Island–whatevers that he'd stupidly drunk. Now he had a massive headache that seemed to engulf his entire brain.

He was back in the real and ugly world. The world where he was a total loser. There was no Sims avatar to pump him up. There was just Emma, somewhere in the hospital laughing at him as she told her coworkers about last night.

Flushed at the thought of his actions being gossiped about throughout the hospital, Roger headed into the IT department and went straight to his desk. Maybe he'd hide there for a week, doing nothing but waiting for his embarrassment to go away.

Well, that was not to be. He looked at today's list from the lawyers and grimaced. This was even more detailed than usual. It would take the entire day—another very *long* day—one he'd wanted to be over quickly and was instead going to drag on forever. He was beginning to feel like the modern-day version of a "gofer"—go fer this, go fer that—only his retrieval tasks were electronic.

Mentally he retreated into his safe zone as he readied himself for the first computer command of the day. In that safe zone, he could convince himself that he was doing something important. That his heroic efforts would save Manhattan Memorial from the clutches of the evil witch Nancy Lexington. That King Jacob would reward his efforts with a worthy prize—running the IT departments of the combined hospitals.

Today's first task, courtesy of Manhattan Memorial's attorneys and the insurance company defending Conrad Westfield, together with Nancy Lexington attorneys, was to dig up any electronic records that Conrad Westfield had kept of Ronald Lexington's surgery.

Fine. Roger would hunt down the files.

Still locked away in his safe zone, he punched the keys skillfully, entering the search using Ronald's patient number, and waited for the systems to respond.

His walk down Fantasy Lane was interrupted by the message on his screen: *File Not Found.*

What? He lurched up in his seat. How could it be not found?

He double-and triple-checked the command he'd entered.

No keystroking errors.

He moved on, trying to search for different files on the same storage array. The list of files quickly populated the screen. How could these files be there but the one he was looking for missing? That answer would have to wait until he had more time. Time to restore the missing file from the off-site electronic backup the hospital maintained.

Roger typed in the URL in his Chrome browser window, entered his login credentials and waited for the authentication process to complete. Next, he went to the matching cloud-based backup drive for the storage array he was interested in, clicked on the directory he was seeking and looked for the date that would cover the operating room video of Ronald's surgery. Many surgeons recorded some of their procedures, either for teaching purposes or for their own edification. Evidently, Conrad recorded all of his surgeries, often critiquing them personally as a way to perfect his craft. Well, good for him, and in this case, good for Manhattan Memorial.

Roger's hands stopped in midair. There was an entire day missing from the sequence. And not just a random day—the day of Ronald Lexington's surgery. Someone had intentionally deleted the video of that surgery, the original and the backup copies, as well.

Quickly Roger picked up the phone and called his contact at the law firm. Before the attorney could answer, Roger quickly hung up, rethinking his first impulse. He needed to discuss this with Jacob—in person. Someone was trying to sabotage the hospital's legal defense. Roger had ways to find out who. He would offer his skills to Jacob, and when he handed him the name of the saboteur, Roger's completion bonus coins would multiply tenfold.

He dialed Janet's extension. She would have to find a way to get him on Jacob's calendar today.

Janet let the phone call go to voice mail.

She was in the middle of something very important—talking to her daughter.

"What do you mean, the cabin burned down?" Diana demanded, sitting across the desk from her mother. "How do you know? How did it happen?"

"You don't need answers to either of those questions," Janet said, not mincing words. "Just know that it's gone. No one else will read about it, except the upstate locals, because there's no link tying us to the cabin."

"Mom." Diana leaned forward, tears glistening on her lashes. "I was born in that cabin. You've told me that story over and over. You raised me there till I was two, and then we went back all the time for weekend trips—just the two of us. I still drive up there sometimes when I need to get away. So do you. You wouldn't be so cavalier about this if it were a surprise or an accident. What's going on?"

Janet pulled out the sheet of paper Casey had given her.

Diana glanced at it, clearly puzzled. "A bunch of computer codes?"

"An encryption key. A page of computer codes. Each one represents one of the women Ronald slept with." She pointed to a code halfway down. "I know that one's mine. Those numbers are the numerical part of the cabin's address."

Diana paled. "Who gave this to you?"

"Forensic Instincts. They're about to figure out the name and detailed background on every one of these women. I'll be exposed—and worse, so will you. There are no options. I *must* find a way to delete my entry from this list. Plus, I have to destroy all my ties to Ronald—even the ones that break my heart." Her expression softened. "All except my most precious one. You're the one blessing he gave me that no one can ever take away."

Diana bowed her head, and her tears came faster. "So you burned down our house."

"I had no choice."

"No, you didn't," Diana admitted softly. "He didn't give you one. He never gave you one." She picked up her head, and there was agony in her eyes. "He hurt you so much. I hate that more than the fact that he never acknowledged my existence. You gave up your whole life for that man. So whatever you did, no one can blame you for—including torching the home he supposedly built for you."

"I'm just doing what I have to do." Janet's jaw set. "The truth about your being Ronald's daughter can never come out. I won't have you in the middle of a scandal."

"The truth about me?" Diana dried her eyes and regained control. "Even I didn't know that truth until six months ago."

"And I never planned on telling you," Janet replied bluntly. "What would have been the point? The truth could only cause you pain—which it has. But when you were up at the cabin, opened that book and the photo of Ronald and me fell out, you asked so many questions. I couldn't lie to you any longer." There was a painful pause. "I still beat myself up wondering which was the worse of the two decisions—keeping you in the dark all those years, or breaking down and telling you the truth."

"It was a lose-lose situation. I always wanted to meet my father, even though you said he was just a brief affair and you broke up before he knew you were pregnant. I guess ignorance is bliss. I missed out on so much from a man who didn't want me, anyway." Diana blinked back tears. "In any case, my emotional baggage is hardly the issue now. We've got to get your name off that list."

Janet's expression was grim. "My copy isn't the problem. The data is stored on the Forensic Instincts' computer server, which makes it impossible to tamper with.

Casey Woods asked me to help her crack this code. I have to pretend I couldn't do it and pray that neither can they—at least long enough for us to hire someone who can hack into and corrupt their system."

"Who do we know who can do that?"

"I'll figure it out. There's got to be a supertechie here who wants a wad of cash. We just have to find him or her."

"What if Forensic Instincts decrypts the file first?"

"Then I'll switch gears and beg for their discretion. Of course I'll become a suspect, but they can't prove anything. And I'm far from alone on their suspect list."

"But will they tell Madeline? Especially if they're working for her now?"

"Not if I do my job right."

Preoccupied and deep in thought, Janet scowled in irritation when her phone started ringing again. It had rung three times during her talk with Diana, and now twice more since Diana had gone back to work. She'd ignored it all five times, since the only emergency call she could be receiving would come from Jacob, who by now would have stormed into her office with whatever was on his mind.

Still, she should have listened to her voice mail. This was a critical and precarious time in her life.

She reached over and picked up the phone. "Janet Moss."

"Where have you been?" a male voice demanded. "I've been trying to get in touch with you all morning."

Janet blinked. "Who is this?"

"Roger Lewis."

Roger Lewis. The IT guy Jacob had appointed to

work with the lawyers. What could he possibly want so urgently from her?

"What can I do for you, Roger?" she asked evenly.

"It's what *I* can do for *you*. I need an immediate appointment with Mr. Casper. Is he there? The receptionist wouldn't let me in to see either one of you."

"You came down here?"

"Well, you weren't answering your phone, so yes. I attempted to knock on either your or Mr. Casper's doors, but I was tossed out. So I'm calling again."

"Mr. Casper is tied up all day today." Janet glanced at Jacob's electronic calendar. "I can try to fit you in tomorrow at about nine-thirty...."

"I said *now!*" Roger almost shouted the last word. "I have crucial information I need to share with him."

"About the lawsuit?" Janet was starting to get a little uneasy.

"Of course about the lawsuit," he snapped. "Is Mr. Casper in his office now?"

"Yes, but he's meeting with our attorney."

"Better still. I'm on my way to his office. Please let me through."

Five minutes later, Janet met Roger in the reception area.

"I've told Mr. Casper you're on your way to see him," she said. "For your sake, I sincerely hope this is a true emergency."

"It is. Now may I go in?"

Janet nodded, preceding Roger to Jacob's door. She knocked, and then poked her head into the office. "Roger Lewis is here to see you."

"Send him in," Jacob called out.

Roger rubbed his sweaty palms on his pants. He was visibly nervous. But he was also a man with a mission.

He walked inside Jacob's office and shut the door in Janet's face.

"Roger." Jacob rose from behind his desk. "You know our attorney, Stephen Diamond."

"Yes, sir, we've met." Roger shook the attorney's hand. "I'm glad you're here. The information I've uncovered is something you both should know about immediately."

"What is it?" Jacob's forehead creased.

"I was doing my first task of the morning, going through the hospital files on Conrad Westfield's surgeries. Evidently he had them all recorded."

"That doesn't shock me," Jacob responded. "Some surgeons prefer to do that, via the cameras in the O.R., so they can review them later or use them in a teaching capacity."

"I didn't know that," Stephen Diamond said. "We should review the video recording of Ronald Lexington's surgery immediately. It might show us something that Conrad was negligent about when he operated."

"That's why I'm here." Roger stood up straighter, still proud of his discovery. "I ran through the entire list of surgical recordings. The file containing Ronald Lexington's surgery has been permanently deleted—not just the original, but the backup copy, as well."

"How do you know that's the surgical recording that was deleted?" Stephen demanded.

"From the date and location. Video recordings of surgeries are all stored on a specific drive, with each date as a separate directory. This was the date of Mr. Lexington's operation, and there's no file with his name on it at all. In fact, that entire day of surgeries was deleted. There's just an empty directory."

"The only reason someone would delete those files is if there was incriminating information on it." Jacob rubbed the back of his neck. "Shit."

"That's not necessarily bad," Stephen said. "Remember that, assuming there was any wrongdoing, we need to shift the blame off the hospital and onto Conrad Westfield. If he committed medical malpractice wrongful death, and the rest of the hospital employees are innocent, then he takes the fall—Manhattan Memorial doesn't."

"But he couldn't have deleted that file," Jacob countered. "He was in a mental health facility."

"He was?" Roger asked in surprise.

"Forget you heard that," Jacob snapped. "It's confidential."

"Anything can be done electronically," Stephen continued. "Conrad had a computer with him, didn't he?"

"I assume so," Jacob replied.

"Then he's not off the hook." Stephen turned to Roger. "Are you sure that there's no way to recover the file or its backup copy?"

"None," Roger replied. "It's completely deleted from our databases."

"Then we have to find a way to get it elsewhere," Stephen said. "Or to prove that Conrad—or an ally of his—deleted it."

Jacob's eyes widened. "You mean Madeline?"

"Anything's possible." The attorney pursed his lips. "But before we start making extra work for ourselves, let's start with the easy route. Conrad wasn't a teaching surgeon, was he?"

Jacob shook his head.

"Then we have to assume he made those recordings for his own purposes."

"I'm sure that's true," Jacob replied. "Conrad was a perfectionist. He must have been reviewing his work and scrutinizing it."

"Then let's see just how obsessive he was." Stephen picked up the phone and dialed. "Edward Markham, please. This is Stephen Diamond."

A moment passed.

"Hello, Mr. Markham. We've come across a situation, and we're hoping we can be on the same side on this one." He went on to explain what Roger had found—or not found—and to stress the significance of this.

"I'm sure your client would want to help us both out if he could, since it could only benefit him." A pause. "Exactly. What I was wondering is if Dr. Westfield happened to keep copies of those videos of his surgeries, since I know how diligent he was about reviewing his work." Another pause. "I appreciate that. Please let me know immediately after you speak with him....Good. I'll look forward to your call."

Outside Jacob's door, Janet backed away, feeling her insides twist. This was the worst-case scenario, the very thing she had feared from the beginning.

Of course Madeline would know where those videos were. She was the most methodical and organized person Janet had ever met. So if Conrad was in the dark, his ex-wife wouldn't be.

Janet had to intercept this problem. She had to get her hands on that video recording before everyone else did.

32

Ryan walked into his lair and sat down at his computer station.

Casey had heard nothing back from Janet Moss, so the woman was obviously not having any luck figuring out Ronald's coding system.

That didn't work for Ryan. Sitting around and waiting made him crazy. Everyone else seemed to be guarding Madeline and Conrad, while he was spinning in neutral. He'd picked up nothing incriminating at the Lexington house—just a lot of ranting and raving from Nancy Lexington that pointed to her being a nut job, but not a murderer.

It was time to check out the current results of his keystroke-logging software. So far there'd been nothing exciting.

Firing up his computer, Ryan called up the keystroke logger management interface.

He scrolled through the log file…nothing major from most of the bigwigs, but Roger Lewis had been a busy boy. Ryan grimaced. He'd probably been sending emails to an online lonely hearts club, weeping about his shattered relationship with Emma.

A minute later, he changed his mind. No whining over Emma. The guy had obviously decided to throw himself into his work. His input was all hospital business.

Brow furrowed in concentration, Ryan reviewed Roger's keystrokes. The guy had been trying to retrieve files. What files in particular? Ryan intended to find out.

He opened up a Telnet session, tunneling right through the hospital's firewall. Using the admin credentials he had forged, he had the same access Roger did. Now to replicate what that shithead had done. It was a long and painstaking process.

Success. Ryan scanned the screen and found the same thing that Roger had—a file was missing and its backup had been deleted.

Checking a little more thoroughly, Ryan put together the pieces and bolted upright in his chair. Based on similar directories and files on the same storage device, the missing file was one of many missing files that had contained video recordings—recordings of surgeries performed the same day as Ronald Lexington's surgery.

Someone had erased the files.

What the hell was on that video recording that someone wanted to make vanish?

Jumping out of his chair, Ryan took the steps two at a time until he reached the conference room.

Casey and Claire were in heated conversation. Marc was pacing the room, and Hero was sitting up straight, visibly tense.

Ryan burst into the room. "I need to talk to you."

"Wait in line," Casey said. "I'm mediating a disagreement. Claire wants to call off Emma ASAP and get her out of the hospital in case Roger tries something even more violent. Marc thinks it would be too obvious if she abruptly vanished, plus it would be one less pair of eyes on Madeline. I'm inclined to agree with Claire. Madeline is well-guarded by professionals—a role that Emma's not equipped to fill. There's nothing more that she can do for us there. And after that ugly experience with Roger, I don't want to put her in harm's way. Who knows if Roger is going to retaliate—"

"Get Emma out of there," Ryan interrupted. "She doesn't need to face that asshole again. And I didn't come in here just to talk to *you*. I need the whole team to hear this."

Abruptly Casey switched gears and focused on Ryan. "You found something. What is it?"

"A pretty explosive something." Ryan explained what he'd discovered when he retraced Roger's keystrokes.

"So the video recording is missing," Casey said. "Is it possible there's another copy?"

"Madeline said that Conrad was obsessive about his work," Claire reminded them. "Could he have made a copy and taken it to Crest Haven with him?"

"There's only one way to find out." Casey reached for the phone and dialed Conrad's number.

Conrad answered on the second ring. "Hello?"

"Conrad? It's Casey Woods. I don't mean to be abrupt, but I need to know if you made a copy of Ronald Lexington's surgery."

"That's odd," he replied. "My attorney called earlier and asked me the same question."

Casey's warning bells went off. "Did he tell you why?"

"Because the hospital's counsel was requesting it. I assume they're looking for something to save the hospital, although I'm not sure what that means for me. I doubt the video is going to help them. I've scrutinized it over and over. Still, I'd welcome a review by my peers. I probably should have asked some of my colleagues for their opinions a long time ago. Perhaps they'll see something I overlooked. Maybe then I can live with myself and go on with my life."

"So you did make a copy," Casey said.

"I made a copy of every one of my surgeries. Watching them gave me a chance to study my technique and see if there was anything I could improve upon." Conrad choked up a bit. "As I said, I watched Ronald's surgery again and again before I was in such a dark place that I admitted myself to Crest Haven."

"Nothing looked out of the ordinary?"

"I couldn't find an error no matter how closely I studied the video. I doubt the hospital's attorney will, either. But for the sake of the attorneys on both sides and the insurance company that's defending me, let them pursue it. I welcome the scrutiny."

"Do you still have a copy of the video recording?"

"I believe so. But truthfully, I'm not sure where. My apartment was trashed. Madeline and I had just divided up our property, and I have no clue where my discs ended up."

"You didn't take them with you to Crest Haven?"

"Definitely not."

"Would Madeline know where to find them?"

"I'm not sure. I left her a voice mail. She must be on shift at the hospital, so her phone is on silent. I can call you as soon as I hear from her."

"Please do," Casey said. "Let us know even before you call your attorney. It's crucial."

Marc had stopped pacing and was staring off, eyes narrowed. "That must be what the killer was looking for when they ransacked Madeline's and Conrad's apartments. In both their places, the DVD collections were totally trashed. The intruder must have assumed that Conrad made a copy of Ronald's surgery. If so, there's something big on that recording—big enough for someone to ransack two apartments and then try to kill Madeline and Conrad."

"Do you think Conrad is lying about having spotted what's on there?" Claire asked.

"No." Casey shook her head. "Conrad is focusing on his part in the surgery. I'm sure he doesn't have a clue if there's a detail he's missing. And Madeline has probably never even watched the video."

"If anyone finds out that the hospital's on to the missing video recording and that Conrad made a copy, then Madeline's danger level just went way up." Marc looked grim.

"Casper would keep it completely quiet," Ryan said. "Trust me, no one's heard a word about this but him, Roger and the hospital's attorney. Plus, nothing's changed. There's *still* no one who knows where the video recording is."

"Except maybe Madeline."

"We'll find that out soon enough," Casey said. "Patrick's stationed outside the hospital. I'll have him hunt Madeline down and ask her." She studied Marc's anxious expression. "Patrick won't let anything happen to her, Marc."

She took out her cell phone to call him.

"Yes, Casey," he answered immediately.

"Is Madeline in the hospital?"

"Yes. She's been on duty for two and a half hours."

"Where is she?"

"Dave checked on her about ten minutes ago. She's in the E.R. patching up a car accident victim. Why?"

"I need you to find the first inconspicuous moment to pull her aside. Don't make a big deal out of it, and make sure no one gives it a second glance. Ask her if she knows where Conrad's videos of his surgeries are. Give me a call with the answer while you're still with her."

"Video recordings. That's what the intruder was looking for when they ransacked her place and Conrad's." Patrick made the connection in a heartbeat. "What's on there that you're looking for?"

"Ronald Lexington's surgery."

"Of course." Patrick's wheels were turning. "That makes total sense. There's something on that video that's going to burn someone's ass, bad enough to kill for it."

"That's where our thoughts were headed, as well," Casey said.

"Conrad doesn't know where they are?"

"Nope. Between the material possessions that were divided during the divorce and the trashing of his apartment, he has no clue of anything other than the fact that the video exists and that he watched it repeatedly before he went to Crest Haven."

"Do the hospital attorneys know about all this?"

"Yes. So I'm sure they'll be checking with Madeline next. And if she should know…"

"Then her safety is even more compromised. Got it. I'll catch her the minute she steps out of the E.R."

* * *

It took a lot longer than Patrick had hoped. But clearly the car accident victim required more than just a patch-up.

Patrick walked down to the closest Au Bon Pain, bought himself a cup of coffee and sat down at a table, waiting.

A steady flow of people moved up and down the corridors, and the E.R. waiting room itself was overflowing. Patrick had to admire Madeline and all the E.R. personnel for their ability to handle pressure and multitask. They'd do well in the FBI.

An attractive middle-aged woman with a large handbag rushed by him, clearly on her way to some vital destination. As she passed, her handbag swung out, knocked over Patrick's cup of coffee and then dropped to the floor.

The coffee and the contents of the handbag spilled out everywhere, brown liquid splashing over leather and all the other items that landed on the floor.

"Oh, I'm so sorry," the woman gasped, nervous and flustered. She squatted down and started to collect her dripping personal items. "Dammit." She sat back on her heels, clearly having changed her mind.

She adjusted her glasses and looked up at Patrick. "I'm going inside to get a bunch of napkins." She rose to her feet. "I'm also buying you another cup of coffee. How do you take it?"

"Please, that's not necessary." Patrick politely declined her offer. "I was just finishing up, anyway."

"Obviously that's not the case. You had three-quarters of a cup of coffee left." She flashed a self-deprecating smile. "I should know. It's all over everything, thanks to me."

"Still…"

"How do you take your coffee?" she repeated. "Otherwise, I'll just have to guess."

Patrick had jerked his chair backward reflexively. Now he picked up the few napkins he'd taken and began wiping the table. "Just black. And I greatly appreciate it."

"Not at all." She walked around the eating area and into Au Bon Pain.

Patrick continued to sop up his coffee, glancing repeatedly over at the E.R.

There was still no sign of Madeline coming out.

Madeline herself was puzzled.

She'd finished taping up the car accident victim about fifteen minutes ago. She'd been about to strip off her gloves and come out when Diana Moss had appeared, slightly bent forward and asking for her help.

"What's the problem?" Madeline had asked in surprise. Diana had smiled shyly at her once or twice since her return, but that's where any sign of reconnecting had stopped.

"I have a bad pain in my lower abdomen. It started a few days ago and has been getting progressively worse. It's unbearable now. I don't want to make a big deal out of it, but could you do a quick check and maybe have an X-ray done?"

"You're thinking appendicitis?" Madeline asked.

Diana nodded.

"That's nothing to fool around with. Come in and I'll have the technician do an X-ray. Then, if it's necessary,

I'll page a doctor." She paused. "Why didn't you ask one of the surgeons to take a look at you?"

"They're very busy right now. Besides, if it turns out to be nothing, I don't want to be sent home to rest and sit around. I need to work."

"Then let's hope it's nothing." Still thinking it was odd that Diana had chosen her, of all people, to approach, Madeline took Diana down to the X-ray room.

Janet bought the cup of coffee at the same time as she saw Diana disappear through the E.R. with Madeline.

She walked over to the island that held the milk, sweeteners and coffee accoutrements. She helped herself to a handful of napkins, and then glanced around. Nobody nearby.

She removed the plastic lid off the coffee cup long enough to drop the sleeping pills in. Quickly, she stirred the beverage, and then snapped the lid back into place.

She headed out of Au Bon Pain and back to Patrick.

33

"Everything looks fine, Diana." Madeline studied the X-ray the technician had taken. "I don't see any glaring problem. But make an appointment with one of our gastroenterologists. You should have a complete rundown and a thorough exam."

"I will." Diana was shrugging into her hospital uniform. "I appreciate you doing this. It was the fastest and most discreet way for me to find out if I was in immediate trouble."

"No problem." Madeline walked with Diana as they headed out of the E.R. "I'm heading for the lounge to get a cup of coffee. Want to join me?"

"There won't be time for that." Janet's voice came from directly behind Madeline. "Diana has to go back to the surgical wing." Janet's open coat brushed against Madeline's arm, and a blunt object jabbed her in the back. "You and I, on the other hand, have to take an urgent drive."

"Mom…" Diana stood there for a moment, looking nervous and unsure. "Maybe there's another way…."

"There isn't." Janet shoved the object firmer into Madeline's back. "Let's go."

That's when Madeline realized that the object in Janet's hand was a gun.

"Janet, what the hell are you doing?" she gasped, watching in shock as Diana turned and walked off.

"Escorting you to your car. Once we're inside, I'll give you instructions. I'll even answer your questions, if you'd like. But right now, we're going to walk to the rear staircase and head down. I've got the gun hidden in the flap of my coat. That doesn't mean I won't use it. So be a good girl, just like you always are, and do as I say."

"My God, it was you?"

"Walk." Janet gave her a little shove with the pistol.

Woodenly, Madeline did as Janet ordered. She headed for the stairwell, located one corridor away. She felt surreal, people passing by, chatting, rushing somewhere, or drinking cups of coffee and waiting for loved ones. The PA system was paging doctors and nurses, punctuated with the squeaks of the orderlies' carts as they pushed them around and the wail of a crying baby.

No one knew what was happening. No one had any idea that she was being held at gunpoint, being kidnapped—or worse.

She felt the jab of Janet's weapon and continued on her way.

Marc glanced at his watch for the fifth time in ten minutes.

"Hasn't it been a long time since you called Patrick?" he asked Casey.

"No, Marc." Casey couldn't help but feel compassion at the anxious expression on his face. "It's been less than an hour. If Madeline is dealing with a serious injury, it could take a lot longer than we'd like. Patrick is within eyesight of the E.R. He'll get to her the instant she walks out. We have to have some patience."

"Patience. Yeah. Right."

"We haven't heard from Conrad, either, Marc," Claire said in that soothing voice of hers. "That means he's waiting, too."

"I know. And you're right." Marc glanced at Casey. "And you were right about my personal feelings getting in the way. I have no objectivity right about now."

"I wouldn't expect you to." Casey was frank. "We're invested in our client, and we're on pins and needles. You're in love with her. If you weren't a wreck, I'd be shocked."

The main telephone line rang.

Casey grabbed it. "Forensic Instincts."

"It's Aidan." He didn't mince words. "I cracked two of the encryption keys."

"And?"

"The first woman's name is Francine Ryder."

The other employee besides Valerie Pintar to lose her job over Ronald.

"No surprise," Casey said. "And the other?"

"Janet Moss."

Casey sucked in her breath.

"I take it that was a lucky break?"

"Yes. I need everything you have on her—now."

"I figured as much. I'll put everything on a USB drive and be there in half an hour."

"Thanks." Casey hung up the phone and looked at the team. "Aidan cracked two of the encryption keys. One is Janet Moss."

"So she *was* sleeping with Ronald," Claire murmured.

An odd expression crossed her face. "Something's not right."

"With Madeline?" Marc demanded.

Claire's eyes narrowed in concentration. "Madeline and Janet. There's dark energy lurking there."

"Shit." Marc took a long stride toward the door.

"Wait, Marc," Casey said. "Madeline's still in the E.R. So she's safe. Aidan is on his way over. Let's get all the information. Then we'll act."

Janet sat in the backseat with the pistol pointed at Madeline's head.

"Drive."

"Where?" Madeline's shock was still so acute, she could barely speak.

"You tell me," Janet said. "Where are the video recordings?"

"The video recordings?" *Focus. Try to make sense of what Janet is asking for.*

But she couldn't.

All she could think about was the gun aimed at her head, and the nightmarish reality that she'd never get out of here alive. *Oh, God. Oh, God.*

Panic replaced shock. Terrified tears slid down her cheeks. How was she going to save herself? She was trapped in her car with a crazy woman holding a gun. No one knew she was missing. No one knew where she'd gone.

She didn't know where she was going or what the hell Janet was babbling about. Video recordings? *What* video recordings?

"Don't play stupid with me." Janet's voice seemed to come from far away and yet way too close. "I know you. You're a perfectionist. You know where everything is—and that includes Conrad's videos. Now turn on the damned car!"

Madeline jumped, and then tried three times to put the key in the ignition.

Finally she succeeded, and the engine roared to life.

She tried to think past the pounding of her heart. "Conrad's...you mean the recordings of his surgeries?"

"Of course that's what I mean," Janet snapped.

"Why..." Madeline wet her lips with the tip of her tongue. "Why do you want those?"

"Not *those*. *It*. One recording."

"The recording of Ronald's surgery." Slowly, what Janet was demanding pushed through Madeline's white panic. "Is there something on it that incriminates you?"

"That's not your problem." Janet was getting impatient. "You know where the recordings are stored."

Madeline wasn't about to play Russian roulette with her life. Maybe, if she gave Janet what she wanted... Who was she kidding? Madeline knew Janet was guilty. Once Janet got what she wanted, there was no way she could let Madeline live.

Still, if she refused, Janet would just shoot her on the spot.

Bile rose up in Madeline's throat. No. She had to fight for time, then maybe she'd find a chance to break away.

"Yes. I know where the recordings are stored," she said.

She could feel Janet's relief fill the car.

"Where are they?"

"In a Manhattan mini-storage on Second Avenue, way downtown."

Janet pressed the gun closer to Madeline's head. "Why so far? You live on the Upper East Side."

"Because the closer one didn't have the size unit we needed."

"Damn," Janet said. "That's going to take us at least a half hour in traffic. They'll be looking for you by then."

"I can't help that," Madeline replied. "But I'm the only one who knows that information. Even Conrad doesn't know where I stored the recordings. He was already on sabbatical when I made the arrangements."

Janet's gaze flickered to Madeline's purse on the passenger seat. "Give me your purse."

The panic resurged, although Madeline complied, placing her purse into Janet's waiting hand. "If you're looking for the key, it won't help you. There's a security check at the mini-storage. The management knows me there. You won't be able to get to the storage unit."

"Point taken. Which means you're still useful." Through the rearview mirror, Madeline could see Janet's eyes narrow as she tossed the purse on the backseat next to her. "Start driving. And I know the city like the back of my hand. So don't do anything stupid."

Marc had already punched in the code on the Hirsch pad and opened the front door when Aidan came striding up to FI at a near-run.

"Upstairs. Conference room," was all Marc said.

The two men took the stairs to the main conference room. The whole team gathered around the table as Aidan sat down at the computer—which was already fired up—and inserted the USB drive.

"Yoda, display the whiteboard," Casey commanded.

"Whiteboard displayed," Yoda replied, just as a virtual white board appeared on the wall.

Aidan called up the files on the keyboard and indicated the two-line list.

"Janet Moss's file is twice the size of the other women's. That clued me in to the fact that she was significant in your investigation." He pressed a button and opened Janet's file. "Here's all the information you need."

Page one appeared on the wall.

"I don't give a shit about the sex poses," Marc said impatiently. "Lexington could have screwed her upside down for all I care."

"Wait," Aidan told him.

He scrolled through the pages, and about five pages in, the pertinent data started showing up.

First came the fact that Ronald had met Janet at a medical seminar he was speaking at, and she was attending to learn more about hospital career opportunities.

"Look at the date of the seminar," Casey said. "That was almost twenty-nine years ago. Janet's only been at Manhattan Memorial for twenty-six years."

"So we're talking about a very long-term relationship that started before Janet even walked through the hospital doors." Ryan's brows were knit as he concentrated.

"Janet got pregnant a few months later," Claire exclaimed, pointing. "My God, that means that Diana is Ronald's daughter."

"The question is, did he know…yes, he did," Casey said, studying the next pages, which were a lengthy accounting spreadsheet. "He paid a chunk of money for Janet's medical bills and living expenses."

"Yeah, and he stashed her away near Belleayre Ski Center in upstate New York at the end of her pregnancy and through the first few years of Diana's life," Marc added.

At that, Ryan moved to a second computer. "Yoda, give me another screen."

"Done, Ryan."

A second virtual whiteboard appeared. Ryan punched furiously at the keyboard while the others continued talking.

"No wonder Janet made her way up the ladder so quickly once she came to Manhattan Memorial." Casey leaned forward, still studying the spreadsheet and the notes attached to it. "Ronald was not only paying her an exorbitant salary with huge raises, but he was promoting her like crazy—right up to being his assistant."

"Talk about buying silence," Marc muttered.

"Guys, look at this." Ryan's head shot up and he stared at the second screen. "Yoda, please display."

"Yes, Ryan."

The data popped up. It was a Google search of the local area near the ski center. A recent news item appeared in the list. Ryan clicked on it, opening it on the screen.

"A ski lodge cabin burned to the ground last night," Ryan said. "No sign of foul play, just an unfortunate accident."

"Bullshit." Marc was rippling with tension. "Janet is trying to destroy all her ties with Ronald. She's guilty as hell."

"I also just ran her car," Ryan added. "She drives a black Town Car. That fits the description of the car that was parked outside Madeline's apartment building."

"I'm going to the hospital and grabbing that bitch." Marc wasn't going to be stopped this time.

"Fine," Casey said. "But before you go, tell me—why is Janet doing all this now? She's had years to deal with the fact that the man she clearly loved was racking up women like sex trophies. She can't hurt him—he's dead. Has she suddenly decided to avenge his death? Why? And what's the tie to Madeline and Conrad that would make her try to kill them?"

"None of this makes sense." Claire had that faraway look in her eyes. She was picking up on some unknown energy.

"Aidan, scroll to the next page," Casey requested.

He did as she asked.

"Dammit," Ryan said. "There's a motive to kill Ronald. Diana just found out the truth about her father six months ago. Maybe she fell apart and that—together with Janet's own pain and resentment—pushed Janet over the edge."

Casey frowned. "Let's run with that. Ronald had already given Diana a great job at the hospital. And he was still paying Janet huge chunks of money. But that might not have been enough to appease her, not when her daughter was totally shattered."

"Fine. So Janet killed Ronald." Marc was still hovering by the door. "How? Did she drug him before the surgery?"

"That never would have escaped Conrad's attention or the anesthesiologist's," Casey said, shaking her head. "Uh-uh. In order to kill Ronald, Janet would have needed access to the O.R. She didn't have it."

"But Diana did," Claire said quietly.

Everyone's head jerked around to face her. She looked sickeningly certain.

"Diana was the circulating nurse during Ronald's surgery," she said. "That means she was the first one in and the last one out. She'd have time alone in the O.R. before the surgical team came in." Another faraway look. "I only met Diana briefly at the dedication ceremony, but I sensed that she was like a lost little girl. Back then, I assumed it was because her mother was so overprotective and her job was so new. Now that we're focusing on her, I'm picking up a whole different energy. She was broken. Empty. Something psychological and heavy."

"Diana must have had some kind of psychotic break when she found out that Ronald was her father," Casey said. "And why wouldn't she? She's a gentle, sensitive girl. This news must have hit her like a ton of bricks. She'd been hurt. And the mother she adored was treated abysmally, and ultimately dumped, daughter and all. No amount of financial Band-Aids can make that go away."

Claire shook her head sadly. "The Lexington happy family—something she'd never be part of   must have constantly been rubbed in Diana's face. From what we're reading in Janet's file, Ronald wouldn't so much as recognize her as his child. That's something even Janet couldn't fix."

"What Janet could fix is finding a way to cover up her daughter's crime." Casey turned to Marc, who was already opening the door. "There's something on that recording that incriminates Diana. That's what this is about."

"Call Patrick and the cops. I'm going to the hospital." Marc paused. "Ryan, what's Madeline's Apple ID and password?"

Without so much as a blink, Ryan gave it to him.

Marc took off at a dead run.

"Speaking of Patrick…" Casey glanced at her watch. "It's been too long. I'm calling him."

The phone rang and rang. No answer.

"Shit. Something's wrong." Casey punched in Dave's number.

The security guard answered on the first ring. "Yes, Casey?"

"I've been trying Patrick. He's not answering. Did he come out? Has Madeline come out?"

"Neither." He sounded alert and ready. "Madeline hasn't left the hospital. As far as I know, Patrick is waiting for her. Do you want me to go in and check?"

"No. I don't want you leaving your post in case Madeline misses Patrick and comes out on her own. Stay put. I'm calling the police."

She hung up and dialed the telephone number of a contact she had at the nineteenth precinct on the Upper East Side.

"Harvey? It's Casey Woods. I need your help." She gave him only the details he needed to know, stressing that Madeline's life was in danger, and that Patrick—who was standing guard outside the E.R.—wasn't answering his phone. "Please send a couple of squad cars over to Manhattan Memorial and see what's up. We're on our way, too. Thanks."

She hung up and grabbed her purse.

"We'll get the car," Ryan called over his shoulder as he and Claire raced downstairs to get their coats.

Aidan rose and met Casey's gaze. "If you need me, I'm here."

"We're okay, but Marc might need you. I'll keep in touch. And, Aidan, thank you so much for everything."

He shook her hand. "I'll hang out with Hero and wait to hear from you. Good luck."

Casey nodded, and then dashed after her colleagues.

34

Janet shifted impatiently in her seat. They'd traveled exactly one and a half miles in twenty minutes.

"Get around this traffic," she ordered.

"How?" Madeline was trying to keep her hands steady and her focus on the road. "If I drive on the sidewalk and run people down, that's not going to get you what you want. It's going to get me arrested." She dashed away the tears on her cheeks quickly so Janet wouldn't notice. Madeline was desperately trying not to show weakness in front of this woman. It would give her even more power.

"You said you'd tell me what this is about," she reminded Janet. "What's on that recording that would make you kill Conrad and me to get it?"

"I needed you dead if you knew what was on that tape. Clearly that was a waste of my time and energy. I just should have kidnapped you and beaten the truth out of you. We would have ended up here a lot sooner."

"Then why didn't you?"

"Because it was a last resort, you idiot. No one knew anything. Now I'm going to have to get my hands dirty."

Another icy shiver ran up Madeline's spine.

"Did you know that Diana is Ronald's daughter?" Janet asked conversationally. "Did you know that he and I were together for almost twenty-nine years?"

"What?" Madeline jerked back in surprise, making the car jerk, too.

"Easy," Janet cautioned. "No fender benders."

"If you and Ronald were together, and Diana is his daughter…"

"Then why didn't he stay faithful to me and raise our child by my side? Why didn't he leave Nancy, whom he didn't give a damn about, and marry me, rather than stay put and father two children with that bitch? Because he was a coward, that's why. Nancy had all the power and influence from her rich, political family. Ronald swore to me that that didn't matter, that we'd be together—all three of us—just as soon as he could arrange for a divorce. Well, that divorce never happened. And he never even acknowledged my child as his. He just paid for us to live very comfortably, far away. He kept me beholden by promoting me up the employment ladder until I could be his assistant, all the while helping himself to a dozen women along the way."

"You stayed with him, anyway?" Madeline was processing the information as rapidly as she could, simultaneously inching the car along. "Did you love him that much?"

"Yes." For the first time, there was raw pain in Janet's voice. "I adored him. I would have done anything for him—including look the other way when he hooked up with one woman after another. I was his staple. His official 'other woman.' But God help me, he was worth it."

"How did Diana cope with this all these years?"

"She didn't. I never told her the truth. She found out

on her own about six months ago. She was beyond devastated. She fell apart right before my eyes."

Janet loved her daughter, even more than she loved Ronald. Was it possible…?

"Did you do something to Ronald before his surgery that caused him to die?" Madeline asked carefully.

"Me?" Janet's voice rang with shocked denial. "I could never hurt Ronald. I could hate him as much as I loved him. I could resent him. But I could never, ever kill him."

"Then why do you want the recording…?" Again, Madeline's voice trailed off. "It was Diana. She did it. She did something before the rest of the team came into the O.R.—something that killed her father. And whatever it was is on that recording. What was it?"

Janet didn't answer. She looked far away, and her face was contorted with pain.

"Oh, my God." Madeline squeezed her eyes shut for just an instant, then reopened them to focus on the truck that had just cut her off. "Oh, my God," she repeated.

Snapping back to the moment at hand, Janet pressed the barrel of the gun to the back of Madeline's head. "She's *not* a murderer. She's a wonderful person."

"You've been protecting her. You trashed both Conrad's and my apartments looking for the tapes. You tried to kill us both to shut us up about information we never had."

"I did what was necessary."

"How did you get past Crest Haven's security?"

"It's amazing what a professional uniform, a self-assured attitude and a big smile will do for you."

Madeline shook her head in amazement. "And now you're going to destroy the recording."

"Not just the recording—you, too, if you don't get us to that mini-storage fast." Janet leaned forward. "Traffic's moving now. Talk time is over."

Madeline didn't say another word. She just accelerated slightly and drove down Second Avenue and toward her destination.

The Forensic Instincts team tore into the hospital parking lot three minutes after the police.

Casey had called Madeline's cell phone five times. Voice mail. Voice mail. Voice mail. Her phone could be on Silent while she did her work in the E.R., but Casey doubted it.

Dave jumped up as the entourage arrived. "What can I do?"

"Just stay out here until I call you." Casey was already walking through the revolving door, Ryan and Claire in her wake.

The cops took off for the E.R. Casey was scanning the area for any sign of Patrick.

She spotted him weaving away from the tables at Au Bon Pain.

"Patrick!" She was by his side in a dozen steps, holding on to his arms to steady him. "What happened?"

"Some woman," he slurred. "She knocked over my coffee and bought me a new cup. She must have drugged me."

By then, Claire and Ryan had reached Patrick and Casey. Ryan went around to Patrick's side and slung Patrick's arm over his shoulders. "Easy, guy. I've got you."

"The woman who drugged you," Casey said. "Middle-aged, attractive, glasses, hair up in a chignon?"

Patrick nodded. "That's her. Who is she?"

"I'll fill you in later. Did you see Madeline leave the E.R.?"

"Not before I passed out, no." Despite Patrick's glazed eyes, he looked grim. "Did that bitch take her?"

"We think so, yes."

Casey paused as Emma came crashing into them. "What's going on? Marc came barreling through here a little while ago, demanded to know if I'd seen Madeline, and then—when I said I hadn't seen her—he took off."

"Took off for where?" Claire asked, brows drawn.

"Wherever Madeline is," Ryan replied. "He took her Apple ID and password. That means he's using the Find My iPhone app to track her down."

Detective Harvey Zimmer strode out of the E.R. "The woman named Madeline Westfield left with another nurse maybe forty minutes ago."

"Another nurse—Diana Moss?"

He nodded. "That's the name they gave me, yes. They also said that a tall guy was in there a few minutes ago asking the same questions. He told them it was an emergency, so they gave him the same information they gave me."

"Marc's on his way to Madeline," Casey murmured. "But who's forcing her to go wherever she's going, Janet or Diana?"

"Have both of them paged—one at a time," Patrick said. He was starting to look and sound like himself again. "Start with Diana. My guess is that Janet did the heavy lifting and took Madeline."

Casey did as he suggested, and the PA system sounded a few minutes later, paging Diana Moss to the E.R.

The police ducked down, their Glocks ready, Harvey's

minirecorder on and ready to tape anything incriminating that Diana said.

Diana came hurrying down the hall, her hands shaking as she reviewed her patient updates. She was clearly upset by something, and Casey doubted it was her chart.

Sure enough, Diana glanced up in time to see the FI team standing there, and she came to a dead halt, all the color draining from her face. She looked around furtively, like a fly who'd spotted a spider and was searching everywhere for a means of escape.

"Don't run, Diana," Casey called out. "It's useless. There are a lot more of us than of you. You won't get away. And we're talking to you *now*."

Accepting the inevitable, Diana lowered her chart and walked toward them as if she were walking to hell.

Twice more, she stopped, close enough so Casey could see that she was dying to bolt.

The second time, Harvey rose, along with two other cops, all with pistols raised.

"On your knees," he said. "We don't want to hurt you."

"All right," Diana said in a whisper, dropping her chart and falling to her knees.

"Hands on the floor in front of you," Harvey commanded.

Diana complied.

Harvey strode forward and took hold of each of Diana's wrists, pulling them behind her and slapping on handcuffs.

Casey stepped forward and helped her to her feet. "Harvey, I know this is your job, but I need some information. My client's life is at stake. Please—let me ask Diana some questions unofficially."

Harvey stared at her for a moment, and then nodded. He motioned for the cops to move out of earshot.
"You have three minutes while I call this in," he informed Casey.

"Thank you." Casey turned to Diana, going straight
for the jugular. "Where's your mother? Where did she
take Madeline?"

Like a dam that burst open, Diana shattered. She
bowed her head, and her shoulders began heaving as she
sobbed and sobbed. "I'm sorry. I'm so sorry. Please don't
hurt my mother. She was just protecting me. I did it. She
didn't. She never would have. She loved him so much."

"What did you do, Diana?" Casey edged a glance at
Harvey, who was calling his precinct, but she knew he
had one ear on the conversation.

"I killed Ronald Lexington. I didn't plan to. I just had
to. It was torturing me. It still is. Who he was. Who I
am. How could he be such a bastard? And me—how
could I do such a thing? But he knew. All these years,
he *knew.* And he never said a word. Never made a gesture. Never even glanced my way. He passed me in the
hall again and again, and his gaze never even flickered
in my direction to see if I was all right, if I was happy, if
I resembled him. What kind of soulless animal doesn't
care about his own child? And how could he treat my
mother like dirt under his feet?"

Sobs racked her body. "I didn't plan to, not until
the day of the surgery. I watched his wife and grown
children gather around him, hugging him and offering
support. I should have been in there, too. My mother
should have been the woman at his side. But she wasn't.
I wasn't."

A pained pause. "Ronald Lexington needed to die.

His family needed to know what it was like to live without a father...without a husband. So I took care of it. I added some diethyl ether to the saline solution. It compromised the glue and dissolved the sutures in the back of the heart. There's no way that Conrad could have saved him."

With that, Diana dropped back down to her knees, rocking back and forth as tears drenched her face, seeped onto her uniform. "I'm sorry...so sorry...."

Passersby had stopped, craning their necks to see what was going on.

"Keep moving," Harvey interrupted his phone call to order. "Police business."

The onlookers hurried off.

Harvey walked over to Diana. "Get up, Ms. Moss. You're being arrested for the murder of Ronald Lexington. It's time to go to the precinct now." Despite the severity of his tone, he held her handcuffed arms so she could struggle to her feet.

Casey waited only long enough for Harvey to read Diana her Miranda rights before she approached her.

"Where's your mother?" Casey asked.

Diana shook her bowed head. "I don't know."

It took all Casey's willpower not to grab her and shake her. "Your mother wants that recording to save you. Where is it? Where is she taking Madeline?"

"I truly don't know. I swear."

"Dammit."

"I've got her," Ryan said. While this conversation had been going on, he'd typed in Madeline's Apple ID and password. Now, the Find My iPhone app showed both Ryan's and Madeline's iPhones on a map on Ryan's screen. He zoomed in to see where Madeline was at the moment and saw that she was on Second Avenue at Saint Mark's Place.

He repeated the same method to trace Marc's phone. Marc was about a quarter mile from Madeline.

"Let's go," he told the team.

"What's the address?" Harvey asked.

Ryan supplied it.

"Good. Darrell and I will follow you." Harvey turned to his other two men. "Take Diana in. I'll call for backup once I know where we're headed. But we're not coming back without Janet Moss."

"Please don't hurt my mother," Diana begged in a watery tone. "She was only trying to protect me. Please don't hurt her."

"We'll try our best." Casey was already in motion.

"I'm coming, too," Emma announced.

"As am I," Patrick said.

No one tried to stop them. With Diana being led away by two policemen, there was no point in their staying here.

It was time to save their client.

35

Manhattan Mini-Storage was fairly quiet at this time of day.

Madeline pulled her car into the loading area of the narrow, gray building. She turned off the ignition.

"Now what?"

"Do you think I'm an idiot?" Janet replied. "You're doing the work. I'm holding the gun. Now let's go."

They made their way inside the building, followed procedure on gaining access to Madeline's storage unit and then headed there, Janet's pistol jabbed firmly in Madeline's back the entire time.

"Open it," Janet commanded, the minute they'd reached their destination.

Madeline did as she was told. It took her a few tries to fit the key in the padlock hanging on the metal door as her hand was shaking so hard. She was nearing the end of the line. The minute Janet had that recording in her hands, she was going to kill her.

She had to buy time. Time to think of a plan of attack. Time to pray that Marc was somehow on his way to save her.

She turned the lock, swung it open and lifted it off.

Then, she pulled open the heavy metal door, wincing as it brushed against her ribs.

Ignoring Madeline's discomfort, Janet held out her hand. "Give me the lock and the key," she said.

Madeline handed both to her.

Stuffing them in her coat pocket, Janet gestured for Madeline to lead the way. "Now, let's go inside and find that recording."

There was plenty of room for the two of them, just as Madeline had feared. The extralarge unit she'd rented was ten feet by ten feet—the size of a small bedroom. Even with everything stored in there, a clear path to the items and lots of empty space remained.

Janet could easily shoot her in here, slam and lock the door behind her and vanish in Madeline's car. No one would hear a few popping sounds, not in Manhattan where the taxis, buses, construction work and crowds were loud enough to block out an alien invasion.

Madeline's cold, dead body wouldn't be found until the stench of her rotting flesh permeated the storage facility.

She wiped that thought from her mind. Her job right now was to stretch out the time it took her to produce that recording and to try to catch Janet off guard.

Madeline made her way down the middle of the unit, brows knit as she stopped to study one box after another.

"Hurry up," Janet ordered. "And stop pretending you're confused. You know where every damned thing in the world is. You could single-handedly organize the entire hospital. Plus, you've labeled every box."

Madeline squeezed her eyes shut, wishing at that moment that she were a disorganized slob.

"Look what we have here," Janet noted aloud. She

waved the pistol at a stack of three boxes a little way down from where they stood. "If I'm correct, those are labeled Conrad's Tapes, are they not?"

Son of a bitch, Madeline thought.

"Yes," she said. "My guess is that one of those three boxes has what you want in it. The problem is, I don't know which one."

"Then we'll look through them all." Janet jabbed the pistol into Madeline's back again, shoving her the short distance to where the stack of boxes was. "Take down the top box. We'll start there."

Gingerly, Madeline reached for the box, favoring her ribs as she did. Her visible discomfort gave her time to get a firm grasp on the fifteen-pound box until her hands were locked securely around it.

In one sweeping motion, Madeline whirled around and flung the box at Janet with all her might.

With a yelp of surprise, Janet fell back, landing on some rattan terrace chairs. The pistol clattered to the concrete floor, spinning in circles and sliding away.

Both women lunged at it at the same time, hitting the floor together.

Ignoring the sharp pain in her side, Madeline scrambled to her knees and crawled, stretching her arm out as far as it would go.

Her fingers brushed the barrel of the gun.

She was inches from grabbing it when Janet's knee came up, slamming into Madeline's ribs as hard as possible.

Crying out in pain, Madeline crumpled in a ball, rocking from side to side and gasping air into her lungs.

That didn't stop her. Pain or not, she fought to regain her momentum and succeeded. She grabbed hold of Janet's legs, dragging her backward while she dodged Janet's kicking and the intended blows of her high heels.

"Let go of me, you bitch!" Janet said, panting as she struggled to reach the pistol, which was just out of her reach.

Madeline wrapped one arm around Janet's legs and yanked harder, using her other hand to slam a fist into the small of Janet's back—once, twice, three times—ignoring Janet's howls of pain, desperate to stop her from reaching the gun first.

Janet went rigid, temporarily crippled by the blows, and Madeline used those precious seconds to hoist herself past Janet and grope for the weapon.

Her fingers had just wrapped around the butt of the gun when Janet reached up and punched her so hard in the face that Madeline saw stars.

She moaned and fell over onto her back, losing her grip entirely and giving Janet free access.

Janet took full advantage.

She grabbed the pistol, rolled over and sat up, aiming the gun at Madeline, who was still crunched on her back.

"Sit up."

"Drop dead." Madeline wasn't dying without a fight. "You want the recording? Go get it. But you'll never find it without my help."

"Fuck you," Janet gasped, barely able to speak. "I can go through boxes and find that tape all by myself. Goodbye, Madeline." She aimed the pistol.

"Drop it!" a masculine voice boomed out. "Or I'll put a bullet straight through your head before you take another breath."

Janet started, peering quickly over her shoulder and

seeing Marc looming over her, a Glock aimed at her skull.

"You're a big Forensic Instincts fan," he said. "You know who I am. I'm the former navy SEAL. The one who can empty a round of bullets in you before your finger ever touches the trigger. Just try me. It won't take a hell of a lot to make me do it."

White-faced and terrified, Janet dropped the gun and held up her hands.

Marc strode over and scooped up the pistol. "And by the way," he added, glancing at the weapon, "your safety is still on. Now get up."

He continued holding his gun on Janet as she staggered to her feet, but his gaze darted to Madeline. "You okay?"

She nodded. "I am now."

As she spoke, the sound of police sirens filled the air.

Marc glanced around and found a couple of electrical cords secured with twist ties. He picked up one cord, gripped the twist tie between his teeth and pulled hard until it gave way, releasing the cord. He spit out the twist tie and repeated the process with the second cord. Then he reached over to snatch one of the rattan chairs that had tumbled to the ground.

"Sit down," he ordered Janet, slamming the chair into an upright position.

She eyed his gun, the rage in his eyes and then sat.

Using one strong hand, Marc yanked her arms behind her, then pocketed his weapon so he could tightly bind her wrists and then her ankles.

He studied his handiwork and nodded. "That'll hold you while we wait for the FI team and the police to find us."

He turned his attention to Madeline. "Come on, sweetheart." He squatted down and lifted her gently in his arms, rising to a standing position. "Don't move. We'll get you fixed up."

The Forensic Instincts van screeched into the storage lot the same time as the police cars did.

They interrogated the attendant at the front desk for the location of Madeline's storage unit. Getting what they needed, they all quickly proceeded to the unit.

Reaching the open door, they stopped short, seeing Madeline clasped in Marc's arms and Janet securely bound by electrical cords in a chair.

"You guys are slow," Marc said drily. "I was about to leave you a note, drop this bitch off at the precinct myself and rush Madeline to the hospital. Looks like I'm going to have to conduct some remedial tactical-skills training at our office."

Casey slid her pistol back into her handbag and stifled a grin.

"Nice work, navy SEAL," she said. "But just know you had first-class backup right on your heels."

Her humor vanished as she looked at Madeline, whose entire face was swollen and bleeding and who was contorted in pain in Marc's arms.

"I'll call the paramedics," Harvey said, reaching for his cell.

"Not necessary." Marc waved away the gesture. "I'm taking Madeline straight to the hospital. Once she's been treated, you can interview her. Until then, forget it."

Madeline shot him a look. "Do I have a ventriloquist?" she asked.

"Cute," Marc muttered. "Very cute."

A small smile, and then Madeline turned her head to face Harvey. "I'm okay. I can give you a statement now."

"No, ma'am." Harvey shook his head. "Your friend Marc is right. You need medical attention. We'll meet you at Manhattan Memorial after we take Janet Moss in. She can join her daughter. We're questioning her right now."

"You have Diana?" Janet looked more horrified than she had when Marc was holding a gun on her. "Please, let her go. I'm the guilty party. I'll tell you everything."

Harvey arched a brow. "Including how your daughter killed Ronald Lexington?"

Janet's face fell.

"Speaking of which," Ryan said, walking into the storage unit. "Before Marc carries you off, Madeline, where can we find the recording of the Lexington surgery?"

"The second box down," she replied. "That has the video recordings of last year's surgeries. You should find Ronald's about halfway down." She paused, gritting her teeth against the pain for as long as she could. "But I still don't know what's on there that will incriminate Diana. If she did something, Conrad would have seen it, either during the surgery or when he reviewed the tape."

"It's not about *seeing* it. It's about *hearing* it," Ryan replied.

They all turned to look at him.

"While we were in the van, I did a full rundown on Diana Moss. Evidently she's an audiophile and does blog posts on current, in-depth computer software. She's really sharp—I've seen her posts, which by the way are done under the name Trix. In her most recent post, she mentioned that she'd just tried out new software called

Audio Detracktor. Fortunately, so did I. The software separates sounds into discreet audio tracks so you can hear each one clearly and separately from the others. It's awesome. Let's use it on Conrad's recording of Ronald's surgery to see what it gives us."

"Later," Marc said firmly as he felt Madeline wince. "We're going to the hospital. Bring whatever equipment you want there."

36

The Manhattan Memorial E.R. staff labeled Marc the biggest pain in the ass they'd encountered in years.

He didn't give a damn. He hovered around like a mother hen while Madeline was examined, X-rayed and taped up. The ribs had been rebroken and there were bad contusions, not only on her ribs but on her face, chest and abdomen. She had cuts and scrapes everywhere, and it took quite a while to stop all the bleeding. The bruise on her face was swelling badly, and the nurse, Roberta Sanders—whom Madeline apparently knew well, and who was chatting with Madeline as if the professional ostracism of the past week had never happened—had applied an ice pack to the swelling.

"I gave you something strong for the pain," Roberta said, "as well as something to help you rest. So don't be surprised when you conk out."

"Gee, it's like being on the other side of an E.R. table." Madeline gave a weak smile. "I'll be a good girl and rest. I'll drink plenty of fluids, too. Can Marc please stay with me?"

Roberta's brows rose. "I don't know why you'd want him to, but sure. Just buzz if you need me. Or if you want me to toss him out."

Madeline's lips twitched again. "Thanks, Roberta. I will." She eyeballed Marc once Roberta had left. "My reputation in the E.R. is destroyed forever, thanks to you. Do you have to be such a tyrant?"

As she spoke, she reached out and took Marc's hand, linking her fingers with his. "I love you," she whispered. "Thank you for saving my life."

He brought her fingers to his lips and kissed them. "You scared the hell out of me."

"Maybe. But I knew you'd come." A huge yawn. "Tell your team they can come in whenever they want. The pain is subsiding. And other than being a little tired..." Madeline's voice trailed off. She was sound asleep.

She awakened a few hours later to see an entire computer set up and the whole FI staff in her E.R. room. How could they all fit? she thought groggily.

"Good morning, sunshine," Ryan greeted her. "How do you feel?"

Madeline blinked and looked around. She wasn't in her E.R. room. She was in one of the big hospital suites that was usually reserved for high-profile, wealthy patients.

"I'm okay. The pain is better. What am I doing here?"

"You're a VIP now," Claire said with a smile.

Marc was sitting by Madeline's side, hunched forward in a leather chair, staring at her as if she were a porcelain doll. "Hey," he said softly.

"Hey back." She smiled.

"You look better. There's some color in your cheeks. But you're going to be waited on by yours truly for the next few weeks."

One brow rose. "Do you cook any better than you used to?"

"No."

Everybody laughed.

"The police want to take your statement," Patrick told her. "But they're giving us a few minutes so you can see—and hear—what we did."

"The recording," Madeline said, suddenly wide-awake.

"Yup. Here it is." Ryan pulled out his iPad and opened the first audio track. He then backed away so Madeline could hear.

The picture remained on the spot where Ryan had set it. It was the tail end of the tragedy, and Conrad was reopening Ronald's chest, desperately trying to stop the bleeding that was soaking the entire O.R. table.

The audio played.

"I need more suction," Conrad was demanding. *"Now."*

Ryan pressed the second track.

There was a flurry of activity as the surgical staff all raced to do their jobs.

Then the telltale third track.

The voice was quiet, but thanks to Audio Detrack-tor, it was crystal clear, and it was definitely Diana's.

"Would you just die already?" she said under her breath. "What I did can't be fixed. So die. Make our pain go away."

Ryan stopped the recording. "There you have it. The last piece of evidence the cops need."

Madeline's eyes had filled with tears. "This is such a tragedy. No matter how justified Diana's feelings were, she had no right to take a human life. I'm glad she's in police custody. As for Janet…" Madeline sucked in her breath. "She told me everything. I can fill in all the details."

"And you will," Marc said. "Later. Right now, I'm giving the cops five minutes with you. And if your strength peters out before then, I'm tossing them out, too. Janet and Diana are both in custody. They can't hurt you or Conrad anymore. The details on everything Janet said can wait." He paused. "By the way, I called Conrad. He was stunned, but he's very relieved that you're okay. He'll probably visit tomorrow. I asked him to wait."

"Did you tell him about us?" Madeline asked.

"I'll leave that to you. It's your right to say whatever you choose to."

"Thank you for that." Madeline squeezed his hand. "He's a good man, Marc. He's going to be very happy for us. You'll see."

"Hey, are there wedding bells in the near future?" Ryan jumped in to ask.

"Oh, Ryan," Claire groaned.

"What?" Ryan looked genuinely puzzled. "They're crazy about each other. They have been for a decade. And they're not getting any younger."

"I give up." Claire threw up her hands.

Casey coughed, trying not to laugh. Patrick was struggling to keep a straight face, as well.

"Gee, thanks," Marc replied. But he grinned, for once unbothered by Ryan's inappropriate comments. "How about letting Madeline and I talk about it first? Then we'll let you know."

"Cool," Ryan said.

At that moment, Emma burst into the room, sans her candy-striper uniform.

"Free at last," she said, spreading her arms wide. "A civilian yet again." She looked immediately at Madeline. "How's our patient?"

"Healing nicely." Madeline clearly enjoyed Emma's enthusiasm. She glanced at Casey. "It's time for me to put in my two cents in a way I have no right to. I know Emma has a month and a half left of her probation, but in light of her amazing contribution to this case, I vote for cutting down some of that time."

"I definitely agree," Claire echoed at once.

"Yeah, me, too, you little brat," Ryan said. "Although God help Yoda."

Marc and Patrick were both nodding.

Seeing the team's reaction, Emma almost jumped up and down. "Casey?" she asked.

Casey didn't contemplate for long. "Probation over," she announced. "You are now officially a member of Forensic Instincts."

"Awesome!" Emma looked around eagerly. "Now I've been dying to know—do I get to choose my own business cards? No offense, but all of yours are kind of boring. I saw a cool purple-and-pink design online that I'm crazy about. Do I need approval? Or can I just order them?"

There was a cumulative groan as the team prepared themselves for Hurricane Emma and the next adventure that awaited Forensic Instincts.

* * * * *

Acknowledgments

Once again, I was fortunate enough to consult with the most extraordinary professionals in their fields, all of whom were an integral part of my creating the authenticity in *The Silence That Speaks*. I thank them all for their skill, time and patience:

Valluvan Jeevanandam, MD, Chief, Cardiac & Thoracic Surgery, The University of Chicago Medicine and Biological Sciences

Hillel Ben-Asher, MD

Angela Bell, Public Affairs Specialist, FBI Office of Public Affairs

SSA James McNamara, FBI Behavioral Analysis Unit, retired, Behavioral Criminology International

Dan Olson, Chief of the FBI Laboratory's Cryptanalysis & Racketeering Records Unit (CRRU)

John Quinn, Deputy Director of Marines SIT, Pentagon

My agent, Robert Gottlieb

My editor, Paula Eykelhof

And, as always, my family, whose love and support defy words

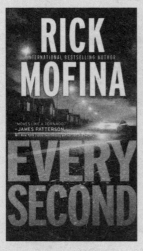

**Discover the next heart-pounding
Krewe of Hunters story from
New York Times bestselling author**

HEATHER GRAHAM

**Can the same killer strike again—
a hundred and fifty years later?**

Estes Park, Colorado, is a place of serenity. But it wasn't *always* so serene. Shortly after the Civil War, Nathan Kendall and his wife were murdered there, leaving behind a young son. The crime was never solved.

Now, historian Scarlet Barlow works at a small museum attached to a B and B, in the same building where that murder occurred. She came to Colorado after her divorce from FBI agent Diego McCullough, a new member of the Krewe of Hunters.

When Scarlet unwittingly photographs the victims of a recent murder, the police look at her with suspicion. Then the museum's historic statues begin to *talk* to her, and she knows it's time to call her ex-husband. Diego heads to Estes Park, determined to solve the bizarre case that threatens Scarlet's life—and to reunite with the woman he never stopped loving.

Available now, wherever books are sold!

ANDREA KANE

31610	THE STRANGER YOU KNOW	___$7.99 U.S.	___$8.99 CAN.
31445	THE LINE BETWEEN HERE AND GONE	___$7.99 U.S.	___$9.99 CAN.
31327	THE GIRL WHO DISAPPEARED TWICE	___$7.99 U.S.	___$9.99 CAN.

(limited quantities available)

TOTAL AMOUNT	$ _____
POSTAGE & HANDLING	$ _____
($1.00 for 1 book, 50¢ for each additional)	
APPLICABLE TAXES*	$ _____
TOTAL PAYABLE	$ _____

(check or money order—please do not send cash)

To order, complete this form and send it, along with a check or money order for the total above, payable to MIRA Books, to: **In the U.S.:** 3010 Walden Avenue, P.O. Box 9077, Buffalo, NY 14269-9077; **In Canada:** P.O. Box 636, Fort Erie, Ontario, L2A 5X3.

Name: _____

Address: _____ City: _____

State/Prov.: _____ Zip/Postal Code: _____

Account Number (if applicable): _____

075 CSAS

*New York residents remit applicable sales taxes.
*Canadian residents remit applicable GST and provincial taxes.

MIRA®

www.MIRABooks.com

MAKI1115BL

REQUEST YOUR
FREE BOOKS!

2 FREE NOVELS
FROM THE SUSPENSE COLLECTION
PLUS 2 FREE GIFTS!

YES! Please send me 2 FREE novels from the Suspense Collection and my 2 FREE gifts (gifts are worth about $10). After receiving them, if I don't wish to receive any more books, I can return the shipping statement marked "cancel." If I don't cancel, I will receive 4 brand-new novels every month and be billed just $6.49 per book in the U.S. or $6.99 per book in Canada. That's a savings of at least 19% off the cover price. It's quite a bargain! Shipping and handling is just 50¢ per book in the U.S. and 75¢ per book in Canada.* I understand that accepting the 2 free books and gifts places me under no obligation to buy anything. I can always return a shipment and cancel at any time. Even if I never buy another book, the two free books and gifts are mine to keep forever.

191/391 MDN GH4Z

Name	(PLEASE PRINT)	
Address		Apt. #
City	State/Prov.	Zip/Postal Code

Signature (if under 18, a parent or guardian must sign)

Mail to the **Reader Service:**
IN U.S.A.: P.O. Box 1867, Buffalo, NY 14240-1867
IN CANADA: P.O. Box 609, Fort Erie, Ontario L2A 5X3

Want to try two free books from another line?
Call 1-800-873-8635 or visit www.ReaderService.com.

* Terms and prices subject to change without notice. Prices do not include applicable taxes. Sales tax applicable in N.Y. Canadian residents will be charged applicable taxes. Offer not valid in Quebec. This offer is limited to one order per household. Not valid for current subscribers to the Suspense Collection or the Romance/Suspense Collection. All orders subject to credit approval. Credit or debit balances in a customer's account(s) may be offset by any other outstanding balance owed by or to the customer. Please allow 4 to 6 weeks for delivery. Offer available while quantities last.

Your Privacy—The Reader Service is committed to protecting your privacy. Our Privacy Policy is available online at www.ReaderService.com or upon request from the Reader Service.

We make a portion of our mailing list available to reputable third parties that offer products we believe may interest you. If you prefer that we not exchange your name with third parties, or if you wish to clarify or modify your communication preferences, please visit us at www.ReaderService.com/consumerchoice or write to us at Reader Service Preference Service, P.O. Box 9062, Buffalo, NY 14240-9062. Include your complete name and address.